Autumn Maze

Jon Cleary, an Australian whose books are read throughout the world, is the author of many novels, including such famous bestsellers as *The Sundowners* and *The High Commissioner*.

Born in 1917, Jon Cleary left school at fifteen to become a commercial artist and film cartoonist – even a laundryman and bushworker. Then his first novel won second prize in Australia's biggest literary contest and launched him on his successful career.

Seven of his books have been filmed, and his novel, *Peter's Pence*, was awarded the American Edgar Allan Poe Prize as the best crime novel of 1974.

Jon Cleary's most recent novels have been *The City of Fading Light*, *Dragons at the Party*, *Now and Then*, *Amen*, *Babylon South*, *Murder Song*, *Pride's Harvest* and *Dark Summer*.

Acclaim for *Dark Summer*:

'A well-crafted, stylishly written page turner with lots of social observation, colour and strong characterization'   *Sun Herald*

Murder Song:

'The author's close attention to detail, his imaginative powers, and his great gifts as a storyteller alone will ensure that this book receives a wide welcome'   *Canberra Times*

BY THE SAME AUTHOR

The Sundowners
The Phoenix Tree
High Road to China
Season of Doubt
The City of Fading Light
The Pulse of Danger
The Beaufort Sisters

FEATURING SCOBIE MALONE

Helga's Web
Ransom
The High Commissioner
Dragons at the Party
Now and Then, Amen
Babylon South
Murder Song
Pride's Harvest
Bleak Spring
Dark Summer

JON CLEARY

AUTUMN MAZE

This edition published by Grafton Books, 1999

Grafton Books is an Imprint of HarperCollins*Publishers*
77–85 Fulham Palace Road,
Hammersmith, London W6 8JB

ISBN 0-261-67191-X

Printed and bound in Great Britain by
Mackays of Chatham PLC, Chatham, Kent

**To Larry Hughes,
a deckchair chum from the *Titanic***

Chapter One

The headline next day said, DEATH BY DEFENESTRATION. It was written by a veteran sub-editor who had cut his teeth on alliteration, an old tabloid habit. Strictly speaking, however, Robert Sweden did not die by defenestration, a custom made popular by Italians in the early 17th century: though there was an open window nearby, he was tossed off a balcony. Whatever the exit, the effect would have been the same. A fall from twenty storeys up, though the quickest, is not the best way of reaching the ground.

Rob Sweden was charming, seemingly generous and gregarious; on the surface he had everything that was needed to hide the fact that, underneath, he was an unmitigated jerk, a sonofabitch and a scoundrel. Only a few people, however, knew this about him: including, presumably, the person who killed him.

His watch, an expensive item that gave the date as well as the hour and was guaranteed to function at forty fathoms, a comfort to drowning swimmers still concerned about punctuality, was smashed to smithereens when he landed. His time of arrival, 9.27 p.m., was given to the police by a passing taxi driver cruising for a fare, though not from above.

2

At 1.05 a.m. that same night the duty mortuary assistant at the City Morgue was in the body storage room, checking the Completed Bodies list for the past twenty-four hours. Normally he did the check around 11 p.m., but with the arrival of Robert Sweden's body and another two bodies, he had been busy and two hours had passed before the police had done their paperwork and departed.

Frank Minto was a cheerful man in his late twenties, a half-blood Maori who spent his Saturday afternoons on the rugby field trying to add to the week's roster of corpses. He had arrived in Sydney two years before and soon found work at the morgue; as he said, it was just like Sunday in Christchurch. Working alone at night he joked with his silent audience and would have been insulted if anyone had suggested his humour was macabre. He would have explained that the dead, rather than being offended by his jokes, laughed silently, knowing that their worries, unlike those of the rest of us, were over and done with. He was a fatalist, though he would be surprised when death came to him.

He was joking with a middle-aged corpse, asking if it was comfortable, as he examined it. The corpse had been brought in just after Sweden's body had arrived and he had made only a perfunctory examination of it. It was not his job to do a detailed report, but since he had started work at the morgue he had begun to dream of becoming a pathologist, of getting some professional standing. He was scribbling a note on the tiny wound he had found at the base of the dead man's skull, when he heard the buzzer that told him there was someone at the big door to the morgue's garage and loading dock.

'I'll be back, Jack. Don't go away.'

Whistling a Billy Ray Cyrus tune, he left the body storage room, closing the heavy door to keep in the chilled air, and went out to the big loading dock. It was empty except for his own battered Toyota. Through the grille of the wide, shuttered door he could see the dark panel van outside. He could also see the dim shape of a man standing by the recently installed intercom.

'We have a body. A woman from a car accident.' The man had an accent, but that was not unusual these days. Aussies

2

told him even New Zealanders had an accent, an insult if ever there was one.

'Nobody told me to expect it.'

'The police were supposed to tell you we were coming. Anyhow, here she is. Let us in, please.'

Strapped for money by a succession of State governments that, unlike certain electorates overseas, could see no votes in the dead, the morgue's security had for a long time been a staff joke. Only two months ago three men had walked in, as into an all-night delicatessen, and, after showing him a gun, had asked to see a particular body which had been brought in earlier in the evening. Satisfying themselves that the two bullets in the man's head had indeed killed him, they had thanked Frank, given him twenty dollars, and departed. It turned out later that the dead man had been the victim of a gangland shooting and the three men were just checking the job had been done properly, conducting due diligence before they paid off the hit man.

'Okay, bring her in. Are the cops on their way?' He pressed the switch that opened the big door.

'We thought they'd be here by now.'

Frank Minto went back up onto the loading dock and through to the receiving room where an empty stainless-steel trolley was always kept in readiness. He dropped his clipboard on the trolley, then wheeled the trolley out on to the dock. The panel van had been driven in to the foot of the dock and three men stood beside it, all of them in grey dustcoats, all of them wearing black hoods with eyeholes in them.

The shortest of the three men came up on to the dock, took a gun with a silencer attached from under his dustcoat, said, 'Sorry about this,' and shot Frank Minto twice in the chest.

'Jesus!' said Frank Minto, though he wasn't a Christian; and died.

The other two men clambered up on to the dock and helped the man with the gun lift Frank Minto on to the trolley. Then they wheeled the trolley back into the receiving room.

The killer unscrewed the silencer and put it and the gun back

3

into the pocket of his dustcoat, doing it unhurriedly and with a tradesman's skill. Then he neatly arranged the trolley beneath the camera fitted to the ceiling in the centre of the room. 'They video all the bodies here before they put them in the body storage room.'

'You're not gunna fucking video *him*, are you?' Both of the other men, taller and heavier than the man with the gun, were visibly on edge, even though they still wore their hoods.

'Of course not. But I think he'd like to be waiting in the proper place for his colleagues in the morning, don't you?' He lifted Frank Minto's feet and picked up the clipboard holding the Completed Bodies list. He ran a slim brown finger down the columns. 'Here he is.'

The entry showed: 7 – E.50710 – M – U/K – Canterbury – 29/3 – HOLD.

'He's on trolley number seven, he's tagged E.50710. He's down as "Unknown", so that's good. They've got him marked *Hold*, so that means they don't know the cause of death yet, that would be done by the forensic people in the morning. Get him. The body storage room is through that door and the first door on the right.'

'Aren't you coming with us?'

'I have to find the records and destroy them, I told you that.' The leader sounded irritated. 'Now go get him!'

The other two hoods looked at each other, then one of the men shrugged and the two of them went out of the receiving room. The leader, left alone, went to work with the ease of a man familiar with his surroundings. He turned to the small rack of shelves against one wall, flipped through the videotapes stacked there, found the one he wanted and put it in a pocket of his dustcoat. Then he went out to the adjoining office. Here, too, he worked with the ease of experience, as if certain that everything would be where he expected to find it. He found the register book where all details were entered by the police who brought in the bodies; he tore out the page with the details on the Unknown Male, E.50710, found at Canterbury. He crossed to another desk, searched through a hardboard folder marked CORONER and found what he was looking for: a Form P79A with the same details on E.50710. He put the form and the torn sheet from the register into the pocket with the video-tape. Finally, he sat down before the computer which was on a bench against the wall, switched it on and then destroyed all data for the previous twenty-four hours. He sat back for a moment like a man well pleased with what he had done, though the hood showed no hint of what expression lay beneath its silk. For he wore silk, while the other two men wore black calico.

He stood up, looked around him as if making sure he had forgotten nothing, then he went back to the receiving room and through to the corridor that led to the body storage room. The other two men were just coming out, pushing a trolley on which was a body in an unzipped green plastic bag.

'Holy shit, it's freezing in there!'

'You'd be complaining more if it was heated in there. You should smell the bodies where I come from, the ones they leave lying out in the open because there's no room for them.' The other two said nothing: killers both, they knew he had probably seen more death than they ever would. 'Let's have a look at him.'

He merely glanced at the grey waxen face of the middle-aged dead man; after all, he had never seen him before he had killed him. He lifted the thick black hair and looked at the back of the scalp. 'Good. They haven't even started an autopsy.'

'How d'you know? They might of opened him up from the back.' The man had no idea how an autopsy was done and didn't want to know; he was squeamish about what was done to the dead.

'They'd have taken the brain-pan out.' The leader gestured at the stack of lidded white-plastic buckets along the corridor wall. 'What do you think is in those buckets? Brains.'

The man lifted a lid, then slapped it back on a bucket, his hood fluttering over his face. 'Christ Almighty! That's fucking disgusting!'

'They have to wait to examine a brain. They keep it in formalin for six weeks.'

'Six weeks? Jesus, why so long?'

'They have to wait till it stops thinking.' Silk hood waited for the calico hoods to ripple with laughter, but nothing happened; he went on, 'Usually they never let the relatives know what they've done. Some people, particularly the Christian fundamentalists, get very upset at the idea.'

'So would I. Jesus, fancy having that done to you after you're dead. Okay, what we gunna do with this guy?' He nudged the bagged body.

'Feed him to the sharks.'

3

Tom's school had a holiday; teachers throughout the State had taken a day off to commiserate with each other on the toughness of their lot. Malone had therefore taken a day off to take Tom, aged ten, to the Vintage and Veteran Car Show at Darling Harbour. The fifty-hectare exhibition and convention centre had, on its opening five years ago, been hailed as a white elephant of the future; instead, it had gradually assumed a promising shade of pale, if metaphorical, grey. Malone was a reluctant admirer of it and an even more reluctant visitor to it. It seemed that each time he brought one or all of his children here it cost him a fortune. His hands were bleeding from reaching into his pockets, where the fish-hooks did their best to help him protect his money. ·

'Oh, come on, mate! You've just had three Cokes and three bags of chips.'

'The chips make me thirsty. Geez, you're a drag, Dad. Why does it hurt you so much to spend money?'

'When I'm old and broke and I come to you for a loan, I'll be asking you the same question. Being thrifty runs in the Malone blood.'

'Garn, Mum's always saying how generous I am.'

'Yeah, with my money.'

The banter between them was almost man-to-man; Malone did not believe in talking down to his children. They had stopped in front of a gleaming red machine, a 1904 Type 7 Peerless. Malone, a man for whom a car was something that had four wheels and a baffling source of power under the bonnet that made it go, looked at the car more with nostalgia than admiration or desire to own it; it symbolized the past, simpler and more innocent days. This car belonged to the times of his grandfathers and though he had never known those Irishmen, he knew in his heart he would have been happy sharing their days with them. Still deeper in his heart he knew he was fooling himself. No era had ever gleamed like this car, history had never been as uncomplicated as its workings.

Tom was unburdened with nostalgia. He said to the beautiful blonde model in the blue period dress that complemented the red car, 'How much?'

The blonde looked at Tom's father. 'Does he mean me or the car?'

Malone recognized her. She worked as a casual for Tilly Mosman, who ran Sydney's leading brothel, the Quality Couch. 'Hello, Sheryl. I almost didn't recognize you. You look – vintage?'

'Thanks,' she said drily, and looked down at Tom. 'It's not for sale, honey. It's like me, priceless.'

'How come my father knows you? Are you undercover?'

'Occasionally.' She smiled at Malone. 'Is he going to be a cop, too?'

'I'm trying to talk him out of it. Tom, this is Miss Brown. She's modelled for the police bulletin.'

Tom, young as he was, could be gallant: 'If all policewomen looked like you, I don't think Mum would let Dad come to work.'

'If all policemen were as nice as you, Tom, I'd join the force.'

Then Malone's pager beeped. He cursed silently; he had warned Russ Clements that he wanted a totally free day.

7

'Sorry, Sheryl, we have to go. Come on, Tom, I've got to find a phone.'

'Bye-bye, Tom. If the car comes up for sale, I'll let you know.'

As they walked away, Tom said, 'Geez, what a nice lady. Does Mum know about her?'

'Not unless you tell her.'

Malone found a phone, then had to borrow small change from Tom to make the call. 'You owe me, Dad, don't forget.'

Clements was at Homicide. 'This had better be important, Russ, or Tom's going to have your head.'

At the other end of the line Sergeant Clements sounded truly contrite; he loved the Malone children as if they were his own. 'Scobie, tell Tom I'll buy him a Harley-Davidson for his birthday.'

'Like hell you will. What's the trouble?'

'You heard about that dive off a balcony down at the Quay? John Kagal and Peta Smith've been handling it, but I think you and I'd better come in on it. Romy's just been on to me. She's done the autopsy and she thinks the guy was dead before he went for the dive. She's found a puncture at the base of the skull, it's a neat way of killing someone, looks like it was done with a long needle or a hatpin or something.'

'Who wears hatpins these days? Can't you handle it till I come in tomorrow?'

'There's something else. The mortuary assistant out at the morgue, you remember him, guy named Frank Minto, they found him this morning, laid out on a trolley, with two bullets in him.'

Malone looked out at the narrow waters of Darling Harbour. It was still warm for early autumn, summer hanging on like a spurned lover; bright sunlight flickered on the water, turned the sail of a passing yacht into a triangular glare. A good day to be spending with one's son. 'Go on,' he said resignedly.

'There's more.'

'I'm not surprised.'

The glass walls of the huge exhibition centre suddenly blazed, as if the sun had slipped in the sky. From across the water, in the amusement park, there was a gasp of raucous music; it was abruptly cut off, as if someone had pulled the plug. Tom looked morosely up at him; he knew already that their day together was finished.

'Someone,' said Clements, 'evidently whoever killed Frank Minto, has pinched a corpse from the morgue. I'll wait for you out there. Give my apologies to Tom.'

Malone hung up, looked down at his son. Despite the difference in age, there was a distinct resemblance between father and son. There was the same dark hair, growing the same way, back from the widow's peak; the dark blue eyes that did not try to hide amusement; the straight thick brows. Tom's cheeks were still round and soft, but beneath them was the hint of the bonework in his father's face. Missing was the frown that sometimes appeared between his father's eyes, that marked Malone with the aches and pains, blood and death, of the world in which he worked. A detective inspector in charge of Homicide could never pass for one of the world's innocents.

'Russ sends his apologies. I've got to go to work.'

Tom sighed, but he was used to sharing his father's time with the bloody Police Service. It was the price he paid for having a father who was a cop: Dad could have been an accountant or, for God's sake, a women's hairdresser. 'It's okay. Can I go with you? Other kids' fathers take 'em to work, sometimes.'

'I've got to go out to the morgue. You wouldn't want to go there.'

'Why not?' He had a ferret's curiosity.

'Because it's full of dead people and dead people don't like kids staring at them.'

'How would they know?'

Malone clipped his son under the ear, put his arm round his shoulders. 'There's plenty of time for you to meet the dead. Don't rush it, mate.'

9

Half an hour later, having taken Tom home to Randwick and delivered him to Lisa's disapproving stare, he drew up outside the morgue in Glebe, one of the city's inner areas. The entrance was in a quiet side street; he wondered what the residents thought of having so many dead neighbours, transients though they all were. He went in the front door, was recognized at once by the man behind the counter.

'G'day, Inspector. You heard about Frank Minto? Geez, it makes you wonder. You'd think you'd be safe in a place like this, wouldn't you?'

Russ Clements was in Romy Keller's office, neither of them acting like the lovers they were. Romy was German-born, dark-haired and, in both Clements' and Malone's eyes, beautiful. Clements was big and untidy, like a bag of clothing on its way to the dry cleaners, unhandsome but with a big pleasant face that appealed to a lot of women old enough to need a little tenderness. Which was what Romy saw in him, and more.

Romy kissed Malone on the cheek, then went round behind her desk and sat down. Two years ago her father had proved to be a murderer; with Clements' help she had weathered the blow. She had been on the verge of leaving the morgue's staff, but had been persuaded to stay on in the State Health Department and was now deputy director of the Institute of Forensic Medicine. Her eyes, when gay, were resplendent; but here at work she toned down the light in them. She was a woman used to men, alive and dead: they had few secrets for her.

'Seems we have something of a mess here, Scobie. Poor Frank Minto – why would anyone want to kill him? If they wanted to steal a body, for God knows what reason, they could have just tied him up.'

'Maybe he tried to stop them?'

She shook her head. 'After those thugs came in some months ago and showed Frank a gun and demanded to see a body, we had a meeting and decided that if anything like that happened again, nobody was to stand in the way. Frank was a sensible man, he wouldn't have put any value on a corpse, not to the extent of trying to hang on to it. No, whoever it was shot him in cold blood. They didn't put any value on a living body.'

'They must've put some value on the corpse they stole?' Up till now Clements had sat silent; sometimes Malone had the feeling that the big man saw Romy as his superior. Which was wrong: in his own way Russ Clements was as competent, or more than that, as Romy.

'We won't know till we find out who they stole.'

Malone raised an eyebrow. 'You don't know?'

'It was a male, unknown,' said Romy. 'Middle-aged, Mediterranean look, no identification at all on him. He'd worn two rings, one on his left wedding finger, the other on his right little finger. They'd been pulled off, the skin was scraped on the little finger. His clothes are in a bag outside, but I gather they'll tell you nothing.'

'All good stuff,' said Clements, 'but off the rack. It could of been bought anywhere.'

'Where was the body found?'

'In a park by Cook's River, out at Canterbury. Some kid and his girlfriend found him last night, about eight p.m. They called the locals, the Campsie D's are in charge of it.'

'So why are we in on it? Have they asked for us?' Local police protected their turf jealously.

'Not so far. But whoever took the body, took all the records of it.'

'They even wiped out all our data on the computer,' said Romy. 'Whoever it was knew their way around a morgue. But they forgot one thing. The cops who picked up the body still have their notes. I called them earlier.'

'Could it have been an inside job?'

Romy shrugged. 'Maybe. But I don't think anyone here would have killed Frank Minto.'

Malone looked at Clements. The big man was still uncharacteristically quiet, his attention more on Romy than on Malone.

11

Had they had a row, were together now only because of their work? 'Russ? *Russ?*'

Clements gathered himself together. 'I'll start questioning the staff, but like Romy says, I don't think it's an inside job. Too obvious. You asked me why we're in on this. Tell him, hon.'

Romy smiled at him, as if she enjoyed being called *hon*, even on duty. But there was something wrong with the smile, a wryness that took the affection out of it. Then she looked back at Malone.

'There was a note in Frank's pocket, a scribble addressed to me. Frank took his job more seriously than it looked – he was thinking of studying pathology, though I don't think he really had the education for it. Anyhow, he would often do a more thorough examination of a body than just checking it in.'

'What did his note say?'

'He found a puncture at the base of the skull of the body that's missing. This morning I did an autopsy, a preliminary one, on a body that came in last night about two hours before the other was brought in. He was supposed to have jumped or been pushed off a balcony twenty storeys up – the body was a mess. But I think he was dead before they tossed him off the balcony. There was a puncture at the base of his skull, too. It's a subtle way of killing, but it would have to be done by someone who had some medical knowledge. You flex the head forward as far as it will go, then you push a broad needle or a thin scalpel into what we call the atlas, the first cervical vertebra. That's what they did to Mr Sweden and, from Frank's note, I'd say the same was done to our unknown male from Canterbury.'

'Who is Mr Sweden?' Malone asked Clements, all at once wondering if the big man and Romy were playing some sick joke on him. 'Not our –'

'*That's* why I called you in. No, he's not our new Police Minister. He's Derek's son.'

Malone swore under his breath; he belonged to a dying

12

school that didn't swear in front of women. Even some of the hookers he knew respected him for it, since they met few gentlemen in bed or the back seat of a car, even a Mercedes.

'I think I'll go on sick leave.'

Chapter Two

❖❖❖❖❖❖❖

1

As they walked out into the still-warm day some dark clouds were boiling in from the south-east; a few fat drops of rain caught the sun as they fell, turning the air into a thin gold mesh. A van came down the street and turned into the morgue's loading dock: another delivery, another death. Two women stood talking at the gate of a house on the opposite side of the road, but neither of them gave the van a glance.

Malone said, 'It's none of my business, but have you and Romy had a row?'

'Not exactly,' said Clements. 'It was just – well, she told me this morning she's ready for marriage.'

'She *proposed* to you? Amongst the stiffs?'

'Well, no, not exactly. We weren't in where they keep the bodies. We were in the murder room, but it was empty.'

'What did you tell her?'

'Nothing so far. I was still digesting it when you walked in.'

'That's why you looked like a stunned mullet. It's about time you made up your mind, son. You've been going with her, what, two years now? You're never going to get anyone as good as her.'

'It was just a bit sudden.'

'Sudden? Two bloody years, you're up to your eyeballs in love with her and it's *sudden* when she tells you she'd like to get married? How long are you going to wait? Till the two of you are laid out side by side on trolleys back in there?' He nodded over his shoulder.

'You're starting to sound like a real bloody matchmaker.'

14

'Wait till I tell Lisa, then you'll find out what a real bloody matchmaker is. Righto, where do we go from here? You dragged me away from a day with Tom, I hope you've got something organized?'

'All right, don't get snarly just because I don't wanna be hasty about getting married. You got your car? I caught a cab up here, a Wog who wanted to take me via Parramatta till I showed him my badge. Then he said the ride was on him.' He grinned; sometimes he relished his prejudices. 'I think we should go down and have a look at the scene of the crime.'

'Which scene?'

'The one down at The Wharf. You'd rather go there than out to Canterbury, wouldn't you?'

'The Wharf? You mean this bloke Sweden, the son, had an apartment there?'

'No, it's his father's and his stepmother's. She's one of the Bruna sisters.'

'You're ahead of me.' Malone led the way towards the family car, the nine-year-old Holden Commodore. Lisa and the children were pressing him to buy a new one, but as usual when it came to spending money, especially large sums, he said he couldn't find his cheque-book. 'Who're the Bruna sisters?'

Clements was a grab-bag of trivial information. 'Don't you ever read *Women's Weekly*? The Bruna sisters are our equivalent of the Gabor sisters, Zsa Zsa, Eva and the other one –'

'You mean you don't know the other one's name? It's Charlene.' Malone was heading the Commodore downtown.

'These three sisters came originally from Roumania, I think it was, when they were kids. They all married money. Several times, with each sister. They're good-lookers, they're rich and if any of them are there at the apartments, I don't think they'll give you and me the time of day.'

'How are you so well informed on them? Do you have a gig on the *Women's Weekly*?' Malone had his own gigs, informers, but none on a women's magazine.

'I started taking an interest in them when I found out who they were married to. There's this one whose place we're going

15

to, she's married to our Minister – he's her second or third husband, I forget which. Then there's one married to Cormac Casement – his money's so old it's mouldy. She's his second wife and he's her third husband. And then there's the youngest, she's married, her third husband, to Jack Aldwych Junior. Yeah, I thought that'd make you sit up.'

Malone nodded, trying to picture Jack Aldwych, once Sydney's top crime boss, on the verge of the local social scene. Then he dropped the image from his mind, turned to getting the next few hours, maybe weeks, into step in his mind. They passed the University of Technology, a tall grey building that could not have generated much optimism in the hearts of those who entered it. Malone had to slow as a group of students, ignoring the traffic, crossed the wide main street at their leisure, jerking their fingers at those motorists who had the hide to honk at them. A larger group was gathered in front of the university's entrance, massing for another demonstration. Demos were becoming frequent again: against further cuts in student grants, against undeclared wars, against the recession. Rent-a-Crowd, Malone guessed, was doing business as good as it had done back in the Sixties and Seventies. He slowed the Commodore down to walking pace as a student, flat-topped, wearing jeans and a sweater three times too large for him, crossed in front of the car, daring the driver to run him down.

'If he knew we were cops,' said Clements, 'he'd of laid down in front of us.'

Malone ignored the student, waited till he had passed and then drove on. The student had his troubles; there was probably no one of his age who didn't. But Malone had his own: 'The Police Minister's son, the son of our best-known crim, a missing stranger who died the same way as Sweden's son – you got any more you want to throw in the pot with that stew?'

'Not at the moment,' said Clements.

'These – Bruna? – sisters. Is there anything dirty against them?'

'Only that they marry for money. I don't think that's a crime, not out in the eastern suburbs.' Clements came originally from

Rockdale, an area that those in the east would have trouble finding on a map. Australian cities are no different from those overseas: they condense the national prejudices, their suburbs tribal grounds of contempt and dislike for each other. 'I don't think we have to worry too much about Aldwych Junior, either. As far as I know, he's got a clean nose.'

'He was mixed up in that case with Romy's father. We never pinned anything on him, but I'm sure he wasn't clean.'

'Well, he is as far as the record goes. Don't start complicating things. We've got enough to worry about.'

The Wharf had been built during the Eighties, in the boom times when people thought the money-tree would fruit forever. It was a circular glass- and granite-faced tower, twenty-four storeys high that, though towered over by the office buildings along Circular Quay, gave the impression it was the only one where you would find quality inside its walls. The marble foyer inside the brass-and-glass front doors suggested you were entering a bank, a small exclusive one where no deposits under a million were accepted and then only as a favour.

The doorman, releasing the security lock to let them in, recognized Malone and Clements; they had been here before to interview a suspect in another case. 'Remember me? Col Crittle. We been over-run with police this morning. You'd be the umpteenth.' He was a burly man with a head of thick grey hair combed flat and an easy smile, the sort of doorman elderly widows could feel secure with. At least a quarter of the owners were elderly widows, the sort who never had to cut dead branches off the money-tree. 'You want the twentieth floor. It's all one apartment, Mr and Mrs Sweden's.'

'Were you on duty last night when the accident happened?'

'They tell me it wasn't an accident. No, thank God I wasn't here. It was the night feller, Stan Kinley.'

'He still works here?' Names stuck in Clements' memory as much as events; Malone had told him that on Judgement Day he would be asked to call the roll. He caught Malone's eye and said, 'He was the guy we saw when we came here to see Justine Springfellow. She still here?'

17

The doorman shook his head. 'She moved out a coupla years ago.'

'Where did Mr Sweden, the young one, fall?'

'Around in the side street. Your fellers've got it cordoned off with tapes. I'm waiting for them to tell me when the council blokes can scrub out the stain. He made a real mess.'

As soon as they stepped into the glass-and-brass lift Malone had a feeling of *déjà vu*. Last time, they had come to interview Justine Springfellow who had turned out to be not guilty of the murder they had been certain she had committed. *Let's have better luck this time.* The lift stopped at the twentieth floor and they stepped out into a small lobby. In front of them were double doors of thick dark walnut, each with a lion's head in brass in the middle of it. A young uniformed policeman stood beside the doors, his authority somehow diminished by their solidity.

He nodded at the two detectives, went to open the doors. 'Hold it a moment,' said Malone. 'Who's in there?'

'The Physical Evidence team have gone, sir. There's one of your men from Homicide – Kagal? – and Sergeant Greenup.'

'No media?'

'They came last night, after it happened. A couple came back this morning, trying for an interview with the Minister, but Sergeant Greenup told 'em to get lost.'

'Good old Jack. He got his sledgehammer with him?'

The young officer grinned; he knew the reputation of his sergeant. Clements said, 'Who else is in there?'

'Mr and Mrs Sweden. Mrs Sweden's sisters – I dunno their names.' Like Malone, the young officer evidently did not read the *Women's Weekly*. 'And one of the Minister's minders, his press secretary, I think.'

'Quite a crowd.'

'It's a big apartment, sir. Oh, there's someone else. Assistant Commissioner Zanuch.'

Malone wondered why a junior officer should almost forget the Assistant Commissioner, Administration, but he made no comment. He himself did his best to forget Zanuch and usually succeeded. One's mind worked better when the AC was not occupying even the remotest corner of it.

Malone and Clements went in through the big doors, pulling up instinctively as soon as they were inside the apartment. They were on a landing, fronted by a dark walnut railing that matched the front doors; four steps led down each side to the main level. One half of the apartment was a living and dining area, a huge expanse that looked out through a glass wall, across a wide terrace, to the harbour and the north-east. Behind the dividing wall that ran right across the apartment lay, Malone guessed, the bedrooms and service rooms. The furniture was a mixture of modern and antique, a cocktail of decor that didn't turn the stomach. The pictures on the long wall were also a mix, but none of them clashed. Malone, a man any interior decorator would have hung on a wall in a dungeon, was nonetheless impressed. He was in *rich* territory.

All the people in the room were grouped at the far end. Assistant Commissioner Zanuch detached himself from them and came quickly towards the new arrivals. He was ten years older than Malone but didn't look it. Tall, handsome and arrogant, he gave the impression of being a banker in uniform rather than a police officer. His uniforms were custom made by the city's most expensive tailor and the Police Service's guess was that the insignia on his shoulders were all solid silver, he would not have been comfortable with less.

'What are you doing here?' He had a beautifully modulated voice but there was an edge to it now. 'We haven't yet decided whether it was an accident or homicide.'

Malone smelled politics at once.

'Oh, it was homicide, sir.' Both men had kept their voices low; the faces at the far end of the room were turned towards them like small satellite dishes, blank of expression. 'We've just come from the morgue. The opinion there is that young Mr Sweden was dead before he was tossed off the balcony. I'm taking charge of the case.'

It was a challenge, and both of them knew it. The two men, because of the difference in rank, had had little to do with

19

each other, but there was an antagonism that came to the surface on the rare occasions when they met on business. Malone could not stand Zanuch's open ambition, his mountaineering amongst the political and social heights around town; the Assistant Commissioner had no time for Malone's casual attitude, his apparent clumsiness in the minefields of respect for authority. All they had in common was that they were both good policemen.

'You're sure?'

'Yes, sir.'

They were stopped from further discussion as Derek Sweden came down the room towards them. Malone and Clements had never previously met the Police Minister; their political bosses came and went like seasonal viruses. Sweden was in his mid-fifties, bony-faced, bald and as elegantly dressed as Zanuch, but not in uniform. He had been in politics for twenty years without ever achieving his party's leadership; he had at the same time managed to make money in property. The son of a political father and a mother who voted as she was told, it was said that he had shaken every hand in the State, including that of the head chimpanzee at Taronga Park. He had always been a State politician, but with the stunning defeat of his party in the Federal election two weeks ago, which had left party members on a merry-go-round, with each man stabbing the back of the man in front of him, it was rumoured that Sweden had set his sights on Canberra and the national playing field.

He shook hands with the two detectives, voters both.

'I'm sorry we have to be here, sir,' said Malone. 'Our sympathy on your son's death.'

'Thank you. From Homicide? What is this, Bill?' He looked at Zanuch. 'I thought we'd decided it was an accident. What's going on?'

'When Detective Kagal said that, I think he was trying not to make waves in front of the womenfolk.' Zanuch might well have been a diplomat as well as a banker or a dozen other professionals. Sometimes he wondered why he had chosen to be a policeman. 'Tell the Minister and me what you know, Inspector.'

'Not that much, sir –' Then Malone went on to explain what Romy had told him and Clements, though he did not mention the stolen corpse and the suspected similarity of its death to that of Robert Sweden. 'Your son could've been dead before he was tossed off the balcony.'

'*Tossed* off?' Sweden looked at Zanuch as if to say, *What have we got here?*

'Sorry. Thrown off.' Malone could have chewed on his tongue; it had a habit of getting away from him, like a snapping dog, every time he came up against authority. He saw the look of irritation on Zanuch's face and knew another black mark had been posted against him.

'So what are you proposing?' said Sweden.

'We'd like to look around, with your permission. The PE team will have done its job, but I just like to look over things myself. Then we'd like to ask a few questions?' He glanced at Zanuch.

The Assistant Commissioner did not interfere in public; but he was visibly annoyed. 'If you must.'

'Dammit,' said Sweden, even more annoyed, 'I don't want anyone questioned! Not now, not today. Christ, we're still getting over what's happened –'

Zanuch looked at Malone. 'Can't it wait?'

'I suppose so, sir. But the more time we waste, our chances of catching the killer get slimmer.' *You know that, even if you've never worked in Homicide.*

For a moment the Minister might just as well have been at the other end of the room with the still-watching group: the AC and his junior officer were locked in their own small tussle. Clements stood silent and aside, his face blank.

Sweden interrupted: 'Killer?'

'Yes, sir,' said Malone.

Sweden, it seemed, was having difficulty coming to terms with the mere fact that his son was dead; that he had been murdered was piling too great a weight on his emotion. He looked blankly at Zanuch.

The Assistant Commissioner, contrary to the national habit, took the long view: the way this present government shuffled its cabinet, this current Minister might not be in power when the Commissioner's post became vacant. 'I think Inspector Malone should do it his way.'

Sweden shook his head, seemed about to make an angry retort, then changed his mind. 'Go ahead, Inspector. Ask your questions.'

'Where is Sergeant Greenup?' Malone asked Zanuch.

'In the kitchen, I think. He's not a detective.'

'No, sir. But he's had thirty years' experience. I'll talk to him first. I'll talk to Detective Kagal, too.'

'You're going to keep us waiting?' Sweden was incredulous; he might just have been told that he had been dumped for pre-selection for the seat he had held so long.

'I'm afraid so, sir. Until the two men out in the kitchen put me in the picture, I won't know what questions to ask.'

Sweden looked at Zanuch, then back at Malone. 'Do you vote Labor?'

Malone grinned. 'Mr Zanuch thinks I'm a communist.'

The AC's smile was like that of a baby with wind. 'Better get cracking, Inspector.'

Malone and Clements left them and went through an archway into the other half of the apartment. As they did so, Clements muttered, 'Are you trying to get us sent to Tibooburra? You go there on your own, mate.'

Tibooburra, in the far north-west of the State, was the city policeman's equivalent of Elba or St Helena. 'If this case gets any muddier, I think I'd rather be out there. Hello, Jack. John. What d'you know?'

The uniformed sergeant and the young detective were in the kitchen. It was a good-sized room and looked as if nothing more than a slice of toast had ever been cooked in it, as if it were waiting for the photographer from *Good Living* to arrive. It was all stainless steel and white Formica, the only colour in the copper bottoms of the pots and pans hung like native arte-facts above the central work-island.

'G'day, Scobie. Russ.' Jack Greenup was in his fifties, grey-haired and overweight, a cop from the old school. He had played rugby league when he was young and still believed in the direct approach; he had never tried to sidestep, to run around a man in his life, not even when his own life depended on it. 'We haven't talked to the silvertails inside. John and I had a few words with the maid.'

'Where's she?'

'In her room, right at the back.' John Kagal was the youngest and second newest member of Homicide, its only university graduate. He was good-looking, dark-haired and aerobics-trim, always impeccably turned out. Malone knew, with resigned amusement, that the young man would some day be Commissioner, possibly succeeding Zanuch. By then Malone hoped he would be in retirement. Or Tibooburra. 'There are four bedrooms and three bathrooms on this side of the apartment. Oh, and this kitchen and a pantry in there.' He nodded to a side door. 'There's a rear door in through the pantry from the service lift.'

'It's bloody big.' Jack Greenup had been born in and still lived in a two-bedroomed cottage out in Tempe where *big* was anything that had a second storey.

'What did the maid have to say?'

'I talked to her. She's a Filipina. She said young Sweden came here last night, his parents were out at the opera, and he told Luisa, that's her name, Luisa – you're not gunna believe this – Luisa Marcos, he told her she could have the night off. He gave her fifty bucks to go to the movies.'

'Fifty bucks,' said Greenup. 'He was telling her to get lost, looks like.'

'So he was expecting someone here?'

'I'd say so,' said Kagal.

'Did you ask the parents about that?'

Kagal shook his head. 'I got the feeling that the AC didn't want any questions asked. That's between you and me.'

'Of course.' *Don't tell me how to run the squad, son. You'll get your turn after I've gone.* 'The night doorman, Kinley, did he say anything about letting anyone in?'

'No. We've got a list of last night's visitors to the building. Not all their names, but who they were visiting. Here it is.' He tore a page out of his notebook and handed it to Clements. 'I'd like it back, Russ.'

'Sure,' said Clements, who didn't like being told the obvious by a junior officer. 'Any signs of a struggle?'

'None out in the living room. He was tossed off –'

'Thrown,' said Malone and grinned as Kagal looked blank. 'I've just been ticked off for saying he was tossed off. You've been warned.'

Kagal nodded. 'Okay, he was *thrown* off, there's a small balcony at the back, off the main bedroom. It overlooks the side street where he was found.'

'The main bedroom? Mr and Mrs Sweden's? Any signs of a struggle in there?'

'No. But there are signs in the second bedroom, where young Sweden occasionally spent the night. He has – had a flat out at Edgecliff, but occasionally he'd bunk down here, keeping his stepmother company while his father was away interstate or wherever. Maybe they knocked him on the head, then tossed – threw him off the balcony.'

'No,' said Clements, who had been taking his own notes, even though Kagal would feed his notes into the running sheet on the computer back at the office. He told Kagal and Greenup what Romy had found in her autopsy. 'He was surgically done in, looks like.'

'Righto, let's go in and talk to the silvertails.' Malone grinned at Jack Greenup, the old proletarian. 'You remind me of my dad, Jack.'

'Must be salt of the earth. You wanna talk to Luisa?'

'You'll have got everything out of her?' He looked at Kagal, knowing the younger man would have done exactly that. 'No, leave her be. If we have to, we'll get back to her. We can't keep the mob inside waiting too long. Stay here, you two, make yourselves some coffee.' He looked around the kitchen again; he would have to tell Lisa about it. 'Don't mess up the place.'

He led Clements back into the other half of the apartment. The silvertails, some seated, some still standing, all turned at once, all, it seemed to Malone, on the defensive. Zanuch's face was the only one that showed neutral.

The two detectives were introduced by the AC; there was a formality about it, almost as if this were some sort of social gathering. 'I don't think you two ladies need to be interviewed. This is Mrs Casement and Mrs Aldwych, they are Mrs Sweden's sisters.'

'We'll stay.' Ophelia Casement was familiar to Malone now that he saw her close-up. His two daughters, Claire and Maureen, made a mockery each week of the social pages of the Sunday newspapers; they would measure the amount of dental display at functions, supposedly sane people grinning like idiots at the camera, and occasionally would show him the results. Mrs Casement, it seemed, was a standard feature in the make-up of every social page. But even at a glance Malone knew she was no idiot. 'Rosalind needs us here.'

'Of course,' said Rosalind Sweden from where she sat on a long couch.

'We've always supported each other,' said Juliet Aldwych.

Ophelia, Rosalind, Juliet: Malone hadn't read Shakespeare since he had left school, but he remembered the names. Once, aged thirteen and going to an all-boys' school, he had been forced to play Ophelia in a school production; his voice had been breaking then and he had alternated between an alto and baritone rendering of her speeches. As he dimly remembered it, at least two of the Shakespeare girls had been hard done by; none of these three looked the worse for wear. Ophelia, he guessed, was the eldest, in her mid-forties, still beautiful and aware of it. Rosalind would be the middle one, four or five years younger, bearing a remarkable resemblance to her elder sister. Juliet was the youngest, in her mid-thirties perhaps, dark-haired where her sisters were blonde. They were a very handsome trio, as sure of themselves as money and beauty could make them. He wondered what lay behind the facades, behind the years past.

25

'How are we going to do this, Inspector?' That was Rufus Tucker, the Minister's press secretary. Malone had known him when he had been a scruffy young crime reporter; now he was twenty kilos heavier, he had groomed himself just as minders groomed their rough-edged masters, he was a smooth-whistling whale in a three-piece suit. He had the reputation of slapping down smaller fish who tried to bait his master. 'I think it would be best if you just spoke to the Minister alone.'

From the moment he had entered the apartment Malone had been manipulated. Ordinarily he would have spoken to each person alone, but the old perversity took hold: 'No, we'll take everybody together.' He had to shut his mouth before the runaway tongue added, *The more the merrier*. Thinking like the fast bowler he had once been, he bowled a bean ball, no fooling around looking for a length: 'Did your son mention to you that he was having trouble with anyone, Mr Sweden?'

Sweden had composed himself, almost as if he were facing a television camera; he was a regular guest on *7.30 Report*, where politicians came and went like store dummies, on exhibition but never saying anything. He had been in politics long enough to appreciate that, when faced with the inevitable, you took the shortest course home, even if it was crooked. 'No, not at all. He was, I think anyone will tell you, a very popular, hard-working young man.' He appealed to his wife and sisters and the three women nodded like a wordless Greek chorus. Though, of course, these were three girls who had risen out of the chorus. 'If my son was murdered, as you seem to suspect, I have no idea who would have done it. None at all.'

'Unless it was someone who broke in?' said Rosalind. 'It's happening all the time these days.'

Malone glanced at Clements. It was an old ploy: keep changing the bowling, keep the batsman off balance. He still thought in cricket terms, though he no longer played the game. Clements said, 'There's no sign of forced entry, Mrs Sweden.'

'Rob could have opened the door, expecting someone else.'

'They still would've had to get in through the security door downstairs. The night doorman doesn't mention any visitor for your stepson.' Clements looked at the list Kagal had given him. 'There was a visitor for you, Mrs Casement. You live here?'

'We have the penthouse,' said Ophelia Casement, making it sound as if she and her husband lived above the clouds, up where the hoi polloi never reached; Malone saw a slight smile on the face of Juliet, the youngest sister. 'We may have had a visitor, I'm not sure. I was out, but my husband was home. People from his office often drop by at odd hours. It's just across the road there.'

She nodded west, towards the end of the long curved glass wall; the vertical edge of the tall Casement building showed there like a sun-reflecting border. A jigsaw was falling into place in Malone's mind. He was not ignorant of the men and money that ran this city, but homicide detectives rarely, if ever, had to sort out the skeins of power.

'Rob liked girls.' Juliet had a throaty voice. To Clements, a late-night movie fan, she sounded like the crop of actresses out of old British movies, when they all tried to sound like Joan Greenwood. To Malone, a man with a biased ear, she sounded phoney. 'Perhaps one of them came here and brought someone? A boyfriend followed her?'

'Rob was told he was never to bring girls unless we were here.' Rosalind sounded like a headmistress.

'I'm sorry, Inspector –' Juliet made a poor attempt at looking innocent. 'I'm playing detective. Forgive me?'

'The doorman says he didn't let in any visitors for Mr Sweden. But we think Mr Sweden must've been expecting *someone*.'

'What makes you think that?' The Minister's voice was sharp.

'Detective Kagal has interviewed your maid. She says your son gave her fifty dollars to go to the movies. We think he wanted her out of the way.'

'Fifty dollars to go to the movies?' Ophelia made it sound

as if, up in the penthouse, she added up the housekeeping money every night.

'Rob was generous, you know that,' said Rob's father, his voice still sharp. 'Money didn't mean anything to him, easy come, easy go.'

'He was generous to a fault,' said Rob's stepmother, the sound of violins in her voice, and Malone waited for honey to run down the walls. It struck him that though Derek Sweden was upset by his son's death, the three women and Rufus Tucker appeared to be labouring to show any real grief.

'What did your son do, Mr Sweden?'

'He was a broker on the Futures Exchange – or he was up till a few weeks ago. He worked for a brokerage office owned by my brother-in-law, Mr Casement. A few weeks ago he transferred to Casement Trust, the merchant bank side of the corporation.'

Malone nodded as if he understood; but he would have to ask Russ Clements, the human data bank, to explain what futures brokers did. Russ, he knew, would also almost certainly know what Cormac Casement did. 'Mrs Aldwych mentioned that he liked girls. Did he have a regular girlfriend?'

'No,' said the stepmother. Rosalind was as composed as her two sisters, but whereas the other two were relaxed in their chairs, she sat stiffly, even primly, on the long couch. She wore a simple black woollen dress, as if already prepared for the funeral, but the double strand of pearls lying on her full bosom suggested she might also be prepared for lunching out. 'He preferred to play the field. He had no difficulty in getting girls to go out with him. He was a very handsome boy.' She looked at her husband, then suddenly smiled; it was so unexpected, Malone wondered if what had gone before was no more than an act. 'Your looks, darling.'

Her two sisters nodded in agreement; Sweden looked unembarrassed. Then Tucker glanced at his watch, a large old-fashioned gold hunter that he had taken from his waistcoat pocket. 'Minister, I think we'd better be going –'

Sweden looked distracted; there was no doubt his shock and

grief were genuine. But he would never let himself fall apart; he was not called The Armadillo as a joke, his crust could withstand mortar bombs. He had been bending over the couch, his hand on his wife's shoulder, but now he straightened up, even squared his shoulders like a bad actor. 'There is a Cabinet meeting –'

'Oh God,' said Ophelia, 'can't politics be forgotten for a day? They won't miss you, Derek.'

'Yes, they will,' said Sweden firmly and with some asperity. Since the unexpected election defeat a couple of weeks ago the Conservative coalition had, it seemed, been meeting every second day for post-mortems. To be absent was to miss the chance of being influential.

'You go, darling.' Rosalind turned her head to look up at her husband; with the movement she turned her back on her sisters. 'I was going to lunch at the Rockpool with Juliet and 'Phelia, but I'll stay in now.'

'We'll cancel,' said Juliet. 'We'll all stay in and have lunch here.'

'No, we'll have it upstairs,' said Ophelia. 'Something light. I have no appetite, anyway.'

Crumbs, thought Malone, she'll give us the menu in a moment –

'An omelette. Asparagus.'

Malone looked at them critically, but decided none of the three sisters was feather brained. Like Sweden they would never fall apart, they would face the world with teeth bared and it was up to you to tell whether it was a smile or a threat. He put them on the list of suspects, out of prejudice more than evidence, and said, 'Well, that's all for the moment. There'll be more questions – there always are. Where do you live, Mrs Aldwych? Here in The Wharf?'

'No.' Juliet looked amused. 'Are we all on a list of suspects or what?'

'Not at all,' said Zanuch, literally stepping into the conversation; he moved a pace forward. He had been unexpectedly quiet during Malone's questioning and it struck Malone only now that the Assistant Commissioner was only on approval here in this circle. 'I'm sure Inspector Malone has no thoughts along those lines, right?' He looked at Malone: it was an order.

'Of course not, sir. It's just for the record, just in case.' He was looking east past the AC, down the harbour. Out at sea, beyond the Heads, he could see a giant waterspout, a dark frightening funnel. It was unusual and he wondered if it was some sort of omen.

'I live at Point Piper,' said Juliet. 'Wolseley Road.'

One of the toniest addresses in Sydney: where else? 'Of course. I've met your husband.' Then the tongue slipped its leash again: 'And your father-in-law.'

The AC looked as if he were about to take another step, or two or three, into the conversation; but Juliet said sweetly, 'Old Jack? The best of my fathers-in-law. He's the third.'

'Minister,' said Tucker, gold watch held aloft as if about to clock Sweden in a sprint to Parliament House. 'It's getting on, we should be moving –'

Sweden looked at Zanuch, ignoring Malone. 'Is that all then, Bill?'

Zanuch, too, ignored Malone. 'For now. But there's bound to be other questions, if it *is* a homicide –'

This time the tongue was trapped firmly inside Malone's teeth. It was Clements who said, 'It's homicide all right, sir. The deputy director of Forensic was sure of that.'

'They make mistakes –'

'Not this one, sir. She's my girlfriend.'

Chapter Three

✦✦✦✦✦✦✦✦

1

All the men had gone and the three Bruna sisters were alone. Said Rosalind, 'You two didn't show much concern over Rob's death.'

''Lind,' said Ophelia, 'your stepson was a shit.'

'Why did Cormac give him a job then?'

'Because he wanted a favour from your Derek, something political. You scratch my back, I'll scratch yours. Or your son's.'

Rosalind did not question that. She and Juliet nodded understandingly; they were, after all, Roumanian, though long removed. They had arrived in Australia when Juliet was six months old, Rosalind five years old and Ophelia ten, but there were centuries of intrigue in their blood. Their mother, Ileana, had come of a family noted for its political chicanery; she had died of sunstroke six months after her arrival in Sydney, sad to depart but happy in the thought that her daughters would grow up in a community where the politicians of the time were as buyable as those back home. She had been ten years older than her sculptor husband, Adam, and, though not expecting to go so soon, had told him she would die before he turned to chasing younger women. He, distraught at the thought of losing her, had asked for advice on how to bring up their daughters. She, with her last breath but still aware of the world's opportunities, especially amongst the native barbarians, had murmured, 'See that they marry rich.' The sisters had done their best to honour their mother's wish. The blood of their mother's family ran like liquid gold through them, their vote was always buyable if the price was right.

'Did Derek arrange it? The political favour?'

'I suppose he must have. Cormac doesn't tell me everything that goes on, though I'm often tempted to ask.'

Ophelia was the impulsive one of the three sisters. On the spur of the moment she had asked Cormac Casement to marry her; a spur of a different sort had been that he had as much money as her dreams were made on. They had gone to bed on their second meeting, she experimenting with an older lover, wondering if his technique would be so simple as to be puritanical; he wondering if his heart would stand up to the demands of what the feminists called a 'woman in her post-menopausal prime'. Each had surprised the other and a month after they had met she proposed. He, not given to impulsiveness, further surprised himself by accepting.

'But Cormac did say something last week that I didn't take much notice of. He said Rob was up to something and he'd have to speak to him.'

'Rob was always up to something,' said Juliet. 'Or up something.'

'Don't be vulgar,' said Rosalind, who could be as vulgar as any gypsy when her temper got away from her. Aware of this, she had cultivated a cautiousness that sometimes made her seem much more callous than her sisters. 'He liked girls, but that's healthy. Or it used to be.'

Juliet, who even as a child in a bath had liked to make waves, said, ''Lind, he liked *women*, not just girls. Any age. His fly was permanently unzipped.'

Ophelia, who could catch a nuance as if it were floodlit, said, 'You too?'

The two sisters, the youngest and the eldest, exchanged glances, then both looked at Rosalind. 'He got me into bed four or five times,' said Juliet. 'He was a marvellous lover, so long as he kept his mouth shut. He always sounded like that loud-mouthed football commentator. He would give a description they could hear down in Melbourne. As if I didn't know what was going on. What about you, 'Phelia?'

'The same. I always felt I was in the middle of an All Blacks–Wallabies scrum.' She knew that rugby was played in Roumania and, though she had no interest in the game, she went to rugby internationals with Cormac because he had in his youth been a representative player and still followed the sport. She never went to rugby league matches, that was the peasants' game. Her mother would have approved of her discrimination. 'Twice was enough. I blew the whistle after that, told him the game was over. Well?'

The eldest and the youngest waited for Rosalind to comment. She sighed, then nodded. 'Me, too. His step-mother.' She was less Roumanian than her sisters, almost as if a Methodist had somehow got into the bloodstream. At times she even displayed a conscience, something her husband found disconcerting. 'Just the once. Too noisy. It's the first time I've been *cheered* for what I was doing to someone.'

'Did he ever suggest he might tell Derek?'

'Never. Derek would have killed him –' Rosalind broke off sharply and she frowned. 'God, why did I say that?'

'Do you think Derek found out?' said Juliet, scooping up some small waves.

Rosalind shook her head vigorously. 'He would have spoken to me first. He's like that. He can be sweet, but he'll always blame the women for everything.'

'Balls,' said Ophelia, who had fondled more than her share. 'It takes two to seduce.'

'Did Cormac suspect anything between you and Rob?'

'No. When he told me he thought Rob was up to something, I wondered for a moment if he meant with me. But Cormac, dear old soul, can be read like a book – there wasn't a glint of suspicion about me. I've never understood why they say the Irish are like the Roumanians and vice versa. They're children, really.'

Her sisters nodded: innocence had never bothered them. At their convent school in Rose Bay the nuns had been convinced that, in succession, all three of them were headed for Hell.

The sisters had been unperturbed. That was where most of the rich finished up, anyway.

'So who killed Rob?' said Juliet. 'Or would it be better if we didn't know?'

2

When Malone and Clements came out of The Wharf they turned into the side street. Two council workers in overalls were cleaning the pavement, scrubbing it with hard brooms. The Crime Scene tapes had been removed and there was no sign of any police. Two young girls paused on the other side of the street, shuddered and moved on, heads close together in a whisper, as if the council workers were gravediggers throwing the last sod on Rob Sweden.

One of the sweepers leaned on his broom and looked at the two detectives. 'You guys stopped for a bit of ghouling?'

Malone had never heard the gerund before; the recession had brought the educated to the gutter. 'We're police, not ghouls.'

'Sorry.' He was a young man, young enough to be the son of his fellow worker, who looked as if he had been sweeping the streets all his life. 'This job is shitty enough, without having to clean up something like this.'

Malone looked up at the stack of balconies above them. 'They must've tossed him out wide so he wouldn't hit the lower balconies.'

'It was a neat throw,' said Clements. 'Three feet further out and he'd of landed on any car parked here.'

The young cleaner was still leaning on his broom, an occupational habit. 'Are you guys always so clinical about something like this?'

Malone wanted to tell him how they felt when they investigated the murder of a child or a woman, but all he said was, 'It's like you and your street sweeping, it's a job.'

'You put your finger on it, mate.' The older worker had

stopped sweeping, leaned on his broom with the ease of long practice. 'I keep telling him, don't ever look too hard at what your broom picks up. Right?'

'Right,' said Clements, and he and Malone grinned at each other and walked back down the short hill.

'Where to now?'

Malone paused on the corner, looked along Circular Quay and up at the tall tower of the Casement building. 'While we're down here, why don't we drop in on Mr Casement? Young Sweden worked for him.'

They crossed the road, stopping to allow a group of Japanese tourists, herded together by their guides as if the local natives were expected to attack at any moment, to make their way towards a waiting cruise ferry at one of the wharves. Clements, a man who couldn't help his prejudices, shook his head but said nothing to Malone. The latter, who fought his inherited prejudices and usually won, just smiled at the Japanese and was rewarded by the bobbing of several heads.

'Our salvation,' he said.

'Japs?'

'Tourists.'

The Casement building, like The Wharf, had been built in the boom of the early Eighties. There were fifty storeys, seven of them occupied by Casement Trust, the merchant bank, and Casement and Co., the stockbrokers. In the big entrance lobby there was enough Italian marble to re-fill the Carrara quarries; thick columns soared three storeys, like branchless marble trees. An overalled cleaner with a toy broom and a tiny scoop shuffled about the lobby keeping the marble dirt-free and butt-free. Visitors were welcome, but expected to be impressed or else.

A uniformed security guard asked the two detectives if he might help them. 'We'd like to see Mr Casement?'

'You have an appointment?' The guard looked at a book on his counter. 'Nobody is allowed on the fiftieth floor without an appointment.'

Malone produced his badge. 'Is that a good enough reference?'

'It's good enough for me. I'll see if it's good enough for Mr Casement's secretary. She's the Wicked Witch. Don't quote me.'

There was a short conversation with the Wicked Witch, a wait, then the guard put down the phone. 'It's okay. Ask for Mrs Pallister. It's about the ugly business over the road, right?'

Malone just nodded, then led Clements along to the private lift pointed out to them by the guard. They rode to the fiftieth floor in ten feet square of luxury: no marble, but top quality leather for which any craftsman would have given his awl. The carpet on the floor looked as if it were newly laid each morning, fresh from the merino's back. Clements looked around admiringly.

'I think I've got a split personality. I get into something like this and I hate the bastards it's made for, yet I *like* it.'

When they stepped out of the lift they were in a reception area that suggested luxury was the norm on the fiftieth floor. A dark-haired receptionist turned from her word processor and gave them a pleasant smile. 'Mrs Pallister is expecting you.' *Not Mr Casement is expecting you*: everybody these days had minders. The receptionist stood up, opened a door in the oak-lined wall behind her. 'The police.'

The police went through into an inner office, three walls oak-lined and the fourth a floor-to-ceiling window that looked out on to the harbour. A blonde woman sat with her back to the view, a paper-strewn desk in front of her. The mess on her desk contrasted sharply with her too-neat appearance. She rose as the two men came into her office, but that was her only hint of politeness.

'Gentlemen.' Her vowels came from eastern-suburbs' private schools, but there was an edge to her voice that suggested it could cut throats if needs be. 'I think it would have been better if you had telephoned so that I could have fitted you into Mr Casement's schedule. He can give you only ten minutes.'

'We'll keep that in mind,' said Malone, instantly forgetting it.

Mrs Pallister was middle-aged and would have been attractive if she had not frozen her face ten years before. Divorce had turned her 180 degrees; her career had become her life. She made forty-five thousand dollars a year, ten thousand a year less than Malone made as an inspector, but she had the air of an assistant commissioner. 'Mr Casement is a busy man.'

'Aren't we all?' said Malone.

She looked at him down her nose, which, snub as it was, rather destroyed the effect intended. She led them through into an office that surprised Malone with its lack of size; he had expected to be led into a luxurious auditorium. But this room was not much bigger than the Wicked Witch's, though there was no denying the luxury of it. Even to Malone's inexpert eye, the paintings on two of the walls were worth a fortune: a Streeton, a Bunny, a Renoir and a Monet. The mix showed that the man who worked in this office did not want to be disturbed by any *angst*-spattered artwork. The furniture was equally comforting, rich in leather and timber. This was a man's room, but Malone, who was learning to be more observant about surroundings, guessed it had been furnished by a woman.

'Inspector Malone?' Cormac Casement stood up from behind the large desk that was almost a barricade. 'This is about poor Rob Sweden's death? A dreadful accident.'

He was twenty-five years older than his second wife, but, as the old shoe-polish advertisement said, though he was well-worn he had worn well. He was shorter than Malone had expected from the photos he had seen of the older man, just medium height and barrel-shaped. He had thin iron-grey hair, a square face that sagged under the chin, and he wore designer glasses that looked out of place on him, much too young for him, as if he were wearing Reeboks on his small dainty feet. The eyes behind the glasses, however, suggested they could open a steel safe without any twirling of a combination lock. His wife was wrong when she claimed she could read him like a book. There were some pages of him still uncut and only he knew what, if anything, was written there.

'Not an accident, Mr Casement. It was murder. We've just come from giving Mr and Mrs Sweden the bad news.'

'Murder?' Casement did not look surprised; which surprised Malone. 'Really? Oh well . . .' He sat down again, waved to the two detectives to take the chairs opposite him. 'You never can tell what's going to happen with today's youth, can you?'

'Do you know much about today's youth, Mr Casement?'

'Only what I read in the newspapers.' The old eyes were steady behind the young man's glasses. 'If you're asking me what I knew about young Rob, the answer's not much. You should be asking someone who worked with him. The general manager of our stockbroking firm, for instance. He would be the one who saw Rob from day to day.'

'He transferred to your banking side a few weeks ago.'

The glasses flashed as he lifted his head. 'Did he? I didn't know that. I don't have any executive position in the bank any more, I'm just chairman of the board. I only saw him on social occasions, he never mentioned it.'

'How did he strike you? On social occasions?'

Casement pondered; he appeared as if he had never really been interested in young Sweden. 'Gregarious, I suppose one would say. He was very popular with the ladies.'

'Any particular one?'

Casement shook his head. 'Not that I noticed.'

'Was he ambitious? I mean, he worked for you, would he have gone far in your corporation, the stockbrokers or the bank?'

'I really don't know, Inspector. I told you, I'm only involved at board level, the day-to-day stuff is behind me. To tell you the truth, I was never interested in the boy's future.'

Cormac Casement came of a rare species in the country's pioneer society, the rich Irish. He was not one of the bog Irish, not one of those driven out of Ireland by the potato famine of the 1840's. An ancestor had landed in the colony of New South

Wales in 1842 and been given a large land grant on the southern slopes a couple of hundred miles south of Sydney. Wool had been the first interest, but gradually the family had widened its grasp, into cattle, mining, sugar and banking. There was no major corporation in the nation that had not had a Casement as an original investor. Society, which is a corporation in itself, had taken them up; or rather, the Casements allowed themselves to be taken up, for, though Irish, they had been gentlemen and ladies long before the colonials had learned how to handle a full teacup or an empty compliment. Theirs had been *old* money when the later fortunes of other colonists were still just dreams based on mortgages.

'Did he appear to you to take drugs?'

'Why do you ask me that?'

'You're an observant man.'

Casement shook his head, turned away and looked out through the big window behind him. The glass here did not extend from floor to ceiling; Casement wanted some privacy, did not want to be spied upon by someone with binoculars. Still, the view was breathtaking. A container ship was passing under the Harbour Bridge, its decks half-empty; exports this year were still down, the foreign debt steady on the graph like a dead man's heart signature. He was too old to be distressed by election results, though he had been disappointed when the Coalition had, as every cliché-ridden columnist put it, snatched defeat from the jaws of victory. The country would continue to go downhill under Labor; he could not bring himself to believe that men from the wrong side of the street could run a country. He turned back to the two detectives, glad of his age, glad that, though born rich, he was not starting life over again.

'You shouldn't be asking me about Rob. I took as little notice of him as I could. I tolerated him because of his father and because of my wife. I didn't like him at all.'

'That's an honest opinion, Mr Casement.'

'You make it sound as if you haven't heard too many honest opinions this morning.'

'You could say that. But we're used to them, aren't we, Russ?'

Clements had been taking notes in his peculiar shorthand; he looked up and smiled. 'It's the other opinions that help us more than the honest ones.'

The shrewd eyes abruptly showed amusement as Casement remembered the Eighties. 'I wish there had been more honest opinions a few years ago.'

'Did you have a visitor at home last night?' said Clements.

'Why do you ask?'

'We're trying to find out how the murderer got into the building. The security is said to be pretty tight.'

'It is. Or it has been up till now. Except –' He stopped. 'I haven't thought about it before. It could be better down in the basement, in the garage. The service lift comes up from there. Yes, Alice?'

Mrs Pallister had silently opened the door from her office without knocking, stood there like a headmistress. 'Time to leave for your luncheon. Your ten minutes are up, Inspector.'

Malone had an elaborate look at his watch. 'Doesn't time fly! Well, thank you, Mr Casement. Maybe we can come back when you have more time.'

'Telephone first,' said the Wicked Witch.

'No, no, Alice. Let them come whenever they wish. I'm interested in how Inspector Malone and Sergeant Clements will proceed from here. Anything for a change,' said Casement and sounded wistful.

At the door Malone paused. 'Are you related at all to Roger Casement?'

'The traitor? Or the patriot, depending on your point of view? You know something of Irish history?' Casement seemed surprised that a cop should know anything of history outside of police files.

'A little. My mother was Irish-born and my father likes to think he was. At least he says he was conceived in Ireland.'

Casement smiled. 'No, I'm not related to Sir Roger,

40

although I've always admired him. Honour is always to be admired, don't you think?'

'Honour and justice don't always mix. Any cop will tell you that. The British hanged Sir Roger, they said that was justice.'

'Well, let's hope justice is done when you find young Rob's murderer.'

When the two detectives had gone, Casement said, 'Cancel that lunch, Alice. I have no appetite, for food or those dreary people I was going to lunch with.'

'You're upset by those two policemen coming in here, aren't you?'

'Don't start guessing my feelings, Alice. You sound like my wife.'

'I've been guessing your feelings for ten years. That's what private secretaries are for, isn't it?'

'Alice, Alice –' He shook his head, spun his chair slowly and looked out the window, at nothing. 'Make me some tea and a sandwich. And cancel the rest of the day. I think I'll go home and hold my wife's hand.' He swung his chair back again. 'What are you smiling at?'

'You haven't needed to have your hand held since you were two years old.'

He smiled, humouring her. 'That wasn't what I said. I'm going home to hold my wife's hand, not she hold mine.'

Going down in the lift Malone said, 'How much would he be worth?'

Clements shrugged. 'It'd be anybody's guess. Even the so-called experts, when they put him on that Rich List in that financial magazine, they're only guessing. Could be half-a-billion, a billion, maybe more. People like the Casements hide what they're worth. Not to dodge taxes, but just because they think it's vulgar to let anyone know. I'd be the same,' he said with a grin.

'So one of the Bruna sisters did all right for herself?'

'All three of them have. She's just done better than the others.'

They came out into the sunlight; the earlier clouds had disappeared. Three or four smokers, the new lepers, stood near the entrance, snatching a few puffs of cancer before they went back to their non-smoking offices; butts lay about them like scraps of fossilized lung. That, of course, was the impression of Malone, a non-smoker.

He paused, looking across at the lunchtime crowd moving towards the cafés along the Quay. Along the waterfront itself parents with children, tourist groups and loafers drifted with slow movements, as if responding to the harbour's gentle tide. Buskers sang or played instruments; with the recession, busking had become a new form of self-employment. Malone remembered stories his father had told him of the Depression: Con Malone had sung in the streets, 'Mother Mchree' torn limb from limb by a tuneless baritone. The Good Old Days: they were coming back, dark as ever. But at least here the sun shone, nobody starved, there was music instead of machine-gun fire. Europe was crumbling, Russia was falling apart, the Serbs and the Croats and the Muslims of Bosnia were making their own hell.

Malone crossed the road, Clements hurrying to catch up with him, and dropped a dollar in the violin-case of a young girl playing some country-and-western number. He looked at Clements, who reluctantly took out a fifty-cent piece and dropped it in the violin-case. 'I hate that sorta music,' he said as they walked away. 'Where do we go from here?'

'I'm having lunch first. Or luncheon. Over a meat pie, you can tell me whether you think someone in the family killed young Sweden. Or had him killed.'

'And what about Frank Minto and the stiff stolen from the morgue?'

'You've just spoiled lunch.'

42

At Casement & Co., Stockbrokers, the general manager was not available. 'He's up at the Futures Exchange, that's in Grosvenor Street.'

'Did you know Rob Sweden?' said Malone.

The pretty girl, an Indian, behind the reception desk closed her big dark eyes for a moment, opened them again, then nodded. 'We're all –' She gestured with a graceful hand, looked for a moment as if she might weep. Then she recovered: 'Yes, I knew him.'

'Did you ever meet him outside the office?'

'You mean, did I go out with him?' Her father had been a Bombay lawyer; but she was more direct. Circumlocution never got you anywhere with Australians, they didn't understand the uses of it. 'No, he never went out with any of the girls from the office. He was – discreet? – that way. He always treated us politely. No, you know, harassment.'

'A gentleman?'

'Oh yes. They're scarce today.' She sounded as if she might show them her bruises.

'Not amongst us older types,' said Malone, thanked her and he and Clements left.

The Futures Exchange was hidden behind the facade of a building that belonged to another age, when a future had no value to anyone but the person whose dream it was. The building had been gutted and turned into a temple owned and run by the money-changers: Jesus Christ would never have got past the security guards at the entrance.

Malone and Clements, being police and not messiahs, were admitted. They found Jim Ondelli, Casement's general manager, in the ten-year-bond pit. He was in his early forties, thin-faced and curly-haired, his trader's vest of purple-and-pink stripes worn over what looked to Malone like a very expensive shirt. He handed his clipboard to a younger man, a mere boy, and came towards Malone and Clements.

'You're from the police? They rang me from the office.'

Malone introduced himself and Clements. 'Is this a good time to talk?'

'Oh sure, no worries. The bond market, especially the ten-year-one, is pretty slack at the moment, everyone's waiting to see what the Japanese are going to do. What can I do for you? I mean about Rob Sweden. Poor bugger.'

It was like being in an aviary; or, as Clements, a chauvinist, would have described it, at a women's luncheon party. Chatter chipped the air, shouts bounced like invisible rubber balls. Ondelli led the two detectives under a balcony where, somehow, the noise was less overwhelming.

'Are you doing what young Sweden did?'

'Yeah. He was one of our traders, not the best but good enough. He might've developed, I dunno. I tried him on several of the pits, they all handle a different commodity. He wasn't quite quick enough for the really volatile pit, say the share-index one over there.'

'Was that why you transferred him to the bank?'

'That was his own idea, not mine.'

'What would he have earned?' said Clements, a punter.

'Here? It varied. He'd have earned less at the bank. The clerks here, the young ones hoping to be traders, they're usually on around forty thousand a year. A trader like Rob would get sixty to a hundred thousand, depending on how good he is. The "gun" trader – that kid over there, for instance –' Ondelli pointed to the share-index pit, where a group of traders, most of them young, stood in a semi-circle facing another young man in a green-and-white jacket. 'That kid is as good as anyone on the floor. He's with –' He named one of the major banks. 'He has the money to play with. When he bids, the others jump in – that's why they're watching him as if he's some sort of orchestra leader. He'd be on a hundred and fifty thousand, probably plus bonuses.'

The two detectives looked at each other and Ondelli grinned. 'It's bloody obscene, is that what you're thinking?'

In these times, yes. But all Malone said was, 'We're in the wrong game.'

Ondelli went on, 'This is, in effect, no more than a gambling den, a legitimate one. It has its uses, though. It can guarantee a price for a farmer, for instance, for his produce, say six months down the track. It can protect him against a poor harvest or a glut harvest – up to a point, that is. We can do nothing about the low prices right now for wool and wheat. As for the rest of it –' He shrugged. 'It's gambling, a casino.'

'How much money passes through here each day?' Clements, the bookies' friend, was hooked: this was one form of gambling he had never examined. It also opened up the possibility that, somewhere on this crowded, noisy floor, lay the reason for Rob Sweden's murder.

'The transactions? We're the ninth largest futures exchange in the world. We handle about seventy thousand transactions a day, about thirty billion dollars' worth.'

The two detectives, feeling more poverty stricken by the moment, looked at each other again. Then Malone said, 'What would the largest do?'

'That's the Chicago Board of Trade. It does a million transactions a day. There's also the Chicago Mercantile Exchange. Between them they do just on sixty-five trillion dollars a year in contracts. That's sixty times the value of all the shares traded on the New York Stock Exchange.'

Malone looked at Clements. 'You going to leave the bookies and try your luck here? He's the scourge of the bookies,' he explained to Ondelli.

'Can anyone make money on the side here?' asked Clements.

'You mean trade for themselves? No, that's a no-no. The Exchange is very strict on that. Rob Sweden wouldn't have been into that.'

'What about scams?' Ondelli frowned as if offended and Clements added, 'I'm not suggesting young Sweden was in any scam. But can they work them?'

'Sure,' Ondelli admitted. 'Any business where money is traded, there's always the opportunity for a scam. Cornering the market in something, for instance. That's been tried every-

45

where. The Japanese invented the first futures market, in Osaka back in 1650, and they invented the first corner about the same time.'

'What about other scams?'

Ondelli looked dubious. 'I dunno whether I should be telling you all this, I'm putting a bad odour on the Exchange. Ninety-nine point nine per cent of what goes on here every day is honest trading. But there's the exception, there always is. A futures exchange is a convenient place for laundering money, you know what I mean?'

'We know what you mean,' said Malone. 'Go on.'

'Say someone wants to launder a million dollars, some drug dealer or some guy who's wondering how he can avoid tax. He picks some trader who's got a blind eye, gives him the million and tells him to trade in some futures that are never going to move, something like New Zealand wool futures or North American lumber. They're not volatile, they go up or down only a few cents, but they're nothing to get excited about. The guy leaves his money with the trader for, say, a month, three weeks. Then he comes back, says he's decided to get out of the market. The trader writes him a cheque for a million dollars, less commission, a *clean* cheque, and the guy walks away with his money all nicely laundered.'

'Who polices something like that?'

'The Exchange itself. It has an audit staff, they keep an eye on everything going on. See those screens up there above each of the pits? That young girl in the middle of each pit, they're kids virtually straight out of high school, she records every transaction that takes place in her pit. She speaks into that mike she's wearing and the computer translates her voice into those figures you see on the screen. That information goes around the world simultaneously, to every major futures exchange – a guy in Chicago or Tokyo or London knows at once what's happening down here in Sydney. Everything on those screens comes before the audit staff and over a week or a month they pick up any blips in what should be normal trading. They inform the trading broker in question and he has

46

twenty-one days to reply. If he can give no satisfactory answer, he goes before a tribunal of the Exchange's chief executive and two outside members of the board. They can fine the broker up to a quarter of a million dollars and take away his licence. At the same time he might be investigated by the Securities Commission, that's a separate thing. They can prosecute the broker and he can get up to five years in jail. The Exchange is self-regulating, but it's tough. Not like some of these other self-regulating bodies.'

'Has anyone been caught laundering money?'

'Not as far as I know. But that's not to say it hasn't happened.' He looked at them shrewdly. 'You're not telling me Rob Sweden might've been into something like that?'

'So far we're not suggesting anything. Why did he transfer to the Casement bank?'

'That puzzled me. He wasn't the banking type – he wouldn't get the excitement in the bank's foreign currency department that he got here. He just sprung the news on me.'

'You know he was murdered?'

There was one of those inexplicable moments when the world is suddenly silent: the noise in the pits abruptly stopped, as if everyone on the floor had heard what Malone had just said. Ondelli gave an audible gasp and his eyes almost disappeared as his thick brows came down. Then the noise started up again and his voice was only a whisper: 'Murdered?'

'Yes, he was murdered before he was tossed off that balcony.'

'Jesus!' Ondelli shook his head; his curls bounced. 'It'll be the talk in the pub this evening. So does that alter the picture on Rob? Do you mean something here –' he waved a hand around him '– maybe had something to do with his death?'

'Could be,' said Malone. 'Here's my card. If a blip, as you call it, comes up on those screens in the next week or two, a scam or something that Rob Sweden might've been connected with, let me know.'

Malone and Clements went back to Homicide in Surry Hills. Homicide, Major Crime Squad, South Region was in a refurbished commercial building that had once been a hat factory; Sydney, the oldest of the colonies, had long ago given up trying to keep all its services in government buildings. One advantage to working in the Hat Factory was that big heads from Administration rarely ventured there.

Malone rang Lisa to see if he was still in the doghouse. Her voice was cool: 'Tom says he understands, there's duty and all that.'

'What's he doing?'

'He's in his room listening to the radio. They're playing that Ice-T song about killing cops. He's dancing to it, seems to be enjoying himself.'

He sighed. 'You should've married someone on the dole, they're home all the time.'

'Oh, now we've joined the New Right, have we?'

'I dunno why, but I still love you.'

But when he hung up he knew he had been forgiven; seventeen years of marriage had inured Lisa to the vagaries of a cop's wife's life. The children sometimes had trouble adjusting to his abrupt coming and going, the broken promises on outings; but Lisa, despite her own occasional annoyance, acted his advocate with them. He was well aware and grateful that she was the rock on which the family stood.

He called Peta Smith in to his small corner office. She came in, briskly cool but with an understated deference to him. She was twenty-nine, a year older than John Kagal, attractive without being either pretty or beautiful, with thick blonde hair cut short, a wide jaw and alert blue eyes. She always wore, no matter what the season, a suit and a blouse; she was neat. She had been with Homicide six months and had proved as efficient as any of the men; yet Malone, aware of the chauvinism amongst the majority of the men under him, was protective of her and so hindered her chances to show how good she was. He was uncertain of her feelings towards him, whether she resented his protection of her.

'Peta –' He explained that there now might be a connection between the Sweden murder and that of the missing corpse from the morgue. 'The Rocks station will run the day-to-day stuff on the Sweden murder and Campsie will do the same on this feller they picked up out at Canterbury. But I want you to keep a flow chart, bringing in the bits and pieces from The Rocks and Campsie.'

She nodded. 'The media are starting to ask questions –'

'Check with Russ, then you handle 'em.' She got up to go, but he checked her: 'Down at The Wharf, did you have a look at the service entrance to the apartments?'

Again she nodded, briskly. 'I went down in the service lift, it goes right down to the basement garage. The PE team had been down there, but said they found nothing.'

'What's the security like?'

She grimaced. 'Pretty lousy, considering what it's like in the rest of the building. There's a grille door at the top of a ramp, it's operated electronically by a card-in-the-slot. There's a smaller door in that large one, its latch is loose, anyone could open the door. It's a joke, security down in that garage.'

'One other thing – would anyone hear the service lift when it's going up or down? I mean from the front desk?'

'I checked that with the doorman. He said no, everything in the building is supposed to be for the comfort of the tenants. Silent lifts, things like that.'

He sat back. 'Peta, do you ever fall down on anything?'

'Only in the guys I choose.' She smiled and left him wondering if she was having love trouble here in Homicide.

Clements came in with the preliminary report from the Physical Evidence team on the Sweden case. 'They haven't come up with much. There are fingerprints all over the apartment – evidently the maid goes pretty light on with the duster, she just re-arranges the dust. Fingerprints will check 'em out with everyone who comes and goes in the apartment, including all those we talked to this morning. I asked 'em to get Cormac Casement's – that'll go down well with the Wicked Witch when our guys walk in with their little pads.'

'Anything else?'

'They found a trace of blood on the fancy coverlet in the

second bedroom, where there might of been a struggle. Just a faint smear, as if a needle or something with blood on it had fallen on the coverlet. It's a fancy pattern, they say, and the killer could of missed the smear in it. There's nothing else. If Rob Sweden had a visitor he knew, we don't know if he offered him a drink. The maid said she washed up all the glasses this morning, Mrs Sweden told her to. Evidently Mr and Mrs Sweden had a drink when they got home from the opera and the uniformed boys were there to tell them what had happened. I'd have a drink, too.'

'Righto, I've told Peta to start drawing up a chart. The Rocks can set up a command room, it's on their turf. I don't know why their D's weren't there when we were down there.'

Clements bit his lip, an old habit. 'Wayne Murrow gave me the word on that.'

Murrow was a senior constable with the Physical Evidence Section. 'Yes?'

'Seems that AC Zanuch got in first. He laid down that it was to be handled directly by Police Centre. I think he also suspected it could be more than an accident. He wants to keep a rein on what goes on.'

'Fred Falkender's not going to like that.' Falkender was the Assistant Commissioner, Crime, one of the seven ACs and no less senior than Zanuch, though without his ambition. Politics was part of the weather in this State and Malone could see the clouds already beginning to loom.

'Scobie, let them work it out between them. Pull your head in.'

'It's right in, I'm not starting any fights on this one. We'll do the donkey-work and let them up above make the decisions. In the meantime we'll start talking to everyone connected to young Sweden. We'll do them individually. The three sisters, their husbands – who do you want?'

'Not the women. I've got Romy on my mind at the moment. One's enough.'

'Propose to her and all your worries will be over. Righto, I'll take the sisters. I'll also take young Jack Aldwych. We'll leave Casement, we've got enough out of him for the moment.'

'That leaves me the Minister. Thanks.'

'No, we'll skip him, too, for a while. There's someone else you've forgotten. The cove they pinched from the morgue. If he was killed by the same method as young Sweden, then I'll bet on it, he was connected to him. Try your luck.'

Frank Minto was on the running sheet in the computer, but he was likely to be overlooked if pressure increased on the Sweden case. It was not true that death made a level playing field.

4

That morning, coming back late from its all-night fishing, a trawler turned seawards to dodge the huge waterspout heading for it. It dragged in the last of its nets: in it was a badly mutilated leg.

'We t'ought the spout, it gonna send us down,' the Italian skipper reported to the police. 'We said the prayers, pretty hard. Da spout, it missed us. Den we look in da net and dere was dis horrible t'ing!'

Though the leg was badly mangled, the foot was intact. Attached to the big toe was a tag, the figures on it almost washed out but decipherable under a microscope: E.50710.

Chapter Four

◆◇◆◇◆◇◆

1

That evening Malone took Lisa and the three children to the Golden Gate, a restaurant in Chinatown. Lisa recognized the outing for what it was, a penance for sins of omission, but she said nothing. Any sense of guilt that could make him spend money on the children was all right by her. She was not extravagant and ran their home with old-time Dutch thrift, but at times Scobie's attachment to a dollar, as if it were an organ of his body, upset her. Money was to be saved, sure, but it was also to be spent.

The restaurant manager knew Malone, though the latter was not a regular customer here; the manager knew every police officer in the central business district. With an illegal gambling club on an upper floor of the building, it was politic to recognize the enemy, declared or otherwise.

The manager came back to their booth after he had taken the Malones' orders. 'Inspector, Mr Aldwych's compliments and he would like you and your family to be our guests.'

Malone looked towards the back of the restaurant, saw Jack Aldwych seated alone in a booth. The silver-haired old man nodded and raised a hand in salute. Malone nodded, then turned back to the manager. 'Thank Mr Aldwych, but no. He'll understand.'

The manager smiled, a Chinese smile that gave nothing away. 'Of course, Inspector. Enjoy your meal when it comes.'

When the manager had gone Claire said, 'Why did you do that, Dad? That was rude.'

'I'm supposed to be the rude one in the family,' said Maureen.

'You are,' said Tom.

Malone looked at his three. Claire, almost seventeen, beautiful (in his eyes) and (also in his eyes) about to be ravished by sex-mad thugs masquerading as ordinary decent young Australian men. Maureen, going on fifteen but already with one foot in the doorway of adulthood, pretty but unconscious of it, both eyes wide open, but not with innocence, to the world. And Tom, who at ten was beginning to realize that being a cop's son was not all fun.

'The man who offered to pay for us is part-owner of this restaurant, but he was once the biggest criminal in the country. A cop can't take favours from a man like that.'

Maureen had raised herself in her seat, taken a polite look at Jack Aldwych, who gave her a small wave. She sank back. 'I read about him in the papers. He's retired, it said.'

'People would still look at it the wrong way.' *Especially now.* This very week two senior police officers were being investigated for having lunched with two top crims.

Claire gave him a smile and patted his hand. 'Well, it's nice to know you're not bent.'

'Thanks,' he said and looked at Lisa. 'What more can kids say about their father than that? Now, when dinner comes, eat everything, since I'm paying.'

'We knew you'd say that,' said Maureen and produced a plastic bag. 'So I brought a doggy-bag, just in case.'

They had almost finished dinner when Jack Aldwych, tall and well-dressed, looking more like a slightly battered banker, of whom there were many these days, than a man who had murdered and ordered murders, came past their booth. Lisa put out a hand.

'Mr Aldwych, we haven't met. I'm Lisa Malone and these are our children. We'd like to thank you for your offer of dinner. It wasn't meant to be a rude refusal.'

Aldwych smiled at her. He liked good-looking women and

this was a good-looking woman: blonde, well-figured, quietly dressed, with a frank but intelligent face. There had been a time when, intent only on the male enemy, cops and other crims, he had made little attempt to understand women. Except, of course, Shirl, the wife, whom he had understood and loved.

'Mrs Malone, it's a pleasure to meet you. And you, too.' He looked around the booth at the three children; then at Malone: 'Scobie, I understand. I wasn't offended – I read the papers. It's just a pity a simple gesture is suspected. I don't mean you, you know who I mean.'

'Sure, Jack. You well?'

'Hoping to live till I'm a hundred. I'll buy you all dinner on the day. By then I should be respectable.' He smiled again at the children, then at Lisa. 'Goodnight, Mrs Malone. The children are a credit to you. So is he.'

He winked at Malone and passed on. Claire said, 'What a nice old man! It's hard to believe –'

'Believe it,' said Malone, 'whatever it is. Why did you do that, darl? Stop him?'

'It was spur of the moment,' said Lisa. 'I've been hearing about him off and on, bits and pieces, for – what? – three years now. A wife gets curious, whether she is married to a policeman or not. I just wanted to see if he was real.'

'Is he?' said Tom.

'Yes, he is. Very real.' And she looked across the table at Malone. Somehow, he thought, she had seen inside Jack Aldwych, seen the ruthlessness, dormant now maybe, that had been his nature for so long. 'But why did you bring us here?'

'Because it's the best restaurant in Chinatown. I'd just forgotten he's a part-owner. Righto, now here's the worst part of the evening. The bill.'

Going through their usual mockery of him, the two girls opened their purses and Tom put his hand in his pocket. Their mother said, 'Put your money away. If he doesn't pay, we're all leaving home.'

Malone grinned and even left a tip, a bounty that left the Chinese waiters unimpressed. It was only five per cent, but it was almost a mortal wound to the donor.

2

Next morning Chief Superintendent Greg Random, Commander of the Regional Crime Squad, came across from Police Centre to the Hat Factory. Malone had just called the morning conference when Random walked in.

'Don't look at me like that,' he said. Tall, lean and grey-haired, laconic as a recorded weather report, he had once been in charge here at Homicide. 'You must have expected me.'

'It crossed my mind,' said Malone. 'Who suggested it? AC Zanuch? Or the Minister?'

'It was my own idea. Get on with it.'

There were six Homicide staff at the conference, plus two detectives from The Rocks and two from Campsie. Malone introduced the outsiders to Random, then nodded to Clements to open the meeting.

'So far we haven't got out of the barrier,' said the big man. 'The missing corpse has turned up, or part of it. But we still dunno who he is or where he came from.'

'There's nothing in Missing Persons,' said Peta Smith. She was sitting with her knees together, her longish skirt covering them, giving the newcomers from The Rocks and Campsie no opportunity to appreciate her good legs. 'It's early days yet. Maybe so far nobody's missed him. Andy Graham is keeping an eye out.'

'Someone, somewhere, is going to miss him soon,' said Malone. 'You think he came from your area, Mick?'

Mick Griffin was one of the Campsie detectives, a young redheaded giant who on Saturday afternoons, when he wasn't throwing his weight at crims, threw the discus in inter-district athletic meetings. 'I don't think he came from around our way, Inspector. We've been to all the pubs and clubs and showed the photos of him taken when he was found by the river. Nobody could tell us anything. We've talked to the girls on the beat on Canterbury Road, we thought he might of been an outsider trying to muscle in on the pimps there, but they told us there's been no trouble for months.'

'He doesn't have to have had a record,' said John Kagal.

'No,' said Malone, 'but I'll bet Sydney to a brick that whoever did him and young Sweden in has a record. Or if he hasn't, he's building up to one. This isn't a domestic, these two were killed by a pro. Have you dug up anything in young Sweden's flat?'

'I went out to Edgecliff yesterday afternoon,' said Kagal. 'His flat is in one of the older blocks out there, but nicely furnished. Looks like he went for the good things. His car is a BMW 525, we found it yesterday morning still down in the garage of The Wharf.'

'What did you find at his flat?'

'These.' Kagal emptied a large plastic envelope on to the table round which they sat. 'There was a lot of the usual stuff in the closets and drawers – there were ten suits, for instance. All imported stuff, Italian.' Kagal sounded envious. 'Zegna, Armani.'

'They're expensive, right?' Malone bought his home-grown wardrobe off the rack at Fletcher Jones or Gowings, usually at sale time.

'Even I know that,' said Clements, another poor fashion-plate.

'Could we get off the style notes?' said Random. 'What you're saying, John, is this man lived above his means?'

'Not necessarily,' said Malone, getting in first. 'He made sixty thousand a year, plus bonuses. He could've spent every cent of it. Young fellers do.'

The young fellers around the table shifted uneasily. Kagal went on, 'He must have liked the ladies – his bedside drawer had enough condoms in it to cover every cock in the eastern suburbs. Sorry, Peta.'

She said nothing, but Malone said, 'Nicely put, John. Just don't put it on the computer. Go on.'

'There are these American Express card account statements. He made a trip to Manila last month, stayed at the Manila Plaza, that's a five-star hotel.'

'He could've gone there for his firm.'

'Yes, except I checked the dates. He flew out on the Friday night, came back on the Sunday. I rang Casement's, they said they'd never sent him overseas on business.'

'Could he have gone on one of those sex tours?' asked one of the men from The Rocks.

Kagal shook his head. 'I don't think so, not when he was getting so much here at home.'

'Anything else?' said Malone.

'There's this.' Kagal pushed a cheque-book and bank statement across the table. 'There are deposits every fortnight. The same amount, obviously his salary cheques. But look at the other deposits. Where did that money come from?'

Malone looked at the statement: there were three deposits, each of five thousand dollars. 'Bonuses?'

'I checked with his office. The bonus is paid once a year, in June, just before the end of the financial year. He hadn't received this year's yet.'

'Could it be money he made trading on the side?' said Random.

Malone shook his head. 'That's not allowed and, as far as we know, young Sweden never tried it.'

'Could it be gambling winnings?' said Peta Smith.

Clements, the gambling man, said, 'Five thousand each time? Your winnings are never as regular as that.'

'You're listening to the expert,' Malone explained to the others. 'Anything else, John?'

Kagal produced another envelope, dropped one item on the table, a second cheque-book. He did it with some flair, like a magician producing a second rabbit from a small hat. You show-off young bastard, Malone thought; and out of the corner of his eye waited for some reaction from Greg Random. But the older man's lean, gullied face showed nothing.

'That account's in another name. Raymond Sexton. R.S. Same initials. It's supposed to be difficult to open a bank account now without proper identification, but it can be done. Look at the deposits. Eight thousand, nine thousand five hundred, eight thousand again, seven thousand eight hundred. There's just over seventy-two thousand dollars deposited in that account in the past three months, all in amounts under ten thousand dollars. That way the bank doesn't have to inform the tax people.'

Malone picked up the cheque-book, glanced at the name of the bank. Then he looked at Clements. 'Well, waddiaknow! Our old mates down at Shahriver Credit International.'

'They're in our territory, aren't they?' Terry Leboy, from The Rocks, was a young blond-headed man almost as well-dressed as Kagal.

Malone nodded. 'We had something to do with them a coupla years ago. They're shonky – plenty of capital, but they don't care particularly who their clients are. So far they haven't been closed down. Maybe they've been keeping their noses clean. Except –' He tapped the cheque-book on the table. 'Young Sweden was up to something. Try the bank. Find out if the deposits there by Mr Sexton were in cheques or cash. These statements don't show.'

'Do we tell 'em we think Sexton and Sweden are the same man?'

'Sure, why not? If they're trying to keep their noses clean, they'll lean over backwards to be co-operative. Be polite.'

Malone gave out instructions to the other detectives and everyone left the table but Malone, Clements and Random. There were other Homicide men working on other cases in the big room. Random rose, jerked his head and led the way back into Malone's small office.

'Close the door.'

Malone did so. 'We're in trouble, right?'

'Not yet.' Random took a pipe from his jacket pocket and put it between his teeth. Malone, in all the years he had known Random, had never seen him light it. He had begun to suspect that the older man, the least actorish of men, used it as a prop. 'The Minister is making noises.'

'What sort of noises? Does he want us to call off the investigation?'

'I'm not sure.' Random sucked on his pipe. 'There are waves coming down from above, from Bill Zanuch, even from the Commissioner, that I can't fathom. The government's got a majority of two, it's had a few messy cock-ups the past couple of months, it doesn't want its boat rocked again. If the Minister's son was involved in something shonky, if the Minister knew of it –'

'Do you think he did?'

Random shrugged, sucked on the pipe again. 'Your guess is as good as mine.'

Malone and Clements looked at each other. They had been this route before, with a Labor government, with past and present Conservative coalition governments. In any democratic State, politics is always ready to interfere; that, Malone was convinced, was what democracy was about. Power had to be protected, to a political party it was as precious as motherhood. So long, that is, as the mothers voted the right way.

'Greg,' said Clements, 'we can't just let this lay. We've got another four unsolved murders out there, ones that have got nothing to do with the Sweden case.' He nodded through the half-glass wall to the big room. 'If we drop another one in the Too Hard basket, the media will be on us like a ton of bricks. They're ready to pile the shit. There's those four young coppers accused of stealing drugs, there's the suspected cover-up by our two senior blokes –' He bit his lip. 'Nothing may come of those, we dunno. But I'd rather protect the service than take care of the Minister. *Four Corners* is just itching to make another TV documentary that makes us look fools. If the media starts querying why we're back-pedalling on the Sweden case, we might as well pack up, take our superannuation and go fishing.'

Random looked at Malone, held up a finger. 'My finger in the wind tells me you feel the same way?'

Malone nodded. 'Let's do it our way, Greg. If the boat has to be rocked, too bad.' He sighed, leaned back in his chair, stretched his legs; he was not relaxing, just trying to ease the sudden tension that had taken hold of his limbs. 'I've reached a point where I don't care a stuff about politics. I think I might welcome being shifted out to Tibooburra.'

'Don't write it off as a possibility.' Random stood up, put his pipe back in his pocket. 'Okay, go ahead. But keep me informed all along the way, everything you come up with, including stuff you won't put in the briefs. I'll make the decisions, understand?'

'You don't think I want to make 'em, do you?' Malone grinned, but there was stiffness in his facial muscles, too.

As soon as Random had gone, Malone tried some politics of his own. He rang Fred Falkender, AC, Crime. 'Sir, I'd like to come over to Headquarters and talk to the Minister. I thought I'd better tell you first.'

'Does Chief Super Random know?'

'He's told me to pursue the Sweden case my own way,' Malone half-lied.

'You mean you haven't told him you're coming over here? Scobie, you really are a pain in the arse.' Falkender had worked his way up from the ranks; there wasn't a trick he did not know. Still, he laughed. He was always laughing, but the unsuspecting had too often found it was just a smokescreen. The Assistant Commissioner was too experienced to believe that all was laughter in the human comedy. 'Okay, come over. See me first, I'll find out if the Minister wants to see you.'

When Malone reached Administration Headquarters several blocks away, Falkender was coming down the corridor from another of the offices occupied by the seven assistant commissioners. 'I've just been talking to AC Zanuch.'

Malone looked warily at him. 'Yes?'

'Don't worry, I'm running you, no one else.' Falkender was built like a bowling ball and as hard; he had skittled more opponents and competitors than he had bothered to count. He presented a jovial face to the world, but he was as shrewd as any long-time politician and he knew more about the law than anyone else in the service. 'You want to tell me why you want to see the Minister?'

He had led Malone into his office, but both men remained standing. Malone knew at once that there was no guarantee Falkender would allow him to see Derek Sweden. 'We've dug up something on his son that doesn't look too good.' He went on to explain all the new details that had been added, or were about to be added, to the running sheet on the Sweden case. 'The son wasn't murdered by some break-and-enter stranger. He was murdered by someone he knew and for a reason. There's also this corpse that was stolen from the morgue. Looks like he was killed by the same method, a needle or a scalpel or something in the back of the neck. There could be a connection.'

Falkender was usually an almost non-stop talker; but he had listened patiently while Malone gave him the facts. Now he folded his plump hands in front of him and rolled his thumbs. He was silent a moment, no joviality at all in his bright blue eyes. Then, 'If that's the way it is, you have to see the Minister,' he said, abruptly taciturn for a change. 'Okay, let's go.'

They went up to the Minister's office, a large suite that fitted the ministerial ego. Up till a few years ago, Police Ministers had been well removed from their department; when one of Sweden's predecessors had insisted on moving into the building, he had been as welcome as one of the city's top crims. The situation had settled down somewhat since then, but there was still a suspicion that, with their boss virtually sitting on top of them, the service could become politicized. Malone and Falkender walked into Sweden's office prepared for the worst.

Sweden was a coat-off, shirtsleeves Minister; it was not a pose for media cameras, he was a genuine worker. He waved Falkender and Malone to chairs, offered them coffee, then sat back. 'I'm as busy as a girl when the Yank fleet's in and I'm about as stuffed. I hope you have some good news, Inspector.'

Malone looked at Falkender, who nodded; he noted that the AC had not laughed or even smiled since they had met downstairs in the corridor. 'Well, Minister, it's like this –' He went on to tell Sweden what he had told Falkender. 'It's not good news, I'm afraid.'

Sweden's desk was the sort that Malone always thought of as being furnished by a woman. There was the gold desk set, the gold-embossed leather barrel for pencils, the gold-embossed leather writing pad, the blotting-roller, the address book, the diary; the desk looked like a Dunhill show-case, stacked with paraphernalia that few men ever bought for themselves. Sweden picked up a gold-plated letter-opener, a business stiletto.

'You're accusing my son of being some sort of criminal, is that what you're saying?'

'I'm not accusing him of anything so far.' Malone's tone was as sharp as Sweden's; he couldn't help it. He glanced at Falkender, expecting some sort of rebuke, but the big round face was impassive. 'All I'm giving you, Minister, are facts that are *real*. I hope we can give you more when our men have come back from the bank I mentioned. You don't know anything about Shahriver, do you?'

Sweden's dark narrow eyes seemed to darken even further; then he put down the letter-opener and leaned forward. 'Yes, I know about it, we've discussed it in Cabinet a couple of times. The Minister for Finance has his eye on it. That's all I know about it. I certainly would never have suggested to my son that he do business with it. You still have to convince me that the bank statement in that name – Sexton? – that it's actually a statement of my son's account with the bank. I hope you're not going to let something like this out to the media, Fred?'

Malone waited for Falkender to back down; but the AC, Crime, bent his knee to no one. 'Inspector Malone is not out to make political capital of this.'

Sweden banged his desk; his bony face abruptly looked ugly. 'Jesus Christ, I'm not talking politics! We're talking about my *son*! Is that all you think I'm capable of, worrying about the fucking politics of it?'

'I'm sorry.' Falkender at least sounded genuinely contrite.

There was a knock at the door and Tucker, the minder, the guardian of the gate, was there, though a little late. 'Minister, I would've been here if I'd known –'

'Beat it, Rufus.' Sweden waved a rude hand, hardly glancing at the press secretary. 'I'm okay. I'll let you know when I want you.' He waved the hand again and Tucker, red in the face, disappeared, shutting the door with some force. 'Bloody minders, they think you can't survive without them. All right, Fred, I'm sorry I flew off the handle. But, Jesus, I'm still in shock –' He looked at Malone. 'You're used to murder, I suppose? I'm not.'

Malone had learned to cope with murder, but he hoped he would never become *used* to it; that way lay barbarism. 'Did your son ever give any hint of being in trouble?' He was quiet but persistent, certain now that Falkender was not going to obstruct him in the interests of harmony here at Headquarters. AC Zanuch, he was equally certain, would now have been on his feet leading the way out of the Minister's suite. 'Did he ever make any unexplained trips anywhere?'

Sweden picked up the stiletto again; it was, Malone remarked, an ideal weapon for puncturing the base of a man's skull. 'Rob was always going away on unexplained trips, usually with a girl. They were unexplained because I never asked about them. I did the same sort of thing when I was young. Didn't you?'

'I couldn't afford it, not on a constable's pay.' There was the tongue again; he smiled to take the edge off it. 'Rob made a quick trip to Manila last month, a weekend trip. Would you know why?'

'No.' The stiletto was steady, its point pressed against one palm.

'This isn't a smart-arse remark, Minister, but your son wouldn't have gone there on one of those quick sex tours. He went there, I think, on business. His own business, not his firm's. They've said they never sent him overseas, he wasn't experienced enough.'

Sweden looked at the stiletto, then carefully set it back on the desk, as if he had just realized it was a weapon. He leaned forward again, finger pointing. This was how he attacked the opposition in the Bear Pit, the State Parliament: Malone had seen clips of him on television. 'Inspector, I am not going to help you besmirch my son's name. All I want from you is to find his murderer.'

Malone's tone was measured: 'That's what we're trying to do, Minister. Murder, unfortunately, is rarely a nice clean job, there's always dirt around the edges. Mr Falkender will back me up there.'

Falkender, rather than acting as if he had been put on the spot, as indeed he had, spoke up. 'That's true, Minister. We'll do our best not to spread any dirt. But we think your son's murder is connected to another on the same night.'

'Whose?'

'We don't know,' said Malone. 'The body was stolen from the morgue. It's been in the papers.'

'I haven't had time to look at the papers today. Or yesterday's. It's probably there in that file of clippings. A corpse stolen from the *morgue*? Christ, what next?'

Malone wondered why the Police Minister's press secretary didn't insist his master look at all crime reports as soon as they appeared. So he told Sweden what he knew of the missing corpse and why they thought its murder was linked to Rob Sweden's.

'That's bloody ridiculous! You're linking Rob to some stranger –'

'He's a stranger to us, Minister, but he may not have been to your son.'

Sweden looked at Falkender; the top of his bald head was glistening, though there was no sweat on his face. But he was angry, ready to boil: 'I hope these sort of insinuations are not going to be broadcast?'

'We don't work that way,' said Falkender in a voice that suggested he was giving a lecture to a Minister still new to the job.

'Okay, I'll see the Commissioner.' Sweden's own tone

suggested that he knew the chain of command. 'In the meantime, no press conferences on this, not till you have solid evidence. If the media want to hear about my son I'll get Rufus Tucker to arrange it and I'll do the talking.'

Falkender stood up. From long experience of politicians, he recognized a brick wall when it was being built. 'Inspector Malone will handle this with his usual discretion, Minister. You'll get a daily report on how he is progressing.'

Going back to Falkender's office Malone said, 'Thanks for that bit about my usual discretion.'

Falkender grinned, his face relaxing for the first time. 'Don't make a liar of me. What d'you reckon?' He jerked his head back towards the Minister's suite. 'Is he just a father doing the usual, protecting his son's good name?'

Malone lowered his voice; no one knew where the ears were in an empty stairwell. 'I think he knows a lot more than he's told us.'

Falkender nodded. 'But be discreet, okay?'

3

In the Opposition Leader's suite in the annexe to Parliament House, Hans Vanderberg, The Dutchman, was seeking material for his last hurrah. He had been Premier of New South Wales for twelve years, running the State almost like an old-time American ward boss; his heroes had been Boss Tweed and Frank Hague and Jim Curley; he knew the names of all the political bosses but only three or four of the Presidents. He had discovered, only a year or two after he had landed in Australia from Holland back in 1948, that real political power does not work on the large stage. Being Prime Minister gave you pomp and ceremony and national headlines, but no PM ever had the power that a truly ambitious State Premier could achieve. The Dutchman had almost had a stroke when all his power had been taken away from him by a mere hundred votes in the last State elections.

'What d'you know about this young Sweden case? They say it's murder.'

'It is.' Roger Ladbroke had been Vanderberg's press secretary for ten years. He had often thought of resigning, of going back to being a political columnist, but in the end always decided that he was a natural masochist and no editor would ever give him the exquisite pain The Dutchman could inflict. It was a consolation that the bruises never showed on him; he always just smiled when the State roundsmen asked him how he continued to put up with the abuse and insults to his education. Some day, when The Dutchman was dead, he would write a book and he possessed secrets that no roundsman could even guess at. 'But as far as I can gather, they have no clue as to who did it or why.'

'His old man connected with it?' Vanderberg played with the quiff of hair that was the cartoonists' delight. He was an ugly little man, shrunk by age, his clothes hanging on him like a wet wash; he was loved only by his wife, but that was enough. 'I tried to give him some sympathy this morning, but he just wiped me.'

The ex-Premier's sympathy was like strychnine: best in small doses.

'There's some skulbuggery in it, I can smell it. Keep sniffing around.' He had never believed that anything was crystal-clear, except his own perceptions.

'Hans, we can't make capital out of a family tragedy. The papers would be on to us like a load of shit.'

'We handle it delicately, son.'

Ladbroke shook his head invisibly at that. The Dutchman's idea of delicacy was how the Chinese had handled Tiananmen Square.

'Use your contacts, find out what's going on. Who's in charge of the case?'

'As far as I can gather, both Assistant Commissioners Falkender and Zanuch seem to have a hand in it.'

'That means they're trying to hide something.' The old man raised his nose, like a hound pointing.

'The man who's actually in charge of the case is that guy, Inspector Malone. You remember him?'

'The honest one?' Vanderberg flattened his quiff. 'He wouldn't tell you the time of Friday –'. No one, not even Ladbroke, was ever sure that The Dutchman did not deliberately mangle everyday phrases. 'We've got to upset the apples, son. Time's running out.'

'The government's got another three years to run.'

'I wasn't talking about them. I was talking about me. I'm getting on, Roger. If we wait for the full term to run, I'll be eighty by the next election. I want to toss out these bastards, get back in, set up things the way I want 'em, put Denis Kipple in my place and then I'll retire. Gracefully.' The thought of his doing anything gracefully seemed to amuse even him: he gave a cackling laugh. 'Get cracking, son. A stitch in time is worth the needling.'

Ladbroke couldn't wait for the graceful retirement. But he would miss the old sonofabitch.

Chapter Five

◆◆◆◆◆◆◆◆

1

In a waterfront apartment out at Point Piper, a narrow diamonds-and-pearls-encrusted finger jutting into the southern waters of the Harbour, another old man was having lunch with his son, his daughter-in-law and his daughter-in-law's father. This weekly lunch was a ritual with Jack Aldwych and he looked forward to it, though he could have done without today's extra guest, Adam Bruna.

'I *adore* this view!' Bruna clasped his manicured hands and gazed out at the Harbour. 'Why don't you move over this side, Jack? Why do you have to live way out there in the Outback, Harbord or wherever it is?'

It amused Aldwych that he might have felt at home here on this tiny peninsula. It had been named after a colonial naval officer, a rake who laid women like stepping stones and who, when it came to making money, had as much dedication to principle as he had to celibacy. Aldwych had never been a womanizer, but he had had little regard for principle if it stood in his way.

'I couldn't afford to live over here.' He was one of the country's richest men, albeit one who never appeared in the rich lists. Wealth based upon prostitution, bank hold-ups, extortion and fraud was not publicly assessable, although in the Eighties fraud had been an almost acceptable method of becoming rich. Aldwych's wealth, thanks to Jack Junior's management, was now squeaky clean, but the smell of its origins still clung to it in certain quarters. 'I could never afford an apartment like this.'

Jack Junior and Juliet had paid three million for the apartment, a price that had shocked Jack Senior almost as much as the day, long ago, a judge had given him five years for attempted murder when everyone knew it was no more than an attempt to teach a welsher a lesson. It had been Juliet who had spent the money, but Jack Senior had said nothing; if she, and what she did, made Jack Junior happy, then there was nothing to be said. At least for the time being.

'Oh, I don't mean you would have to buy something like *this*!' Bruna fluttered his hands. He was a handsome man, as good-looking as any of his daughters; small and compact in build, always beautifully dressed, if a trifle flamboyantly for Aldwych's tastes, he had sharp eyes and a smile that winked on and off as if on a rheostat. He was not homosexual, but he had exaggerated gestures and expressions that had at first confused Aldwych, a man of prejudice whose hands had the stillness of holstered guns. Bruna had once been a sculptor and still occasionally exhibited a piece or two, but his main source of income, apart from his daughters, was a gallery he owned in Woollahra. He had tried to sell Aldwych a small Giacometti, but the older man liked his statues, as he called them, rounded and in marble. The two fathers-in-law were not compatible, but so far not at war. 'But this would be *nice*. I hope you'll leave it to your dear old dad, darling, if you go first. You and Jack,' he added with a smile towards Jack Junior.

'Don't let's talk of dying,' said Juliet. 'Not this week.'

Aldwych looked at her across the table. They were lunching on the apartment's small terrace, sheltered from the unseasonal sun by a large umbrella; the Harbour was a silver glare, a black-clad windsurfer stuck in the middle of it like a table ornament. Aldwych was the only one not wearing dark glasses. Juliet's gold-framed glasses were flattering, but not revealing. 'Have the police talked to you yet about Rob Sweden's murder?'

'Just the morning after it happened, not since then. Do you think they'll come to see me and Jack?'

'You can bet on it.' He ate some ocean trout; Juliet, a smart

69

girl, knew what her father-in-law liked and did not like. 'You remember who's in charge?'

'An Inspector Malone. A nice man, I thought.'

'He is.'

'Did you ever have anything to do with him, Jack?' Bruna had the Eastern European curiosity born in those who came from the crossroads of history. He knew Aldwych's history and was not embarrassed by it. In the art world you met all types, never questioned where their money came from, otherwise you would lose half your sales. He knew that many of his, paid for in cash, had been a means of laundering the client's money but, like many an art critic, he never looked behind the paint.

'Not officially,' said Aldwych, smiling to himself at how pious he sounded.

'There's no reason why he should trouble us.' Jack Junior had been quiet; he was the sort of diner who concentrated on his food. He was as tall and as well-built as his father, but he had a tendency to put on weight; Juliet now had him on a diet. They had been married twelve months and he was deeply in love with her, but lately the thought troubled him that she had taken over the running of his life. In the nicest possible and loving way, of course. 'We had absolutely nothing to do with Rob and the way he lived.'

'That's not quite true, darling.' Juliet was dressed in light-weight cashmere today, with a little gold in the ears and on both wrists, nothing too eye-catching except to her father and other jewelry assayers. Aldwych was no expert, though in the past his hauls had frequently included gold and gems, but he was becoming adept at sizing up Juliet and the way she spent Jack Junior's money. *His* money, for he was still Chairman of the board, though none of the figurehead board members of Landfall Holdings knew that; they thought Jack Junior was the Chairman, just because he sat in the chair. Aldwych watched Juliet as she went on: 'Rob often came to me and 'Lind and 'Phelia for advice. Social advice.'

'You mean advice on women?' said her father.

She smiled at him, as if he were the only one of the three men at the table who understood the relations between men and women. 'Yes. He was juggling about six or seven girl-friends.' Or nine or ten, if one counted herself and her sisters. She did not regret going to bed with Rob, an affair for her was of no more consequence than a luncheon engagement, but Rob's death, and the manner of his dying, might prove that his ghost would be more trouble than his living self had been. 'He looked upon us as women of the world.'

'Which you are, of course,' said her father, and his smile winked on again as he looked at the two Aldwych men. 'When they were small girls, that was what I decided they would be. Women of the world. It just turned out to be a smaller world than I'd planned.'

'Meaning Sydney?' said Aldwych, who loved his home town, even though he had robbed it blind. 'Would Roumania have been a bigger, better world?'

'Touché.' Bruna smiled again, but it was more forced this time. It was forty years since the Brunas had escaped from Roumania, smuggled aboard a ship out of Constanta that had taken them down to Istanbul. After the fall of Ceauşescu three years ago he had thought of paying a return visit, his roots stirring again, watered by memories, but in the end he had known there was nothing to go back for or to: the past of his own and Ileana's family was dead. 'No, not Roumania, old chap. Europe, all of Europe.'

'Europe has nothing but trouble,' said Aldwych.

Then the cook-housekeeper, who had arrived from Roumania after the fall of Ceauşescu and still couldn't believe her luck in getting out of Bucharest and falling into a job like this, came out on to the terrace. She looked frightened, as well she might, considering her previous experiences: 'Two policemen. Secret ones.'

'Secret ones?' said Aldwych.

'She means they are not in uniform,' said Juliet. 'They must be detectives.'

'Malone, I'll bet,' said Aldwych and looked with a certain

71

pleasure as Malone and Clements were ushered out on to the terrace. 'Scobie! We were just talking about you.'

'Have you had lunch yet?' said Juliet. 'Won't you join us?'

'Thank you,' said Clements, who, always hungry, would have joined cannibals if invited.

The two detectives sat down and, over small talk, were served fish by the housekeeper, who looked as if she were being called upon to serve the Securitate. Malone was between Juliet and her father, Clements between the two Aldwych men. Clements took wine, but Malone asked for just water.

'You'll like that wine, Russ,' said Aldwych. 'It's our own. We have a half-interest in a small vineyard up in the Hunter. That's our '86 semillon.'

Malone was savouring the ocean trout. 'You seem to go in only for half-interests, Jack.'

'Keeps our name out of the papers,' said Jack Junior, and his father nodded in smiling agreement. 'Why are you here, Inspector?'

Malone cleared his mouth of fish. 'We're finding out a few things about young Rob that worry us.'

All the forks at the table, except Clements', paused in mid-air. 'Such as?' said Juliet.

'Seems he had sources of income outside of his salary and bonuses at Casement's.' He looked across the table at Jack Junior. 'Did he ever do any moonlighting for you, Jack?'

Jack Junior put down his fork, aware of his father's watchful eye. Eighteen months ago, in his one venture outside the law, he had almost run afoul of Malone. He had been involved with another strong-minded girl then and it had been his father who had broken up the relationship and saved him from making a fool of himself and, probably, doing time behind bars. 'I don't want to speak ill of the dead –'

'Why not?' Bruna's smile flashed around the table. 'Isn't that the best and safest time?'

Jesus, thought the elder Aldwych, no wonder Roumania fell apart.

Jack Junior ignored the interruption: 'I wouldn't have a bar of Rob, Inspector. Not in business.'

'Why not? As Mr Bruna says, let's speak ill of the dead. Maybe we'll learn something.'

'He was too unreliable, I always had the feeling that if he could make money on a shonky deal, he would.' It was his turn to sound pious; he saw the faint glimmer of a smile at the corner of his father's mouth. What surprised him was that his wife, too, seemed on the point of smiling. 'He was a borrower, too. He put the bite on me a week after my wife introduced me to him.'

'You didn't tell me that,' said Juliet.

Malone interrupted before a husband-and-wife diversion could get in the way: 'Did you lend him any money?'

'No. I told him I only lent money at the going rate and with firm security.'

'That's the only way to be in business,' said Aldwych and winked at Malone. 'In our business, right, Scobie?'

'I didn't think you were still in business, Jack. Our business.'

Juliet glanced sideways at the policeman beside her, then across at her father-in-law. She had no experience of how the law and the criminal element worked. She did not read crime novels, watch crime films or television series, never read crime stories in the newspapers. She was not naive and knew that the world only went round because the good and the evil recognized they were two sides of the same coin and the toss was often a matter of luck. It intrigued her that these two men appeared to have a working arrangement and she wondered if Inspector Malone was corrupt. That thought intrigued her, too, because corruption fascinated her.

'A figure of speech, Scobie.'

'Did you know him, Jack?'

'Never met him. Mr Bruna here knew him, didn't you, Adam?' Aldwych threw a right hook, playful to be sure, but he wouldn't have minded if it had hurt.

'Oh yes, I knew him. I always thought he was perfectly charming. He never tried to borrow from me,' he told Jack

73

Junior. 'Perhaps he knew that gallery owners live from hand-to-mouth.'

'Stop crying poor mouth,' Juliet rebuked him.

'Was I doing that? How vulgar.' The smile was intended to blind them all.

The two detectives finished their fish, joined the others in the baked cheesecake dessert served by the still apprehensive housekeeper. Aldwych, never having known Rob Sweden, was the spectator here at the table and he sat back to enjoy it. 'No dessert for me,' he said, and almost said, *I'll sit back and watch*. 'More wine, Russ?'

'No, it's a beauty, Jack, but I'd better not. I'm driving.' Then he looked at Bruna, knowing it was time he took up the bowling. 'Did Rob ever do any business with you, Mr Bruna? I understand you're a very successful gallery owner?'

'You're interested in art?' Bruna made no attempt to hide his surprise at what the modern cop got up to in his idle time.

'No, I just do my homework.'

Top marks, thought Aldwych with malicious pleasure.

'I should imagine in the gallery game, a lot depends on recommendations and introductions, right? Did young Sweden ever bring you any customers? He operated in circles where people, young people, have money to spend.'

'We call them clients, Sergeant, not customers. Customers go to supermarkets. Young people with money to spend – and they are scarcer than they used to be, much scarcer – if they buy art at all they buy paintings, not sculpture. I exhibit paintings, but mostly sculptors' work. They buy as an investment and sculpture, if it's not from a big name, is not looked upon as much of an investment. No, Rob never brought me any *clients*.'

'So how did you know him?' said Malone.

'Oh, I met him occasionally here at Juliet's. And Jack's,' he seemed to add as an afterthought. 'And he would come to exhibitions at my gallery. He knew a lot of pretty girls, models, nobodies but *pretty*, and they always make an exhibition

74

opening more attractive. They distract the husbands while the wives buy things.'

The smile this time had all the blandness of a smear of white blancmange. What a snob, thought Aldwych who, for all his sins, had never been a snob, not even towards the police. But the bastard was hiding something, those dark glasses were hiding more than his eyes.

'So he never brought a – a client, someone who wanted to pay a lot of money for a painting or piece of sculpture? But pay in cash?'

'No.'

'Do you ever get any clients who want to pay in cash?'

'Occasionally.' The dark glasses were as opaque as darkest night; by some trick of light nothing was reflected in them. 'But they are never strangers.'

'No names, no pack drill?' said Malone.

Then Bruna took off the glasses, squinting a moment as he adjusted to the sunlight. He had dark artful eyes that, Aldwych guessed, could match a buyer and a painting in seconds, far faster than any artist could paint, even a graffiti dauber. 'It's not unusual, Inspector, for buyers to ask for anonymity. It protects them from burglars. Pictures are always being stolen, they can always be sold to buyers who are even more anonymous than the original owners.'

'Does the tax man ever enquire into any of this?'

Bruna pushed away his half-eaten cheesecake. 'You have spoiled my lunch, Inspector.' The smile flashed again. 'We Roumanians are like the South Americans, we think taxation is a social disease that should never be mentioned in polite company.'

'Is that what you think, Jack?' Malone looked at Aldwych.

The old man spread his hand on his chest; the Pope could not have looked holier. 'Scobie, I haven't missed a tax payment in I dunno how long.'

'How about twelve months?'

'Scobie, I'm an honest man now, won't you ever believe that?'

Jack Junior said, 'I don't think you should insult my father.'

His father waved a quietening hand. 'It's all right, Jack. Mr Malone and I understand each other. Better, maybe, than any of the rest of you here at this table. Except you, Russ.' He looked around, but Malone and Clements were only on the periphery of his gaze; he was focussed on Jack Junior, Juliet and Adam Bruna. He was smiling, but it was an old crim's smile, full of guile and cynicism. 'It puzzles you, Julie, how Mr Malone and I understand each other, right?'

'Yes, it does.' She was not afraid of her father-in-law. She had only a sketchy idea of his history; Jack Junior, naturally, did not boast of his father's record. She made her own on-the-spot judgements of those she met and she had already filed her verdict on Jack Senior. He had killed and would kill again if necessary; he had retired, but his moral superannuation was flexible. He would kill, she was certain, if it meant saving his son from some awful fate. 'You appear to be genuine friends.'

'Are we, Scobie?'

'We seem to be heading that way,' said Malone; but everyone at the table recognized the caution in his voice. He pushed back his chair. 'I think we'd better be going.'

'You won't stay for coffee?' Juliet didn't want the detectives to leave. They might be dangerous, to whom, she didn't know; but they had made the day interesting. Lately she had started to become bored, which can happen when you discover you have married the wrong partner.

'I'll come down with you.' Aldwych rose, pulled down his waistcoat. He always wore a three-piece suit; Shirl, his wife, had always insisted that he should camouflage what she called his Australian belly. Shirl was dead now, but in various ways, he still paid his respects to her every day.

'Can we give you a lift?' Clements asked.

'No, there's a hire car waiting for me downstairs. I never drive, never did. I always had a wheel-man. I used him in getaways,' he explained to Juliet and her father. He delighted in shocking the straights of the world, though he had his doubts about how straight Bruna was. He ignored Jack Junior's frown of disapproval. 'Take care of yourself, Julie. And of Jack.'

She kissed him on the cheek. 'I'm taking care of you, too, you dear old man.'

Going down in the lift Aldwych said, 'She's a great bullshit artist, my daughter-in-law. Women have always been better at it than men. It took me a long time to find that out.'

'Me, too,' said Clements, who, until he met Romy, had changed relationships almost as often as he changed his shirts. 'I never understood why there weren't more con-*women*.'

'Maybe there were. Maybe they were so good, they never got caught.'

The two chauvinists nodded at each other while Malone said, 'What about *Mr* Bruna?'

'You notice his hair? He not only sells to the blue-rinse set, he's one of them. You think I'd look better with a blue tint, Russ?'

'It'd suit you, Jack. No bullshit.'

'Jack,' said Malone, 'that wasn't what I meant.'

Aldwych looked at him quizzically. 'Scobie, are you trying to recruit me as a gig? Don't waste your time, son.'

'Russ and I are trying to solve three murders. Yeah, *three*. You read about the corpse that went missing from the morgue?'

'How about that? Stealing stiffs. Even I never went in for that. So what's the connection with young Sweden?'

'We don't know, except that they were both done away with by the same method. A sharp instrument here –' Malone touched the back of his neck. 'It's not a common way of knocking someone off.'

They had reached the ground floor, walked out through the lobby into the short circular driveway where a white Mercedes with HC plates and darkened windows stood waiting. A uniformed driver got out and opened the rear door. But Aldwych paused out of earshot of him. 'Scobie, Russ, I know nothing. That's the truth. If I find out anything that'll help you, I'll let you know.'

'But?' said Malone.

'But what?'

'But not if it concerns Jack Junior, right?' The old man's face went suddenly stiff and Malone went on, 'Jack, I'd never ask you to inform on your own son. But he almost got himself into bother with that girl Janis Eden eighteen months ago. She's still loose, you know.'

'He hasn't seen her, I can promise you that. I scared the shit outa her and she took me at my word. I'd come outa retirement if ever she came back and started making trouble.' A roughness had crept back into his voice, anger, controlled though it was, scraping the skin of the gang leader he had been.

'Righto, I take your word on it. But if you hear anything on any of the others . . .'

'What others? The whole clan? Juliet's sisters and their husbands? You think Cormac Casement would get himself involved in something dirty?' He shook his head. 'You're barking up the wrong tree there, Scobie.'

'What about Derek Sweden?'

Aldwych shrugged. 'Your guess is as good as mine. I vote for him, or anyway his party, because I'm a conservative. What are you grinning at, Russ? You wouldn't expect a bloke who's earned his money like I did, you wouldn't expect me to be a socialist, would you?'

'I'm with you all the way, Jack,' said Clements, still grinning. 'It's these lefties like Scobie who bugger up the system.'

Malone, whom no party would have bothered canvassing, said, 'Jack, about Derek Sweden?'

'I dunno for sure. Maybe his scams now are only political ones, but he made his money originally with some shonky development deals. There, that's all I'm gunna tell you. I'm gunna have trouble getting to sleep tonight, giving information to coppers. But it's been nice seeing you both. Look after yourselves.'

The two detectives escorted him to his hire car. 'How do you fill in your time, now Jack Junior's married?'

'Read. I'm catching up on my education. Political history, crime biographies, stuff like that – they're often much the same thing. And watch TV and videos. I'm gunna watch *Pretty*

Woman tonight for the second or third time. It's a great fairy story, that. A virtuous hooker can find true love if the john is rich enough. Some of the girls who used to work for me must of laughed themselves sick at it. Home, James.'

'Yes, Mr Aldwych.'

He wound down the dark window and winked at them as he was driven away. He had reached a serenity that some old men achieve. Since it was neither senility nor spirituality, it had to be amorality.

2

When Malone and Clements got back to Homicide Andy Graham was waiting for them with some encouraging news.

'A missing person. A lady has been in touch, says her husband's been missing for three days. His description fits that guy who went missing from the morgue. Her name's –' He checked his notebook: 'Mrs Kornsey, Leanne Kornsey. She lives out at Lugarno. I'll go out there now –'

Malone was about to say yes, then thought of Mrs Kornsey being told that all that remained of her husband, if it was he, was a foot and half a leg. Andy Graham, a well-meaning young man but as subtle as a bullock, was not the one to send on such an errand. 'Never mind, Andy, I'll go. It could be a bit awkward –'

Graham might be unsubtle but he was not unintelligent. 'Thanks, Scobie, I wasn't looking forward to it.'

'You want me to come with you?' said Clements.

'I don't think so. If this *is* her husband, one-on-one is better.' He never relished these sort of visits, but they came with the job. He remembered how grateful he used to be when Greg Random was in charge of Homicide and had to do this sort of dirty work. 'You're coming to dinner tonight, you and Romy?'

'Yeah.' Clements sounded unenthusiastic.

'What's the matter? You afraid Lisa is going to lean on you, get you to propose to Romy over our dinner table? Forget it. I've told her it's none of her business and I'll put her on a charge if she interferes.'

'What charge?' Clements managed to smile.

'Corruption, extortion, I'll think of something. But you can't go on putting the girl off. Make up your mind and soon.'

He drove out to Lugarno, south of the city, in his own Commodore, the photo of the dead man in a folder on the seat beside him. He found the Kornsey address, in a quiet street overlooking the George's River. The district had first been developed by an immigrant who, with the cataracts of nostalgia, had seen a faint resemblance in the landscape to Lake Lugano in his homeland. The Kornseys' street was a mixture of houses, some modest, some with pretensions to being mansions, none of them on very large lots, all of them fronted with well-kept gardens. The Kornsey house was on the river side of the street, backing on to rough bush that ran down to the water. A large tibouchina tree stood in the front garden, its deep purple bells looming like a lenten cloud; its colour, Malone thought, was appropriate for the occasion but he would have preferred a more nondescript ornament. The house was one of the less pretentious ones, but it was solid brick, two-storeyed with a double garage on the ground floor and a waterless fountain on the opposite side of the path from the tibouchina. The house was painted white and had a blue-tiled roof. The mat on the fancy-tiled porch actually said WELCOME in worn blue letters, but the heavy grille of the security door suggested the welcome was subject to qualification.

A small blonde woman opened the front door, peered out through the grille at Malone. 'Yes?'

'Mrs Kornsey?' Malone introduced himself, showed his badge. 'May I come in?'

'It's bad news, right?' She hadn't touched the lock on the security door, as if she wanted protection against even bad news.

'I'm not sure till you've seen the photo I have here.' He held up the folder, but didn't show the photo. He did not want her collapsing on him and he unable to get to her because of the door.

She hesitated, then unlocked the door and stood aside for him to enter. Then she led him through the house and out to a sun-room overlooking the river. She didn't offer him coffee or a drink, just sat down heavily on an upholstered cane chair and looked across at him as he sat down opposite her.

'Not there, please. That is Terry's.'

Malone moved from the chair to a lounge, part of the brightly coloured suite. Mrs Kornsey was about forty, he guessed, though she wouldn't admit to all those years. She might have been good-looking in her youth, but she had gone the wrong way about preserving her looks. She had spent too much time on the beach, the sun had leathered her. The blonde hair was too brassy and there was too much of it, the make-up was too thick; she wore Ken Done separates that should have been separated by at least a mile, the colours clashed so jarringly. Her voice had been roughened by drink and cigarettes and her bright eyes thinned a little as if she were short-sighted. Even as he looked at her eyes she put on a pair of bright-blue-framed glasses that seemed to cover half her face.

Malone took out the photo and passed it to her without a word. She looked at it, at the dark-haired man lying on the grass, his eyes shut as if against the glare of the flash. She frowned, took off the glasses, frowned even more, then gasped, 'He's *dead*?'

'That's your husband? Terry Kornsey, that's his name?'

She nodded; then abruptly began to weep. She lowered her head; he saw the dark roots in her hair and felt cheap at noticing such a blemish. She wept noisily, in great gulping sobs: they were echoes of similar situations but they still hurt his ears. He sat quietly, not moving to comfort her; he had learned that, sometimes, that was the wrong thing to do. Some women were fiercely protective of their space, where they loved or grieved or just shut out the rest of the world. From even the brief time he had been in the house, he judged that Mrs Kornsey would never shut out the world, she *needed* it; but he

81

acted cautiously anyway. Once, early in his experience of these situations, he had comforted a widow and she had refused to let him go, phoning day after day till he had had to ask for a counsellor to go see her and take her off his back.

At last Mrs Kornsey wiped her eyes, blew her nose and put her glasses back on. She was a small round-figured woman, though not plump; she seemed suddenly to have got smaller. 'Where is he now? Terry?'

He said as gently as he could, 'Mrs Kornsey, there is not much – I mean, all we have –' He stopped, then recovered, tried to keep his voice as steady and sympathetic as he could. 'All we have of your husband is his foot and part of his leg.'

She frowned again; the blue-framed glasses slipped down her nose and she looked almost comically schoolmarmish. 'You've only got –' She couldn't bring herself to dismember her husband. 'Oh God, *how*? You've got that photo *there*, then you try to tell me there's only –' She shook her head. 'Is this some bloody great sick joke?'

He said nothing, looked out at the river below them. The George's River was notorious for the sharks that came upstream; there had been swimmers taken in the past, but people were less foolhardy now. He wondered if Terry Kornsey had known about the sharks and pondered what it would be like to be eaten by one. At least he had been devoured dead, not alive as the unlucky swimmers had been.

He looked back at the widow, who had pushed her glasses back up her nose and was glaring at him. 'Mrs Kornsey, it's a strange story –' He told her all they knew about her husband. 'Someone murdered him, then his body was stolen from the morgue –'

'Holy Jesus!' She was stupefied; she sat very still, as if he had knocked her out and she had not fallen over. Then abruptly she stood up. 'You want some coffee? Come into the kitchen.'

The kitchen was not large, but it appeared to have every appliance that any cook, or team of chefs, might have called for. Unlike the kitchen in the Sweden apartment, this one looked *lived* in. Mrs Kornsey saw Malone looking around:

'You looking at all the gadgets? Terry was American, he loved gadgets. The garage, his workshop, is full of 'em.'

'He was American? What did he do? I mean, his job?'

'He didn't do anything. Except gamble, though he didn't do that full-time, I mean he wasn't a *professional* gambler. You know, he did SP and that. He'd go down to Wrest Point occasionally, I never went with him. Tasmania didn't appeal to me, there's nothing to see but old jails and churches, they're not my cuppa tea.' She was talking too fast, hardly drawing breath. 'Cappuccino? We got anything you want. Cappuccino, perc-u-lator, plunger, you name it, we got it. Cake? It's home-made. Terry made it, some sorta Italian cake.'

'Was he Italian-American?'

'I dunno. He didn't have any family. He told me his mother and father were killed in a terrible fire, their home just blew up, gas or something, and he come out here seven or eight years ago to put it all behind him. We been married four years. Sometimes he'd have nightmares, dreaming about what happened to his parents. *Murdered?*' The cappuccino machine hissed, then stopped; she twisted her head and looked over her shoulder at him. 'Why would anyone wanna murder him? He was quiet, but everyone liked him. *Really* liked him. Some of the girls at the club told me how lucky I was.'

'What club is that?'

'The St George Leagues Club. We'd go there once a month, maybe twice. Terry was quiet, like I said, but he'd take me wherever I wanted to go. Except to Surfers. There.' She handed him his coffee, slid a plate across to him with a large slice of cake on it.

'Surfers Paradise?' They were seated on stools on opposite sides of a breakfast bench. 'Why wouldn't he take you up there?'

'I thought he'd love to go, gamble at Jupiters, but he always said no. He said the gamblers there, them that come in from overseas, were outa his league and he didn't wanna be tempted and play for stakes that were too high. He wasn't *mean*, but he was careful with his money. I always had the impression

83

that he'd been used to a lotta money before he come out here. It was like he was doing his best to live on something less than he'd been used to. I'm talking too much,' she said and shut up, compressing her rather full lips.

'It's a way of relieving the shock.' He sipped his coffee, nibbled at the cake. 'What did you live on?'

She looked at him sharply. 'That's a pretty personal question, isn't it?'

'Yes, it is. We often have to ask questions like that. I'm trying to find who murdered your husband, Mrs Kornsey. But it seems to me I first have to find out who your husband *was*.' He held up a hand. 'No, don't jump on me. Do *you* know who he was, where he came from, his family history, all that?'

She had stiffened; but now she slumped on her stool again. She shook her head; the spray-stiffened mass of hair didn't shiver. 'I'm sorry. You're right, I didn't know him, not really. We were happy, you gotta believe that. We really loved each other. You married? Happily married?'

'Very. With three kids.'

'We had no kids, I've always been sorry about that. We decided we were both too old to start a family. Terry was fifty-three, that's what he said he was. I'm – well, it's none of your business, is it?' A small smile creased her mouth. 'No, I guess I didn't really know him.'

'Where did you meet him?'

'In a coffee lounge up in Hurstville. I was the manageress. He'd come in once a week for morning coffee, we used to kid each other, one thing led to another . . . You know how it is . . . How did we live?' She had decided to trust him. 'I dunno, to tell you the truth. He used to get money from the States every month. I never saw it. He said it was from a trust fund, something his parents had set up for him, he said his father had been in the printing business. It used to come into the Treasury Bank in Hurstville, he had an account there. He'd give me money to run the house and for things for myself, I had my own account. We're not *rolling* in money, but we're comfortable. There are two cars out in the garage, a Honda

Accord, that's mine, and a Mercedes.' She waved a hand around her, not just at the kitchen but at the whole house. 'This is not bad, right? It's all good stuff, none of your Joyce Mayne bargains or your K-Mart specials. Terry took care of me.' Then the eyes behind the glasses dimmed again, she bit her lip and shook her head. 'Jesus, *why*?'

'We'll do our best to find out. Do you have any photos of him?'

'No, I don't. God, is that the only one's gunna be of him?' She nodded at the folder into which Malone had put the police photo. 'Were you gunna give me a copy?'

'No, that's not the drill. So you don't have a photo of him at all? That's strange, isn't it? Not even a wedding photo?'

'Yeah, we had a wedding photo, but, I dunno, it disappeared. Terry was odd about having his picture taken, he said it was bad luck. He used to make a joke about it, that he was like them African natives, they believe you take a photo of a man and you steal his soul. But he never would stand in front of a camera.'

'You said Terry was fond of gadgets. Could I have a look at what's out in his workshop? Did he have a computer, for instance?'

'There's one out there, he used to lock it away in the safe.'

'Safe? He had a safe out in the garage?'

'It's cemented to the floor. He kept the computer in it and some other things, expensive tools. There's a bit of burglary around here sometimes, 'specially since the recession.'

She led him out the back door of the kitchen and towards a door into the garage. Malone noticed that the garden was carefully tended; a row of rose bushes, the last rose of summer gone, had been freshly pruned. A neat strip of lawn separated the house from a swimming pool; the pool furniture looked as if it was already stacked for the coming winter, a big umbrella furled till next summer. Three Chinese rain-trees stood in a row, their bright-green leaves turning yellow. It seemed that Terry Kornsey had not been expecting to die, had been preparing for the seasons of another year.

The blue Honda and the silver Mercedes, one of the large models, were as well-kept as the garden, shining with new wax. The floor of the big garage was spotless; there were drip-trays under each of the cars. In one corner, in an alcove that appeared to have been built on, was the workshop. There were two benches and Malone, though no handyman with tools, guessed they carried every appliance a do-it-yourself handyman would need. He opened a big steel tool-box; in it were enough spanners, screwdrivers, drills and what-have-you for Kornsey to have dismantled the *QE2* on his own. Malone wondered what trade Kornsey had followed in the United States, in that other mysterious life he had kept from his wife.

'Where's the safe?'

Mrs Kornsey slid back a panel under the higher of the two benches: there was a large safe, its base anchored in the concrete floor. 'Don't ask me to open it. It's a combination job and I dunno the combination.'

'I'm no safe-cracker, I'll have to send someone out here to open it.'

'What do you expect to find?'

'I don't know, Mrs Kornsey. Maybe we'll find out who your husband was. *Really* was.'

The glasses slipped down her nose again; she pushed them back with scarlet-tipped fingers. 'I oughta be angry with you, but I got the feeling you're actually trying to help me, right? But I dunno I wanna know who Terry really was. He was my husband, that was the man I knew, and he loved me, like I loved him. What does the past matter, now he's dead?'

He put a hand on her arm; she didn't draw away. 'I'll try to make it as soft as possible, try to see you don't get hurt any more than you are right now. But if we don't find out who killed him, there may be more murders. There's another murder already we think is connected to Terry's.'

'Another?' She looked at him as if he were deliberately trying to increase the torture. 'Who?'

He told her. 'Did Terry ever mention the name Sweden to you?'

'Never. You mean the politician's son, there was a piece in the paper about him? Terry hadn't the slightest interest in politics. I once asked him what he thought of President Bush and all he said was, President Who? No, he wouldn't of known anyone named Sweden, definitely.'

'Well, I can't do anything more till we get that safe open. Terry didn't have any papers in the house, did he?'

'No, all his papers and things are in there.' She slid the panel back to hide the safe.

Malone wondered why her husband had been so secretive; but there was a limit to the number of darts you could throw at a widow still suffering the shock of his murder. 'I'll ring you when someone is on the way out to open the safe. It'll probably be this evening. You'll be home?' She nodded. 'You got someone to come and stay with you?'

'My sister'll come over, she lives at Cronulla. I'll be all right,' she said, recognizing his concern. 'I'm no jellyback.'

'I'm sure you're not.'

She worked her mouth, as if it had suddenly gone dry. 'What about Terry's, er, foot and leg? Do I have to, er, reclaim it to bury him?'

'I honestly don't know. Do you want, er, it?'

She shook her head, undecided. 'I'll think about it.'

He left her standing like a shadow behind the security door, walked through the purple shade of the tibouchina and out to his car. He drove across to Hurstville, found a parking spot in the busy shopping centre, went into the Treasury Bank and asked to see the manager. Treasury was one of the smaller chain of banks that had emerged in the Eighties during deregulation of the industry; it was also one of the survivors, catering to small depositors. Malone had to produce his badge; evidently he looked like someone seeking a loan and he would have had to take his place in the queue. On his way into the manager's office he passed five people sitting in a line of chairs, their faces dull and pinched with their troubles; mortgages, debts, bankruptcies stamped on them like club tattoos.

Inglebath, the manager, was middle-aged and had a face and

figure that suggested he liked a drink or two or three. He had prematurely grey hair that made his mottled face more conspicuous. He wore black thick-rimmed glasses that looked more like camouflage than a help to his sight. But if he was a drinker, there was none of the usual drinker's bonhomie; when he smiled, it was a bank manager's smile, cynical and I've-heard-it-all-before.

He had not heard what Malone had to tell him. 'Good God! Really? I only met him a couple of times, but he seemed – harmless?'

'Maybe he was harmless, Mr Inglebath. You don't have to be harm*ful* to be murdered, not these days. The trouble is, we don't seem to know much about who he really was. I'd like to see details of his account.'

'I'm afraid I can't do that, Inspector.'

'This isn't a Swiss bank, is it? The Treasury Bank of Zurich or somewhere?' He did not like Mr Inglebath, who seemed intent on being obstructive.

Inglebath smiled, was suddenly friendly. 'Inspector, I'm not trying to be obstructive. Incidentally, you're wrong about Swiss banks. They are much more co-operative than they used to be when it comes to questions of secret accounts. I'll let you see Mr Kornsey's account, but you'll have to show me a warrant first. And I'd like written permission from *Mrs* Kornsey. I presume there *is* a Mrs Kornsey?'

'He never mentioned her?'

'Not as far as I know, but I can have my assistant manager check that.' He made a call on his inter-office phone, hung up and looked back at Malone. 'We have no record of there being a Mrs Kornsey. We have no home or business address for him, just a box number at the local post office. He opened his account here seven years ago, before all the tax mullarkey we now have to go through.'

Malone asked if he could use the manager's phone, then called Clements. 'Russ, send someone out here with a warrant for us to look at the account of Terence Kornsey. And get someone out to the Kornsey place at Lugarno, someone to open a safe there. Try the Fraud Squad, they're cracking safes all the time. I want it done *now*. Anything happening your end?'

'Someone just tried to burn Cormac Casement alive.'

3

Kelsey Bugler and Kim Weetbix were neither revolutionaries nor did they even belong to a gang. They just hated the rich because they themselves were not rich. Given the option of being poor and revolutionary and being rich and rapacious, they would have opted for the latter. Each of them had been out of work for eighteen months and they had grown tired of trying to live on the dole, waking up each morning to a day that they knew was going to be worse than yesterday. Hopelessness had started to give way to hate against anyone better off than themselves.

Kel Bugler was a fifth-generation Australian, though, if pressed, he would not have bothered to trace the generations back past his parents, who had kicked him out of the house when he was sixteen. He was tall and thin and might have passed for good-looking if surliness had not been his most prominent feature; he had long dark hair tied with a rubber band at the back in a pony-tail and there was a botched tattoo on the back of his left hand. He was twenty-two years old and had no training in any trade except mugging and he was still an apprentice at that.

Kim Weetbix had never had a home to be thrown out of. Her father was an unknown American soldier; not *the* Unknown Soldier, just a cypher. Her mother, now dead, had been a Saigon bar-girl. Kim had arrived in Australia with the first boat-load of refugees, a scared but resourceful fourteen-year-old; she had escaped from the camp where she and the other refugees had been taken and she had been on the run ever since. She had begged, stolen, sold herself and managed to scrape up enough money to buy herself forged papers; she had taken her second name off the box of the first food she had been offered in the immigration camp. The hustler selling her the papers, a patriotic Aussie trying to enlarge the national consumer market by encouraging immigration, had looked at her quizzically, then given her her naturalization. For his price, of course. Kim was tall for an Asian girl, but that could be attributed to her father, whoever he was; she was never to find out, but he had been a high school basketball star and at six feet six an easy target for a Viet Cong sniper. She had good looks, was almost a beauty, but she had long ago set her face in stone against the world. She had twice as much intelligence as Kel Bugler and what she saw in him only she knew.

When they found the small door could be opened in the big grille door of The Wharf's garage, they couldn't believe their luck. They crept down into the bottom level of the basement garage, intending only to break into the cars they found there, taking whatever came to hand. They were disappointed when they reached the lower level and found only two cars and a truck: a Mercedes, a Bentley and a utility that, said the sign on its sides, belonged to B. PAKSON & SON, PAINTERS. In the back of the truck were several cans of paint and two cans of thinners: nothing worth stealing, since Kel and Kim were neither artists nor decorators.

Then they saw the old geezer, carrying a briefcase, get out of the lift at the far end of the garage and walk towards the Bentley.

'We'll do him!' Kel was not over-intelligent but his mind was like a fox's, quick on reflex.

They were both wearing black leather jackets, worn jeans and cheap trainers. Each of them had a woollen scarf round his neck against the chill wind that, they were sure, always waited round the corner for them; they had even begun to hate nature, though this warm autumn perversely mocked them. They pulled the scarves up to cover their lower faces; they looked like the masked figures one saw on television almost every night of the week, the Arab, French, German stone-throwers, the brother- and sisterhood of protestors. But they

90

had no cause other than grabbing a wallet from the elderly man now opening the door of the Bentley and throwing the briefcase on to the front seat.

Cormac Casement half turned as the two figures came up in a rush behind him. He went down under the blow across the back of his neck. As he fell he rolled over, lay on his back and looked up as the masked man knelt on him, fumbling for his wallet while the other attacker, a girl, snatched the gold watch from his wrist.

Cormac Casement had never worn an expensive watch in his life till his second wife had given him one; for him a watch had always been only something that told the time and its cost neither hurried time nor made up for the loss of it. He also was old money, so old he was pre-credit card. He was well known and knew he was; he frequented only places where he was recognized. Clothiers, clubs, restaurants: he ran accounts at all of them and never needed a credit card or cash. His wallet was as flat as a visiting card; all it contained was his driving licence and two ten-dollar notes, emergency money. He would have been much safer with Kel and Kim if he had been carrying a roll of notes and a venetian-blind of credit cards.

When Kel saw how little there was in the wallet, fury suddenly took hold of him. He stood up and kicked Cormac Casement in the ribs; the old man yelped with pain and tried to roll away. 'Where's your fucking money? You gotta have more than this!' Kel had a very narrow view of the relationship between the symbols of wealth and actual cash; anyone who drove a Bentley should have a bank of ready money in the boot. He kicked Casement again. 'Where is it, shithead?'

Kim stuffed the gold watch into her pocket, then snatched the briefcase from the front seat. 'Maybe there's money in this! Come on, let's get outa here!'

'No!' Kel's fury had grown, he was storming with anger and hate.

He spun round the front of the Bentley and ran the few yards to the painters' truck. He grabbed one of the cans of thinners and ran back to where Casement still lay on the ground, holding his ribs. 'On your feet, arsehole!'

He ripped off the cap of the can of thinners, dragged Casement to his feet and thrust the can at him. 'You gunna burn this heap, fuck you! Start splashing!'

Casement looked at him blankly; he could not bring himself to believe the hatred in this young man. He was not horrified at having to burn his car; his horror was that this young savage could hate him so much. Kel shouted at him again, hit him across the face and Casement staggered against the car, splashing thinners over the bonnet. Kim stood aside, saying nothing; but above the mask of the scarf her dark eyes were troubled. She was capable of hatred, she had experienced enough degradation to have built up a store of it, but she could control it. It worried her to see that Kel had no leash at all on himself.

Cormac Casement emptied the can, splashing thinners on the car from front to rear. He felt nothing at what was about to happen to the expensive car; possessions meant little to him. He stood back, inadvertently stepping on Kel's foot as the latter lit a match and threw it on the car. Kel let out a shout of pain and shoved Casement against the car as the thinners burst into flame. Casement screamed as his hands were engulfed by fire and he fell away, trying to put out his burning hands by burying them in his armpits, much as he would have done if they had been frozen.

'Serve you fucking right for being rich, arsehole!'

Then Kelsey Bugler and Kim Weetbix ran up the ramp leading out of the lower level of the garage.

Chapter Six

◆◆◆◆◆◆◆◆

1

'Did you see Casement?' said Malone.

'They wouldn't let me see him.' Clements settled himself at the Malones' dinner table. 'He's in the private section at St Sebastian's. He's in mild shock, they said. We can see him tomorrow.'

'Mild shock, that all? I didn't think anything would shock him.'

'It could of been the burning of his car. It was a Bentley turbo.'

'A write-off?'

'Total. John Kagal tells me it's four hundred and sixty thousand dollars' worth. That'd shock *me*.'

'All right,' said Lisa, putting the first course of pumpkin soup on the table. 'No shop talk.'

'What's it like being married to a policeman?' said Romy; then gave Clements a conciliatory smile. 'Just a routine question, Sergeant.'

Lisa sat down. The children had already eaten and retired to their bedrooms to do their homework. Lisa had an old-fashioned sense of discipline that Malone, if not the children, appreciated. She was appalled when she read stories or heard from old schoolfriends in Holland of the expansively liberal attitude of the burghers of Amsterdam, her home town; she was far from prudish and was liberal in many of her attitudes, but she believed that nothing worked if it was allowed to run off the rails. She ran her home better, she claimed, than most of the police stations she had seen – 'At least I would make the drunks and the hoons clean up after themselves.' Standards had to be paid heed to.

'You have to adjust,' she said to Romy, as if the two policemen were not present at the table. 'It's worse if he's in Homicide. Even so, I suppose that's better than Internal Affairs.'

'Anything's better than Internal Affairs,' said Malone.

'Nobody's talking to you,' said his wife. 'How's the soup, Romy? It's a German recipe.'

'Delicious. I love cooking,' with a sidelong amused glance at Clements, 'but cooking for oneself, there's no enjoyment in it.'

'Geez.' Clements put down his spoon. 'All right, let's get married.'

'You hear that?' Romy looked at the Malones. 'You're witnesses.'

'Refuse him,' said Lisa. 'If he's genuine, he'll ask you again when you're alone. We shouldn't be hearing this.'

'What's the matter with you?' said Malone. 'You've been working on this proposal for two years, now you're objecting to the way Russ has gone about it.'

'It's too casual,' said his Dutch wife. 'Too Australian.'

'That's the way we operate in Homicide. We arrest people casually. *How about coming down to the station, mate, while we charge you?* That's the way we do it. It works.'

The banter was light, but all four knew there had been a commitment. Clements looked slightly bemused, as if he had stepped out of a plane in mid-air and wasn't sure he could work the ripcord on his parachute. Romy looked at Lisa and winked, but there was no smug pleasure on her face. Lisa, a romantic, was the one who looked as if she had been proposed to. Malone, the pragmatist, who knew Clements better than either of the women did, just hoped the big man would not have second thoughts in the morning.

He poured some wine and raised his glass. 'To the two of you. May you be as happy as we have been.'

'We couldn't ask for more than that,' said Clements without

awkwardness and Lisa got up, moved round behind him and kissed him fondly on the cheek, her arms round his neck. Then she looked across at Malone and he saw the glisten of tears and felt the lump in his throat, the sweet cancer of love.

Later, out in the kitchen where Romy was helping Lisa stack the dishes in the dishwasher, Lisa said, 'There'll be a difference for you two. You're both in the same line of work, almost. I could never stomach what you do.'

'You get used to it.' Romy was as practised at the kitchen sink as she was at the autopsy table; plates and bones had much the same fragility. 'Russ and I don't talk about it now. There'll be no need to change when we're married. I get upset sometimes, especially if it's a child, but death is worse for the living than it is for the dead. That's an old saw, but it's true.'

'I know that.' Lisa closed her eyes for a moment against the thought of ever losing one of her children; then she closed the dishwasher, set it going. 'Scobie tells me sometimes what it's like when he has to call on a wife or family and give them the bad news. He hasn't told me anything about it yet, but I think he had one like that today.'

'He did. Russ told me.'

'The government and the public think that all police are paid for is keeping law and order. They don't know the half of it, damn them.'

In the living room Malone and Clements were looking at a television programme on law and order. A politician was working some micro reform on the English language: 'No Austrayan guvment has ever know-en or show-en –'

Malone got up and switched off the set. 'Bugger 'em! When it comes to our work, no politician knows his arse from his elbow.'

'Including our Minister.' Clements was enjoying what he called his cooling ale, his standard after-dinner drink; not for him a port or a brandy, he was Aussie right through to his liver. 'Greg Random was on the blower to me just before I left the office. Zanuch had been on to him and Sweden had been on to *him*. I gather it was our fault someone tried to do in Cormac Casement.'

Malone grinned wryly. 'Isn't it always? You think there's some connection between the other murders and the attempt on Casement?'

Clements shrugged. 'Your guess is as good as mine. It's a different MO, no subtlety about it. But maybe they worked it that way just to confuse us. He was lucky to get out of it, they could of locked him in the car. How'd you get on with Mrs Kornsey?'

Malone told him. 'She knows nothing about her husband, or practically nothing. I'm hoping the safe in the garage will tell us something. Mr Kornsey, whoever he was, had something to hide.'

Then the children came in to say goodnight. Claire and Maureen kissed Clements and Tom punched him gently on the shoulder. 'No kiss?' said Clements, grinning.

'Garn, Dad would arrest me if I did that.'

Then the two women came in from the kitchen and Lisa said, 'Romy and Russ are engaged.'

There was a shriek from the two girls and they rushed at Romy and hugged her. Tom waited till his sisters had stepped back, then he put his arms round Romy, lifted his face and kissed her on the cheek. Then he looked at Clements. 'Okay, Uncle Russ?'

'Okay.'

Clements looked suddenly happy and relaxed, as if his parachute had opened safely.

2

Greg Random had come across to Homicide for the morning conference, but sat in the background, his unlit pipe hanging from one corner of his mouth. Occasionally it rose, like a pointer's nose, as one of the detectives produced another item of evidence.

'We opened the Kornsey safe,' said John Kagal, putting two plastic bags on Malone's desk. 'There were some tools in it, but I didn't bring those back. There's a small computer outside on my desk, one of the latest. I've run through it, but it seems brand new, there's nothing in its memory. He could've been getting ready for some project.'

Malone emptied the plastic bags. There were half a dozen photos; two postcards of Manhattan; an Esso map of New York City, yellowed and cracked; two passports and an airline ticket, first class, to Hong Kong; a bundle of US one-hundred-dollar bills; a bank book and a bank statement; two boxes of headed notepaper; two boxes of ammunition and a Colt .45 automatic. 'The average contents of the average suburban safe?'

'Mr Kornsey wasn't your average suburban Joe,' said Kagal. 'The passports are American, but in different names. Terence Kornsey and Joseph Caccia. Same photo, though, same date of birth. The money, it adds up to twenty-eight thousand dollars. The postcards have nothing on the back of them, so it looks as if he might've bought 'em for sentimental reasons, a reminder of home. The map has a small biro circle on it, out in the borough of Queens. I'd say that was where he came from. The photos are all of him with someone. Some with an elderly couple who could be his parents, one of them with a girl, a real bimbo . . . No offence, Peta. She really is.' He held up the photo.

Without moving closer to look at the photo, Peta nodded. 'I'll take your word for it, John.'

Kagal looked at her a moment, then he picked up the last photo. 'Then there's this one of him with two guys who I wouldn't trust, on face value, with anything worth more than a dollar.'

'What about the notepaper?'

'One for a company called Sue City Investments – there's an address in Hong Kong, plus a box number. The other's for Hannibal Development, same address in Hong Kong, a different box number. No phone numbers, no fax numbers.

Looks like a few sheets and envelopes have been used from each box, but that's all.'

Clements was looking at the gun. 'This isn't brand new, it's been used. He must of thought he might have to use it in a hurry, the magazine is full.'

'Turn it over to Ballistics.' Malone was examining the bank book and statement. 'Why ain't I surprised? Our old mates again, Shahriver International. Three hundred and eighty thousand bucks has gone through his account in the past three months, most of it to, cunning bastards, Overseas Transfer. That tells us nothing.' He picked up the airline ticket. 'One way to Hong Kong. I don't think we need to tell Mrs Kornsey, not right now anyway, but it looks like her hubby was planning to split on his own.'

'Well,' said Random, taking his pipe from his mouth, 'what would you say to Mr Kornsey being Mafia? I think you need to get on to the FBI.'

Random respected the chain of command: he left it to Malone to give the order to Andy Graham: 'Andy, get on to Washington now. Tell 'em what we have and ask 'em if they can add to it.'

Graham was on his feet and out the door like a heavyweight greyhound out of a trap. Random looked after him, shook his head, and the other detectives all grinned. 'I think he'd run all the way to Washington, if you'd let him,' said Kagal.

'Sure,' said Malone, 'but he'd come back with everything you sent him for.'

It was a reprimand and Kagal recognized it, but said nothing. Clements picked up the awkward moment: 'I think it's time someone went over and saw Cormac Casement.'

'I'll do that now,' said Malone. 'You go down to Shahriver, bring in Mr Palady, the boss, and the English bloke who's the general manager. Tell 'em we'd like a chat.'

'What about me?' said Kagal, sounding as if he felt he was being left out.

'Start getting everything together in our computer, straighten everything out. This is starting to look like a Chinese betting shop. You bring the flow chart up to date, Peta.'

When Malone and Random were left alone, the senior man said, 'Do you have any trouble with John Kagal?'

'No. Why?'

'He's smarter than the rest of us, including you and me. Let me know if he gets too smart, I'll move him somewhere else.'

Malone shook his head. 'No, Greg. Russ and I like the competition. We need someone to give all the nasty jobs to.'

'You're a mean bastard underneath, aren't you?'

'Why else would I be a cop?'

They smiled at each other, like actors who knew it was best to write one's own reviews.

3

Between them the three old men, some years ago, had ruled the State. Casement had been king of the financial circles, Vanderberg of the political, Aldwych of the criminal. But they had never been together before, though they had met in pairs in two instances. Jack Aldwych was the odd man out; he had never met The Dutchman before. He had come to the hospital this morning, not because of any concern for Cormac Casement, but because of concern for Jack Junior. A murder and an attempted murder so close to his son was too much for the old crim's peace of mind.

Casement's hands and arms were wrapped in dressing; there was also a burn dressing on his right cheek. He was no longer in shock, but yesterday's experience had marked him for the rest of his life. He had long ago lost his fear of dying, but he had not been prepared for his murder.

'Are you here for my vote, Hans? It's not worth it. I backed the wrong horse three weeks ago.'

'Didn't you all?' said Vanderberg gleefully; anything that set the conservatives back on their arses almost convinced him that God did take an interest in politics. 'But I'm working on you – a vote in hand is better than chasing one in the bush. I've just come back from telling the wheat-and-cow cockies this State government couldn't run a chook raffle. But it was like talking to a mob of sheep. You ever do any jobs in the bush, Mr Aldwych?' He was a politician, not a diplomat: criminals voted, too.

'There was never any real money in the bush, not in my line of work.' Aldwych smiled, amused by this old pol, as crooked, in his own way, as himself.

Vanderberg looked at Casement with an expression that might have been sympathetic. 'Oldies like us shouldn't die violently. Past a certain age, we should be allowed to die quietly.'

'Are you going to go quietly?' said Casement.

'No bloody fear.' The grin, meant to be amused, was just ugly. 'What about you, Mr Aldwych?'

'I'm retired. If I was gunna die violently, it would of happened years ago.' Remembering the attempts on his life and the anguish of Shirl as she had sat by his bed.

Casement had been lying listlessly in his bed when the two men had arrived; he had felt on the edge of his grave. He had also, surprisingly, felt lonely. He had no siblings and there had been no children from his first marriage; he had dozens of acquaintances but no really close friends; there was only Ophelia. He had been surprised at how he had welcomed the two surprising visitors.

Now, watching them, both unscrupulous in their respective fields, he had perked up. His own past was scattered with scruples that, for one reason or another, he had found superfluous. But, compared to these two, he was all honesty and principle. Though conservative, he had never been a snob and these two rascals fascinated him. They were better than any of the medication the nurses had poured into him.

'These two young punks who tried to kill you –' Aldwych put the question bluntly. 'You think they were connected to whoever did in young Sweden?'

'I honestly don't know, Jack. I'm not an expert on killers.'

Aldwych smiled, unoffended; every man to his trade, had been his motto. 'I could start some enquiries –'

'Jack, you know the underworld –' It was an old-fashioned term that dated him. 'Why would anyone from your *milieu* want to kill me?'

Aldwych had to guess what his *mill-yer* was. 'Cormac, it's the *underworld* where people go for a hitman. Did they steal anything?'

'My briefcase. And a watch Ophelia gave me.'

'How much?'

'How much was it worth? I don't know.' He had the very rich's ignorance of price tags, those who don't value trivial possessions; it was he who had paid for the Bentley, but only at Ophelia's insistence; she had said that a Bentley was more chic, less gauche, than a Rolls-Royce. His wife's snobbery amused him rather than annoyed him. Love, if not blind, was often vision-impaired, as the euphemists called it. 'It's the sentimental value, if you like. But it's those kids themselves –'

'I can have some enquiries made,' said Vanderberg. 'I'm not just Opposition Leader, I'm spokesman on police matters.' He was spokesman on *everything*; besides being known as The Dutchman, he was sometimes called Baron Thatcher. 'I've got my contacts –'

Then there was a knock on the door and Malone stood in the doorway. 'I have some questions to ask, Mr Casement –' Then he recognized the other visitors. 'G'day, Jack. How are you, sir?'

Vanderberg remembered everyone; or at least those old enough to vote. 'Malone, isn't it? How are you, Inspector? You in charge of this case?'

Malone was certain the old bugger knew who was in charge. 'Yes. This and a couple of others.'

'We've just been talking about 'em. Maybe we can sit in on the questioning, give you the benefit of our wisdom. Like a Cabinet meeting,' he said and grinned at them all. It was well known that, when he had been Premier, his Cabinet meetings had been called the Chapel of the Twelve Dumb Apostles. He spoke and everyone listened and if any wisdom came out of the conference of minds it had to be telepathic. 'Give you an objective point of view.'

He hadn't had an objective point of view since he had opened his eyes at birth; but Malone's tongue, this time, was held in check. 'Thanks for the offer, sir. But I'm afraid I have to see Mr Casement alone. Later, maybe, I'll get the objective point of view . . .'

Aldwych rose, smiling to himself. Now that gang warfare was behind him, he enjoyed watching any little, or big, conflict between others. Malone had won this small one; he smiled again at the irony of being pleased for a cop. 'Look after yourself, Cormac. I'll have a few questions asked in my *mill-yer* and let you know if I come up with something.'

'Me, too, Jack?' said Malone.

'Of course, Scobie. You know I'm on your side.'

The Dutchman, defeated but showing no sign of it, reached under his chair and produced a cardboard box. 'The wife sent this, Cormac. One of her pumpkin pavlovas.'

Casement did his best to show delight. 'Just what I was looking forward to.'

When Aldwych and Vanderberg had gone, Malone sat down beside the bed. Casement held out the cardboard box. 'You have a family? Would you like to take this home for dessert?'

Malone took the box. 'Thanks, the kids'll love it.'

'What about you?'

'Pumpkin I like. Pavlovas –' Malone shrugged. 'Mr Casement, two of my men have been to see you, got the basics of what happened to you yesterday. I'm here to see if you can add to that?'

Casement looked down at his hands, lumps of white dressing. 'I haven't a clue who they were or why they attacked me. One of them was a girl, of that I'm sure. They had scarves around their faces. What I can't understand is why they hated me so much.' He looked at Malone for understanding. 'I don't think it was just because of what I am –'

'A rich man? It could've been. You're an intelligent man

102

too, you must have some idea of what kids on the dole feel about the distribution of wealth.'

'Are you a communist?'

Malone grinned. 'They're out of fashion now, aren't they?'

'Not everywhere.' On the other side of the world Yeltsin was battling the unreformed hard-liners; in China the old guard still clung to the old credo; in Eastern Europe the true believers had just changed their name by deed poll. But Malone was right: the old labels had lost their glue. 'Still, that was a stupid question. I think the shock I suffered has made me a little stupid. You're right, I'm an intelligent man.'

'Do you always drive yourself? Your age, a car like that?'

'I *like* to drive. I have a driver, but I don't use him all the time. I wish he'd been with me yesterday, he's a husky young chap. So you think it could have been a couple of street-kids going berserk because I wasn't carrying any money on me?'

'That may have been it. A coincidence following on the other two killings.'

'You believe in coincidence?'

'I believe in anything that gives me a clue. In this case –' He shrugged again. 'These kids may have been told to attack you just to confuse us.'

'They'd have chosen smarter kids than these two. Or I would have.'

Malone let that pass. 'Could they have been friends of Rob Sweden?'

'No, they were – punks, is that the word? Rob was a self-centred young bastard. I could use a stronger word, but I don't think it would make any difference – you get my picture of him. But he was not a punk, he'd have sneered at them. He was a yuppie snob.'

'You really had no time for him, did you?'

'I've already told you that, I think.' Casement had been without his glasses, but now he put them on. He still looked wan and tired, but now he had become businesslike, as if Malone's questions were going to need more attention.

'This is delicate, but I have to ask it. What about your wife's ex-husbands? And your sisters-in-law's exes? I think there are five altogether, aren't there?'

'Five, yes. Are you asking if any of them are jealous or something? That they'd want some sort of revenge on the women?' He shook his head. Then he looked beyond Malone and his face lit up; he seemed suddenly younger, yesterday gone from his face. 'Darling!'

Ophelia Casement came into the room in a swirl of skirt and a faint aura of expensive perfume; it was a musky scent, oriental in essence, rich gypsies would have it brewed for her. She leaned across the bed and kissed her husband on the lips, a lover's as well as a wife's kiss. Malone, unaccountably, felt it was for his benefit.

She put a two-pound box of Belgian chocolates on the bedside table, smiled at Malone. 'My husband is a chocoholic.' Then she looked at her husband's hands. 'Oh darling, how are you going to sort out what flavours you want?'

He gave her a bandaged caress. 'I have a very attractive nurse who'll help me out . . . Inspector Malone has been asking questions about your ex-husbands. Yours and your sisters'.'

Ophelia Casement did not seem put out at what some other women might have thought an invasion of privacy. 'Darren and Ron? What could possibly interest you about them, Inspector?'

'I'm trying to find someone, *anyone*, who might've organized the attack on your husband. Perhaps one of your ex-husbands might have grown jealous –'

'I don't think you need to pursue this line, Inspector –'

'No, it's all right, darling.' Ophelia put a hand on her husband's arm. 'Inspector, if you knew my ex-husbands, you would never entertain the thought. Darren is gay, one of the nicest men you could wish to meet – he and I are still the best of friends.' She didn't explain why she, an obviously lusty woman, had married a homosexual, so Malone could only surmise she had married Darren for money. He would have to look into Darren's background. Ophelia went on, 'As for Ron – no, he's too vain to be jealous.'

'Vanity can lead to jealousy.'

She smiled indulgently. 'Not many men would ever notice that.'

'In Homicide we learn to notice a few things. A lot we'd rather not know.'

'It wouldn't lead to any jealousy on Ron's part. He's the sort of man who's bald on top but rubs conditioner on his pubic hair.' It was her sport to shock; but Malone showed no expression. Casement winced, but it was only in his eyes; his wife pressed his arm. 'Ron hasn't given me a thought, I'm sure, since we were divorced. In any case, he lives in Melbourne and Melburnians would think it beneath them to be jealous of anything north of the border.'

Malone still showed no expression and Casement said, 'I have the feeling, darling, that the Inspector thinks you aren't taking this seriously enough.'

'Mr Casement, you are the one who should be taking it most seriously. You and the rest of the clan. I'm the outsider, I don't think anyone is going to try to kill me.' He said it to shock them and it did, even Ophelia.

Her face stiffened and the gay impertinence in her grey eyes died. Like other people Malone had witnessed, she seemed to age when the possibility of her own death was pushed in front of her: dying was for others. He wondered how she had looked last night when she had seen her husband in intensive care.

'You mean you think it hasn't finished? The killing? Oh God.' This time she squeezed the bandaged hand and Casement winced visibly. 'But why?'

'When we find the reason, Mrs Casement, we'll be pretty close to finding the killer. Or killers.' He stood up. He decided to shock them a little further. 'I can put a police guard outside your door, Mr Casement, if you feel unsafe.'

'No,' said Casement, his voice steady, 'we feel safe enough.'

Malone nodded, said goodbye and left, taking the pumpkin pavlova with him. Despite Casement's assurance, he had the distinct impression that the couple were truly afraid, that their confidence had all the crumbly fragility of a pavlova.

When he got back to Homicide the big main room was crowded with visitors, some of them unwilling guests. Suspects had been brought in for questioning on three of the other unsolved murders; with them had come their legal counsellors. Malone recognized one of the solicitors, a man who had made a self-publicized career of criticizing the police for anything and everything they did; Malone was glad that he was too down-market to be involved in the cases he was handling. He went into his office to find it, too, crowded with Clements and the two executives from the Shahriver Credit International Bank. Harold Junor, the general manager, was as big as Clements, an ex-rugby forward with a straight-on approach to everything and a flushed face that looked as if it had spent more time at the club bar than packed down in a scrum. The managing director, Ishmael Palady, was smaller, as dapper as a stand-off half before the rough-and-tumble of a game had started. But the game *had* started and both men knew they had been caught off-side.

'Mr Palady, Mr Junor. We can't go on meeting like this. Not if you want to stay out of jail.'

'Inspector —' Palady was dressed in banker's grey, white shirt and a dark blue tie marked with tiny crests so discreet that it would have been impolite, at least in banking circles, to have asked what club, regiment or school he belonged to. He had been born east of Suez and west of Hong Kong and his blood-stream had as many strains as an old caravan road. He had small, sharp features, thousand-year-old eyes still undimmed and he knew the banking laws of every state from Alaska to Zaire.

'Inspector, Mr Junor and I are here to co-operate with you in every way. I don't think you should be mentioning jail.'

'It was a joke, Mr Palady.' It wasn't, and they both knew it. 'What have we got, Sergeant?'

Clements looked as if his patience, never very thick, had run thin. 'Mr Palady and Mr Junor are trying to stick a little too close to the book –'

'Now hold on, old chap –' Junor shifted his bulk on his chair, a heavyweight parody of a sidestep. 'There are certain rules banks have to hold to. Confidentiality, that sort of thing. We'll produce whatever you ask for, but you'll have to show us a warrant, something that takes the onus off us. You remember that fuss last year about the leaking of confidential info.'

'I think that was slightly different, Mr Junor,' said Malone. 'That was confidential information being *sold* to private investigators and credit organizations. We're not going to *buy* anything.'

Junor flushed, his red face turning almost purple; Palady said, 'I'm sure Mr Junor didn't mean it that way, Inspector. We'll co-operate, but you do understand, I'm sure, we'll need some sort of warrant that, as it were, gets us off the hook on this rule of confidentiality.'

'I can refer the whole thing to the Securities Commission, if you like.'

Palady recognized the threat. 'No, no, there's no need for that. It's just that . . .' Then he spread a hand, giving up: 'What exactly do you want to know?'

'Ishmael –' said Junor warningly.

'Harold, there is an old money-lender's proverb written on the back walls of cupboards all over the world. A bank's principles should never exceed its principal, or what's an auditor for? Ask your questions, Inspector.'

Malone had long ago given up passing judgement on other people's pragmatism: you took your answers and only thought about conscience later. 'Mr Terence Kornsey, first. Nearly four hundred thousand dollars has gone through his account with you in the past three months, most of it sent overseas. Where did it go?'

The two bankers exchanged glances before Junor said, 'To our branch in Hong Kong. It was being held there for Mr Kornsey to collect it. I got the impression it wasn't intended as a long-term deposit.'

'How about earlier? Had he sent any other money overseas?'

'He'd only been with us three months. His first deposit, as I remember it, was a hundred thousand dollars, something like that.' He had a banker's casualness about money; he could have been talking about petty cash.

'Who recommended him?' said Clements. 'He wouldn't have come to you without references, not if he wanted to transfer money overseas.'

Again the bankers looked at each other. Then Palady said, 'I'm afraid we can't stretch the confidentiality rule that far –'

'Was it Mr Robert Sweden?' Malone threw a wild one.

It landed smack in Palady's face; he blinked as if he had been hit. Palady fumbled with it, then looked again at Junor, who seemed reluctant to help him out.

'Come on,' said Malone impatiently, 'he's dead, too. He's not going to come back and sue you.'

Palady at last nodded. 'Yes, it was Mr Sweden.'

'Did you ever transfer any money overseas for him?'

'No,' said Junor, 'he was really a pretty small depositor, by our standards. He mentioned to me once that he intended to lodge a large amount and would want it transferred overseas, but he never got around to it.'

'Who recommended *him*?' said Clements.

Again Palady left it to his general manager; Malone all at once saw him as Pontius Pilate, in banker's grey instead of toga. If Shahriver Credit International were closed down in Sydney, he would survive. He would just pop up somewhere where the rules of banking could still be bent, where there were depositors looking for ways to cheat the tax man.

Junor looked out through the glass wall of Malone's office. The crowd in the outer room was thinning. Two men were going out in handcuffs, escorted by Phil Truach and another detective; the sharp solicitor was patting one of the prisoners on the back, telling him not to worry. If Junor had been looking for some comfort in the outer room, he found none; he turned back to Malone and Clements. At least, so far, he and his managing director were not in handcuffs.

'The recommendation on Mr Sweden came from our Manila office. I don't know who told them he should be accepted as a client. We don't ask those questions of each other,' he said and sounded like someone from an etiquette school.

'Do you have any Filipino clients here in Sydney?' said Malone.

'We have all nationalities,' said Palady.

'That wasn't what I asked.'

Palady pursed his thin lips. 'Inspector, I think you really are going beyond your province –'

'I do it all the time, Mr Palady, I'm a bugger for it. Sergeant Clements will tell you the Commissioner drops me daily little notes about it. But it saves time, Mr Palady. Yours and mine.'

Palady was unfocussed, as if he hadn't got the joke, if there was one; then abruptly he looked resigned. 'Let's do a trade, Inspector. If we tell you all we know, how much will you tell the Securities Commission?'

Malone looked at Clements: there was no offended look on the big face, no look of outraged piety. 'You're not taking notes, Sergeant?'

'No, Inspector. My biro's run dry.' So had his voice.

Malone looked back at Palady and Junor. 'Righto, gentlemen, let's say I couldn't find the Securities Commission if you led me to their front door. What have you got to tell us?'

'We have three Filipino clients,' said Junor. 'They are all in company names. I have no idea what their business is, we've never enquired.' He saw Clements' raised eyebrow and he said rather testily, 'Okay, it may seem slipshod to you, but that's the way we work. We provide a service for those who are looking for a *particular* service.'

'Like laundering money or helping tax dodgers?'

Both bankers looked hurt, though they had to act the part. Malone said, 'Forget Sergeant Clements' remark. He's the moral minority in Homicide.'

'I'd heard you were that, Inspector.' It was Malone's turn to raise an eyebrow and Palady went on, 'After we met you back in 1991, I made some enquiries about you.'

'You make enquiries about cops but not about your clients?'

'No offence was meant, Inspector.'

'All right, none taken. But don't you take offence if I suddenly stop being polite. Get on with it, Mr Junor. Can you name the three Filipino companies?'

'Bataan Importers, that's run by a Mr Suto. Imelda Investments –' He smiled, for a moment looked genuinely amused and relaxed. 'No, no connection to *that* lady. It's run by a Mr Rey, and Imelda is his wife's name, he says. Then there is Pinatubo Engineering, the managing director is a Mr Tajiri.'

'Tajiri? Is that Filipino?'

'No. Mr Tajiri is Japanese, we understand, but his company is registered in Manila.'

'Engineering? What does it build?'

'I have no idea.' Junor's shrug implied he had no curiosity, either.

'Have you met Mr Tajiri?'

'No. All our dealings have been with a Mr Belgarda. We understand he was the original owner of Pinatubo and stayed on when he was bought out.'

'Did Mr Sweden or Mr Kornsey ever mention any of these companies to you?'

'Not that I can recall.'

'Discretion is our trademark,' said Palady. 'We try never to make a connection between one client and another.'

In Homicide there were rarely, if ever, opportunities to admire the suspects. In other criminal fields Malone had, albeit reluctantly, come to marvel at how men (and women) could juggle their morality; that is, if they ever had any to begin with. Which he doubted in the case of Palady. He said with no hint of asperity, 'Do you ever lose any sleep over what you do for your clients?'

'Morality, Inspector, is built on sand. A wise banker never interferes with the foundations.'

'Who said that? Another old money-lender?'

'This one,' said Palady and tried to look modest if amoral.

Then the phone rang: it was Kagal. 'Inspector, could you come down to Casement and Company? Mr Ondelli said to say that one of those blips he mentioned has come up. He said you'd understand.'

Chapter Seven

◆◆◆◆◆◆◆

1

The Police Minister's office was not a temple in his own honour, as it had been for one or two of his predecessors. The walls were not hung with photos of himself with notabilities: there was no shaking hands with the Queen, the Pope, visiting presidents, the Prime Minister, the Premier and any white-collar criminals who had given him their vote before they had been caught. The Minister was not without ego, but he did not need advertisements to massage it.

He was with his wife and Assistant Commissioner Zanuch; he was saying, 'Bill, this has got to be tidied up. The media are having a ball with it, as if it was me who'd been toss – thrown off that balcony.'

'Derek, we're doing the best we can. I talked with Fred Falkender this morning, he's giving out no more to the media than he has to. What you read and hear, if you look at it, it's all conjecture, guesswork. They know nothing.'

'The point is, what do *we* know? This guy Malone, what's he come up with? I look at these bloody summaries –' He gestured at the file on his desk. 'Nothing!'

Rosalind looked at Zanuch. 'Do the detectives have to report everything every day as it happens? I mean everything they find out?'

'They're supposed to. It's all supposed to be in the running sheet, as we used to call it. Now it's in the computer. But that's not to say that some of them don't keep things to themselves till they've checked and sometimes double-checked. That's been happening since we got so much bad publicity over a few bungled jobs.'

'So Malone and his men may know more than they're telling me?' Sweden was noted for his anger; as Minister of another department he had been known to hurl an ashtray at his chief executive. He bounced a fist on his desk. 'Jesus Christ, I'm the Minister here and the victim's father! Who do you have to be to be told the truth?'

Zanuch, like most ambitious men in a bureaucracy, had learned that it was never politic to tell all of the truth; even if one knew it. He tried to be tactful: 'Derek, you've been Police Minister only three weeks. It's the toughest job in the Cabinet – you probably know that, you've been in politics long enough. The Police Service is second only to the Navy in the way it sticks together, it's closer-knit than the Army or Air Force. Ministers before you, from both sides of the House, have tried to hit it over the head and make it come to heel, but it doesn't work. The service itself is partly to blame for the image it has, but politicians and the general public haven't helped. It reckons it knows its job better and how to go about it better than anyone else, that it has the experience and outsiders don't have it.'

He had spoken as if he were an outsider. Sweden, from his own long experience, recognized that Zanuch was playing his own game. 'You make it sound as if the Minister is here as just some sort of figurehead, the one to take the political bumps.'

Zanuch took the slightest of risks; he just nodded. He could feel the ice cracking beneath him; he rose to his feet. 'I'll talk to Fred Falkender, see if he can fill you in more.'

'He probably doesn't know any more than you or I. Tell him I'd like to see Inspector Malone tonight, at the apartment. Six o'clock.'

'I think you'd better tell him. He's the AC Crime, Malone is his man.'

'Okay, I'll do it.' He waited till Zanuch had left the room, then leaned back in his chair and looked at his wife. 'If Leeds retires as Commissioner while I'm still Minister, I'll see that Bill Zanuch takes his place.'

'Why?'

'He'll do what he's told. Even by an outsider.' He sat looking at Rosalind, elbows on the arms of his chair, his hands clasped; judges often sit in the same pose on the Bench. Rosalind suddenly felt uncomfortable, not a common feeling with her. 'I've learned a few things about Rob, myself. I'm waiting to see if they come up in Malone's reports.'

'Such as?' Her discomfort increased, though she showed no hint of it. He *couldn't* know about her one-off affair with Rob.

'I think he was double-dealing at Casement's, on the Futures Exchange. That could have been why he transferred to the banking side, afraid they were catching on to him.'

'Does Cormac know?'

'I don't know. He doesn't have much to do with the day-to-day running of the office. All his time is taken up with the boards he's on.'

'How did you find out?'

He made a steeple of his fingers; he was an archbishop now, though without any religion. 'He used my name, without my permission, to get himself a few introductions. I only found out last weekend, I didn't have time to tackle him about it. The introductions were to people it'd be political suicide –' He stopped, as if the word itself were poison. Then he went on, 'People it wouldn't pay for me to be associated with. An outfit called Pinatubo Engineering that I know the Securities Commission is already investigating.'

She relaxed; though she had looked relaxed all along. 'Seems Rob had us all fooled. And I thought I knew all about men –' She shook her head at her own obtuseness. She had had one previous husband, a doctor with a wealthy practice and a drink problem; the divorce judge had awarded her half the estate and her husband had disappeared into an alcoholic haze somewhere overseas. There had been lovers before the doctor and between him and the politician and, despite her disarming remark, she *did* know all about men. 'Are we going to find out anything more about him?'

'I did find out something else about him. He had an affair with Ophelia.'

How to react? Indignantly, in defence of her sister? Shocked at the treachery of her stepson? She chose to play puzzled: 'What a ridiculous suggestion! Whatever put that into your head?'

'I went out to Rob's flat one afternoon, I just decided to drop in. Just as I got there, I saw Ophelia coming out – she didn't see me. A week later he was at our place, visiting. When he left he went upstairs to the penthouse – Cormac was away in Melbourne at another board meeting. Ophelia was there on her own. Rob stayed a couple of hours.'

'You mean you spied on him?'

'Yes.' He gazed at her steadily. 'Did he ever try to sleep with you?'

'No.' Her eyes were greenish-blue; her gaze was as level as a flat sea and as opaque. 'Are we going to have a row? If so, I think it would be better if we waited till we get home.'

'No, I'm not looking for a fight. I'm sorry, 'Lind – Oh Christ!' The hands crumpled one into the other. 'I don't know why I asked you such a question. It's those bloody sisters of yours!'

'Both of them? It was only 'Phelia a moment ago.'

Unlike her sisters, she had always been conscious of the proper time and place; she was like her father in that regard. She kept waiting for the door to open, for Derek's secretary or that always-bloody-intrusive Tucker to appear and guess at the atmosphere. Below and around them police business went on, all the paperwork involved with murder and robbery and rape (the paperwork in the hands of men, she was certain). Somewhere in this tall hive a busy bee was filing papers, no matter how few, on Rob: nothing with her name on it, she was sure. But Ophelia's? Or Juliet's?

'Love, you know what those are like. They flirt like a couple of nymphos.'

'Have they ever flirted with you? Seriously, trying to get you

115

into bed?' She would stab them through the heart if they had.

He smiled, but it was an effort. 'Relax, they don't play that close to home.'

'You just said 'Phelia was sleeping with your son. My stepson. Isn't that close enough to home for you?' She stood up, pulled on her gloves. She always wore gloves, one of her remaining tributes to her long-dead mother. Ileana had insisted that ladies always wore gloves, that when she had been a young girl in Bucharest before the war (there had been only two wars for Ileana, World Wars One and Two; no other wars had touched her) she had changed her gloves three times a day and she had had two hundred pairs. Rosalind drew on the gloves, drawing on Ileana's ghost. 'I'll see you at home. You are wrong about 'Phelia. And Juliet, too.'

Like her mother she could lie, to deceive herself as well as others.

2

Malone had never been in the dealing room of a merchant bank; indeed, he had never been anywhere near a stockbroker's. He had seen movies, *Wall Street* and *Bonfire of the Vanities* and had read Tom Wolfe's book, but now he was seeing the *actual* it seemed more unreal than the fiction.

It was like an orgy of youth, though he didn't see it in those terms. Young men, and women, in shirtsleeves, expensive shirtsleeves, shouted at each other; at phone-connected other brokers on other floors, on opposite sides of the city, the country, the world, they shouted even at the green-lettered terminals immediately in front of them. Malone could make nothing of what was being said, the language was just one long roar that only God and Mammon, for once on a network, could understand.

Ondelli, in a blue shirt with a white collar and a fashion-of-the-moment tie that resembled a length of regurgitation, led Malone round the edge of the boiling ring.

'Tokyo's jumping!' he shouted. 'The yen's on the rise again!'

Malone just nodded. He hated to shout and he had no answer anyway: he had never *seen* a yen. This was another world where, if he was to believe the social commentators, the rise and fall of the Eighties had begun. He wondered how large had been the shouting mob back in those hectic years, and when he and Ondelli were beyond the hubbub, in a narrow glass-walled corridor leading to the general manager's office, he asked the question.

'Back then we had three floors, we gave practically everyone a job who came in and asked for one. We had money running out of our ears, what did another paycheck matter? Or five or six or ten?' Ondelli shook his head. 'It'll never happen again, not in my day.'

'But some time in the future?'

'Sure. Why not? What else have we got to look forward to? Greed's a recurring disease, we all suffer from it.' He grinned, but he had said it without shame. 'You're a cop. Do you think human nature ever learns anything from its mistakes?'

Malone conceded the point, paused before the closed door of Ondelli's office. 'These fellers you caught, are they bad buggers or just greedy?'

'Greedy, that's all, I think. They're out of a job, anyway. I just fired them.'

He opened the door, ushered Malone into a medium-sized office where four terminals and a chart, rather than pictures, graced the walls. The furniture was Italian modern, all sharp angles at crotch-level, designed to make *castrati* of careless clients. The big window behind the desk looked uptown into sun-blazing walls of other windows. Malone wondered who, if not the general manager, had the harbour view on this floor. In this town having a harbour view was the same as having your name on a roll of honour.

Kagal rose as Malone and Ondelli came in. His university tie and Malone's police tie made them look like undertakers against the other three ties in the room. 'Inspector, this is Roger Statham and this is Leslie Bute.'

Their youth surprised Malone, though he should have expected it. Neither of them looked more than twenty; Statham looked even younger, a schoolboy. He was tall and thin, still acne-scarred, with long blond hair and deep blue eyes that now looked bewildered and embarrassed. Bute was shorter, broader, dark-haired, a young bull who still had his balls but was shocked at how close he had come to losing them. Besides their flowered ties, both young men wore bright red braces, like some sort of regimental regalia. They stood up respectfully, as if they had both come from homes or schools that had taught them manners. Malone at once sensed that neither of these boys had the in-built antagonism to cops that he had become accustomed to. They would be helpful.

He told them to sit down, then took a seat beside Ondelli, on the manager's side of the desk. 'I'll talk with you later, John,' he said to Kagal. 'Let's hear what Mr Statham and Mr Bute have to say.'

Both young men cleared their throats; then Bute said, 'First, Inspector, I'd like to say we're not criminals. At least I don't think we are.'

'Mr Bute, I'm not here looking for crims. I'm here for information.' He glanced at Ondelli. 'Detective Kagal told me there'd been some blips.'

'Roger and Les were dealing with Rob Sweden. He got them in evidently because he needed to spread some money.'

Malone looked back at Statham and Bute. 'Righto, explain.'

The two young men exchanged glances, then Bute said, 'Rob came to us about three months ago, right?' Statham, who seemed to have trouble finding his voice, nodded. 'He said we could make some money on the side if we helped him out. He had a client who wanted to clean up some money, he said.'

'Have you done this before? Cleaned up money?'

'Geez, no!' Statham found his voice, cracked and worn; he sounded as shocked at his own behaviour as at being caught. 'I dunno why we said yes . . . '

'Greed,' said their boss, not accusingly but like a specialist offering a diagnosis.

Statham nodded, almost as if glad of the interpretation. 'Yeah, that's it.'

'How much did you make?' Malone asked. 'On the side?'

'Not that much,' said Bute. 'Rob said we'd make more as time went on. We made twenty thousand each.'

'What do you normally make a year?'

'Sixty thousand. Sometimes more, with bonuses.'

Malone looked at Kagal. 'We're in the wrong game, John.'

'Yeah, but we get the bonus of occasionally being shot at.' It was heavy-handed, but it made the three Casement men look, if not feel, uncomfortable.

'How was the money to be laundered, Mr Bute?'

'Rob had this client. He deposited a million bucks, each of us had to handle a third. We were buying North American lumber futures –'

Malone looked at Ondelli, who said, 'Like I told you.'

'How come this wasn't picked up before now, if it started three months ago?'

Ondelli looked only slightly ill at ease. 'Inspector, I don't think you appreciate the money that passes through this office. Rob was smart, he split the money. Three hundred, three-fifty grand, that's not a large amount in our terms. It'd run by the observers without causing any real blip.'

'So when did it cause a blip?'

'When the client called in the money and we had to write the cheque. A million two. The call came late yesterday afternoon and if I hadn't talked to you a coupla days ago, it probably wouldn't have registered.'

Malone, the counter of pennies, marvelled at a mind on which a million two (even the amount sounded unfamiliar) wouldn't register. 'Who was the client?' The three Casement men exchanged glances and Malone snapped, 'Don't give me any confidentiality bullshit, I've had enough of that for today. Who was the client?'

'Pinatubo Engineering,' said Ondelli.

Going back to Homicide Malone said, 'Check on Pinatubo, John, they've got to be registered here.'

'Will do.' Kagal sometimes sounded as if he were in the army; when he became police commissioner he would also be a field marshal. 'What about those jerks, Bute and Statham? Do we refer them to the Fraud Squad?'

When he was commissioner he would sweep the city clean . . . 'John, never give yourself more work than you have to. Let Fraud find them themselves. They've lost their jobs, that's good enough for me.'

Kagal said nothing for a while, then he looked sideways at Malone. 'You think I'm an eager beaver, don't you?'

Malone had never ducked bumpers, even though he had been a poor batsman. 'You are, aren't you? I don't hold it against you. I'd rather an eager beaver than a lazy bugger who bludged on his mates all the time. But you have to draw a line. What satisfaction would you get out of all the time and paperwork you'd spend on getting those two kids to court? And when you got 'em into court, it's a fifty-fifty chance the judge'd give them a slap on the wrist and put them on a bond for twelve months. Too many of our judges have a reluctance to go heavy on white-collar crims. No, John, slow down, that's all I suggest. Police work was never meant for sprinters.'

Kagal digested that; then he smiled. 'I sometimes find you a pain in the arse, sir, but still I admire you.'

'Likewise,' said Malone and for the first time liked the young man.

Back in the office he did his own paperwork; then sat back and gazed at the note he had found on first coming back to his desk: *AC Falkender called. You are to see the Minister at his apartment at 6 p.m. Lucky you.* The note was in Clements' large scribble.

Then Clements came into the office. 'You got the note? You going for cocktails?'

'I'll bet that's what his wife serves – cocktails. If I'm lucky, I'll get a stale beer. Why the hell me?'

Clements dropped his bulk into the chair opposite Malone. 'John Kagal told me about Pinatubo. I've already checked on it, as soon as Palady and Junor left. It was registered here two years ago, its full name is Pinatubo *Medical* Engineering. It was managed by a Mr Belgarda, Ramon Belgarda. If Mr Tajiri has anything to do with it, he's not down as a registered director or executive. Their offices are down in William Street. I've been down there, it's two rooms above an empty car showroom. Nobody home, the door was locked. I've been on to Romy. She's just rung me back. Pinatubo used to import medical equipment into this country – operating tables, trolleys, stuff like that. There's some of their stuff out at the morgue. Romy has made a few enquiries. As far as she can gather, Pinatubo hasn't been selling medical equipment for at least six months, maybe more. It could of been set up as a front for –' He shrugged: take your pick of a dozen choices.

'These kids I talked to at Casement's, they said they knew nothing of Pinatubo. I believe them. They never met Tajiri or this other bloke – Belgarda? Rob Sweden was their only connection. I asked them if Sweden had ever mentioned Kornsey or Caccia, whatever name he used, but they just looked blank.'

'He's connected to it all, though.'

'Of course he is. But how? Money is the key to this. It's the be-all and end-all for these people, and I mean the lot of them. They are either born to money or they're born to make it, they marry for it or they kill for it. Or are killed.'

'The commos must miss having you as their spokesman. You've taken in the whole capitalist system there.'

'Romy once told me something, on our first case with her. She said when looking for the cause of death in a homicide, she started from the outer limits, eliminating everything as she went along that might've or might not have caused the death, till she got to a core of probable causes. I think we should do the same with these cases. How're you going with her, anyway?'

They had known each other so long and so well that neither of them was ever fazed when the conversation went off at a tangent. 'D'you mean am I having second thoughts about proposing to her? Yes. But I always have second thoughts about everything, even whether I'll have a piss.'

'So, leaving aside whether you piss first time up, how do you feel now you've asked her?'

Clements bit his lip, then nodded. 'I'm happy. So's she.'

'Good.' Then Malone looked up at Andy Graham in the doorway. 'Yes, Andy?'

'Nothing from the FBI yet.' He scraped his feet, as if about to take off for Washington to find out what was delaying them.

'Waco, Texas,' said Malone. 'That's probably all that's on their mind, Waco.'

The horrific end to the siege of the religious cult at their headquarters in Texas had thrown up a glare that had gone right round the world. The FBI itself was now under siege for its handling of the long stand-off, but Malone's sympathy, like that of most cops, was with the law enforcement men. It was an old cliché but true: hindsight was the perfect example of twenty-twenty vision. And no one was ever as decisive in their criticism as those who did not have to make a decision.

'Keep at them, Andy. But gently, try some Aussie diplomacy.'

'What's that?' said Clements.

'Our request is probably going through the system, same as it does here. The Yanks have as many bureaucrats as we do. More, probably.'

'You think I should try going through their embassy in Canberra?'

'Forget that, that would only add to the system. We could be here till Judgement Day and I don't think that's on the calendar yet.'

Graham disappeared and Clements said, 'You're being extra patient, aren't you?'

'No, I think I'm like you. I'm having second thoughts. I've got the feeling that if ever we solve these cases, make the connection, we'll be wishing we were at Tibooburra.'

4

The door to the Sweden apartment was opened by Luisa, the Filipino maid. She was in her thirties, plump, plain, but not unattractive with a flat-cheeked face and long-lashed dark eyes that had a remote look about them, as if she had not entirely left the slopes of Zamboanga, her home province. She ducked her head to Malone, but gave him no smile of welcome, instead looked apprehensive. Malone wondered if she was an illegal, if Sweden, unknowingly, was like those White House executive nominees who had neglected to check on their servants' credentials. But illegal immigrants were not Malone's province, he had enough bother with the natives.

There was a smile of welcome from Rosalind Sweden, who came forward hand outstretched. 'Inspector! How nice to see you again. You've met my sisters,' she said, as if he were the dim sort of man who went through life never remarking the women he met.

'Of course,' said Malone, irritated, and perversely spread the suavity like honey. The three sisters, collectively, were formidable and he decided the best way of combatting them was with silk gloves. Unlike most Irishmen, he was not afraid of a woman, but in the plural he preferred to treat them with caution, which is the way even Latin men do.

'My husband has been delayed, he's been held up by some demanding constituent. It comes of representing an electorate like this.' She waved a hand as if they were in the middle of an unemployment camp. Malone had never bothered to check his Minister's electorate and he wondered what the poorer voters would think of their member living in a pad like this.

'Are you any closer to solving Rob's murder?' said Juliet.

Malone held up his finger and thumb half an inch apart.

123

'We're making progress. Homicides are rarely solved the same day. Except domestics,' he added, putting salt in the honey.

'Domestics?'

'When a wife kills a husband,' said the Police Minister's wife. 'Or vice versa. I'm learning the jargon since Derek has been bringing home papers from the office.'

Malone had never shown a paper from the office to Lisa in all their married life. 'You find the papers interesting?'

All three sisters caught the note in his voice; they had been reading men's voices since kindergarten. 'Of course, Inspector. I did a year of sociology at university.' It had been a waste of time, she had soon discovered there were no rich sociologists. 'But I suppose you look at the papers differently. You *write* them.'

So far he had written none on the Sweden case. 'I'm sure you'll find the papers on your stepson interesting when they're all in. Especially if I can link up his murder with another one.'

That sat them up; he actually thought he heard Ophelia's girdle creak. They looked at each other, then gave him the glare of a concentrated gaze. '*Another* murder?'

'Have any of you heard of a man named Terry Kornsey? Or he might've called himself Joseph Caccia. He was an American.'

There was a flicker in only one of the three pairs of eyes: Ophelia's. Then all three heads were shaken. 'The names mean nothing to me,' said Rosalind. 'Julie? 'Phelia?'

'No.'

'Was he a friend of Rob's?' said Juliet. 'Thanks, Luisa.'

The maid had brought in some canapés to go with the drinks she had served. Malone had noticed that she had poured the drinks with the measured skill of a barmaid. He had asked for a light beer and she had poured it without choking it with a heavy collar.

'Rob never brought any of his friends here,' said Rosalind. 'Except girls. Very pretty girls with nothing between their ears.' A description that had never fitted her or her sisters.

124

'Maybe I should talk to some of them. Can you remember their names?'

'Not their surnames. They were always Caroline or Felicity or Joanna.'

'Nice North Shore names,' said Ophelia. 'Murderers never have names like that, do they?'

Come to think of it, no they don't. 'You follow the crime stories in the papers?'

'Only since my brother-in-law has become Police Minister. Hello, Derek, we're talking murders.'

The look of disapproval on Sweden's face as he came down from the front door was blatant. 'Jesus, 'Phelia, do you have to turn everything into party chatter? A whisky, Luisa, a double.'

'My, we are in a mood.' Ophelia stood up. 'I think it's time I went back to the hospital. I'm bringing Cormac home tomorrow. We'll have a nurse come in, just in case. Goodbye, Inspector. Good luck with your inspecting. Are you handling my husband's case?'

'Only indirectly, Mrs Casement. I think it's been entered in the papers as assault, not homicide.' It was cruel: they both knew it, but she didn't blink.

She put on a hat, drew on gloves: it was like watching someone getting ready to go out to face the 1950s. The hat reminded Malone of the large-crowned caps worn by Soviet generals, who looked as if, if a wind blew up, their heads would spin away in the updraft. But Ophelia would never lose her head any way at all.

'Nobody will kill Cormac. He'll die in his own time,' she said and left. Winds would blow round her, but never through her.

Sweden took Malone into a small study; Rosalind called after them, 'Do you want us, too?'

'No,' said her husband, 'this is police business.'

Malone was at once wary, wondering in what sense this was police business. He followed Sweden into the study, closing the door when the Minister gestured for him to do so. A quick glance around the room gave Malone a new look at the

Minister: unless the bookshelves were there just for show, Sweden had wider and deeper interests than Malone had suspected. There was what looked like a whole shelf of political history, national and international; a book by Gough Whitlam was somehow stuffed between two volumes of a biography of Lyndon Baines Johnson, a juxtaposition that would have sent the ex-President cross-eyed. There were books on music, art and there were two shelves of what Malone, lately converted to reading, took to be serious fiction: Bellow, Greene, Malouf. Then he saw the two vases of flowers and the small triptych of the three Bruna sisters on the wall. He guessed this was as much Rosalind's room as her husband's, this was where she read *the papers*.

Sweden slipped off his jacket, took off his tie (a police tie, Malone remarked), sat down and motioned Malone into the chair on the opposite side of the small, neat desk. He sipped his drink, taking his time, looking at the detective with deliberate scrutiny that was insulting. Malone held his temper.

At last Sweden said, 'So what do you know that hasn't been in your reports?'

They were one-on-one, outside police precincts; Malone let his tongue go: 'What makes you think I'm holding anything back?'

Sweden was about to take another sip of his drink; the glass was stuck halfway to his mouth. 'Don't let's you and I get off on the wrong foot, Inspector.'

'I think we've already done that. You're accusing me of holding something back on your son's case.'

'Aren't you? I've looked at the summary briefs, there's bugger-all in them. You want another beer?'

Malone put down his empty glass. 'No, thanks. Look, you're the father as well as the Minister. I've learned a few things about your son that smell – would you want me to put those in the reports before I've had time to double-check whether they're true or not? I'm a father, too. That comes first, before being a cop.'

Sweden put down his glass, leaned forward. The small room

was warm and there was a shine of perspiration on his bald head. 'Okay, point taken. So what have you learned?'

Malone told him, waiting for an explosion of indignation; but there was none. Sweden listened without interrupting, then sat back and was silent for a full minute. Then he nodded. 'I knew all that. Not about the other two kids being involved, just my son. I found out a couple of weeks ago.'

'What did you do?'

'I blew the shit out of him.'

'To what effect?'

'I don't know. He took it pretty quietly, more so than I'd expected. We were never the best of mates, even though he was an only child. We never fought, but somehow we were never close. When his mother died, he thought I didn't waste any time in marrying again. What I'm telling you doesn't go out of this room, okay?'

'So long as you don't report me to my AC for talking back.'

Sweden shook his head, looked on the point of smiling. 'Jesus, Malone . . . Have you ever thought of going into politics? Never mind, don't answer that.'

'How did you find out what your son was up to?'

'That firm you mentioned, Pinatubo. When it set up in business here two, three years ago, I was Minister for Health. I had to okay a couple of contracts for them, medical equipment for a hospital and the city morgue, as I remember it. They seemed okay to my department at the time. Then all of a sudden they stopped submitting bids and we started to hear rumours about them.'

'What sort of rumours?'

'That they were really owned by the *yakuza*, the Japanese crims. We have no proof, they're still being investigated by the Securities Commission, but the last thing I wanted was Rob being associated with them. I don't think he knew who he was really dealing with, he sometimes wasn't as smart as he thought he was.' He picked up his glass, finished his drink. 'If this gets out, the Opposition will make all the capital it can out of it. And our majority's so slim. Do you know Hans Vanderberg?'

Malone grinned. 'Do you mean do I know what he's like? Sure I know. When he was Police Minister . . . Well, never mind.' Political histories are written; but histories of the relations between ministers and their departments never see the public light. Yet the past, even yesterday, is thick with gossip, innuendo, suspicion and often downright hatred. A hypocritically clean sheet was always opened to the new Minister . . . 'This other case, the body stolen from the morgue, it's connected to Pinatubo. I can't find any connection between your son and the dead man, his name was Kornsey, but there is one somewhere along the line. You've never met Tajiri, the feller who supposedly runs Pinatubo now?' Sweden shook his head. 'What about Belgarda, the original manager? He'd have been running it when you signed those contracts with them.'

'Once I met him, but I can't remember him. He came to some reception we gave, when they got their first contract. I can't help you with any detail about him. As a Minister you meet hundreds of businessmen like him.'

'We presume he's a Filipino. So's your maid, isn't she?'

Sweden's raised eyebrows went up beyond what would have been his hairline in the past. 'Luisa? You've already questioned her.'

'Not me. Can I talk to her now?'

'Sure.' Sweden stood up. 'In here?'

'No, I'd rather talk to her out in the kitchen, alone. All right?'

A narrow hallway led from the study out to the kitchen. Sweden led the way, pushing open the swing door into the kitchen and calling, 'Luisa!'

The kitchen was empty, cold and clinical as a morgue but with no bodies, not even one. Luisa was gone: her bedroom, too, was empty. The closet doors were open, there were empty spaces amongst the clothes on the racks. The rear service door to the apartment was slightly ajar, as if Luisa, leaving, had not wanted its closing to be heard.

Out in the big living room Rosalind said, 'She's not there? But I spoke to her five minutes ago.'

'Maybe she's gone downstairs for something,' said Juliet.

'I don't think so,' said Malone. 'She's packed a bag and left. Does she have a car?'

'No.' Sweden was perturbed. 'Do you think she's connected to Pinatubo, too?'

'I'm not even making a guess at this stage. Could be. Probably. How did she come to you?'

'From an agency,' said Rosalind. 'She came to us five, six months ago. She had excellent references, I took her on right away. Good help is so hard to get these days, despite the recession.'

'We have the same trouble in the Service,' said Malone; he saw Juliet smile, just a twist of her full lips. Rosalind and Sweden didn't smile and he went on, 'Did you talk to her about your stepson's murder?'

'Of course not. It was none of her business.' Rosalind sounded haughty.

'I think it may have been very much her business.' He glanced at Sweden. 'She told one of my men that your son had given her fifty dollars to go out to the movies. Maybe he gave her nothing, we had only her word for that. Maybe she let the murderer in, then went out, to be out of the way when it happened.'

All at once Rosalind lost her composure; she shivered. 'God, it's all getting worse! It's – *bizarre*! Frightening!'

Juliet put an arm round her. 'Be calm, darling. Nobody else is going to be hurt. That's right, isn't it, Derek?'

She addressed the question to her brother-in-law, but looked at both men. The answer was in their faces.

Chapter Eight

✦✦✦✦✦✦✦✦✦

1

Saturday afternoon Malone was playing tennis down at the public courts at Coogee with Keith Cayburn, his neighbour, and two other men with whom he played regularly. He looked forward each weekend to the exercise, serving powerfully, hitting hard on both forehand and backhand, not really caring whether he and his partner won or lost, just intent on getting the past week out of his system. He was a natural player, but, as in his cricket, he might have been better had he taken the game more seriously. But for him sport was *sport* and dedication was not in his weekend lexicon. Even as he crossed over between games on this Saturday afternoon, a well-known marathon runner ran by on the road outside, all sinew and bone, legs pumping, face gaunt and aged by dedication, running willingly into arthritis, crippled knee-joints and an early grave. Malone, who knew the runner, gave him a derisive wave and the athlete raised an answering arm, like that of a drowning iron-man swimmer.

'Inspector Malone?'

Malone frowned, not recognizing the newcomer who had appeared at the back of the court. He was tall and athletic-looking and his hair had gone grey along the temples since Malone had last seen him. 'Sergeant *Kenthurst*?'

'Superintendent now.' He had a long-jawed bony face, a dark military-style moustache and quick brown eyes that were frank rather than foxy. 'I'm sorry to interrupt, but . . . '

'Can it wait till I finish the set? We're nearly there.'

Malone's concentration had been distracted; the set took

longer than expected, mainly due to his errors. What was Kenthurst doing here on a Saturday afternoon, all the way up from Canberra? Had the Federal police suddenly become involved in the Sweden case? He hoped not. The stew had already become too thick and another cook in the kitchen was the last thing he wanted. When the match was over, he and Keith Cayburn had lost it.

'Sorry, Keith, I blew that. I'll sit the next one out, get someone else to take my place.'

'Police business?' Malone nodded and Cayburn said, 'Do you get extra pay if you bring a crim to justice at the weekend?'

Malone grinned, went across to Kenthurst and led him to some chairs at the side of the clubhouse. Kenthurst waited till each of them had opened his can of light beer, then said, 'Terry Kornsey, you were making enquiries about him?'

'To the FBI in Washington. You acting for them now?'

'We do, but not on this one. The US Marshals' Service has been in touch with us. Kornsey was *their* pigeon. They've been looking after him under their Witness Protection Scheme.'

'What was he – Mafia?'

Kenthurst nodded. He was dressed in a navy blazer, tattersall-checked shirt, police tie, cavalry twill trousers and desert boots; he looked like a staff officer from Duntroon, the military school near Canberra. A major-general, at least; Malone wondered what a superintendent's pay was compared to his own. There was no rank of inspector in the Federal service. 'He turned informant against the Mob in New York, his evidence sent three of the bosses to jail for life. He's been in Australia seven years under the Protection Scheme. His real name is – *was* Vincent Bassano.'

'Did you people know he was here?'

'No. They don't take us into their confidence on those things. We knew nothing of him till they contacted us this morning. My commander put me on a plane for Sydney after we'd talked to them. I'm sorry about spoiling your afternoon, but I have to be back in Canberra this evening, the Prime Minister is having a dinner for senior officers.'

131

Can't miss that, can we? 'How did you know where to find me?'

'Your wife told me.'

Malone hated the thought of Lisa being disturbed for police business, especially on the weekend. 'What do the Yanks want us to do?'

'They don't want any more than the usual paperwork.' Kenthurst smiled, his teeth very white under the dark moustache. 'That he's officially dead and buried –'

'He's not, not yet. All we have of him is a foot and half a leg.'

'That should satisfy them. I'd guess they work the same way as us, get the paperwork done so his name can be removed from the payroll. They paid him full subsistence for two years. Then he's bitten them for odd sums since then.'

'He was adding to it, you know. He'd raised capital from somewhere, he was using it to deal on the futures exchange.'

'Do you think his Mafia mates caught up with him? They blew up his parents while he was giving evidence. Bombed their house, killed them both. Nice types.'

Malone pulled on a sweater against the cool of the afternoon as the sun moved round behind the clubhouse. From over at Coogee oval, a hundred yards away, there came a roar as someone scored a try in the rugby match being played there. A youth and a girl leaned against the wire netting at the end of the court, watching a mixed doubles match; the boy and the girl each had a hand grasping the netting as if trying to hold themselves upright while their passion for each other weakened their knees; their other arms were wrapped round each other, hands groping over buttocks like horny crabs. From the courts there came the soft thump of a ball on racquet and the occasional shout or squeal. An ordinary Saturday afternoon as background to talk of murder and Mafia; but Malone knew the world was painted in colours as juxtaposed as these. 'They could have, but we've got no evidence. At the moment our lead suspects are Japanese and Filipinos.'

'Japs? You mean the *yakuza?*' Kenthurst twisted his thin lips, the moustache wriggling. 'We don't want *them*. They're here, we know that, but so far they've kept a low profile. The PM has been preaching closer trade ties with Japan, but there's a limit.'

Malone grinned. He had met Kenthurst five years ago for the first and only time and found the man humourless and stiff with Canberra starch and superiority; promotion and time had humanized him. 'Spoil his dinner for him tonight, tell him who we think are now in business.' He stood up. 'Between you and me, Ron, I'm having to treat this case pretty gently. It's linked with the homicide of young Sweden, our Minister's son.' Kenthurst pursed his lips. 'Don't mention that at the dinner tonight or it'll curdle the vichyssoise. We've got no evidence of a direct link, but if the Yanks have anything that might help on what they know of – what was his name? Bassano? If they have anything, I'd be grateful for it. Are you the one handling things direct with them?'

'For the time being. I don't think it's going to last more than a week or two.'

'Stick with it, as a favour to us. I don't want this spread around any more than is necessary. I've got a Minister, two ACs and an Opposition Leader breathing down my neck and I don't like the smell of any of it.'

Kenthurst put out his hand. 'Let me have what you have, the bare bones. Enough to satisfy my chief and the US Marshals' Service. Then we'll see what turns up when I put some questions to the Yanks.'

'A fax'll be on your desk Monday morning. Why did they send you all the way up here instead of just getting me on the phone?'

'That's where I'm to ask you a favour – for the US Marshals' Service. They don't want it broadcast that they've been hiding ex-Mafia out here, they'd rather the less people know about the Witness Protection Scheme, the better. If you can work it, they'd like it if you can keep Bassano's history out of your report.'

'That's asking a lot.'

'They appreciate that. But there are political implications –' He came from the city propped up by political implications; Canberra would fall down, a hollow shell, if politics, implied or otherwise, deserted it. 'The Brits started this country by dumping their unwanted crims out here. You can imagine what the Lefties would make of it if the Yanks started doing the same thing.'

'How many protected ex-Mafia do they have out here?'

'I have no idea, they'd never divulge that. Maybe none, now Bassano's dead. Maybe a dozen. You notice how basketball, baseball, the American games are catching on out here?' He smiled to show he was just kidding. 'So far the only ones who know who Bassano really was are my commander, you and I. Phone me Monday, don't fax.'

'I'll have to tell my boss, Greg Random. He's the one who decides what goes further.'

'Is he likely to make waves?'

'Greg? He wouldn't make a wave if he farted in his bath.'

'You should move to Canberra. You speak the language.'

'What's it like down there, now Labor's been re-elected?'

'Peculiar. The rumour is that Cabinet has made a mass appointment with a psychiatrist – with Medicare, of course – to see what will happen to their pysches if they act gracious in victory. They've only been taught to put the boot in.'

Kenthurst left to go back to Canberra, another planet. Malone went back on court and played badly. The Mafia and the *yakuza*: who needed them to call the shots? He mis-hit a forehand drive into Cayburn's back, causing another wave, this time of indignation.

When he got home, exercised physically and mentally, Lisa said, 'Did that Federal man catch up with you? More trouble?'

After his shower he sat on the side of their bed in his underpants and told her; if the US Marshals' Service thought wives should be forbidden its secrets, then none of its marshals could be married. She sat opposite him in the bedroom's one

tub chair, a slim leg showing through the opening of her bath-
robe, her hair still wet from her own shower. She looked
beautiful and desirable, but he had other things on his mind.
'How do you fancy Tibooburra? Out there I'd be my own boss,
just checking the rabbit-proof fence, drying out the occasional
drunken drover . . . No Mafia, no *yakuza*, no politicians, no
greedy money-hungry bastards –'

'You're getting angry.' She got up, came across and stood
in front of him, opened her robe and pushed his face against
her breasts. 'There, have a nibble.'

He did. 'You're disgusting. You think sex is the answer to
everything. Where are the kids?'

There was the sound of a key in the front door. 'There they
are now. Tough luck, old chap.'

She closed her robe and went out to greet the children, while
he, half-aroused, sat on the side of the bed and wondered
how many other frustrations he would face in the coming
weeks.

2

'Our Premier is a bugger for stating the irremediable obvious.'
Jack Aldwych was showing the benefits of his retirement reading, though he was careful how he got out *irremediable*. 'That's
as distinct from telling the truth.'

Bruna looked at him with surprise. 'Such cynicism! You
could be East European.'

'Is that supposed to be a compliment?' Aldwych was in good
humour.

'Of course.' Bruna, too, was in good humour. He always
was when his daughters, any one of them, entertained him in
the manner for which he had raised them. He loved these
outings on the Harbour, moving majestically past lesser craft
crowded with hoi polloi. Somewhere back in his lineage there
was an ancestor who was an asterisk in the *Almanach de Gotha*,
that bible of snobbery, and he had inherited the talent of

waving at the peasants with the proper kindly condescension. The peasants, at least those on the harbour, usually replied with a hoi-polloi finger.

Jack Junior and Juliet's cruiser was a fifty-two-footer with two 450-horsepower diesels and an interior that always made Jack Senior think of a floating brothel, though he had never been aboard one of the latter. He had no idea what it had cost Jack Junior, but whatever the cost, it would have been too much; Aldwych himself had never gone in for expensive toys. Juliet had decorated it, not letting taste get in the way of its luxury. She spent money wisely; that is, never from her own purse. This was a company boat, something her father-in-law would not know till next year's accounts were in. In the meantime she wooed him with its luxury, trusting that he would fall in love with it and not complain about the cost. She had misread him.

She came and sat beside him under the awning on the aft deck. Her father had got up and gone into the saloon to put his arm round his woman for today, a grey-, almost white-haired beauty who was notorious as an always-available free-loader. There were two other couples on board, two young executives of Landfall Holdings and their equally young wives. Juliet knew that the two old men in her life liked to look at attractive young women; she knew her father was lecherous, but she could never be sure of Jack Senior.

'Enjoying yourself?'

'I'm expected to, aren't I?' His smile was friendly; but he could have smiled like that as he killed someone. He was still dangerous, she was sure of that, but the danger of him thrilled her. Had he been thirty years younger she would have married him instead of his son.

She put a silky hand on his hessian one. 'Jack, dear, why don't you trust me?'

'Why wouldn't I trust you?' He had been interrogated by police and lawyers, the best of both breeds; he wasn't going to be thrown by a woman less than half his age.

'You don't trust women at all, do you?'

In the saloon he could see the white-haired woman responding to Bruna's fondling hand; he was a prude when it came to sexual advances in public. 'I trusted Jack's mother.'

'Jack's told me about her. Hers was the only law you respected. She must have been a strong woman.'

Shirl hadn't been; but he said, 'She had to be, to put up with me. You and your sisters are all strong women.'

'How did you know that?' She didn't simper or look coy, that was beyond her.

'Observation.'

'You ran the prostitution –' She hesitated.

'Racket?'

'Well – yes. Did you choose the girls?'

He smiled; she was naive after all. 'Does Derek choose the clerks in the Police Department? I was the Minister for Prostitution . . . Back in the Middle Ages did you know there were Ministers for that? It was all well organized. So it was here in Sydney when I ran it. There were no Wogs and Chinks trying to muscle in with their half a dozen girls. All the hookers up the Cross belonged to me. That was before prostitution got out to the suburbs.' He looked up as Jack Junior came down the stairs from the wheelhouse. 'Jack, we're talking about the good old days, when the economy was on the straight and narrow.'

'Prostitution,' said Juliet. 'The straight and narrow.'

Jack Junior grimaced; then changed the subject: 'They're burying Rob on Tuesday. Are you coming to the funeral, Dad? I'll come and pick you up.'

'I don't think so. Juliet, could you let me have a word with Jack?' He was more than just a guest on the boat; he was the admiral. The words were a request, but the look was an order. 'Just a few minutes.'

She squeezed his hand to show him she was doing him a favour, then went into the saloon, gently lifting her father's hand off the white-haired woman's buttock as she went past. Jack Junior looked after her. 'You shouldn't dismiss her like that.'

'She and I understand each other . . . Jack, this Rob business, it's getting dirty.'

Jack Junior was not surprised; though he tried to go straight, there was inherited larceny in his blood. 'I thought it might. What have you found out?'

'I rang up a few old mates. Scams are going on and it's not the local boys who are pulling 'em off. The Japs and the Filipinos, they say, but they don't have any proof. I asked what about the Triads or the Vietnamese, but they said no. Has Julie told you that the Swedens' Filipino maid has disappeared?'

'Yes. D'you think the Asiatics tried to do Cormac in?' Like most Australians, those of the third, fourth or fifth generation, he lumped together three billion people, of fifty-plus languages, a dozen skin tones and half a dozen cultures. He was not uneducated or ignorant, just white and prejudiced. Though to be fair, until he had married Juliet he hadn't known there was any difference between Roumanians and Hungarians, neither of them was to be trusted.

They were now moving up the Lane Cove river, one of the many inlets of the Harbour. Up on their left was Hunters Hill, the narrow peninsula with its narrow streets and narrower lanes, its stone houses built by French and Italian masons and its air of superior respectability. Aldwych had once thought of buying one of the grander houses, but it had been Shirl who had vetoed the idea. She knew whom respectability would and would not accept.

'I made some enquiries about what happened to Cormac. I spoke to Les Chung. Just in case the Japs had employed a coupla local punks, to confuse the situation.' He shook his big head. 'It looks like what Cormac said it was, a coupla kids trying their luck.'

'But Jesus – trying to *burn* him! Even you wouldn't have done that when you were young.'

'Thanks. You wanna be cut outa my will? Jack, the point is, watch it. If the Japs and the Filipinos are in on this, there may be more to come. I don't think Rob was the only one in this family involved in this mess.'

138

'What makes you think that?'

'Didn't you know I had a sixth sense? I got stabbed a coupla times, but never in the back . . . Hello – Emily, isn't it? Here, sit beside me.'

Emily Karp, the white-haired beauty, could have been an aunt of the Bruna sisters; she had spent almost sixty years flirting with men. 'You said that like a king.'

'I used to be one,' said Aldwych, smiling at her. He felt sorry for her: all she had was her beauty and, when one looked closer, one could see that beginning to crumble around the edges. 'You must have been a dazzler when you were young.'

'Now now?' She looked up at Bruna, who was standing with legs wide apart, keeping his balance as the boat rocked in the wake of a passing speedboat. 'Am I fading, Adam?'

'Not in my eyes, my love.'

Aldwych felt seasick, and not from the rolling of the boat. 'I've got cataracts.'

She gave him a smile that, in his younger days, would have swollen his balls. 'You're forgiven, Jack. We should have dinner together some time. Adam only calls me when there's no one younger. We're two of a kind, Jack. Over the hill – but the youngsters don't know what the view is like from the other side.'

All at once he was unfaithful to Shirl: he wished he had met this woman sooner.

She went back into the saloon with Bruna and Jack Junior said, 'You're not going to fall for her line, are you?'

What line did you fall for from Juliet? Or Janis Eden? There were more young fools than old fools. 'I'm too old for that.'

'I've been thinking about what you said. What makes you think someone in the family is mixed up in Rob's murder?'

'Because no one, except Rob's father, seems really upset. Families get upset when someone who belongs to them gets murdered. I *know*. Even crims' families don't take it the way this lot has.'

'They're all going to the funeral Tuesday.'

'Have you ever watched a State funeral? They bury some

prominent bloke and ninety-five per cent of the mourners are there to be seen, not to weep tears over him. Rob's funeral is gunna be a little State burial. There'll be the family and all the pretty girls he laid and maybe one or two of his workmates. And the only one who'll be looking really upset will be his father. No one else is gunna weep for the young shit.'

Jack Junior was sometimes shocked by the hardness in his father; but it was that that had kept him alive, had made him successful. 'The police will be there.'

'Of course. If you see Scobie Malone or his sidekick, Russ Clements, tell 'em I'd like to see 'em.'

'Are you going to tell them what you think about the family?'

'I might.' He smiled; it was hard to tell whether it was malicious or fatherly. 'I'm just gunna make sure they don't point a finger at you.'

3

Kelsey Bugler and Kim Weetbix lived in a squat, one of a row of condemned terrace houses in a squalid street in Redfern. The houses had been marked for demolition by the local council four years before, but somehow each year's budget could not find the money for the wreckers to move in. So squatters, street-kids and winos and one or two eccentrics who kept to themselves, had moved in and taken over the decrepit dwellings. There were certain sections of Redfern, no more than two kilometres from the heart of the city, that had been taken over by the Aborigines, but there were no blacks in Bulinga Street, despite its aboriginal name. The squatters and the Kooris distrusted each other with equal bigotry.

The houses were two-storeyed, seemingly leaning against each other for support; the two end houses leaned outwards, ready to fall down at any moment. It had once been a neat terrace, but all the iron-lace, like dead vines, had been stripped from the balconies; indeed, most of the balconies themselves had gone, their floorboards torn up for firewood. None of the houses had glass in their front windows; if the spaces were not boarded up, they gaped like silent mouths. All the houses had front doors of a sort: the original doors in some cases, sheets of corrugated iron in others, a truck's rear door in the house at the far end. No electricity or gas was connected and several houses were no more than blackened shells, where the occupants had burnt themselves to a cinder with fires they had lit to cook meals or warm themselves. Kel Bugler didn't mind his surroundings, but Kim Weetbix hated them. Even the pits of Saigon, eight years ago, had never made her feel as degraded as this house and this street did.

Monday morning she was not at home when the killer called; she was trying to raise money at a pawnshop on Cormac Casement's gold watch. Bugler was upstairs in the back room that he and Kim called home, whenever they thought of that word. There was a stained mattress on the floor, two stained and frayed blankets and two pillows that were an aberration: they had snow-white pillow-cases. Kim, as a twelve-year-old, had worked in a Saigon laundry; she could not lay her head on a dirty pillow. The rest of the room was bare but for a car seat, stuffing sticking out of its vinyl upholstery like weed growing out of a rock, a small spirit stove and a rickety-legged chest of drawers in which their food was stored. Their meagre wardrobe was hung on nails on the scabbed walls, like parts of cadavers who had lived here before them.

Bugler was lying on the mattress, Casement's briefcase on the floor beside him, reading the sports pages of a newspaper he had stolen from the local newsagency. His team, Balmain, was running second last in the season's rugby league competition; nothing, it seemed, was going right in this fucking world. Sometimes at night he wept silently at what the world had done to him; though he had not the intelligence to analyze it, he had found that self-pity made you feel better. Once, when Kim had heard him weeping, he had tried to explain it to her, but she had just listened with that fucking Asiatic mask of hers and in the end he had belted her out of frustration. She had told him then that if he ever hit her again she would leave him.

That was when his intelligence had for the moment burst into flame, flickering though it was: he had known then that, if she left him, his fucking world was finished.

He looked up over the newspaper as the man, soft-footed, came into the room, closing the squeaking door behind him. He was thin, not very tall and he was pulling a black silk hood, with eye-slits, down over his face. Bugler sat up, more puzzled than, as yet, afraid.

'Who the fuck are you?'

'It's who you are that matters.' The voice had an accent, but Bugler had never had an educated or sensitive ear. 'You're the one who tried to kill the old man by setting fire to him. Correct?'

'Where'd you hear that shit? What old man?' He was wondering if he could dive from the mattress and bring the man down in a tackle. But the sight of the gun in the man's right hand held him back.

'You talked too much, young man. You shouldn't have boasted what you and your girlfriend did.'

That had happened Saturday night. An angry Kim, on their way home, had snapped at him for letting his mouth run on. They had been up at the Cross, sharing a joint with another couple while they looked for drunks they might roll, and Kim, searching for a handkerchief, had taken the gold watch from her jacket pocket. *Where'd you get that?* the other girl had asked, and Bugler, mouth loose as always, had told her. Now he couldn't believe that this guy with the gun had got to that couple and squeezed the information out of them.

'Who gave you that crap?'

'Your friends, so-called. A little cash . . . ' He rubbed finger and thumb of his left hand together. 'It didn't take much effort to find you, young man. The description of you fitted street-kids – it was only a matter of knowing where to look. I was a street-kid myself once, in another place.'

'Okay, so you know I tried to burn the old guy. So what d'you want? Did he send you?'

'A man like that?' The hood moved from side to side. Then

he picked up the briefcase, saw that the two combination locks had been forced. He cursed in Spanish, though Bugler didn't recognize the language. Then he reverted to English: 'Did you understand the papers in here?'

'What the fuck if I did?' But the defiance was paper-thin: Bugler knew the man was going to kill him.

'You really are a nuisance. You have complicated an already complicated situation. It's a pity your girlfriend is not here, but I cannot wait around for her. Let us hope she takes a hint from what she sees when she comes back.' He put down the briefcase, took a silencer from his pocket and fitted it to the gun with a smooth practised hand. 'Sorry about this.'

Then he shot Kelsey Bugler twice in the chest, picked up the briefcase and left, removing the silk hood as he went out the door.

4

The pawnbroker's shop was in an old, narrow arcade in the heart of the city; an arcade too old and narrow to have been taken over and rebuilt into a small cathedral by developers, as some of the other city arcades had been. The pawnbroker himself was old and narrow in build, but not in his thinking; he saw the world through a wide-angled gimlet eye. He was also old-fashioned: he offered Kim Weetbix the old fence's going rate of fifteen per cent on stolen goods.

'I didn't steal it. It was my mother's watch.'

'This is a man's watch.'

'An American gave it to her. My father.' She rarely, if ever, used the word, even thought it: she said it now without shame or pride.

The old man looked at the watch again. 'Fifteen hundred dollars, take it or leave it, love.'

'Two thousand?' She wouldn't plead with him, there was too much pride in her to whine. He shook his head with its shock of white hair and she surrendered. 'Okay, fifteen hundred. You're a robber.'

'So are you, love. Birds of a feather. Don't come back to redeem it, it won't be here.' He would wait for the usual discreet advertisement, then sell it back to the insurance company, no questions asked, no information given.

He handed Kim the money. She took it without thanks and left the tiny shop. Ten minutes later Jack Aldwych walked in: three-piece suit, English trilby hat, custom-made shirt, Grenadier Guards tie (made in Hong Kong).

'Jack, you look a million dollars! You back in the business?'

'G'day, Manny. No, I just been calling on a few old friends, old mates like yourself. You're last on my list.'

'You gunna have a reunion? I heard you'd retired. Jack, I gotta say it, you look *respectable*! Like a retired judge, no less.'

'Thanks, Manny. You always had the best eye in the business for real quality, for value. I didn't know you had any social values. I'm looking for something, Manny. A gold watch, a Piaget. And a briefcase, a Vuitton.' He pronounced it a Voo-itton. 'You seen 'em?'

'It's *yours*? The watch?' The pawnbroker's voice cracked. 'Holy Christ, the kid was in here not ten minutes ago, a bit of the Chink in her. A half-caste, I'd say.' They were both old enough to use the old term. 'She said her father was an American.'

'She leave her name?'

'Jack, you know there's no name with stolen goods. There, that it?' He had produced the watch. On the back of it was inscribed: *From O. to C.*

'That's it. How much?'

'Two thousand.' His gaze couldn't have been more honest.

'Manny –' Aldwych shook his head. 'You know down to a dollar what this would cost at Hardy's. You still operate on the old fifteen per cent – my other mates told me, Manny, they all know you. What did you give the girl? Fifteen hundred?'

'You haven't lost your touch, Jack. Yes, fifteen hundred. You can't blame me for trying, these are tough days.'

144

'You wouldn't have tried it in the old days, Manny, or I'd have had your neck.' He took fifteen one-hundred-dollar notes from his wallet and laid them on the counter. 'What about the briefcase?'

'The watch was all she brought me. Take my word, Jack.'

'Have the coppers been here yet?'

'Not yet.'

'You never saw me, Manny, okay? Nor the watch. Take care. When are *you* gunna retire?'

'I can't afford to, Jack. I got three sons and a daughter, all trying to be honest, all on the dole.'

5

When Kim came home and found Kelsey Bugler dead, she did not scream or faint or panic in any way. She sat down on the torn car seat and looked at him, chest bloodied, sprawled on the mattress, looking more peaceful than she had ever seen him. She had seen enough death in Vietnam as a young child not to be horrified by the sight of a corpse; but she was surprised and puzzled that someone should take the trouble to kill Kelsey in this way. She had known that he would never reach middle age, let alone ever become an old man, but she could not understand why he should die like this. This was an execution, as she understood it: she had seen such results before.

She threw a blanket over Kelsey, leaving his face uncovered, gathered up her belongings, which were few, and put them in her cheap duffle-bag. She looked for the briefcase and for the first time noticed it was gone. That fact further puzzled her; and chilled her. Who would bother to come here to this squalid squat and kill for a briefcase?

Then she said goodbye to Kelsey Bugler in her own language, went out of the house and down the street to the nearest phone-box. From there she called the local police station, not saying who she was, just telling them where to find a young man's body.

When she came out of the phone-box she stood irresolute. For the first time she realized that, in his own peculiar way, Kelsey Bugler had been some sort of signpost, even if pointing in the wrong direction. Now, she was lost.

Chapter Nine

❖❖❖❖❖❖❖

1

William Street is a broad avenue running from the centre of the city up a hill to Kings Cross. Traffic heading up it, towards the wealth and social snobbery of the eastern suburbs, goes through a tunnel under the sleaze of the Cross, as swimmers dive under a river's pollution. On the left-hand side of the long slope are several tall office blocks, a four-star hotel and a mix of shabby shops that were to have disappeared in a grand boulevard plan that somehow kept slipping off the drawing-board. On the right-hand side the buildings are old and dilapidated, some of them looking as if they are only held together by the FOR SALE and FOR LEASE signs plastered across their fronts. There had once been a dozen or more car showrooms on this side, but now there are only three or four. At the bottom of the slope are the Rolls-Royce showrooms, outside of which at night the hookers parade in skimpy outfits that do nothing for the image of Rolls or Royce.

The building housing Pinatubo Medical Engineering was halfway up the hill, on the right-hand side. At eleven o'clock on the Monday morning the hookers were still at home, getting over the labours of Sunday night services. The two empty showrooms on either side of the stairs that led up to Pinatubo had once sold expensive imported cars; flash young men, flashing money and machismo, had come here and bought Maseratis and Lamborghinis with all the flair of youth who were certain tomorrow would never come. Now tomorrow had come and a length of tinsel ribbon on the dusty showroom floor was all that glittered where chrome had once blazed, and the young men had disappeared into debt and oblivion.

'Even the girls are having closing-down sales,' said Clements. 'You can get a knee-trembler on your credit card these days.'

He and Malone, armed with a court order, were waiting on the estate agent who leased out the building. A taxi drew up and a woman got out, paid the driver, waited for her change, then came towards the two detectives, juggling her handbag and a small briefcase.

'I'm Sophie Rutter. You're from the police?'

She was in her late thirties, her out-of-fashion ultra suede suit stretched tightly across her plumpness, her dark hair cut urchin-style around her good-natured face. There was a brisk-ness about her that made Malone suspect she viewed everyone she met as a prospective client.

'What's the problem?' She had opened the street-level door, was leading them up a steep flight of stairs to the first floor. 'I didn't know our tenants had done a flit till you phoned us. How about that?'

There were two suites of offices on the first floor: Pinatubo Medical Engineering and Lava Investments, both entry doors showing the same style of lettering. 'Who leased that one?' Malone asked.

'Lava? It's leased by the same tenant, Mr Belgarda.' She opened the door into Pinatubo. 'You still haven't told me what the trouble is.'

'We think Mr Belgarda and his companies may be involved in some shonky business.'

'Then why is Homicide investigating it?' Both detectives looked hard at her and she said, 'Come on, when your message was passed on to me, it said to ring you back at Homicide if I couldn't meet you.'

Clements said, 'Have you ever thought of becoming a cop?'

'I might, if business gets any worse than it is. Has Mr Belgarda been killing someone?'

'We don't know. What do you know about him?'

She waved a hand around the Pinatubo office. The outer

room was as expensively furnished as the inner office; both were a contrast to the shabbiness of the building. The furniture was frigidly modern: glass tables on stainless steel legs, black leather chairs with the same stainless steel legs, a lounge with a low back designed to accommodate sitters with no heads, lamps that looked like missiles. There was only one picture on the wall in the inner office, a colour photograph of Mount Pinatubo in eruption. Malone could not see the selling point of such a picture, but then he had never been a salesman, not even of himself.

'Mr Belgarda had money to spend. He never quibbled about the rent, didn't ask for any concessions. Today, you get a tenant like that, you grab him, right? They all want at least three months free rent, they want a re-paint job, you name it, they want it before they'll sign a lease. Not Mr Belgarda. He took a twelve months' lease, it's still got five months to run.'

'Did you ever meet a Mr Tajiri?'

'Tajiri? What's that, Italian?'

'No, Japanese.'

She shook her head. 'We have Japanese clients, but no Tajiri.'

'What about next door?'

'No, I never heard the name mentioned there. Let's have a look.'

Lava Investments was as well furnished as Pinatubo, in the same style. The picture on the wall this time was of Mount Fujiyama. 'They liked their mountains,' said Clements.

'Maybe Mr Tajiri did use this office,' said Mrs Rutter, 'but I never saw him. Mr Belgarda took a twelve months' lease on this one, too. All he asked for was more power outlets. For these, I guess.' There were four video display terminals on a bench along one wall of the inner office. 'I came here one day, I was out there in the other room and this door was open. There were four or five guys sitting in here looking at those screens. It looked to me that they were screening stock exchange prices, something like that. I've seen 'em in movies, you know?'

'They've gotta be connected to some central information point,' Clements told Malone. 'If they do carry stock exchange prices. Or futures . . .'

'What was Mr Belgarda himself like?' said Malone.

'Very pleasant. And *polite*! Geez, they don't make 'em like that any more.'

'Thanks,' said Malone, politely.

She grinned, an urchin on her way to middle age. 'You know what I mean. He was almost – smarmy? Not quite, but almost. Every time he'd ring up about something, he'd say, Sorry about this, no matter how trivial it was.'

'Give us a description of him.'

'Well, about medium height – don't ask me to give it in centimetres. I know what a metre is, but not a centimetre. I left school before we really got into metrics.' That put her in her forties, then. 'He was a Filipino, but I suppose you've guessed that. Not bad-looking, you know, in their sort of way. There's different sorts of good looks, right?' she added, as if she had suddenly thought they might report her for racial discrimination. 'A sharp dresser, God knows what his suits must've cost. Not flashy, though – well, not *too* flashy. Oh, he had a moustache, one of those old-fashioned thin ones, like you see on old film stars like Clark Gable and William Powell.'

'Before my time,' said Malone.

She gave him the urchin's grin again. 'Put a moustache on Sergeant Clements and you'd know who I'm talking about. Clark Gable.'

In a minute she's going to offer to let me take up the rest of Belgarda's leases. 'Let's have a look at what's in the filing cabinets. You want to open them, Clark?'

There were two cabinets, steel disguised as teak, against the wall opposite the display terminals. None of the drawers was locked; none of them contained anything. The drawers of the desk were also empty. Clements drew the same blank when they crossed the small landing into the Pinatubo office.

'Seems the only thing they didn't take was the furniture.' Clements slammed shut the last drawer in the desk in the

Pinatubo inner office; the sound was like that of a pistol aimed at the back of the departed Belgarda. 'When did you see him last, Mrs Rutter?'

'Friday – well, I didn't exactly *see* him, I spoke to him. This month's rent was overdue, just a few days, and I rang him to remind him. He was normally so prompt. He was polite, as usual, said it would be in the mail immediately. It turned up this morning. Why would he send the rent if he intended doing a moonlight flit? It is murder, isn't it? I mean, that's what you want him for? Or is he the one who's been murdered?'

'He's still alive, we think,' said Malone, but told her no more. 'Who worked for him? He must've had staff.'

'Just two girls, that was all I ever saw, one in here, the other across in Lava. Whether he had anyone else, I dunno. I never knew exactly what either firm did.'

'Did he come with references, guarantees?'

She dug in her briefcase, produced a thin folder. 'His bank guaranteed him, Shahriver Credit International. I checked with them, I'd never heard of 'em, they said he was okay.'

'We've heard of them, they're rolling in money.'

She looked at him shrewdly. 'Is that sarcasm? Never mind . . . Funny thing is, all the rent cheques were drawn on another bank, Treasury Bank.' She looked at him again. 'There isn't a solider bank in town than Treasury. Why didn't his guarantee come from them?'

'You do want to be a cop, don't you?' said Clements.

'Did you have a home address for Belgarda?' She shook her head and Malone went on, 'The girls who worked for him? You knew their names?'

'One was Maryanne, she worked here in Pinatubo, I never knew her full name. She'd answer the phone, you know, the Yank way we have now? Pinatubo Medical Engineering, Maryanne speaking,' she said in an affected voice. 'As if anyone wants to know Maryanne or Sherylanne or whoever. But when Mr Belgarda signed the lease, he asked if I knew where he could get staff. I put him on to an agency, Delta Staff. You could try them.'

151

'What about across the hall?'

'I think Lava brought their own girl, a Filipino like Mr Belgarda.'

Then Malone's beeper gave its warning. Clements picked up one of the phones on the receptionist's desk, put it to his ear, then handed it to Malone. 'It's still connected.'

Malone dialled Homicide, got John Kagal. 'Scobie? Another homicide, this time in a squat in Redfern. Two gunshot wounds. The tip-off, Redfern says, came from a girl who hung up as soon as she told them where to look. It's a young guy, it's a long shot, but he fits the rough description we have of the guy who tried to burn Mr Casement. He's been sent to the morgue and soon's he's been tested for HIV, Dr Keller will take the bullets out of him and send them to Ballistics. We'll check if they came out of the same gun that did in the morgue attendant. You coming back here?'

Do you need me? Malone wanted to ask. 'Russ and I are on our way now. In the meantime get in touch with an employment agency, Delta Staff, ask them if they sent anyone to work for Pinatubo Medical Engineering and Lava Investments – got that? I want their names and home addresses, pronto.'

He hung up, turned to Clements. 'Another one.'

'Another murder?' Sophie Rutter all at once looked worried. 'Mr Belgarda, has he killed someone else?'

'We didn't say he'd killed anyone.'

'Inspector, I'm not dumb. The fact that you haven't answered my question has answered my question. Is he dangerous? I mean, am I likely to . . . I mean, for talking to you?'

'You're in no danger, Mrs Rutter,' said Malone and hoped he was right.

2

When they got back to their unmarked car, which Clements had parked in a nearby lane, there was a parking ticket stuck under the wipers. He tore it up and dropped it in the gutter.

'That's the fifth this month. I'm beginning to think they're harassing me. Where to – back to the office?'

'Let's drop out to Redfern first.' Coming down the stairs from the Pinatubo office he had explained Kagal's call. 'There may be nothing for us, John's probably covered it all, but we'll have a look.'

'Does he get in your hair? He does in mine. He's so bloody thorough.'

'Mate, we're getting old.'

Redfern, each time he had to visit it, made him feel even older. It had always been a tough beat for a cop; the local elements, a democratic lot, had run their own version of law and order. But over the last few years the nature of the district had changed, there were boundaries within its boundaries. Blacks had no time for whites, whites had no time for blacks and neither had any time for the police. There were citizens, black and white, who were trying to hold the small region together, but Malone, on his occasional visits, saw Redfern coming apart at the seams. Cities, he had decided, died at their heart, as if the life-blood flowed away from it and did not re-circulate.

There were two police cars in Bulinga Street and Crime Scene tapes still decorated the second house from the end of the dilapidated terrace, a crude parody of the bunting that one saw outside houses about to be auctioned. The Physical Evidence team had done their job and gone, but a small group of watchers, mostly youths and girls, glad of anything to fill their empty days, leaned against the battered iron railings on the other side of the road. A detective was questioning two youths in tattered, shapeless sweaters and torn jeans, while two young uniformed men stood in the background.

'G'day, Inspector.' The detective was Sergeant Sid Guyatt, turned fifty in years and girth inches, a plodder who believed that if you stood in one place the world, and its suspects, would always come round again. He had known Malone and Clements for years, but he believed in rank in front of outsiders, which meant all voters outside the police service. 'I been talking to these two young gentlemen, but they're not talking back. The locals tell me these two don't belong around here. So I been asking them why they're hanging around.'

The two young gentlemen were an odd pair. Neither of them was out of his teens, but they looked as if they had been scarred by every year since they were born. One was tall and thin to the point of emaciation, his head shaved, a safety-pin in the lobe of his ear; his black, stained sweater hung on him as if it were empty. His companion was short and fat, his black hair combed down past his shoulders, a wispy beard hanging from the upper of his two chins like strands of black cotton. Both of them wore reflective aviator glasses, expensive shades that only accentuated the derelict look of the rest of their attire.

Malone said, 'Did you know the deceased?'

'The deceased?' The tall thin one's lips curled under the mirrors. 'What's that?'

Malone had left his hat in the car. He took out his comb, leaned forward till his face was only six inches from that of the tall youth; then he combed his hair in the mirrors of the glasses, patted it in place and leaned back. It was TV cop stuff, but it worked: the two young uniformed policemen smiled and the tall youth flushed with anger. Across the street someone laughed and the youth turned and jerked a finger at the group.

'I think you'd better answer our questions, son, or maybe we're going to break your mirrors and give you seven years' bad luck.' Again it was cheap stuff, but these kids understood it better than any polite questioning.

'That'd be just your fucking form, wouldn't it?' He looked over his shoulder at the watchers by the iron railings, as if expecting applause, but their gaze gave him no encouragement. He was another outsider.

Malone looked at the shorter, fatter youth. 'You got anything to say, son? We've had a murder here. You wouldn't want to be charged with being an accessory, would you? Take off those glasses.'

For a moment it seemed that the youth was going to defy Malone; then he took off the glasses, squinting a little in the bright sunlight. He had surprisingly big eyes in such a chubby face, sad brown eyes that were beginning to show fright. 'Look, we only come here to warn Kel –'

'Kel?' Malone looked at Guyatt.

'Kelsey Bugler. His wallet was still in his jeans, he had an out-of-date driving licence.'

Malone looked back at the fat youth. 'Go on – what's your name?'

'Billy.'

'Billy what?'

'That'll do. Billy What.'

'And what's your name, Curly?' Malone looked at the skinhead.

'That's right. Curly What.' The sneer looked like a permanent distortion of his lips.

Clements, the Late Night Movie fan, said, 'They think they're Abbott and Costello, that was one of their baseball routines. Who's on first, What's on second and on third Idunno.'

The two youths and the two young policemen all looked blank. Malone said, 'Clark Gable, Abbott and Costello, all in the one morning? . . . Righto, Billy. Why'd you come here to warn Kel?'

The fat youth looked up at his companion, who had turned the mirrors down on him. 'Ah shit, mate, what's the point? Fuck it, I'm gunna tell 'em the truth . . . This morning a guy comes up to us in the Cross, where we hang out, he was asking about Kel, though he didn't know his name. Just said he was looking for a guy and a girl who'd done over a friend of his. We knew who he meant, Kel had told Damien here and his girlfriend. The guy sorta stood over us, but he offered us money. So we took it. Then we got sorta worried about Kel and we come over here to warn him. But we was too late . . .'

'How much did he give you? Thirty pieces of silver?' It was Clements' turn to sneer.

'Get fucked,' said Damien, but he flinched as he saw Guyatt bunch a fist that could fell a bullock.

155

'Describe the man,' said Malone.

'Jesus, what if he comes after *us*?' The fear was plain now in Billy's big eyes. Malone wondered how long the kid had been on the streets, if he was beyond redemption. But that was a social worker's problem. 'He could find us easy enough –'

'Keep your mouth shut,' said Damien.

'You keep yours shut,' Malone told him. 'Righto, Billy, describe the man.'

Billy hesitated, looking up at his mate, then he said in a rush, 'He was a dude, real flash. Asian of some sort, they all look alike to me. Maybe a Vietnamese, a Thai, I dunno. A bit taller'n me, with a moustache. And a very soft voice, but cold, you know what I mean? Put the shits up you.'

'You've just cut our throats,' said Damien.

'No,' said Guyatt. 'If you get it, it'll be bullets.'

Billy looked ready to run and Malone put a hand on his shoulder. 'Hold it, Billy. Who was Kel's girlfriend?'

'Did I mention any girlfriend?' He was abruptly cautious, under Damien's thumb again.

'Yes, you did. Come on, Billy, don't fartarse about. Maybe the bloke is after her, too. Let's find her.'

Billy looked at Damien again, but the latter had turned his head, was facing up the street, blank dark mirrors where his eyes should have been. The short fat youth pulled at his own sweater, as if trying to get out of it, then he said, 'Okay, her name is Kim. I dunno her second name, we never use 'em, they don't matter anyway. She's half-Vietnamese, that's all I know, a good-looking bird. She was Kel's old lady. Tell you the truth, I dunno why.' Damien turned his head, looked down at him; Billy glared back. 'Well, shit, you said the same yourself.'

'Did she use drugs?' The kids could often be traced through the dealers.

'I never saw her on anything. No, I don't think so. Can we go now?'

Malone looked at Guyatt. 'You want them, Sid?'

The burly detective looked at the two with distaste. 'I don't think so. We got enough of our own around here without bringing in outside trash.'

'Up yours,' said Damien and led Billy away down the street, the short fat youth putting on his glasses again, both of them, Malone mused, going back to a life that didn't merit being mirrored.

After a look at the derelict houses, a cursory search that depressed both men, Malone and Clements left, promising to let Guyatt know if they came up with anything on the murder. After all, it had occurred on his turf and would go down on his running sheet. No detective liked a running sheet where no bottom line was drawn. That was the accountancy of crime.

3

Aldwych brought a basket of fruit to Cormac Casement; Shirl had nurtured a few social graces in him. He also brought the gold watch, neatly encased in a small box. 'Don't ask me where I got it, Cormac.'

Casement took the small box with his bandaged hands and passed it to Ophelia to open it. She was impressed: 'Jack, I don't know how you managed it, but thank you so much. When you called, I had no idea this was what you were bringing . . . '

Aldwych had never been invited to the Casement penthouse; but he had not been embarrassed at inviting himself this afternoon. Most of his life had been a series of self-invited visits: to petrol stations early in his career, then to banks, to anywhere where money could be picked up at the point of a gun. Today, however, he had no gun and had not come looking for money.

'If the cops notice you have it back, Cormac, you can tell 'em where you got it. No, on second thoughts, only tell Scobie Malone. Don't tell any reporters. Especially don't mention my name. I wouldn't wanna embarrass you.'

All three smiled, unembarrassed. Casement, over the last ten years, had met white-collar criminals, ones he had recognized long before their crimes had become public; they may not have been as deadly in dealing with their victims as this old man opposite him, but they had been just as ruthless and evil. Ophelia had known no criminals, but she had lived her life without ethical restraint; she also had a fond respect for anyone successful. And there was no doubt that Jack Aldwych had been successful.

'The briefcase?' asked Casement.

'No luck there, I'm afraid.'

Casement put the question a little hesitantly: 'Did you find the kids who stole it? Who did this to me?' He held up his hands.

'That's what I wanted to talk to you about.' Aldwych looked at Ophelia. 'Do you wanna listen to us talking business?'

'Yes,' she said easily, taking one of the bandaged hands in hers.

Casement smiled at Aldwych. 'Jack, I don't share my business problems with her, but this is *our* problem. You're not really going to talk business, are you?'

Aldwych sat back in his chair. Though he could well afford it, he did not live in surroundings as luxurious as these. Ophelia, it seemed, spent her husband's money even more lavishly than her younger sister spent Jack Junior's. This big living room was filled with a mixture of European and Oriental antiques; somehow the mix did not look like a badly tossed salad. Even the pictures on the walls seemed to complement each other: a 15th century Japanese print by Motonobu did not clash with a winter landscape by Monet. Aldwych knew none of the artists nor recognized any of the furnishings, but he had somehow acquired a sense of taste. He had, for instance, never had a man killed in front of his wife and children. Certain things went well in the eye, others did not.

'Yes and no, Cormac. I'm here to protect my son.'

Both Casements looked at him in puzzlement. 'Jack? Why, what's he got to do with this?' Casement held up his hands again: they had become Exhibit A.

'Nothing. But things may be connected in all this mess and I wanna make sure Jack is right out of it.'

'Are you playing detective? Jack, I don't mean to be offensive, but I find that amusing. You, an old retired –' He paused.

'Crim?'

'All right, if you think it fits. An old retired crim playing detective.'

'Cormac, who better than me would know a criminal act? Don't let's pussyfoot around. I'm being careful with my language here, Ophelia.' He grinned at her, as he had at Kate Leigh and Tilly Devine and other old molls. 'I know where to look, where to ask. How d'you think I got that back for you?' He nodded at the watch, now on the ormolu-legged table beside Ophelia. 'I want to know what you knew about young Rob before he was done in.'

A less observant man might have missed Casement's caution; or was it that Ophelia came in before her husband could reply? 'Jack, we knew nothing of Rob's doings before he was – was *done in*. We would have him here occasionally at our parties, but only because he was young and good-looking and he'd bring a pretty girl with him. He was – decoration, if you like.'

'He never talked business with you, Cormac?' His disregard of Ophelia was almost bluntly rude. 'Jack tells me Rob came to him for a loan a week after they met. Did he ever put the bite on you?'

Casement smiled at the old slang; banks now had portmanteau phrases for the same thing but still finished up bitten. 'Not me, no.'

'You, Ophelia?' He tried to give her a kind look, but his eyes were too old and experienced.

'Yes,' she said without hesitation. She patted her husband's arm. 'Relax, darling. I gave him nothing.'

She could lie with all the gravity of a fallen angel; though long removed from it, she came of stock that saw no sin in infidelity. Her mother's female deity had been Queen Marie, though that high-spirited consort had been half-English, half-Russian and her affairs had never been as numerous as gossip said they were. Ileana's own affairs had been tolerated by Adam, since she tolerated his; they knew that their passion for others never equalled their passion for each other. It was just that they enjoyed the spice of variety. Ophelia felt the same way, but she had never attempted to explain it to Cormac, he was too Protestant Irish for that.

'Jack,' said Casement, 'I don't see how anyone could link Jack Junior to all this.'

'Mud sticks. Every reporter in town knows I'm his father. They don't mention it in their columns, they're afraid I might pay 'em a visit. Which I might. Al Capone, you remember him?'

'Not personally,' said Casement and smiled; he enjoyed the company of this old – old crim. 'Did you ever meet him?'

'I didn't get to the States till after the war, he was dead by then. Nineteen forty-seven, I think he died. He was King of Chicago,' he explained to Ophelia, adding with a smile, 'Someone once called me King of Sydney. There was no comparison. But Capone, he said something once. He said a kind word sometimes gets things done. A kind word and a gun *always* gets things done. Something like that. Anyway, it's true.'

'You still carry a *gun*?' said Ophelia.

'Not in years. But I call on a feller in his office who's written something nasty, you think he's gunna know whether I'm carrying a gun or not? Sometimes it pays to have a reputation. Except when they try to pass it on to your son.' He looked at her with suddenly sad eyes. 'Shirl, that was the wife, she'd come back to haunt me.'

Casement said quietly, 'I think I can assure you that young Jack will never be linked to any of this mess. I'll talk to Derek about it.'

'No, leave him to me. I do my own dirty work, Cormac.'

'It won't be dirty work –'

'It could be. I don't think this is your kind of game.'

At four o'clock that afternoon Malone was sitting in his office catching up on that morning's *Herald*. The Balkan stew was becoming bloodier; Boris Yeltsin had just been re-elected captain of a ship that was on the rocks; South Africa stood point-blank in front of the gun; here at home the Prime Minister, pushing for a republic, was charged with tearing apart the fabric of the nation. The metaphors spun like balloons in a whirlwind.

It was a relief when John Kagal came in and said bluntly, 'Another one, Scobie.'

Malone suffered the theatrical pause as Kagal stood in the doorway; he just sat and waited. Kagal, he had heard, had once played Hamlet in a Macquarie University Players' production: Yorick's skull must have grown hair during some of Hamlet's pauses. Kagal at last went on:

'Peta and I traced that secretary who worked for Pinatubo. Her name was Maryanne DaLuca, she lived in a flat out at Petersham. We went out there, found her mailbox still had last week's letters in it. The neighbours said they hadn't seen her since last Thursday morning. There was no deadlock on the door, so Peta and I picked the Yale lock –'

Malone didn't dare ask. Kagal would give a short lecture on how to pick a lock and the point of his report would be delayed even further.

Kagal came suddenly to the point: 'She was lying on the living room floor with two bullets in her. Doc Boon, he's one of the young guys from the morgue, reckoned she'd been dead two or three days at least. That puts it Friday, probably. We're doing the same as on that kid out at Redfern, soon's they've checked for HIV they'll extract the bullets and hand them to the on-call Ballistic guy. My bet is the same gun killed all three – the guy in the morgue, the kid at Redfern and Maryanne. Wouldn't you?'

Malone offered no opinion. 'What about the other girl?' He looked at his notes. 'Teresita something?'

'The employment agency knew nothing about her. But I

checked with a contact I have in the Tax Office, we were at university together.' There had been a commotion last year when it was discovered that several government department officers had been peddling information to private investigators, credit agencies and other outsiders who thought that freedom of information meant anything could be bought so long as the price was right. Kagal smiled: 'It saved time. Going through the proper channels – well, you know, proper channels tend to get flooded, right?'

'Sure. Irrigate where you can,' said Malone, not to be outdone. 'So where is Teresita and who is she?'

'Her PAYE monthly statement from Lava Investments and her tax file shows she is Teresita Romero, she lives in Double Bay in Longmuir. That's a pretty expensive block of apartments – my uncle lives there. Not bad accommodation for a girl on four hundred bucks a week take-home pay. So I got on to another mate in Corporate Affairs this time and he gave me the home address of Mr Belgarda, the managing director of Pinatubo. Same address as Miss Romero.' 'The plot thickens, eh?'

'My very thought.' Malone remained straight-faced. 'When will we know about the bullets?'

'It usually takes about four hours for the HIV test, the blood has to go all the way out to Westmead. I asked them to get a move on, but you can't hurry doctors or pathologists, you know that. They move to their own waltz.'

Malone couldn't top that one; but he'd try one of *his* mates: 'I'll ring Doc Keller, she has clout and can hurry things along.'

'Is it true she and Russ are engaged?'

'I don't think they've announced it. You look puzzled?'

Kagal nodded, smiled. 'Well, you couldn't meet a nicer guy than Russ. But, well, I'd never have said he was the doc's type, would you?'

'You never know with women. They move to their own waltz.'

You mean-minded bastard: meaning himself. But Kagal could take a joke against himself; he raised an approving thumb. '*Touché* . . . So what do we do? I mean about Belgarda?'

'Put out an ASM on him. Tell Immigration to check for him and Teresita on any international flights, ask the Feds to keep a lookout for him at any of the airports in case he tries to go interstate. He comes from Manila and I don't want him heading back there before we can ask him some questions. If you tag him, let me know at once, no matter what time it is.'

'What about Redfern?'

'I've got Sid Guyatt working on that with his blokes. They're looking for the dead kid's girlfriend. She's half-Asian, her name's Kim. She shouldn't be too hard to pick up, unless she's gone interstate.'

Kagal stood up. 'Scobie, what would happen if we never solved these cases?'

'What makes you ask that?'

'It's a can of worms . . . '

Malone took his own long pause; he could never play Hamlet, but he might have played one of the grave-diggers. Digging his own grave . . . 'It's a can of worms, all right. But we'd never be able to keep the lid on it, the politics are too slippery. Some day when you've got pips on your shoulders and silver braid on your cap, you're going to appreciate that fighting crime is only half the battle for us cops. Politics is Public Enemy Number Two.'

Kagal took the advice soberly. 'It'll never change?'

'Not unless human nature changes. And I've given up on that score.'

When Kagal had gone without any further remark, he sat on, uncomfortable with his pessimism.

Then he picked up the phone and called Romy. She promised to do what she could to hurry the HIV tests. At five-thirty, as he was getting ready to leave, she called back: 'Westmead have just called. The boy in the Redfern case, he's HIV-positive. The girl, Maryanne DaLuca, is clean. I'm taking the bullets out of them now and they'll be with Ballistics in half an hour. Russ is with me, he and Jason James from

Ballistics, he'll bring them back. You want to speak to him?'

'No, tell him I'll wait for him over at Ballistics. Thanks for your help, Romy. I love you.'

'I love you, too. But I'm spoken for.' She laughed and hung up. Standing over an HIV-positive corpse, extracting bullets from it, she sounded happier than she had sounded in two years. That was what love could do for her.

He rang Lisa to tell her he would be late for dinner – 'Again?' she said. 'How did I guess?' – and walked across to Police Centre and took the lift up to Ballistics on the fifth floor. Clarrie Binyan was waiting for him, unlocking the security door, then locking it behind him. There were eight thousand confiscated weapons on this floor, an arsenal of temptation that Binyan guarded as if they were sacred relics.

He was looking older, darker; Malone wanted to ask if Aborigines got darker as they grew older, but he refrained. He and Binyan chi-acked each other with racist jokes, but there was a line beyond which neither of them ever ventured. Binyan's mother was a Koori from the east coast tribes and he often referred to her with affection; but he never mentioned his white father. The line was faint, like a finger trace in sand, but Malone never went beyond it. Binyan, this evening, certainly looked older and tired.

He led Malone into a side room where the forensic comparison macroscope was mounted. It was German, made by Wild Leitz, and it was Binyan's boast that, by comparison, it made an eagle's eye myopic. He sat Malone down on the stool in front of it, then placed two bullets under the macroscope.

'These came from the gun that shot the feller out at the morgue. The fired cartridge cases are nine-by-eighteen millimetres, not the usual ammo we see in here. You mentioned the *yakuza* – some of them use a Russian piece, a Makarov. It fires this calibre and it takes a silencer. It could be the make of gun we're looking for.'

A phone on the bench beside the macroscope rang and Binyan picked it up. 'Okay, send them up.' He hung up. 'It's Russ and Jason. I'll let them in.'

He came back in a minute or two with Jason and Clements, who dropped two plastic envelopes on the bench. 'Two slugs from Bugler, the kid out at Redfern. Two from Maryanne DaLuca. Seems our killer can't resist letting off that second shot, just to make sure.'

Binyan took Malone's place at the macroscope, ran the three sets of bullets beneath it, then repeated the process. At last he stood up. 'Same gun. Same pattern, two bullets into each victim. So it's the same feller, I'd say.'

Clements was leaning with his haunches against the bench; he bit his lower lip, his substitute for the furrowed brow. 'What puzzles me, if he's used a gun to kill these three, why didn't he use a gun on Rob Sweden and Kornsey – Bassano, I mean? He stuck them in the neck, a surgical job.'

'We don't know it was the same man,' said Malone.

Clements nodded. 'That's true. But if it's not, what've we got – a team? And what's the connection between all the victims?'

Malone took his time sorting out the answers: 'It looks as if Maryanne got hers because she knew too much about Pinatubo.'

'There's no evidence of that.' Clements was playing defence attorney, an unusual role for him.

'We don't have much evidence on anything, do we? We know young Sweden was up to no good. But we don't know what his killer, or killers, had against him. Bassano – well, the Mafia could have caught up with him and ordered his killing. Frank Minto, he probably did no more than just get in their way.'

'The attack on Casement?'

'Your guess is as good as mine. Maybe it's totally unrelated. What are you grinning at, Clarrie?'

Binyan ran his hand through his greying curly hair. 'I'm just glad I'm not dealing with humans. Bullets and guns, they've got their characteristics, but in the end their motive boils down to one thing – they're designed to kill. It makes our job so much simpler, we don't have to worry about personality or psyche or all the rest of it. But you get me the gun that fired these –' he gestured at the bullets on the bench '– and I'll give you enough evidence to nail the feller who used the gun. Then you can belt the shit outa him and find out the connection between all the murders.'

Malone looked at Clements. 'You see how they'd do it in the tribe? Belt the shit out of him. We're too civilized.'

'We've been telling you that for two hundred years,' said Binyan, grinning. 'Get outa here. I wanna go home to the gunyah.'

'Have you seen his gunyah, Russ? Two-storeyed, out in Dulwich Hill, garage, pool in the backyard, Saturday night is Corroboree Night. They throw another goanna on the barbie, run another video of Madonna . . . Admit it, Clarrie, you like being civilized.'

'Our day'll come,' said Binyan, pushing them towards the door. 'Pick out your sacred site, so we'll know where to bury you.'

Chapter Ten

◆◆◆◆◆◆◆

1

They buried Vince Bassano, alias Terry Kornsey, the next day; or rather, he was cremated, at least part of him. Malone and Clements went to the cemetery on the southern outskirts of the city, to stand outside the crematorium and watch who came to pay their last respects. The morning was grey and cool, a good day for last rites. Malone, who had been to a few funerals, as mourner and spectator, had come to believe that all Australian burials or cremations should be held on autumn or winter days, in seasons that kept the colour sense to a minimum. He had been to funerals where bright dresses, some even sequinned, white safari suits and rainbow ties had suggested the mourners had only stopped off on their way to the spring racing carnival at Randwick. He was as old-fashioned as his mother Brigid when it came to burying the dead.

There was no one amongst the funeral crowd who looked like a Mafia hitman; nor were there any Asians. There were a few broken noses and cauliflower ears, but they belonged to old rugby league players, now fellow members of Mrs Kornsey at the St George Leagues Club. If Terry Kornsey had been as quiet and reclusive as his wife had said, Malone wondered if the club members had come out of respect for her or her husband.

The crematorium was painted a bilious green. Its tall chimney looked like a clock-tower from which the clock-face had been removed, as if acknowledging that time no longer mattered to those going up in smoke through its core. Huge box-gums, trees older than most of the bones in the cemetery, faced the eastern front of the low building; a couple of Roman pines stood at one end of the line of box-gums, like immigrant mourners at a native funeral. It occurred to Malone that Roman pines seemed to be a feature of all the cemeteries he had attended and he wondered why. He made a resolution to find out the reason; but he knew, even as he thought of it, that he wouldn't. Life was full of neglected explanations: no one knew that better than a cop.

As the crowd slowly filtered out of the service chapel, a man detached himself and came towards the two detectives. Malone was surprised to see it was Kenthurst, wrapped in a trenchcoat, hat-brim pulled down all round, looking like a five-hundred-dollar-a-day private eye, Philip Marlowe from Canberra's anything-but-mean streets. 'What are you doing here, Ron?'

'I'm here representing the US Marshals' Service – unofficially, of course. I have to report Vince Bassano is no more, just a heap of ashes. You weren't inside, were you? I kept wanting to laugh. A full-sized expensive coffin with half a leg and a foot in it, going into the oven. I don't know whether any of the crowd in there knew what was inside it –'

'They couldn't have used a child's coffin.'

'No, I suppose not. The widow went up and touched the lid of the coffin, but no one else followed her. So I guess they all knew there wasn't much of Vince Bassano there. It was macabre. Well, he's officially dead now and the Marshals' Service can write him off their books. You here looking for leads?'

Malone nodded. 'And finding none . . . Oh, Mrs Kornsey.'

She had come out of the chapel and stood surrounded by sympathizers. Then, as if to escape from them, she had abruptly pushed through them and come across to the detectives.

'Mrs Kornsey, this is Sergeant Clements, my colleague. And this is Superintendent Kenthurst of the Federal Police.'

Her frown increased the sad look; she was older this morning, faded by grief. 'Federal Police?'

'We don't want to come back to the house, you'll have relatives and friends there. I wonder if we could have just a few minutes with you now? There's some explaining to do.'

A woman, her resemblance suggesting she might be a sister, came towards the group; but Mrs Kornsey waved her away and, stumbling a little on the gravel path, till Clements took her arm, she walked with the three men away from the chapel towards a row of graves.

Malone said, Superintendent Kenthurst is here on behalf of the United States Marshals' Service.' Then he told her who her husband had been and why he had come to Australia: 'He was Mafia, Mrs Kornsey, and we think the Mafia finally caught up with him.'

She shook her head, as if to refuse to believe what they were telling her; behind her, her husband went up in smoke from the crematorium's chimney. 'But Terry was so – so *gentle*. He couldn't have been a killer.'

'He wasn't.' Kenthurst himself was gentle with her. 'From what we got from Washington, he was on the money side. He was their book-keeper, not one of their soldiers.'

'Soldiers?'

They were standing amongst low headstones, most of them markers of those who had died in the Thirties. What had they died of? Malone wondered. Despair, broken hearts, those illnesses of the Depression? There had been no AIDS then, no OD-ing from drugs; there had, of course, been murder, an ancient disease. There were several well-known criminals buried in this cemetery, but none of them had ever had a murder charge proven against him, though Malone and Clements had once pressed such a charge against one of the crims. Malone further wondered if Kornsey would feel at home here.

Kenthurst did not try to explain the Mafia order-of-battle. 'He had no criminal record of violence, Mrs Kornsey.'

'What did you say his name was?' As if abruptly accepting that her late husband had been a stranger; or was fast turning into one.

'Bassano. Vincent Bassano.'

'Then that explains it.'

'Explains what?' said Malone.

'The phone call. Yesterday. A man phoned, asked if I was Mrs Bassano. I said no, I didn't know what he was talking about. Then he said, "Sorry about Vincent," and hung up. I oughta called you, I suppose, but I haven't been thinking too straight since you come the other day and told me –' She half-turned, gestured at the crematorium; Malone couldn't tell whether her gaze was at ground-level or at the top of the chimney, where the smoke was dribbling away as a faint wisp. She looked back at the three detectives. 'Will you catch them? The men who killed Terry?'

'We're trying,' was all Malone could promise.

She turned to Kenthurst; she was gathering herself together. 'You said something about the Americans, their Marshals' Service or something. Will they tell me more about Terry if I write to them?'

'I doubt it, Mrs Kornsey. They're very restricted in what they can put out, even to family.' He glanced at Malone. 'I think Inspector Malone will agree with me, it might be better if you just thought of your husband as Terry Kornsey, forget what he was before he met you.'

'Jesus, you think that's gunna be easy? Anyway, thanks.'

She turned suddenly and walked away from them, towards the woman, her sister, waiting for her by the blue Honda. 'She'll write them,' said Clements.

'Of course. Women are masochists,' said Kenthurst.

Malone grinned. 'When did anyone in Canberra ever guess right about women?'

'When did anyone anywhere ever guess right about them?' said Kenthurst. 'What happens now?'

'We're on our way to another funeral.'

2

Jack Aldwych, for reasons of propriety, and Cormac Casement, because he did not feel well enough, did not attend Robert Sweden's funeral. Premier Bevan Bigelow did attend, working the crowd as if he were at a party fund-raising fête. A short square man with blond hair falling down over one eyebrow, he was known as Bev the Obvious, always with his eye on the larger target, too frequently the wrong one; had he been a polo player he would have hit the horse more often than the ball. He was the perfect stop-gap: thick-skinned, thinly gifted, empty of ideas. He was tolerated by his betters, Derek Sweden amongst them, while they fought amongst themselves to see who was best.

Most of the Cabinet came with the Premier. Police Commissioner John Leeds was there, along with five of the seven Assistant Commissioners. Opposition Leader Hans Vanderberg came, working the crowd with the same diligence as the Premier, even though practically all the mourners were conservative voters. But after the recent Federal election upset, who knew what a swinging voter looked like?

Rob Sweden was buried in a small cemetery in the eastern suburbs, where plots were as valuable as gold reefs. One was lowered into the ground as if being admitted to an exclusive club; Rob was accepted because of his dead mother, whose social connections were better than his father's. It was an old-fashioned cemetery, none of your discreet lawn plots and small plaques; there were marble crosses galore, a concentration of crucifixes, and a chorus of stone angels stood waiting to be called heavenwards. Malone and Clements stood behind three of them, like recent arrivals at Heaven's gate, and waited.

'This is a waste of time,' said Clements. 'The killer isn't gunna turn up.'

'You never know . . . The three sisters look great. Like they're on their way to lunch. Luncheon.'

'At least they're wearing black. But notice, no tears?'

'The only ones weeping are his father and those half a dozen girls who look as if they're going to miss Rob giving them a good time. They're all pretty, he knew how to choose them.'

'Who are the young guys?'

'Mates he worked with. Including the two who worked the scam with him. The tall skinny one looks as if he's in shock.

He's probably never seen a burial before. Look at The Dutchman, he hasn't once looked at the grave. He's sizing up the crowd. Uh-uh, we've been spotted. Here comes Jack Junior.'

He picked his way through the graves towards them, dressed in a lightweight topcoat, hat in hand, sprayed hair as steady in the breeze as a bicycle helmet. 'My dad told me to keep an eye out for you, Inspector. He said you usually turned up for the funerals of murder victims.'

Old Jack would know: but you didn't make a remark like that to his son. 'Did he want to see me?'

'If you wouldn't mind. He said he'd rather not come to Homicide –' Jack Junior smiled. 'I gather he has bad memories of going there once or twice back in the old days. He'd like you to have lunch with him at the Golden Gate. A private room.'

Malone had begun to trust the old crim; but . . . 'I'll bring Sergeant Clements with me.'

For just an instant there was a look of pain in the younger man's eyes. 'He's no longer what he used to be, Inspector –'

'I know that, Jack. But people still have a habit of being suspicious. What time does he want us?'

Jack Junior looked at his watch. 'Now, if you could manage it. He'll be at the restaurant.'

'Are you coming?'

He hesitated, then nodded. 'I think I might. I'll tell my wife –'

'Don't bring her.'

Jack Junior was annoyed. 'I hadn't intended to. But what –?'

'I don't know what your father is going to tell me. It'll be the first time, I think, he's ever given information to a cop. I don't want your wife or anyone else thinking of him as a dog. Do you know what he's going to tell me?'

'No. That's why I want to be there.'

Jack Aldwych Senior walked down the front steps of the big house in Harbord; the white Mercedes with the hire car plates and the smoked windows stood in the driveway. The Aldwych house was the largest in the street, perhaps the largest in the small suburb; it had been built at the turn of the century by a circus family who presumably had wanted room in which to tumble around. Harbord in those days had been much less settled than now; today it was a jumble of modest houses and inexpensive flats spread over a hill that looked out to sea. In the past several Olympic swimmers had lived in the suburb, but their fame had never lasted as long as the notoriety of Harbord's most prominent living citizen. The local elements did not exactly look up to him, except in a geographical sense, since his house was at the very top of the hill, but, now he was known to be retired, there was a tolerance of him that he would not have been accorded in his heyday. Perhaps it had something to do with being beside the sea: respectability, as if the salt air has eroded it, is less strong in Sydney's seaside suburbs than elsewhere.

'Chinatown, James.'

The chauffeur's name was Orlando, but he agreed with the old man's opinion that it was not a name for a chauffeur. He was young, blond, had learned, at great effort, not to talk too much; and was fascinated by this old crim who rode behind him in the darkened car, always, it seemed, at peace with a world which he had screwed any way he could. 'Nice day, Mr Aldwych.'

'At my age, son, you wake up still breathing, every day's a nice day.' He gave the young man a smile. 'That's bullshit wisdom. Take no notice of it, the world is full of it.'

The big gates were opened by Blackie Ovens, the general factotum, though he would have decked anyone who called him that, since it sounded dirty. He had once been one of Aldwych's standover men, an artist with an iron bar, but he too had retired, content to live off the boss for what little he did around the place.

'Have a nice day, Jack. Give my regards to young Jack.'

Aldwych tantalized him: 'Blackie, I'm having lunch with a coupla cops.'

Ovens looked sick. 'You've spoiled my day, Jack.'

The car went down the steep street, past the houses with their windows shut against the wind coming up from the south-west. A postman came up the hill, stuffing bad news into the letterboxes; a youth on a skateboard, long hair streaming in the wind, went down the hill and careered dangerously round the corner and was gone. The Mercedes turned the corner into the street that led down to the main road. The grey Ford Fairlane was waiting for it, blocking the left-hand lane.

Two men jumped out of the Fairlane and came running back towards the Mercedes; at the same time a third man, who had been standing on the corner, appeared from behind the Mercedes. All three were wearing party masks, Groucho Marx triplets with guns. One man snatched open the driver's door and jerked his gun at Orlando.

'Out, sport! Don't try nothing funny or you've had it! Out!'

There was nothing in the chauffeur's contract with the hire car company that said he had to be a hero. He didn't look back at Aldwych as he slid out of the car and, prodded in the back with the gun, walked quickly towards the Fairlane. He got into the back seat, the gunman following him, and at once the Fairlane took off, speeding away with a squeal of tyres.

In the meantime the other two gunmen had got into the Mercedes, one in behind the wheel and the other beside Aldwych in the back seat. Aldwych had sat without moving, his eyes flicking from one man to the other but his face otherwise showing no expression. He was too old for quick physical effort; his age, as much as self-control, kept him in his seat. Nothing was said as the man behind the wheel moved the Mercedes forward and the car went down towards the main road. If anyone in the houses had seen the incident, there was no outward sign; no one came rushing out of a front door, no curtain dropped back into place as someone left a window and went to phone the police. The ambush had taken no more than fifteen or twenty seconds, had been executed by men who appeared practised in this sort of thing. Aldwych, an old pro, had to admire the efficiency of it all.

The driver took off his mask and dropped it on the seat. Aldwych looked at the man beside him. 'You gunna take yours off? You look bloody silly, I can't take you seriously, if you're gunna wear that.'

Without hesitation the man took off the mask: Groucho Marx was replaced by a smiling Japanese. 'You are a cool customer, Mr Aldwych. Are you going to remain cool and sensible?'

Aldwych nodded at the gun in the man's lap. 'I don't have any choice, do I?'

'No, I should say not.' He was tall for a Japanese, just on six feet, slim but with a suggestion that there was muscle under the well-cut suit he wore. Aldwych had no way of guessing a Japanese's age, but the man looked young, perhaps no more than thirty. He looked like a professional: a banker, a lawyer, a doctor; but he could also be a professional killer. He had the bland handsomeness that was almost a look of anonymity. 'We want to talk to you, Mr Aldwych, not kill you. Not unless we have to.'

The car had turned at the bottom of the hill and was moving north. An ambulance came up behind it, siren screaming, and the driver up front moved over and waved it on. The ambulance was followed immediately by a light van, tail-gating it and chopping off the Mercedes as it went to move back into the outside lane. The man behind the wheel blew his horn angrily, but all he got in answer was a finger from the van's driver.

'Goddamned Australians!'

'Why don't you shoot him?' advised Aldwych; then turned to the Japanese: 'Do you have a name?'

'I do, but I don't think you need to know it.'

'You're a Jap, right?'

'Japanese.'

'Okay, Japanese. *Yakuza*?'

The Japanese looked down at his wrists. 'Are you looking

for tattoos? You need flesh and muscle to show off tattoos. It's better, too, if you have no intelligence, but don't quote me. *Yakuza* is a loose term, Mr Aldwych, like Mafia. What did you call your organization when you were king?'

'Don't piss in my pocket, son. How would you know what I used to be?' But he was flattered. 'Okay, which outfit do you work for? Yamaguchi-gumi? Inagawa-kai?'

'You're well informed.'

'I heard about the *yakuza* coming into Queensland a few years ago, when you ran the scam on the bent coppers and the SP bookies and the tax-dodgers, when you took 'em for, what, two, three million in a coupla months? Something to do with red beans on the Tokyo futures market.'

The Japanese smiled. 'It was very smart, but no, we had nothing to do with that. Our organization has a name, but I don't think you need to know it, Mr Aldwych.'

The drive continued in silence. Aldwych studied the driver, another Asiatic: maybe a Filipino? At one time they had all been Chinks to him and even now, with the country full of the yellow bastards, he couldn't tell one from another. He was a true conservative, wondered at how White Australia had been sent down the gurgler by lily-livered liberals.

Finally the Mercedes turned off the coast road that led to the northern beaches, came to a halt in a lane that looked out on a golf course. Aldwych recognized it as Long Reef, a course that ran out to a headland north of a curve of beach. The wind from the south-west had increased and gremlins of dust danced around two golfers in the rough; farther back a man hit off from a tee and the ball seemed to waver and dip in the air like a guided missile. Aldwych, no golfer, wondered why anyone bothered to play the game.

'Why here?' he said to the Japanese. 'Because you Japs are so crazy about golf?'

'Not me, Mr Aldwych. But my friend is very crazy about it.' His English was excellent.

The Filipino, if he was a Filipino, had switched off the engine and turned round. He was older than the Japanese, with cynically amused eyes and a thin moustache of a style that Aldwych thought had gone out years ago; he had known one or two conmen who had worn a lip decoration like it. He was what Shirl would have called a natty dresser, a dude who would look at himself in every window he passed. He smelled faintly of perfume, a habit Aldwych despised in men.

'Why kidnap me?' said Aldwych.

'Sorry about that,' said the man up front. 'But my friend will explain.'

'Mr Aldwych,' said the Japanese, 'why are you interfering?'

'Interfering in what?'

The Japanese smiled. '*Please*. You know what I mean. What were you after besides Mr Casement's gold watch?'

Aldwych, an old hand at being questioned, took his time. The golfers had moved on, leaning into the wind at the same angle as some of the trees that grew along the edge of the course; it did not occur to him to try to attract their attention, he had never called for assistance, even from his own kind. He had his own brand of proud courage. 'You been to see Manny Schmidt? You didn't hurt him?'

'Of course not. My friend just made a suggestion to him and he told us what we wanted to know.'

'Good old Manny. Waddia wanna know from me?'

'You're not thinking of coming out of retirement?'

'It wouldn't be any business of yours if I did.'

'Ah –' It was almost a hawking sound. Aldwych was surprised to hear it: it was like a bad imitation of how Japanese were supposed to speak. 'It would be very much our business, Mr Aldwych, if you came into our field.'

'What's your field?'

The Japanese ignored that one; he said, 'Were you looking for the briefcase?'

Aldwych took his time again. The man up front had lowered the smoked windows a few inches; Aldwych could see out over them. The golfers had disappeared, maybe to look for lost balls, which, he had been told, was one of the pleasures of golf. Below the lane, down to the right, was a small lagoon and marshy wetlands; a sign at the end of the lane said they were on the edge of a wildlife preserve. Down in the marsh a man in waders stood as still as a tree-stump, binoculars to his eyes as a flight of ducks, like a shower of miniature warplanes, came in on the wind. Aldwych wondered how long a body, dumped in the swamp, would remain undetected. He wondered if carrion birds were a protected species. For the crazy bloody conservationists every other form of wildlife seemed to be, except humans.

'Mr Casement's briefcase?' he said, making a guess. 'No, I wasn't. Did Manny offer to sell it to you?'

The man up front said, 'The pawnbroker never had the briefcase. If you weren't –'

'Let me ask the questions,' said the Japanese.

The Filipino worked his lips, as if trying to hold in a rejoinder; his eyes were suddenly still, blankly dark. 'Sorry about that,' he said, but his voice, too, was blank.

The Japanese went on, 'Mr Aldwych, if you weren't looking for the briefcase, what were you after?'

'Do you know I have a son?' The Japanese nodded. 'Okay, all I was doing was making sure he had nothing to do with whatever you guys are up to. You ran young Rob Sweden, right? Come *on*,' as the faces of the two men remained expressionless, 'don't bullshit me. I'm *old*. You think I'm scared of dying? Forget it. You wanna talk to me, we talk straight, no bullshit. Rob Sweden worked for you, right?'

'Yes, he worked for us. A stupid young man.'

Aldwych made another guess: 'He tried to screw you somehow? That'd be his form, from what I've heard. Was that why you did him in?'

The Japanese smiled. 'You don't expect me to answer that, do you?'

'No, I wouldn't of answered it, either.'

'Then why ask?'

Aldwych smiled, his old crim's grimace. 'It must be because I'm retired, I'm thinking *straight*. What about the other guy, the one you took outa the morgue?'

'What other guy?'

But Aldwych had his answer. 'Okay, you know nothing about him, either. But that was where they fished him outa the water, you know that?' He nodded out towards the far point of the golf course. 'Half a leg and a foot. But the police connected him to young Sweden, did you know that?'

'We read about it.'

'No, you didn't. There's been nothing in the papers about the connection.'

The Japanese looked upset at how he had been caught. The Filipino in the front seat looked smug: the questioning should have been left to him.

'The papers dunno they both died the same way, with the ice-pick or whatever you used in the back of the neck.'

'Where did you get all this?' said the Filipino.

It was Aldwych's turn to put up the shutters. 'Don't ask. Not unless you wanna swap one answer for another. Who did the job on both of 'em?'

'As you say, don't ask,' said the Filipino.

'Fair enough,' said Aldwych, satisfied he had got his answer once more. 'Now can you take me back to my driver? I'm going to lunch with a cop.'

The two men looked at each other, their bland faces abruptly creased with frowns. 'A police officer? Who?'

'Inspector Malone. He's heading the investigation on this one.'

'He is a friend of yours?'

'Not exactly.' He was enjoying their discomfiture; it was the first time in his life he had used a cop as a threat. He knew now they had no intention of killing him, not today. 'You want me to tell him about our meeting?'

'You're tempting fate, Mr Aldwych.'

'Maybe I'm turning Oriental like you guys. You tempt it all the time, don't you?'

'Not me,' said the Filipino. 'I'm Catholic.'

'I shouldn't do it, Mr Aldwych, tell the police officer about us. Not unless you want to finish up out there –' The Japanese nodded towards the distant sea. 'Half a leg and a foot.'

Aldwych laughed, a deep rumble with genuine mirth in it.
'Let's get back and pick up my driver. I'm getting hungry.'

The Filipino started up the car, backed it up the narrow lane
on to the main road and they headed back towards the city. The
smoked windows wound up again, shutting them off against the
outside world, Aldwych and the Japanese talked amiably about
the state of the world and how its economy was in the wrong
hands.

'What about your politicians?'

The Japanese shook his head in disgust. 'Corrupt. They can
be bought as easily as women.'

Aldwych wondered why he wished the three Bruna women
were here in the car with them.

4

Malone looked at his watch. 'I'll give your old man ten more
minutes, Jack.'

Jack Junior was worried. 'I don't know what's keeping him,
he's usually so punctual. My mother taught him that after she
heard him called the Crime King. She said punctuality was the
courtesy of kings. That appealed to him.'

The private room at the Golden Gate was one of two at the
front on the middle floor of the three-storeyed building in
Dixon Street, the main artery of Chinatown. Behind them,
separated by a landing, were the restaurant's offices; above,
on the third floor, was the gambling club, called, for tax pur-
poses, the manager's residence. Malone and Clements were
aware of the set-up, but, being Homicide men, they had blind
eyes to what might offend the Gaming squad. Like any sensible
public servants, they did not give themselves any more work
than they had to.

Over the first course of shark-fin soup Clements said, 'Jack,
what was it like growing up as your dad's son? Where did you
go to school?'

'Cranbrook.' One of the most expensive and exclusive of schools. 'I was registered there under my mother's maiden name. But everyone knew who I was, they just never mentioned it. They were probably afraid he'd come and blow up the school.'

'Did he ever turn up for speech day?'

Jack Junior smiled. 'Mum would never let him. She ruled the roost as far as I was concerned.' The door opened and his father came in. 'Dad, where have you been? I've been worried stiff!'

He suddenly looked it and Aldwych was touched. He patted his son's arm and sat down between Malone and Clements. 'Sorry. I got held up. The usual, Lee,' he said to the waiter who had followed him in. 'I'm hungry. How did the funeral go?'

'Quietly,' said Malone. 'How did you expect it to go? Are you going to tell us what kept you? I'm not used to being kept waiting, Jack.'

'Will I tell you?' Aldwych sipped some water. 'They told me not to.'

'Who did?' said Jack Junior.

'A Jap and a guy I'd say was a Filipino.'

Malone put down his spoon and even Clements stopped pouring soup into his mouth. 'Where their names Tajiri and Belgarda?'

'They didn't give me any names.' Then Aldwych told them how and why he had been delayed. 'They dropped me back near Manly golf course. Their sidekicks were waiting there for us with my driver. The poor little coot was shit-scared. I hadda write him a cheque to get him to forget what had happened to him, so he wouldn't tell his firm.'

'How much?' asked Jack Junior.

Aldwych smiled at the two detectives. 'Always keep an eye on the outgoings. Five hundred.'

'Too generous,' said his son.

'I got Casement's watch back for him,' Aldwych said.

'I won't ask how,' said Malone.

'The punks also stole a briefcase. Did you know anything about that?'

The soup plates had been taken away and a lazy susan of mixed dishes had been placed in the centre of the table. As he helped himself with the selective eye of a Chinese gourmet, he who had started in his youth on *dim sums*, Aldwych went on, 'The briefcase seemed their main concern, like they were afraid that was what I'd been looking for.'

Malone glanced at Clements, who shook his head and said, 'There was nothing in the initial report about a missing briefcase. Just the gold watch and his wallet.'

'Jack, you wanted to tell us something else –'

Aldwych picked at his food. 'Scobie, I've got nothing definite, but the word is that something's going on. Not drugs, something else. The locals aren't in on it, that's why the information is so skimpy. I got into this because I wanted to make sure nothing was connected to Jack here –'

'Thanks, Dad.' His son's voice was bone-dry with sarcasm.

'I didn't say you were connected with it.' There was a rasp to his father's voice. 'I just wanted to make sure no one tried to connect you with it, even if only by hearsay. Gossip sticks to our name like shit to a blanket. Excuse me,' he said to the two detectives, 'I forgot we're at lunch. Where was I?'

'Something big is going on.'

'Yeah. But what? I dunno. I dunno whether it's being run by the Filipinos or the Japs, but my money would be on the Japs. You oughta have no trouble picking 'em up.'

'Because they look different to us?' said Malone. 'It's not that easy. What do we do, ask every Neighbourhood Watch committee in Sydney to let us know if some Asian strangers move in? We know where the Filipino lived, but he's already gone through from there. We haven't had a fix at all on the Jap. Both of them could've moved out to Cabramatta, amongst the Vietnamese and the Cambodians and the Thais. We couldn't pick 'em out from amongst that lot, they all look alike to us. If we're going to pick 'em up, it'll be at some airport and there's no guarantee that's the way they'll try to leave the country. Look at that Malayan prince a coupla years ago, the one who took his children away from his wife. He drove all the way up to the Gulf country in north Queensland, took a boat to New Guinea or West Irian, somewhere there, then got a plane to Malaysia. These blokes could do the same when they're ready to skip. The question is, what brought them here? They didn't come down here hoping to win the lottery.'

Clements said, 'Has the scam, or whatever it is, gone through?'

Aldwych shrugged. 'Your guess is as good as mine. But I'd say no. Otherwise why would they have grabbed me this morning?' He stopped eating and shook his head in wonder: 'Grabbed – *me*! In the old days . . . '

'In the old days,' said Jack Junior, 'you'd have probably started a war. Thank Christ they're gone.'

'Amen,' said Malone, grinning. 'Listening to you two is like listening to Attila the Hun's family. Consider yourself lucky, Jack. You're not thinking of revenge, are you?'

'Only through you guys. This is the first time in my life I've ever given information to coppers. So you owe me, Scobie. You too, Russ. It's bad enough the way business here has been selling the country to the multinationals, anything for a quick buck.' He spoke piously, like a man who had never made a quick buck in his life, except for bank hold-ups. 'It'd be the bloody end if we let foreigners take over crime in Australia. I couldn't salute the flag any more.'

The other three patriots agreed and tucked into the sun-dried oysters, the Chinese hopeful omens of wealth.

Chapter Eleven

❖❖❖❖❖❖❖❖

1

'It's a long shot,' said Malone, 'but we'll get the fellers out at Cabramatta to ask around.'

'You think we'll learn anything?' Clements shook his head. 'Those people out there, they still think we're the Viet Cong. They never spill anything on each other, the gangs have got 'em scared stiff. What about Casement, are we going back to him to ask him about the briefcase?'

They had come back to Homicide after lunch. The homicide calendar was looking less cluttered; arrests had been made in two of the cases on it. The running sheet on the Sweden and Kornsey cases, however, was beginning to look like the preliminary notes for a royal commission, those legal enquiries where the wordage grew in proportion to the fees charged by the lawyers engaged. A royal commission, to the police, was another name for what the legal eagles took home.

Malone picked up the phone, got the Wicked Witch. 'Mr Casement is not available, Inspector. He is at a board meeting.'

'Mrs Pallister, tell him we'll be in to see him tomorrow morning at ten –'

'Inspector, I have his diary open in front of me –'

'I have mine open in front of me and there's his name. Ten o'clock. Thank you, Mrs Pallister.' He hung up in her ear, grinned at Clements. 'I wish she were my secretary. She'd even keep the Commissioner out.'

Or an Assistant Commissioner: the phone rang and AC Zanuch said, 'Can you see me first thing in the morning, eight-thirty. I've okayed it with AC Falkender.'

Malone put down the phone. 'What now? Zanuch's stirring the pot again.'

Clements stood up, smiling with the satisfaction of a Christian who had just been told the lion could handle only one meal at a time. 'I'm going home to Romy.'

Malone raised both eyebrows. 'Your place or hers?'

'Hers. I've moved in with her. A trial marriage, I think they used to call it once upon a time. Better not tell your kids. Nice Catholics, I wouldn't want them to think their Uncle Russ was a sinner.'

'Can I tell Lisa? She's a nice Catholic, but she likes sinners. They all do.'

That evening Lisa took a reluctant Malone to see the Sydney Dance Company at the Opera House. He was no ballet fan, believing that humans prancing upright on two legs were nowhere near as graceful as animals, especially members of the cat family, on four legs. Still, he admired the athleticism of Graeme Murphy's company and he managed not to fall asleep. His mind wandered at times to those occasions when he had had to come here to the Opera House for things more dramatic than a ballet, to the murder of a call-girl in the huge building's basement, to that of a singer who had been, with Malone himself, on the hit list of a deranged man. He wondered what other ghosts wandered the building, not prancing on their toes but floating aimlessly looking for an exit. Though he had enjoyed himself spasmodically, he was glad when the lights went up.

They were going down the wide steps outside when a voice called, 'Inspector!' He loved being called by his rank in a public place; a space always opened up as the natives moved away from the leper. He turned round: it was Ophelia Casement, her arm in her husband's. He introduced Lisa to them, the four of them standing awkwardly on the steps while the audience flowed down around them. Ophelia said, 'Do have supper with us. We have a table at Verady's.'

Malone hadn't a clue where Verady's was; all he wanted, anyway, was to get home and fall into bed. But Lisa said, 'That would be nice,' and then the four of them were walking along the waterfront towards the restaurant on the ground floor of The Wharf. Ophelia took Malone's arm as if he were an old friend and he and she walked in front of Lisa and Casement, who kept a respectful but friendly distance from each other.

Malone, working hard to be pleasant, said, 'I'm surprised your husband was well enough to come to the ballet.'

'I thought it would do him good. He loves ballet. He's recovering – he was at a board meeting this afternoon. Cormac is tough, Mr Malone, very durable.' She looked at him sideways and he wondered if there was any sexual innuendo in her words. She was wearing a strong perfume and he was aware of the animal in her. He gave her no encouraging reaction, not with Lisa three paces behind him and reading his thoughts.

Verady's was the sort of restaurant where Malone was glad he was not picking up the tab; financial arthritis would have gripped him from the shoulder down. The place was full, a mix of young people and some older Opera House patrons; in these hard times Malone wondered where the money came from. But then, he had read, even the restaurants in today's Belgrade were full: money or credit cards, like water, could always find an empty vessel. The Casement party settled into a corner booth, the head waiter hovering around like a man on a retainer. Orders were taken, then the four were left alone.

Casement was wearing white gloves to cover the dressing on his hands; he was unselfconscious of them. 'You're a ballet fan, Mr Malone?'

Malone shrugged and Lisa said, 'Just occasionally. Most of the time he's a Philistine. But my favourite Philistine,' she said and smiled a warning smile at Ophelia.

'Why haven't the Philistines founded an international organization?' Casement, it seemed, was doing his best to keep the mood light. 'There are so many of them around the world. They had their own Diaspora, like the Jews, but they never got themselves organized.'

'They try,' said Lisa. She was at ease with the Casements, more so than Malone. But then other people's money and social position had always worried her less than it did him.

Supper was brought, omelettes for three, blueberry pancakes for Malone. He was a sweet-tooth man and he knew they would lie on his chest all night, but he hadn't been able to resist them. In the next booth two young couples had just ordered another bottle of Bollinger and he wondered what they had to celebrate. When he turned his head he saw that one of the young women was Justine Springfellow, who had once lived in this building, whom he had once wrongfully arrested for murder. He looked away quickly, but not before she had seen him and her face had turned to stone.

Ophelia was saying, 'It must be a relief for you to get your mind off your work. And for you too, Mrs Malone.'

Both women seemed wary of each other. 'He never brings his work home,' said Lisa. 'It's a rule. He's broken it once or twice, but that wasn't his fault. Someone once dumped a body in our pool.'

'Ugh!' But it was a muted exclamation; Ophelia neither shuddered nor even looked upset. 'Cormac brings his work home occasionally, but he says he tries to protect me. Business fascinates me. It's the last field for the would-be Napoleons.'

Casement, fumbling with the fork in his gloved hand but refusing any help, smiled at Malone. 'He was never one of my heroes. I preferred De Gaulle . . . My secretary called me, said you wanted to see me tomorrow morning.'

'It can wait.' Then, tired and abruptly irritable, he thought, *What the hell*? 'It was about your briefcase.'

The fumbling hand in its glove was suddenly still. 'My briefcase?'

'You made no mention of it. Had you forgotten it? Did those kids steal it?'

The fork sliced into the omelette. 'I can only assume I forgot it, forgot to mention it. I'd dropped it on the front seat of the car, I think – when the car went up in flames, I suppose I took it for granted the briefcase went up, too. How did you know about it? Have you found it?'

Malone was aware that Lisa was concentrating on her omelette; if she was displeased at his raising police business at the table, she was hiding it. Ophelia, on the other hand, was leaning forward, her interest almost intense. He said, 'Jack Aldwych told me about it.'

'Jack? Did he find it? He brought me the watch they stole –'

'He told me about that. As for the briefcase –' He told them what had happened to Aldwych that morning. The two Casements both leaned forward, their food forgotten; even Lisa stopped eating. 'The two fellers who abducted him asked him if he had been after the briefcase when he went around the pawnbrokers. He said they appeared pretty concerned about it.'

'Did Jack say whether they had it or not?'

'He couldn't tell. What was in the briefcase that would interest them?'

The two couples in the next booth were leaving. As they passed on their way out, Ophelia, who had had her back to them, looked up. 'Justine! How wonderful you look! Oh, this is Mr and Mrs Malone –'

'We've met,' said Malone. 'How are you, Miss Springfellow?'

'Not guilty,' she said and with a nod to the Casements walked quickly towards the door.

There was silence for a moment in the booth, then Casement said, 'Do you get that often? People who never forgive you?'

'Were you in charge of the Springfellow case? Oh my God!' Ophelia wanted to give herself over to gossip, which always reduces one; she suddenly did not look as formidable, no more than a society matron. 'I never connected you with it –'

'No one ever does,' said Lisa, her voice tart, as if the omelette had too much salt in it. 'Perhaps it's just as well.'

'We got the real killer in the end,' said Malone. 'He almost blew my head off, but we got him. I thought she might have forgiven me.' He looked towards the revolving door at the front of the restaurant.

'The female of the species,' said Casement, then ducked his

head apologetically at Lisa. 'Sorry, Mrs Malone, that's an old man's chauvinism.'

'I'm used to it,' said Lisa. 'Old and young.'

She glanced at Ophelia, but the latter, whatever she thought of men, had never put them down. Instead, she patted her husband's gloved hand. 'Darling, you're not old. I was telling Mr Malone how durable you are.'

Malone got the conversation back on track: 'What sort of briefcase was it?'

'Leather. Coach-hide, with combination locks.'

'Coach-hide? That's fairly thick, isn't it? It probably wouldn't burn to a cinder. What was in it?'

Casement pushed his plate away, the omelette hardly touched. 'Just papers, minutes of a board meeting. I can't understand why the men who grabbed Jack would be interested in them. Nothing's going on at –' He named the company, one of the icons of the country's commercial world. He all at once did look *old*; he put the gloves up on either side of his face and stroked the corners of his eyes. 'I'm tired. Will you excuse us?'

Ophelia dropped the society look, was a hospital matron. She gathered up her handbag and stole, was on her feet, helping her husband out of the booth while Malone had a forkful of blueberry pancake halfway to his mouth. 'I've worn you out! I shouldn't have insisted we go to the ballet –'

'No, no, it was a good idea –' They might have been alone. Then Casement, now on his feet, stood still and looked down at the Malones. 'I'm not usually as rude as this, will you forgive me? But all of a sudden I feel I'm going to fall over –'

'They understand, darling. Come on, I must get you to bed. Goodnight, Mrs Malone. Finish your supper. The bill will be taken care of.'

Then they were making their way towards the front door, the head waiter backing his way ahead of them, heads turning at the other tables as the Casements were recognized. Ophelia knew how to make an exit: she straightened up and marched towards the door and Casement all at once had to quicken his pace so that he was not left behind. He caught her in the revolving door and they disappeared, though Malone, mouth full of pancake, would not have been surprised to see the old man come spinning back into the restaurant.

Lisa said, 'Well, that's the first time someone else but you has dumped me.'

'What did you think of them?'

'Her or him? They're not a pair. But he's afraid of losing her.'

'Him? Why would he be afraid of losing her? He's rich, he's powerful – though I don't think he's really interested in power, not the way his brother-in-law, Sweden, is. He's *secure*, the way the rest of us will never be. And he's too old to be lovesick.'

'I hope you're still lovesick over me when you're his age. He's in love, he's afraid of losing her, I tell you. Not that I think she'd ever leave him, not till he's dead. I didn't like her at all.'

'I gathered that. Neither do I.'

'Were you satisfied with his answer about the briefcase?'

'You're playing cop again. No.'

'Let's go home to bed. What do you think of Russ sharing Romy's bed?'

'It's none of our business.'

'Of course it isn't. But I'm glad, anyway. They'll be happier than Mr and Mrs Casement.' She looked up as the head waiter, thin, blond, hands doing a ballet of their own, loomed above them. 'Has the bill been attended to?'

'It will go on Mr Casement's account. He looked so *ill* – was it something he ate? The omelette?'

'No,' said Malone. 'It was something else entirely.'

2

Zanuch's office was hung with photos of himself with prominent people, like diplomas of merit. The feature of each picture was that one's eye was caught by him, not by whoever was with him: the Prince of Wales, the Premier, Dame Joan Sutherland. He appeared to be just that much more forward in the photo, in *bas-relief* compared to the flat image beside him. On his desk was a family photo, of himself, his wife and their two sons: even there he was the dominant figure. It was pointless to wonder if the man ever grew tired of looking at himself.

'You know AC Falkender's gone on leave?'

Malone had a sudden sinking feeling. 'No, I didn't know. That was sudden, wasn't it?'

'His wife's seriously ill.' So am I, thought Malone. 'I'm taking charge of the Sweden and Kornsey cases. The Minister specifically recommended that I do so.' He gazed steadily across his desk at Malone; the challenge was unmistakeable. 'We've got to clear this up, Scobie, and soon.'

'The sooner the better, as far as I'm concerned. Do I report direct to you or through Chief Super Random?'

'Direct to me, it'll save time. Copies of the reports, of course, to Greg Random.' He sat back, in charge. 'So where are we at now?'

Malone told him, including yesterday's abduction of Jack Aldwych.

'Have you any trace on the car they used?'

'Aldwych's driver was smart enough to get the number. They'd smeared the plates with mud, but he managed to pick out the registration. It was a rental job. We've checked, whoever took it out used a fake licence, there was no record of it in the RTA computer.'

'What about the Filipino or the Jap – did they own cars?'

'The Jap didn't, not as far as we know. The Filipino had a Mazda 929, registered to Pinatubo Engineering. We've traced it. He sold it to a second-hand dealer out on the Windsor Road, got a cash cheque for it. If he's got wheels now, they're probably rented.'

'You don't seem to be getting far.' Zanuch's tone was flat.

'All our leads are pretty frayed ones. My wife and I had supper with Cormac Casement and his wife last night –' He waited for a reaction from Zanuch, the social mountaineer, but there was none. 'His briefcase, the one the Jap and the Filipino seemed concerned about, he said he thought it went up with the car when it was burnt out. I checked with Physical Evidence this morning, they said they found nothing like a briefcase, no metal locks, no charred leather.'

'What did he say was in it?'

'He never got around to telling me, just to say it was some minutes of a board meeting, at –' He named the corporation. 'He suddenly had a turn of some sort and he and his wife just up and left, went home.'

'You weren't having supper at their apartment?'

'No, downstairs in the restaurant, Verady's. We met them coming out of the Opera House, we'd been to the ballet.'

Zanuch's eyes opened a little wider, as if he had expected Malone to be a fan of nothing more than break-dancing or even a waltz; but he made no comment. Instead he said, 'Do you think Casement has something to hide?'

'It seems to me that everyone in that family, the sisters and their husbands, has got something to hide.'

'Including the Minister?'

There was a warning there, but Malone took a chance: 'Including the Minister. He's trying to protect his son's name, Jack Aldwych is trying to do the same with *his* son, Casement – I dunno, but he could be protecting his wife. Or vice versa. But there's more hidden there than anyone wants to tell us.'

'Do you expect me to tell the Minister *that*? I'm his surrogate.'

Malone wondered if, except for the downgrading in pay, Tibooburra could be any worse. 'Can you stall him?'

'I don't know. Hans Vanderberg is breathing down his neck like a dragon. You never know what The Dutchman is going to come up with, Labor has more moles than the KGB ever had. What have you got in mind?'

'Finding the girl who was one of the two who burnt up Casement. She's around somewhere, otherwise they'd have killed her along with her punk boyfriend. She might've read the papers in the briefcase.'

'You don't expect Casement to tell you?'

'I think there must've been something else in the briefcase besides those board minutes, something that gave him his bad turn. I could go back to him, lean on him, but he could complain to the Minister and I know who'd get the push. I'd rather try our luck at picking up the girl. I've put out an ASM on her, though our description of her is pretty skimpy. And she could've skipped the State, especially after she found her boyfriend murdered. Our guess is that she was the one who called in to report to Redfern.'

'Can you pick her up through Social Security? If she's a street kid, she's probably drawing the dole.'

'They can't help. Anything on her is sacrosanct under the Privacy Act and the Crimes Act and half a dozen other acts, unless we can prove she's a menace to public security. She's not a serial killer or a terrorist, so she's free.'

'She tried to kill Casement, burn him.'

'According to his testimony, it was the punk with her who did that. No, we've got to take our chances on picking her up through the ASM or one of her mates dobbing her in.'

'All right, do your best. We're between the devil and the deep blue sea or a rock and a hard place, any cliché you want to use. The Premier wants it all wrapped up as soon as possible, the Minister would like it all forgotten and The Dutchman would like it all to turn out much worse than it is. As the *Herald* journalists say, we're in no-win mode.'

Malone abruptly got the impression that the Assistant Commissioner wished he had not become involved, that he had stuck to administration and left crime to the crime specialists. Scaling the heights, he had slipped on a cliff-face. We're on the same rope, Malone thought; but he knew who would fall first and farthest.

When he got back to Homicide there was a message to call Mrs Pallister. She came on the line, her voice as cold as a blade. 'Your appointment with Mr Casement is cancelled. He is under doctor's orders.'

'I'm sorry to hear that. He wasn't well last night.'

'You saw him last night?' Her tone suggested that she knew now who was to blame for her boss's indisposition. 'I'll let you know when Mr Casement will be available.' She hung up.

Malone put down the phone. He looked up at the map of New South Wales on his office wall. Tibooburra was in letters too small for him to read from where he sat, but he knew its location as well as he knew his home address. It was beginning to look like Shangri-La.

3

Kim Weetbix said, 'Mrs Hoang, let me do that.'

'No, no. My job.'

They were speaking in English, Kim's almost fluent, the old lady's broken. Mrs Hoang had been in Australia five years, but the natives frightened her and she had never learned to be easy with them in their language; Kim, for her part, had become rusty in her own tongue. There was, however, a warmth to Mrs Hoang that overcame the communication difficulty and Kim, after two days, felt at home with her. More so than she ever had with her own mother: there had been no home with that cheap bitch.

Kim had come here to this modest Fibro cottage in Cabramatta with Mrs Hoang's daughter-in-law, Annie. The latter worked in a fast-food café in Kings Cross and Kim had got to know her over the past year. She was a cheerful midget of a woman who, you knew, would one day own the fast-food shop, taking it over from the slow-witted Greek who ran it and who would never recognize his exit being greased, not till he was out of the place and Annie Hoang was in charge. She had a husband who worked in a dry-cleaning establishment and two small daughters who were already earmarked for university and professional careers in the 21st century. When Kim had confided to her that she had broken up with Kel and had nowhere to go, Annie had invited her home, one refugee who had made good taking in another who still had to make it.

Mrs Hoang, only fifty but looking seventy, had a face where pain, grief, worry and laughter had resulted in a scribble of lines that obviously distressed her; Kim had already noticed that every time Mrs Hoang passed a mirror she turned her head away. Kim, proud of her own looks, guessed that somewhere in the past was a mirror that held the reflection of a good-looking woman who had been the young Mrs Hoang, before the bombs and the landmines and defoliation sprays had come to Vietnam.

'You get job?' said Mrs Hoang. She was preparing the evening meal, working with the precision of a mortician, the vegetables sliced just so, the chicken dissected clinically.

'When I get to Queensland,' said Kim. 'The Gold Coast.'

'The Gold Coast? Gold is there?'

Kim smiled; it occurred to her that in the two days she had been here in this house she had smiled more easily than in two years with Kel. 'I don't think so. It is just a name for a place. People hope, but only the rich find gold there. Not real gold, just money.'

'Not now. Annie tell me, nobody got money now. You got money?' She had a peasant's directness.

'A little.' She still had the pawnbroker's payment, but she would keep that aside for the moment. She would register for the dole when she got to the Gold Coast; she wondered if the police, or worse still, the killers of Kel, would be able to trace her through Social Security. Maybe she should change her name; but that would mean getting new papers and they always cost money. The price had gone up since she had become Kim Weetbix. She had read only this week that bloodsuckers in the United States were charging Chinese illegals 30,000 American dollars for smuggling them in. 'I'll get a job, Mrs Hoang.'

'Be careful, Kim.' Mrs Hoang knew what could happen to pretty girls; she had seen them leave the village and go to Saigon. 'Stay on feet.'

At first Kim didn't get the meaning of the warning; then she laughed, her first loud laugh in God knew how long. She was laughing when Annie came in the back door, pulling off her cheap raincoat that glistened with the evening drizzle. 'What's so funny?' Then abruptly she said, 'Kim, come inside.'

There was a warning in her voice, not one to laugh at. Kim sobered, put down the kitchen knife she had been holding and followed Annie through into the front bedroom where Annie and her husband slept. They passed the two Hoang girls watching *Neighbours* on television in the small living room, learning about their new homeland from a soap opera where even tragedy was sunlit and everyone washed his or her hair every day and everyone's teeth were perfect. In the bedroom Annie sat down on the bed, with its bright blue sateen coverlet, and looked up at Kim.

'Why didn't you tell me? Your boyfriend is dead. Murdered.'

Kim sat down on the stool in front of the dressing-table. The room was furnished Western-style; the furniture was cheap, discount bargains. Annie had cut her roots to her homeland; she left the sentiment to her mother-in-law. The only picture on the wall above the bed was one of the Virgin Mary, an icon Kim had never understood nor been much interested in.

'What would you have done if I had told you the truth? Still invited me home like you did?'

'No.' Annie was as blunt as Mrs Hoang. 'Did you kill him?'

'No. I don't know who did.'

'He was never any good, a bad one. I never liked him. You should not have stayed with him so long. The police are looking for you.'

'I thought they would be. Did you tell them anything about me?'

'No. Whoever killed your boyfriend, he might be looking for you, too. You have to go, Kim, you can't stay here. I must think of my family.'

Kim all at once hated and envied her; Annie had security, hard-won and shaky though it might be. Kim had no wish for children nor even for a husband; but she had seen what support a family could give. Fragile though it might have been, she had felt a certain security even in just the two days she had been with the Hoang family. 'I'll go tonight.'

'No, no. First thing in the morning, when I'm going to work. You come on the train with me to the city, you catch a bus to somewhere. Where?'

'The Gold Coast?' All the street-kids at the Cross talked of eventually finishing up there, as if it were some sort of earthly paradise, a dream she had never believed in. There was no paradise anywhere.

'You have money?' But Annie made no move towards her handbag, which lay on the bed beside her.

'I'll be all right.' She put her hand on the older woman's. 'I'd have liked you as a sister, Annie.'

Annie smiled, showing her new false teeth. 'You'd have been too much trouble, Kim. You got no faith.'

'In what? God? I could never be religious.'

'No, in anything. Not even in yourself.'

In the morning they left the house at seven o'clock. Mrs Hoang and Annie's husband Willy came to the front door to say goodbye. Willy was a wiry little man with a shock of black hair that stood up as if he were in perpetual fright; like his mother, but unlike his wife, he was afraid of the rough-and-ready local elements. Like Annie, he had taken an Anglo name, wore it as camouflage.

He pressed Kim's hand. 'You take care.'

'Yes,' said Mrs Hoang, eyes alert for danger even in the empty street. 'Beware men, Australian men. No trust any men.' But she patted her son's back to show he was an exception. 'I pray for you, Kim.'

Burdened by their good wishes and prayers, a weight she had never had to carry before, Kim left with Annie for the railway station. She carried a small suitcase Annie had given her, in it everything she owned.

The two women passed a queue of young people outside a McDonalds. 'Are they all waiting for breakfast?'

'Breakfast?' Annie looked puzzled; then she shook her head. 'No, no, they are after a job. McDonalds advertised two jobs.'

Kim looked back at the queue; a hundred or more young faces stared back at her, challenging her to join them. Then she realized they were resenting her; they thought she was one of the fortunate ones on her way to work.

'Fucking slopeheads,' she heard a youth say. 'They got jobs, they work for fuck-all.'

All at once the Gold Coast began to glisten.

4

Suddenly the weather turned cold. Television weathermen reported that it was the coldest May day for a hundred years; reported gleefully, as if it were their own sadistic revenge on all those who criticized their sometimes wrong reports.

Malone got out of bed at six, his usual time for his morning walk. He put on his track-suit and trainers, went out the front door and immediately came back and put on a heavy sweater.

'Come back to bed,' said Lisa sleepily. She loved the cocoon of their bed, especially with his warmth curled into hers.

'Go back to sleep,' he said and went out the front door again.

He was a walker, not a jogger; he had too much respect, he claimed, for his joints and cartilages to pound them day after day on the hard pavements. He walked down to Randwick racecourse, went in through one of the gates, nodding to the gatekeeper, who knew him, and began his usual circuit round the outer rail of the outer track. On the tracks the horses went past in the semi-darkness, seemingly moving in slow motion through the slight mist, the sound of their hoofs as faint as faraway drums. He passed men leaning on the rails, arguing in low voices about the merits of the horses, punters dreaming of fortunes as ghostly as the shapes in the mist. He had never had any interest in horse racing; it was his gentle boast that he hadn't known Phar Lap was dead till he had seen the movie. He had never placed a bet on a horse in his life, never even bought a lottery or sweepstake ticket; he had no faith in fortune's falling out of the sky. Occasionally, just occasionally, he would place a bet in his head that fortune might strike in a homicide case. But that was placing a bet on human nature, another lottery barrel altogether.

He completed his walk, twice round the course, and went home. Lisa was up, preparing breakfast, and the children were having their usual morning squabble over who should use the bathrooms first. Lisa put his bacon and eggs in front of him, poured his coffee. She claimed that the Dutch made the best coffee in the world and he agreed with her.

'What did you think about this morning?' She knew that he spent the walk sorting out yesterday's thoughts.

'What would you say if I asked for a transfer from Homicide?'

'I'd say, praise the Lord. Then I'd have second thoughts. You wouldn't be happy behind a desk.' She kissed the top of his head. 'This business will pass. The next murder will be a nice uncomplicated one. What am I saying? That's callous.'

'You'll never be that.' He rubbed her bottom through her dressing-gown.

'Watch it,' said Maureen as she came in, sat down and reached for the cereal box. 'Not in front of the children.'

'You sound like Mother Brendan,' said Malone.

'Oh God.' Maureen rolled her eyes.

Malone passed her the milk jug; milk bottles or cartons never appeared on Lisa's table. 'Her latest report didn't say much for you.'

She rolled her eyes again. 'I'm not cut out for school, Dad. I should've been born an adult.'

'I thought you were,' said her mother. 'Judging by what you used to do to my breast, you had a full set of teeth at two weeks.'

'Disgusting,' said Maureen and winked at her father. She would, he was certain, wink her way through the troubles of the life that lay ahead of her. He should have been so lucky.

He went to work, came back to his office from lunch to find a lottery prize sitting with its father in the big outer office.

Roger Statham, the young man from Casement's, rose to his feet, nothing co-ordinated, each limb seeming to unfold of its own accord.

'Inspector Malone, this is my father, Matthew. He – he suggested I come and see you.'

Malone looked past them at Clements, who stood in the background. 'Have you talked to the gentlemen, Sergeant?'

'They got started, then I told 'em to hold it. I thought you should hear it.'

Malone led the way into his office. When they were all seated, he said, 'It has to do with Rob Sweden's murder?'

Roger Statham shook his head, looking slightly puzzled at the question, as if he hadn't expected it. His father said, 'Not directly. It has to do with what young Sweden was up to. I'm in banking, I'm with –' He named one of the four top banks. There was a distinct resemblance to his son, though he was not as tall nor as thin; he also had none of the boy's bruised innocence showing in his tanned lean face. He did, however, have that withdrawn look that some honest men get when they learn that trust is an expendable commodity. Malone wondered what sort of disillusion Matthew Statham had suffered in the free-for-all of the Eighties. 'When Roger told me of his suspicions, I knew at once what might have happened.'

'What?'

He had looked at Roger, but the boy said to his father, 'You explain it, Dad.'

Statham looked enquiringly at Malone, who nodded. 'Well, Roger says that young Sweden told him he was on to something much bigger than the laundering of a million dollars. Much bigger.'

Malone looked at Clements, who grinned. 'Better adjust your thinking, Inspector. This isn't small change at the super-market counter.'

'You think I'm talking big money?' said Statham.

'You haven't mentioned any sum yet, but I can feel my wallet curling up in embarrassment,' said Malone.

Statham smiled. 'You must excuse me, Inspector, if we toss

200

large amounts of money around as if they mean nothing. They do. But I'm sure you speak of murder in the same way, it's all in the day's work to you. So are millions to me.'

'Were they to Rob Sweden?'

'Seems he was trying very hard to become accustomed to such sums. I mean, such sums that would belong to him. He and Roger, they dealt every day in big sums but it was other people's money.'

'This was other people's money, too,' said Roger Statham. 'The money Rob was going to steal.'

Malone showed no reaction. 'How much?'

'Twenty-five million.'

'Who from?'

'Casement Trust.'

'How?' Malone looked at Statham Senior, the expert.

'Well –' The banker abruptly had a fit of banker's circumspection, as if he had had second thoughts about his coming here. 'You must understand what I'm suggesting is only a guess. We haven't been to Casement Trust to talk to them. I could hardly do that . . . '

Banks, Malone thought, had once been as much in each other's vaults as it had been possible to be; they had formed one of the most exclusive clubs in the world. Then the Eighties had split the club wide open, banking had been de-regulated and banks, like virgins on Spanish fly, had gone wild in their competition with each other. Now, with many of the newer, smaller institutions already out of business and the older, larger ones still nursing deep wounds, the old incestuous clubbiness was creeping back in. A bank's secrets were its own till it divulged them to the club.

'Tell us your guess,' said Malone patiently.

'Just from remarks young Sweden made to Roger, this could be what was planned. Maybe it's already been done and Casement Trust are keeping quiet about it. It's the manipulation of electronic money. Most people think of money as cash in hand – they never really think of the proportion of their money that moves through cheques. Five out of every six dollars that move in the economy on any given day goes through computers – that's what I mean by electronic money. CHIPS, the Clearing House Interbank Payments System in New York, the biggest of the lot, pushes through over a trillion and a half dollars a day.' He smiled, just a twist of his thin lips. 'How's your wallet feeling?'

'Rolled up in a ball. Go on.'

'Young Sweden talked of twenty-five million. There's no other way he could steal an amount like that than the way I'm describing, electronically.'

'Doesn't the clearing house have some sort of security to prevent that?' said Clements.

'Of course. There's an authentification barrier – each transfer carries a code. If the code is not correct, the line to the transmitting bank is severed. The only way of beating the system is for it to be an inside job. It's happened once – or anyway, it's only been reported once. Two insiders at a Swiss bank in Zurich managed it, working the scam for someone outside the bank.'

Malone looked at Roger Statham. 'Did Rob ever tell you what he was going to do?'

The boy shook his head, a lock of his long blond hair falling down. He was dressed today like his father, in banker's grey; both of them wore the same sober tie, an old school one. Malone wondered if Roger was wearing the bright red braces under the conservative jacket, but guessed not: he had been drummed out of the regiment, if not by Ondelli then by Matthew Statham.

'Not in so many words. But he did say that any minute of the day he could put his finger on any amount I cared to name. I knew what he meant – his computer finger. I said to him, How about twenty-five million? It was just a figure I pulled out of the air. And he looked at me, hard, and said, sort of quiet, How'd you guess? Then he said, That's what I'm after. I didn't think any more of it, I just thought he was bullshitting . . . Then last night, when Dad had a talk to me –' He stopped and glanced at his father.

'It was a father-to-son talk,' said Matthew Statham. 'He's

too big to whip, but I blew the Christ out of him. He's damn near broken his mother's heart, his sister won't even speak to him . . . '

'Is that why you're here?' said Malone quietly, wondering what he would do if he were in the same position with one of his own children. 'You want us to blow the Christ out of him, too?'

'No.' A moment ago Statham had looked on the verge of anger; now he was soberly circumspect again. 'No, it's – it's expiation, if you like to call it that. Trying to make up for what he's done. I understand you have made no charges against him – I appreciate that. For that I thought he owed you something. He's lost his job, but at least he's not going to jail.'

Malone swung his chair round, faced Clements, who had been making notes. 'Sergeant Clements is our residential financial genius in Homicide,' he explained to the Stathams. 'What d'you reckon?'

'I think it's worth a try,' said Clements.

'You'll go to Casement Trust?' Matthew Statham suddenly looked anxious. 'You won't mention where you got your suspicions from? I mean –'

'Don't worry, Mr Statham. We're grateful for your efforts. We'll keep mum.' The four men stood up, crowding the small room. 'Good luck, Roger. Keep your nose clean in future. Open your jacket.'

The boy looked puzzled, but he opened his jacket; his trousers were held up by a belt.

'Stay away from the red-braces set,' said Malone, 'or we'll arrest you for consorting.'

5

'Love your walls, Adam. Pity about the paintings.'

'Unfortunately, my dear, one has to sell the paintings, not the wall paint.'

'Well, must fly! Thanks for the bubbly. Domestic, wasn't it? We're all feeling the pinch, aren't we?'

Then she left with a flash of long legs and a flicker of fingers. She was an artist/writer who trebled as a critic. Her own body of work was anorexic and her sales just as frail, but each week in her column she flung her weak acid at the efforts of others. Normally Adam Bruna tolerated her as one of the hazards of being a gallery owner, but this evening he felt like shouting after her never to come back. He was depressed and not just by the failure of tonight's exhibition.

It had been a disastrous opening, not a painting sold nor even a hint of a possible sale. He walked back to his three daughters. 'They crowd in here, drink one's champagne, and then the bastards and bitches buy *nothing*, absolutely nothing. I'll be out of business six months from now, if this keeps up. I hope the three of you have got some expensive retirement home fixed up for me. On the Harbour and a short walk from Double Bay.'

The three sisters had come without their husbands; the three men shared a common wisdom that kept them away from gallery openings. All the champagne crowd had gone, most of them, no doubt, commenting on the substitution of domestic bubbly for the usual French; the gallery was empty but for the caterers cleaning up and Bruna's assistant who was helping them. The gallery, two large rooms, had that silence that a crowd leaves behind it, a vacuum after the noise had been withdrawn. The paintings on the walls, none with a red Sold spot on it, added nothing to the atmosphere: they were all, it seemed, painted in what Juliet had called 'recession grey'.

'Why on earth did you choose this artist, Pa?'

'Because he has such *promise*. That's why I choose all my artists, the young ones. Their promise.'

Ophelia looked around the walls. 'He doesn't promise much with these, does he? God, there isn't an optimistic stroke in any of them. Couldn't he have painted at least one with a touch of colour in it?'

'You could buy one,' said her father. 'Or two.'

'Not a chance. Cormac won't let me spend a penny, not on extravagances. We've tightened our belts.' She patted the Hermès gold-buckled belt she wore. 'He says we should be setting an example. I don't know who to. But there it is. He would blow his top if I bought something like that.' She nodded at the paintings.

'Cormac blow his top?' said Rosalind. 'I can't imagine that. How is he, anyway?'

'Recovering. He's been upset since they discovered the body of the boy who's supposed to have burned him.' She twirled the champagne flute in her hand. 'Father, haven't you any *real* bubbly? Where's the Taittinger I sent you?'

'You sent him some?' said Juliet. 'I did, too.'

'Me, too,' said Rosalind.

All three sisters aimed their empty flutes like guns at their father. He shrugged and went away, came back with two bottles of Taittinger. 'I was saving it for my retirement. As the natives say, things are crook.'

'Crook or crooked?' said Ophelia, who had never bothered, in all the years she had been here, to learn the native slang.

'I hope there's nothing crooked?' said Bruna, looking around the three of them. A born cynic, he always looked for dirt in corners. 'Have my sons-in-law told you something?'

'Nothing,' said Juliet. 'So things are just crook, as you say. Bad. Parlous. Bloody dreadful.' She raised her glass and drank to her pessimism. 'All this violence.'

'That's what I mean.' Bruna had poured himself some champagne, but so far hadn't touched it. 'It was bad enough, Rob being killed. But then the strangers, too . . . One shudders.' He did, theatrically. 'And Cormac, a harmless old man.'

'Not much older than you.' Ophelia sounded defensive, as if she had been accused of marrying an ancient.

'Is this all connected to your father-in-law?' Bruna looked at Juliet.

'Jack Senior?' She laughed. 'Oh, come off it, Pa. He's *retired*. All right, he must have been a terror at one time, a real criminal. But he's respectable now. Well, almost.'

'He's reformed?' asked Rosalind.

'No, retired. He says there's a difference. If he'd reformed, he'd have a conscience about what he used to do. But he doesn't. At least he's honest about that. A lot of truly respectable people wouldn't be so honest. In politics, for instance.'

'Don't start that,' said Rosalind.

There was tension between the two younger sisters, always had been. Rosalind had never been the free-wheeler that the other two were; she had had her share of marriages, but still one less husband than her sisters had had. Her first husband had died of a heart attack while making love to her, a not unnatural way to go; he had died happy, or at least in ecstasy. He had not been discarded, as her sisters' previous husbands had been, just cremated.

'Derek is as honest as it's possible to be, considering. Politics is compromise and compromise isn't necessarily being dishonest. In any case, this isn't Roumania, the politicians here don't have people bumped off.'

'Darling,' said her father, 'don't put down our country. It was once a wonderful place to live. Your mother loved it.'

'Even so,' said Ophelia, 'they were always, as 'Lind puts it, bumping off people.' She had spoken lightly; then she abruptly shivered. 'Let's stop all this talk about killing. I've had enough of it.' She stood up. 'Coming, Julie? I'll drop you off.'

They gave perfunctory kisses to their father and Rosalind, then were gone. As they walked away down the gallery Bruna looked after them. 'You all have a certain queenliness. You got it from your mother.'

'Don't mention it in front of Derek, he's suddenly become a republican. Political compromise,' she explained. Then she said, 'Why do you praise us so much, to our faces? Since I married Derek I've started to hear gossip about us. A lot of people think we're stuck-up bitches. I don't think I ever heard that about us before, but since I've become a Minister's wife . . . Derek has enemies and I've inherited them by marrying him.'

'Enemies who want to *kill* him?' The caterers and the gallery assistant had gone; Bruna's voice sounded unnaturally loud in the big empty rooms. 'Do you mean they might have meant to kill him and not Rob?'

She usually wore her blonde hair in a chignon, but tonight it was loose; she shook her head and it fell down over her forehead, making her look younger. She also looked abruptly vulnerable. 'Pa, I'm worried. Derek knows more about why Rob was killed than he's letting on. He says no, when I question him. But I'm sure of it, sure that he does know.'

Bruna put down his glass. They were seated on a couch that stood against one wall, under a painting of what looked like a dozen or more wooden stakes in various shades of grey. In front of the couch was a low glass table on which was an unopened order book. He glanced around the gallery, the business part of his mind wondering how he could have expected to sell such a depressing collection in these depressed times. Then he looked at Rosalind, put a hand on her arm. He loved these girls of his, had worked hard to educate them, had steered them through their difficult times. This, however, was the first time he had been truly afraid for one of them. He knew enough of history to know what ambition could do to a man. But, it struck him only now, he didn't really know Derek Sweden.

'Has Derek mentioned to you that he could become Premier?'

She frowned. 'No. You mean he's said something to you?'

'No. I had a chat with someone, never mind who.' It had been another Cabinet minister, a gallery client who liked to snap up bargains at art auctions. Though their hold on government was precarious, there was little or no solidarity in Cabinet. The back-stabbing could have been that usually found amongst Labor factions. Or in Roumanian cabinets. 'They want to dump Bigelow, he's a wimp. He sits on the fence on every issue, they're calling him Cement-Crotch. Derek is the tip to take over from him. But –'

'But what?'

'If you speak to Derek about this, will you tell him where

you got the information?' He always covered his tracks, even in the family.

She had long ago got over any disappointment she might have felt in him; mostly she was amused by his deviousness. But there was nothing to be amused about now. 'You're safe. Tell me what you know.'

He moved a little closer to her, the movement of a born gossip. 'Derek did some insider trading on a takeover – someone on the board of one of the companies gave him the word on it. It was a bribe – the company wanted something done in Parliament and Derek got it through for them. He had to hide the shares he bought, so he warehoused them – the Americans call it parking – at Casement's, had someone put them in their name. Presumably it was Rob. When the takeover went through, Derek made four million dollars. Some might call that peanuts, but right now I'd like such a shower of nuts.'

'Is it illegal, what he did?'

'Of course it is, both the insider trading and the warehousing. If it got out, it would mean the end of Derek in politics. Not to mention being Premier.'

'Who knows about this? Besides whoever told you?'

He shrugged. 'Your guess is as good as mine. Presumably someone in Casement's would know about it. Perhaps one or two in Cabinet, but not the Premier. On the other side, if that horrible man The Dutchman knew about it, he'd have had it all over the front pages by now. It happened six months ago.' He finished his champagne, picked up the unopened second bottle. Waste not, want not: he lived extravagantly, but at other people's expense. 'I think your husband would like Rob's murder to die quietly, for the police to roll up their little blue-and-white strips of tape and disappear. He can never be sure of what they are going to turn up next.'

Chapter Twelve

◆◆◆◆◆◆◆

1

Kim Weetbix waited outside the Koala Motor Inn off Oxford Street for the Greyhound bus to the Gold Coast. It was due to leave at three-thirty and the day had seemed extraordinarily long since she had arrived in the city with Annie on the early-morning train from Cabramatta. She had not gone up to Kings Cross with Annie; better to stay away from her usual haunts. Instead, she had wandered about the city's main shopping centre, tempted at times in the better boutiques to do a little shoplifting, especially when she saw some outfit that would fit her into the Gold Coast scene, all bright colours and glass slippers. Twice she thought she saw patrolling policemen look at her and after lunch, retreating from the main streets, she had found herself wandering across the green sward of the Domain towards the Art Gallery. There, in the big halls, she had felt secure. Even, to her surprise, interested: for the first time in her life she looked at paintings and found some meaning in them.

At three o'clock she was at the bus station, had paid her sixty dollars for a one-way ticket and was waiting for the coach to pull in. Then the drunk approached her. 'G'day, love. You going all the way?'

She had never liked drunks, especially Australian ones, though she had rolled a number. 'Get lost, Jack.'

'Don't be like that, love.' He was in his mid-forties and looked as if he might have been drunk for the last thirty years; his beer belly had not been grown on a fast diet. He had a round red face with the blood vessels seemingly on the *outside* of his skin, deep-set bleary eyes under thick brows, a Mexican bandit's moustache, receding black hair with long sideburns and a sweaty stink that shrank one's nostrils. Enough to turn off any woman: except that he had a roll of notes that, thrown with force, could have knocked any woman flat. He produced the roll. 'Four days on the town, love. You wanna share it?'

'No, thanks.'

'You too good for me?' He suddenly looked dangerously angry. 'Fucking slopehead –'

He tottered, fell back against the wall and let go a belch that turned the air alcoholic. His speech had suddenly slurred and he looked at Kim with eyes that had abruptly become glazed, just tiny orbs of brewery glass. 'Howaboutit?' he mumbled, then slid down the wall and fell on his side, the roll of notes clutched loosely in his hand like a paper grenade.

There were other people waiting for the coach; but they had turned away as the coach now drew into the kerb. Kim glanced around her, saw the turned backs and at the same time saw her opportunity. She bent quickly, grabbed the roll of notes from the drunk's hand, picked up her suitcase and moved towards the coach. She almost fell over with shock when the strong hand clutched her arm.

'Okay, miss.' He had come out of the doorway behind her, one of the Greyhound handlers. He was young and muscular and not at all sympathetic. 'Inside! Don't make a fuss.'

'What's the matter, for Chrissake?' She was all innocent indignation, with the roll of notes still in her hand. 'I was going to bring it in to you –'

'Bullshit,' said the young man. 'We get hustlers like you around here every day in the week. Inside, I said. No fuss, hear me?'

'I wasn't hustling!' She was beginning to panic. She struggled to break free, but his grip was too tight. 'What're you gunna do?'

'Call the police,' he said. 'Tell your story to them, not me.'

'Mrs Pallister told me you were coming,' said Cormac Casement. 'I gather she tried to persuade you not to, but you wouldn't take no for an answer?'

'Afraid not, Mr Casement. How're you feeling?'

'Not the best. But that won't make any difference, will it?'

Malone shook his head. He and Clements had been let into the penthouse by Casement himself; if there was a servant here, he or she was not visible. The penthouse was two-storeyed, the main sitting room rising to a gallery; Malone wondered what two people could do with all this space. If the homes of the other two Bruna sisters were luxurious, Ophelia Casement's apartment went beyond that adjective. It was the sort of surroundings that aroused envy in even the most incorruptible cop. The two detectives, doing their best to hide their envy, managed to look unimpressed. Casement, having lived all his life amongst luxury, did not remark their indifference.

Still, as if afraid of letting the oxen loose amongst all the elegance, Casement led them into a study. This room was all leather and polished wood; two walls were solid with books, many of them leatherbound editions. There were also old prints, many of them sailing ships. It seemed that Casement liked to surround himself with the past. Except for the computer on an antique side-table: the timeless world of finance evidently could not be kept out.

'I used to sail, ocean sailing. I did the Sydney–Hobart a dozen times. Either of you sail?'

Neither of them did. 'I get seasick on the ferry to Manly,' said Clements.

'Did you ever play sport?'

'I played for Easts, rugby league. Inspector Malone played cricket.'

'Of course! Why didn't I connect you with that Malone?' It seemed to Malone that Casement was trying to delay asking why the two detectives had come to see him. 'Do you miss it?'

'Occasionally.'

Casement offered the two of them a drink, but they declined and at last he settled down opposite them in one of the three red leather chairs. His hands were ungloved today, though still coated with gauze dressing. He was wearing a houndstooth jacket, corduroys and an open-necked dark blue shirt, but he did not look at ease, not even in this, his own den. He also, Malone thought, looked ten years older than he had the day they had first interviewed him.

'So?' He was the chairman of the board, calling the meeting to order.

'We've picked up the girl who tried to burn you,' said Malone.

There was no reaction from Casement at first, as if this point wasn't expected on the agenda. Then: 'Has she anything to say?'

'We haven't interviewed her yet. We only got word just as we were leaving to come down here to see you.'

'Where is she? I presume she'd left Sydney?'

'She was about to. No, she's being held at Surrey Hills police station at Police Centre. She's been charged with rolling a drunk.'

'Rolling a drunk?'

'That's not the legal term. She had almost three thousand dollars of some drunk's money when a feller from Greyhound grabbed her.'

'Greyhound?'

'Greyhound buses.' Then it struck Malone that Casement was not ignorant of how drunks were rolled nor of the names of coach lines; he was playing for time, trying to get his thoughts in order. 'You don't look happy that we've picked her up.'

'What? Oh, I am. Of course I am.' He opened his hands on his lap, looked down at them as if now remembering that these were his connection with the girl. 'I don't know that I want to see her.'

'We'll need you to identify her.'

'She was masked, she had a scarf round her face –' Then he

saw the look on Malone's face and reluctantly he nodded. 'Yes, I suppose so.'

'There's something else, Mr Casement . . . '

'I thought there might be. What?'

Malone looked at Clements. 'Fill Mr Casement in, Russ.'

Clements took out his notes, glanced at them, then looked direct at the old man. His look was hard: there were times when he appeared to shed weight, or when bone replaced flesh. 'Has Casement Trust had any money stolen from it in the past three months?'

Casement frowned. 'I don't know. Possibly. What sort of money are you talking about?'

'Twenty-five million.' Clements glanced at Malone and half-smiled: the amount had rolled off his tongue like a small each-way bet. 'How's your wallet?'

'Still in a ball. Sorry, Mr Casement. A private joke.'

'I hope this question you've put to me isn't some private joke.' Casement was building up some irritation. His glasses slipped down his nose and he pushed them back with an awkward hand. 'Where'd you get this from?'

'We can't tell you,' said Malone. 'But we know Rob Sweden had something like that amount in mind. We think he wanted something much bigger than his rake-off from laundering money.'

'How? I mean how was he going to steal so much? The sum is ridiculous!'

'Not the way it's been explained to us. Tell him, Russ.' He left it to the figures man.

Clements explained the method of theft. He sounded expert, as if he had been dealing in electronic transfers all his working life; once again Malone was amazed at how sharply the big man's mind could work when it came to the mathematics of money. 'We'd like to check with Casement Trust, with the bank executives.'

Casement took off his glasses, sat silent, staring at the two detectives, but as if not seeing them. Out in the drawing-room a clock struck the half-hour, like a golden gong. The sound seemed to break Casement's stare; he put his glasses back on and his eyes came into focus again. His voice sounded like a croak: 'There's no need for that.'

The two detectives waited. Silence seeped into the study from the rest of the apartment like smoke, hung heavily. Casement had lifted his hands, rested them on the arms of his chair; they looked like half-roasted birds. His legs were together, but one foot was raised on its ball; his knee started to tremble and he abruptly dropped a hand on it. He looked down at it and managed a smile.

'An 18th century American lawyer once said, A sense of humour is the first requisite in a man; the second best sense is that of silence. This, I think, is when the senses should be reversed.'

He's stalling again, Malone thought; and his own gaze became a stare. Casement got the point: he took a deep breath, as if entering a confessional:

'Yes, the money has been stolen, the sum you named. We know where it is and we are endeavouring to get it back.'

'Have you reported the theft? To the Reserve Bank? The ASC? Anyone?'

'No.'

'Why not? Twenty-five million isn't a sum you mislay every day.'

Casement bridled at the sarcasm; he was far less friendly than he had been. 'That's a smart-aleck remark, Inspector.' Then he made a visible effort to calm himself. 'Banks have had a bad press these past couple of years. There has been a lot of stupid management, incompetence – you name the mistakes, the banks have managed to make them. Not all of them, but far too many of them. If we let out that we've been robbed of twenty-five million by one of our own employees, the son of the Police Minister, indeed a nephew of mine by marriage, what do you think the media would make of that? There have been bigger losses, much bigger, but most of those were due to stupidity or incompetence, lending millions against useless paper collateral. This is just plain theft, the biggest in any

214

Australian bank's history. We could wear it in money terms, but it would cripple us as far as reputation. So we have kept a lid on it, only a few top people at the bank know of it, and we're optimistic we can get the money back before we have to close our yearly accounts.'

'Where from?'

'I'd rather be silent on that.'

Malone felt his own irritation itching him. 'I'm sure you would, Mr Casement. But you seem to forget that Sergeant Clements and I are working on the murder of the young man who's supposed to have stolen this money. There may be no connection in your banker's mind –'

'Oh stop it, for Christ's sake!' A hand slapped the arm of the chair; Casement winced, put the hand gently on his thigh. He was suddenly weary, worse than being merely tired. 'Do you think I'm trying to obstruct you?'

'Frankly, yes.'

'All my life I've had my own way,' said Casement, as if to himself. 'But then I've never had anything to do with the police. From all accounts, some of you act as if you're a law unto yourselves.'

'Just as you must have,' said Malone tartly. 'We cops aren't perfect. But if you don't like us and the way we work, what's the alternative? The army? Try some of the Latin Americans who've come to Australia, ask them what law and order is like under the army. Let's cut out the bullshit and get down to the works. Where's the money?'

Casement, it seemed, had never been spoken to so bluntly; he had, indeed, always had his own way. He flushed; but he had control of himself. He hesitated only slightly, then he said in a flat voice, 'It's in a company account in Hong Kong.'

'The name of the company?' said Clements, notebook ready.

'Hannibal Development.'

'One of Kornsey's companies,' Clements told Malone. 'Would the money have gone through Shahriver Credit International?'

Casement looked surprised; and more alert. 'You seem to have a fix on this?'

'Not entirely,' said Clements. 'But we're not as far behind as you seem to think. Kornsey was the man killed the same night as young Sweden, killed the same way. The one whose body was stolen from the morgue. So now we've made that connection. Are you dealing through Shahriver or direct with Hong Kong?'

'The Hong Kong bank is another Shahriver branch. They're not very reputable, but you probably know that.'

'Are they co-operating?'

'The office here is – or anyway, up to a point.'

'We know Mr Palady, the managing director. That's his form – he co-operates up to a point. But Hong Kong, what about them?'

'They're stonewalling. I fear the money may have gone on further, to another bank in some other part of the world.'

'Manila, for instance?'

There was no reaction. 'We wouldn't know.'

'Who outside your bank knows about the theft?'

Once again Casement hesitated. He obviously was not accustomed to telling any more than he wanted to disclose; Malone could see him as chairman at annual general meetings snubbing questioning shareholders. 'If you must know –'

'We must,' said Malone, patience wearing thin.

'Derek Sweden knows. That's all, as far as I know.'

'Not your wife?'

Casement's neck stiffened. 'Why should she know?'

'I can understand you not telling her about the day-to-day troubles in the bank. But a missing twenty-five million? That's not day-to-day stuff.'

Casement remained stiff-necked for a long moment; then abruptly he nodded. 'All right, she knows. Just the fact, none of the details. The sort of thing I presume you tell your wife about homicides.'

Malone made a pretence of pulling the dagger out of his chest. 'Not quite, Mr Casement. Interest in homicide is morbid, interest in money is not. Now would you come down to Police Centre with us? We want you to identify this girl.'

For a moment it looked as if Casement would refuse to move; then he raised himself awkwardly from his chair. He had suddenly become older, as if he had stepped through a doorway into a climate that had weathered and broken him. 'Jesus,' he said, more to himself than to the two detectives, 'I think I'm getting old.'

'It happens,' said Malone, smug in his early forties, and Clements, on equally firm ground, nodded.

Inside the front door Casement reached for a topcoat and tweed hat, put them on, Clements helping him don the coat.

As they turned towards the door it opened in their faces and Ophelia stood there, key held like a small knife. 'You're going *out*?'

Her husband explained. 'It will only take a little while, darling. Half an hour at the most. Order dinner to be sent up from Verady's.'

'I'm coming with you. I want to see this bitch who tried to kill you.'

'I don't think it would be advisable,' said Malone, though he knew he couldn't stop her.

She took no notice of him, taking instead her husband's arm. 'I let the driver go –' she told her husband; then looked at Malone. 'We've been using a hire car since ours was burnt out. I don't drive.'

'We'll go in the police car,' said Malone. 'It's unmarked, so the neighbours won't notice.'

Casement smiled, blew on a spark of humour. 'You think she cares about the neighbours? She's Roumanian.'

'I love him,' said Ophelia and gave her husband a kiss. 'Now let's go and see this little pyromaniac. Or is there another name for people who set fire to people?'

They drove up through the city, through the drizzle of rain that gave a shine to the lamp-lit darkness. By the time they got to Police Centre, the rain had stopped and been replaced by a cold wind. 'Are police stations cold places?' Ophelia asked as they went up the broad outside steps.

'Only for the guilty,' said Malone. 'We're always very comfortable ourselves.'

Out of the corner of his eye he saw a slight smile from Casement; the old man had taken on some new energy from his wife's presence. They were arm-in-arm and Malone suspected he would be dealing with them as a pair while they were in the station.

The Surrey Hills station was an annexe on the ground floor of Police Centre; like the big building it was only a few years old and not yet soiled by the human waste that went through it each and every night and day. This evening business was in the doldrums, the hour was early, and the sergeant behind the desk gave Malone and Clements all his attention when they walked in with the Casements. A battered housewife, face dark with bruises, sat on a chair in a corner of the charge-room, a small girl, face pale with fear and bewilderment, standing beside her; there were no other customers at the moment. Ophelia looked at the woman and child, then shook her head at Clements but said nothing. The big man was surprised at the troubled look of compassion on the face that, up till now, he had seen only as a beautifully made-up mask.

'G'day, Barry,' said Malone. 'You still got that Viet girl they brought in this afternoon for rolling the drunk, what's her name?'

The sergeant ran a bony finger down a page of the book open in front of him. He was not tall for a policeman and one could see the bones of his shoulders under the dark blue sweater he wore. His face was equally bony, chipped and repaired like an old vase; his nose had been broken three times in brawls with citizens who had later claimed to be law-abiding. 'Kim – you're not gunna believe this – Weetbix. She's downstairs in the cells. You want me to bring her up?'

'I want Mr Casement to identify her in a case we're working on. She's entitled to a line-up, but how long would it take to round up six or seven girls who look something like her? Has she asked for a lawyer yet?'

'She hasn't opened her mouth, except to abuse the policewoman who took her her tea. We're holding her overnight. She's due in magistrate's court tomorrow at ten.'

Some other police had come in from the back offices, two young men and a young woman constable. They looked curiously at the Casements, recognizing them as the sort of visitors not usually seen here in the station; then the policewoman went to the woman seated in the corner. The child cringed away from the woman in uniform and her mother held her close to her.

'We've locked up your husband, Mrs Pockley. Have you got somewhere you can spend the night? I don't think you should go back home, not yet.'

The woman shook her head. 'Nowhere,' she mumbled through swollen lips that didn't hide the teeth that had been broken off. 'How is he?'

'He's passed out,' said the young policewoman. '*He's* not worried, he'll sleep till morning, the bastard.'

'Chris –' said the sergeant warningly.

'Sorry, sarge.' But she obviously wasn't. 'You want the other prisoner brought up here?'

'Take her into the interviewing room.' He looked at Malone. 'You know where it is, Inspector. You can start the tape?'

Malone nodded and led the way out of the charge-room. As they passed the woman and her child, Ophelia stopped. 'Would you be offended if I gave you some money to go to a hotel? A nice place where you can have a comfortable night?'

The battered woman in her bloodstained dress looked up at the beautifully dressed older woman; the contrast, Malone thought, was cruel. Yet Ophelia looked genuinely concerned, she was not putting on a Mother Teresa act to impress anyone. The woman touched her own face. 'I couldn't, not like this. Thanks, but.'

'What will you do?'

The woman shrugged helplessly, shook her head. 'Go home, I suppose.'

Ophelia opened her handbag, took out some money; Malone couldn't see how much it was, but he caught a glimpse of a hundred-dollar note and a fifty. 'Buy yourself a new dress. And something for your little girl.'

Then she followed the three men down the short hallway to the interviewing room. She caught the expression on Malone's face and she read his mind. 'All right, so money may be insulting to her. But what else could one give her? Sympathy? That doesn't salve bruises, Inspector. A new dress may hide some of them. God, you men are brutes! No, not you three. Just men in general. Oh, is this her?'

She turned round as Kim Weetbix was brought into the small room. The young policewoman pushed the girl into a chair, then stood back by the closed door. The room was crowded, but Malone made no complaint; he wanted the Casements out of here as quickly as possible. Clements started up the video tape and Malone said, 'Kim, I take it you've been warned anything you say et cetera . . .'

She looked up at him, her face too impassive to be even sullen; he wondered how a girl as good-looking as this one could have finished up a street-kid. 'I've got nothing to say.'

'Do you recognize this gentleman?'

She flicked a glance at Casement, but said nothing.

Malone said, 'Mr Casement, do you recognize this girl?'

'No,' said Casement calmly, not looking at the two detectives but directly at the girl. 'The girl who attacked me had her face covered.'

'Darling!' Ophelia reared her head back in disbelief. 'It *has* to be her!'

Casement was unmoved. 'I don't recognize her.' Then he looked up at Malone, his gaze steady; he had, it seemed, abruptly regained his strength, had pushed back being old. 'Sorry, Inspector.'

It is not easy for a Celt, when angry, to be impassive; but

Malone was as Orientally blank-faced as Kim. 'Thank you, Mr Casement. That'll be all, then. Thank you for coming.'

Clements made a move to show the Casements out of the room, but Malone shook his head. The young policewoman opened the door and stood aside. It was impossible to catch any expression in Casement's eyes; a trick of light turned the panes of his glasses opaque. But there was fire in Ophelia's eyes, her whole body looked ready to erupt.

'That's all you have to say – thanks for coming? You drag us up here like – like –'

'Like ordinary citizens?' The tongue had slipped its leash again.

'The Minister will hear about this – I'll ring my brother-in-law as soon as we get home –'

'Darling.' Casement took his wife's arm, pushed her out the door. As they disappeared down the hallway, she still loudly complaining, those in the room could hear him saying, 'Darling, let it lie – it'll be better –'

Malone looked at the young policewoman. 'Christine, is it? Chris, don't take that as an example how to handle the public . . .'

'I thought you handled it perfectly, sir. I felt like kicking them both up the bum.'

'They're teaching you that at the Academy? Things never change.' Then he looked at Kim Weetbix. 'Do you want us to kick you up the bum, Kim, or are you going to be sensible and tell us something?'

'Get fucked,' said Kim. 'How's that?'

'It's a start.' Malone sat down, gestured for Clements to start up the video recorder again. 'We're going to make a tape of this interview, Kim. We don't want to ask you anything about the theft charge, that's none of our concern. We just want some information on the briefcase you stole from Mr Casement when you and your boyfriend attacked him.'

'You're wasting your time.' She was utterly relaxed; or looked it.

'Time costs nothing, Kim. We're public servants, it's only taxpayers like you who foot the bill. You pay tax?'

'You're kidding.' But she smiled, almost.

'Who'll bury you when the men who killed your boyfriend catch up with you? The taxpayers? Those fellers are looking for you, Kim. They're looking for the briefcase, too.'

'They've got –' She had become too relaxed; she bit her lip at her slip.

'They've got what? The briefcase?' She remained silent and Malone went on, 'They took it after they'd killed Kelsey, is that it? But you must've opened it, looked to see what was inside? That's all we want to know, Kim. What was in the briefcase?'

Clements came in: 'Kim, according to Mr Casement, it was Kelsey who tried to burn him, not you.'

She was sharp enough to shake her head at that one: 'He said he didn't recognize us.'

'No,' said Clements. 'He said he didn't recognize *you*.'

Malone said, 'He told us that Kelsey was the one who tried to burn him, not the girl. So we're not looking for you on that count.'

'How are your papers, Kim?' said Clements. 'Are you an illegal? Would you like to go back to Vietnam or wherever you came from? We can arrange it, if that's what you want. Have you been in trouble here before? Tell us the truth, Kim. We can always look it up.'

'No, I've never been in trouble.' Only because she had been careful not to be caught; at least up till now. She gave him her honest look: 'And I'm not an illegal.'

'Is Weetbix a Vietnamese name?'

'Only since the war in Vietnam.'

Malone grinned. 'So you're a good citizen?'

Again the half-smile. 'Almost.'

'So tell us what was in the briefcase. Let's say it's a hypothetical case and you had a hypothetical peek inside it. You understand the word hypothetical?' She nodded. 'What did you see, Kim?'

She pondered a while, her long fingers drumming noiselessly on the table in front of her. Then she looked up at him. 'I can't get out of rolling the drunk, can I?'

'You'll be charged, Kim. But you may get off on a bond, as a first offender.' He nodded to Clements, who switched off the video recorder. 'Tell us what was in the briefcase and we'll see what we can do to help you.'

'How?'

'The drunk got his money back, so maybe he can be talked into not laying any charges. The briefcase is more important, Kim.'

She stared at the two detectives, then at last she nodded. 'Okay. We busted the locks on it and had a look inside. There was nothing worth taking, except a gold pen. Kel hung on to that. And there were some papers, business letters and – memorandises?'

'Memorandums. You remember anything from the letters or the memos?'

'There was a letter addressed to some company in Tokyo, Japan. I can't remember the name of the company, Something-or-Other Securities.'

'You're sure? In Tokyo?'

'Sure. The letter was marked Private and Confidential, I remember that. It was on a bank's notepaper.'

'Casement Trust Bank?'

She frowned. 'Yeah, that was it. How'd you guess?'

'We're good at guessing. Can you remember what the letter and memos were about? Can you remember any names in them?'

She shook her head. 'No, they didn't mean anything to me or Kel. All I remember was a figure, money, in one of the letters. Twenty-five million. Kel really went off his head about that. All we got outa the old guy was twenty dollars, two ten-dollar notes, not even a credit card, and here was a letter talking about twenty-five million.'

'What did it say?'

She shrugged. 'I didn't take much notice. Money like that – can you get your mind around it?'

The two men smiled, shook their heads; Malone looked at the young policewoman. 'You, Chris?'

'There's not that much money in the country, is there?'

'If there is, it's all debt . . . Righto, Kim. Is there anything else you can tell us?'

'No.' But there was. There were odd phrases in the bank's letter that floated loose in her mind, that, when she was calmer, she would put together in a pattern. She had no idea what the pattern would be worth, if anything, but you never knew. Never throw anything away, her mother had taught her, especially something you know about other people. Lily, her mother, had been not only a bar-girl but a blackmailer and a police informer. 'No, that's all I know. Will you do what you can for me?'

'Sure,' Malone promised and meant it. 'But I'll want to know where we can find you, Kim. We can't just let you disappear.'

She pondered that, disappointed. 'I want to go back to Saigon.'

'Really?' He didn't believe her. 'Why?'

'It – it'll be safer. And people don't call you names there, like slopehead and worse.'

'From what I hear, they'll call you other things. You're a half-and-half, Kim. Aussies aren't the only racists.'

'Then I'll go to Hong Kong. The rich men like Eurasians, the half-and-halfs.' She was not a romantic, she did not dream; but men, she had learned from her mother, liked to listen to pretty women. 'I'll let you know where I am when I get to Hong Kong.'

Malone grinned, still not believing her. 'You do that, Kim. In the meantime watch out for Kelsey's killers.'

3

Next morning Kim was taken down to Central Court, where, before she could be given a public defender, she was told there was no case against her. The drunk whose money she had attempted to steal did not put in an appearance; unbeknown to Kim and the police, his wife had caught up with him, thumped him, breaking his nose, and taken him and the money back to home and the kids. The case was dropped and Kim walked free.

She came out of the old Victorian courthouse, built like the temple of justice it aspired to be, and stood under one of the plane trees that fronted the building. A few leaves hung on the branches above her like yellow handkerchiefs; fallen leaves had been swept up into heaps ready to be collected. People stood about, swept into groups like the leaves, their faces autumnal with pessimism, as if they expected no joy when they were called into court. Kim looked for Inspector Malone or Sergeant Clements and was disappointed that there was no sign of them; they hadn't, despite their promise, appeared to help her out. A big young man lumbered up the steps from the street and almost ran into the courthouse; it was Detective Constable Andy Graham, but she had never seen him before and did not know that he was Malone's emissary. She stepped out from under the tree, suddenly feeling really *free*, and went down the steps into Liverpool Street.

As she came out of the gates the well-dressed young woman stepped forward. 'Kim? Annie sent me to collect you.'

She was instantly suspicious. 'Annie? Why would she send you? You're Filipino, right?' It was a wild guess. 'What d'you want with me? Get away! I'll yell –'

'Don't do that,' warned Teresita Romero. 'There's a car parked up the street with your friend Annie in it. She's with a friend of mine. If you don't behave, he's likely to hurt her. Let's go and join them, Kim. Be sensible and you'll be okay.'

Kim, afraid, certain she was halfway to being dead but also suddenly afraid for Annie, walked with the young woman up to the white Nissan parked at the kerb. As they approached a man leaned back from the front seat and opened the back door for them, giving Kim a welcoming smile. Teresita pushed Kim in, followed her and slammed the door shut.

'Let's go.'

The driver started up the car and eased it out into the traffic. Kim looked at the woman beside her.

'Where's Annie?'

'I'm an awful liar,' smiled Teresita. 'She's probably at work at that crummy coffee place up the Cross.'

The driver looked over his shoulder at Kim. 'Sorry about this.'

Chapter Thirteen

❖❖❖❖❖❖❖❖❖

1

'I missed her,' said Andy Graham. 'I shouldn't have gone by car. We got held up in the traffic, there's a pile-up in Elizabeth Street, two cars and a bus. Sorry.'

Malone couldn't complain. Despite the State government's and the city council's much publicized efforts at traffic control, for every new rule announced a thousand more cars seemed to be spawned. The Harbour Tunnel had reduced traffic on the Harbour Bridge, only to spew out a gridlock in the inner city. Nobody was going to be denied the use of his car, or what was the point of getting into debt to pay for it? Armageddon would not be a battle but just one last huge traffic jam. Eternity, it seemed, would be history's biggest junkyard.

'Righto, Andy. Keep the ASM on her going, on the coach stations as well as the airports. I don't want her killed, that's all. We couldn't have held her, I just wanted to keep tabs on her. But if she's done a bunk . . .'

'Maybe she hasn't.' Andy Graham hadn't sat down; he never did, unless told to do so. Malone sometimes wondered if the big young detective had been born standing up, bouncing up and down between his mother's legs on his already ungainly big feet. 'I checked if anyone had seen her come out of the court. One of the sheriff's men had. He'd come out for a smoke, he said, and saw her go down the steps to the street – he was looking after her, he said, because she was such a good sort. Some woman, another slopehead he thought, came up to her and said something. The last he saw of them they were walking up Liverpool Street. I must've passed her and didn't recognize her. I hadn't seen her before, you know,' he added defensively.

Malone threw down his pen; he had been making notes before feeding yesterday's report into the computer. 'She could've gone off with anyone. One of the killers, a friend, anyone. . . . Oh, hullo, Mr Junor.'

Clements had appeared behind Andy Graham, escorting Harold Junor from Shahriver International Credit Bank. Graham excused himself and Malone waved Junor to a chair. 'Thanks for coming in.'

'I had very little choice.' Junor looked at Clements, who had seated himself at the corner of Malone's desk; he did not seem to resent the big detective, seemed more resigned. 'I've been left holding the bag, as they say.'

'Mr Palady couldn't come?'

'Mr Palady left this morning, our head office recalled him last night.'

'That was a bit sudden, wasn't it? As I remember it, your head office is in Abadan. Not a healthy place to be recalled to right now, is it?'

'Well, actually, no. He's gone to Hong Kong.'

'To look into this transfer of twenty-five million dollars stolen from Casement Trust?'

Though Junor had spent a good deal of his youth in the front row of a rugby scrum, not an intellectual haunt but a place where your opponents, when not trying to screw your genitals off, tried to mash your brains, he had not lost a talent for quick thinking. He was not fazed by Malone's question; he caught the ball on the full: 'We had nothing to do with the theft, you know. We were merely the conduit, which is what banks are, mostly. I'm surprised you know about it. Casement's have kept it pretty quiet.'

Malone let that pass. 'Are you going to return the money to them?'

'That's why Mr Palady has gone to Hong Kong.'

'Casement's are under the impression that you'd like to hang on to it.'

Junor flushed at that, as if he had been uppercut in the scrum. 'I don't know where they got that impression. Mr Palady and I have talked about it, we've done our best to advise Hong Kong to play it straight and return the money as soon as possible. Head office, I gather, thinks the same way as we do.'

'Has Hong Kong got some sort of autonomy? Is that how your branches work?'

Junor glanced from one detective to the other, grated his teeth together. He was not a born banker, but so few are; the talent has to be bred through generations. He had been recruited because, as a sporting hero in England, he had presented an image of bluff honesty; honesty, even bluff, always looks good in the doorway of any bank, especially one as questionable as Shahriver. He had learned to skirt the truth, if not to be exactly untruthful, but even reputable banks do that; truth is not only the first casualty of war but, too frequently, also of finance. He wanted to lie, but all at once saw the profit in truth.

'What I tell you is just between us?'

'You have no idea how many times we're asked that, Mr Junor. But, righto, go ahead. It's off the record.'

'Well –' He sat back on his chair, took a deep breath. 'Some of our branches have local equity.'

'Here in Sydney?'

'No, we're totally owned by head office. But Hong Kong –' He paused as if wondering if he was pursuing the right course. But he had been left holding the bag and the bag was proving to be heavy. Another deep breath: 'Hong Kong doesn't really bear looking into. Shahriver owns only a third. The other two-thirds are owned by Chinese and Japanese interests.'

'Triads and *yakuza*?'

Caution fell on his face like a visor, as if he had abruptly realized he might be talking dangerously; he frowned, peering at Malone and Clements suspiciously. 'Well, no, I didn't say that. Do you mean you know something?'

Malone went off at an angle: 'When you were last in here,

Mr Junor, you told us that Rob Sweden had never transferred any money overseas, that he was a pretty small depositor by your standards. But he was the feller who transferred the twenty-five million.'

'We didn't know that, then. The money didn't pass through us, it went direct to Hong Kong and his name wouldn't have been on the transfer. We only learned of it two days ago, when Casement's started leaning on us out here.'

'We know the money's gone to one of Mr Kornsey's companies. Has Mrs Kornsey been in touch with you?'

'Well, yes. Not her exactly – her solicitor. She's claiming everything in his name in our accounts.'

'Including the twenty-five million?'

'I don't think she knows of that.'

'Are you going to tell her?'

Junor looked surprised at the question. 'Do you want me to?'

'I don't really care,' said Malone. 'I care when someone is done out of a thousand bucks or ten thousand, especially when it means something to them. But twenty-five million?' He shook his head. 'That's not money, Mr Junor, not the way I understand it. That's just figures.'

There was a sudden silence, broken only by voices in the outer room and the ringing of a phone. Junor looked from one man to the other. He looked less flushed now, less worried. 'So is there anything more?'

'I don't think so, unless Mr Palady comes back with the money.'

'Or,' said Clements, who had been taking the occasional note, 'unless someone from here in Sydney starts applying pressure on you.'

Junor frowned. 'Such as?'

'Oh, half a dozen people. Casement, Mrs Kornsey, your other clients Belgarda and Tajiri, Rob Sweden's father . . . We've got enough candidates lined up. If they do call on you, Mr Junor, let us know. We don't want to be called in on your homicide. Come on, I'll show you out.'

'Thanks for coming,' said Malone.

Junor, on his feet, squeezed out a wry smile. 'You've made my day, old chap.'

When Clements came back, Malone said, 'I think we should pay Mrs Kornsey another visit. She's shoving her neck out too far too soon.'

They drove out to Lugarno through a crisp day, the rain gone, the air positively shining under the slight wind coming up from the south-west. This autumn was proving variable, almost mocking.

The silver Mercedes was standing in the driveway and as soon as he saw it Malone had one of those moments when one's forgetfulness, incompetence, stupidity, call it what you will, hits one right between the eyes. 'Bugger!'

Clements drew the unmarked police car into the kerb. 'What's bitten you now?'

'When Kornsey went missing, did anyone ask Mrs Kornsey how he left home? Why didn't he go wherever he was going in that Merc. or in his wife's car?'

Clements shrugged. 'I can't tell you. There may have been something about it in the Missing Persons report, but I dunno. *You* were the one who talked to her.'

Malone, getting out of the car, looked back over his shoulder. 'Are you accusing me of being slipshod?'

'Looks like it.' Clements got out, looked at Malone across the roof of the car. He could be irritatingly urbane at times, even though it was just a front. 'It happens to all of us.'

They walked up the path to the front door. All the blooms had fallen from the tibouchina tree and had been swept up into a tapering heap that made them look like one huge bloom. The Welcome mat had disappeared from the front step; it had been replaced by a new coir mat with no message at all on it.

Mrs Kornsey came to the door, peered short-sightedly at them through the screen of the security door. Then she put on the blue-framed glasses. 'Oh it's you!' Her voice was like the mat on which Malone stood, blank of welcome. 'Not more bad news, I hope?'

'No. May we come in?'

She seemed to remember her manners; all at once she was flustered. 'Of course! What's the matter with me?' She opened the security door, ushered them into the house, led them through to the sun-room. 'I've been – what's the word? – inundated with visitors since . . . A death brings you together, doesn't it?' She didn't say whom it had brought together. 'Would you like some coffee? Come into the kitchen, I feel better there. It's the only room in the house where I can keep myself busy. I've made so much bloody jam, biscuits . . . '

Malone and Clements settled themselves on stools at the breakfast bar. At one end of the bar there were at least two dozen jars of marmalade, all of them topped with fancy cloth covers. Mrs Kornsey busied herself putting on a percolator and setting out cups. She seemed thinner than Malone remembered her, but her hair was newly done, her sweater and skirt were more than just around-the-house gear and she was wearing costume jewelry, earrings and a bracelet. She would hold herself together from the outside in.

'Have you had any calls, Mrs Bassano?'

She gave Malone a chiding look. 'Mrs *Kornsey*.'

'You know what I mean. From the man who called you, said he was sorry about what happened to Vince.'

'Terry,' she corrected automatically; it was as if she were protecting her own identity. 'No, nobody's called. Why would they?'

'We understand you're enquiring into your husband's estate?'

'Bikkies? They're an American recipe, I make 'em myself.' She put a plate of coconut biscuits in front of them. 'Have you been stickybeaking into my affairs? You've got a hide!'

'We learned of it by accident. We don't like stickybeaking, we both *hate* it, in fact, but too often we have to do it. We only find killers by – well, stickybeaking. Did anyone suggest you try to trace Terry's estate?'

She looked at both men over her coffee cup, the hard look

of a woman who had been hard done by by men. 'Are you trying to make trouble for me?'

'We're here to help you,' said Clements. 'Nice cookies. I have another?'

'Help yourself. How do you mean – help me?'

'We still haven't found the killers,' said Malone. 'We don't want them coming here, paying you a visit. Has your solicitor told you how much is in the estate?'

'Not exactly, he's still trying to add it all up. He's found another bank that Terry had money in, Shahriver International.'

'What's your solicitor's name?'

'Fairbanks, Douglas Fairbanks.'

'Senior or Junior?' Clements, choking on a biscuit, barely got out the question.

She smiled, the first time since they had entered the house. 'I know, it sounds like a joke, but it's his real name. He's just not – dashing? He's as dull as dishwater. He was Terry's solicitor, though I didn't know it till he got in touch with me. His offices are up in Hurstville, next door to the Treasury bank. The only bank I thought Terry had,' she added and for a moment there was a sour, almost spiteful note in her voice. 'More coffee?'

'Terry never discussed his affairs with you at all? Gave you a hint of where his money was?'

'Never. I suppose I was stupid not to ask, but I just – well, I just trusted him, the way you do with someone you love. Or do only women do that?' But she didn't wait for either of the men to answer and she went on, 'He used to get the *Financial Review* every morning, but he said it was just a hobby with him, following the stock exchange.'

'He never mentioned the futures exchange?' said Clements, on his third biscuit.

She frowned. 'Funny you should say that. Only a coupla weeks ago he said something like, There's a future in futures. I thought it was just one of those, you know, smarty remarks you men make to dumb women.'

'You're not dumb, Mrs Kornsey.' Malone got up and looked out through the bars that protected the wide kitchen window. 'I notice that every window I've seen in the house has bars on it. Inside there, there's a sliding security grille across the sun-room's doors. Did Terry ever explain to you why all that security was necessary?'

'He was paranoid about people breaking in. Not for himself, he said, but for me. Whenever someone broke into a house and raped a woman or killed her, he'd throw the newspaper at me and say, See?'

'When were the bars put on, and the grille?'

'I dunno. Three months ago, maybe more.'

'Up till then he hadn't been worried?'

'Well, no. But the last twelve months there's been a lot of rape and murder of housewives. *You'd* know that.'

Malone nodded, still looking out the window. 'Your land runs right down to the river?'

'Yes, we have a jetty down there and a small runabout. Terry'd sometimes go out fishing.'

Some trees fringed the rear of the garden beyond the pool. Someone could come up from the river without being seen from the house. 'Are you still living here alone? No friend or relative has come to stay with you?'

'My niece wanted to, but I said no. I'm all right, aren't I? I mean I'm safe enough, right?' She took off her glasses. 'I am, aren't I?'

'Mrs Kornsey,' he said gently, 'I think it'd be an idea if you went and stayed with someone. Just till this is over, till we get Terry's killer. It's a precaution, that's all.'

She thought about it, then nodded. 'Okay, I'll go to my sister's. In the morning.'

'Why not tonight? Now?'

'She talked to me this morning, she called me. Her and her husband have had a donnybrook, they aren't speaking – it gets a bit tense over there sometimes. I don't wanna walk into her house with things like that between 'em. I'll ring and ask if I can come tomorrow and that'll give 'em time to patch things up.'

Other people, other wars: they went on all the time. Malone nodded. 'Righto. In the meantime get your niece over here to stay the night.'

She lifted her head to peer up at him. 'Jesus, you sound just like Terry! Is someone really gunna try and hurt me? For what? For just being married to him?'

'At the moment, Mrs Kornsey, we don't know why they killed him. We don't think it was the Mafia, after all. It was someone else, we're not sure who. Until we find out, Sergeant Clements and I would feel better if we knew you were safe. We can get you police protection –'

'No!' Her hand knocked her cup, spilling some coffee. 'No, I won't have that, not if I'm gunna stay with Carmel. Joe, her husband, would go off the deep end – he can't stand cops, he's always saying . . . Sorry, I don't mean you. No, no police protection . . . ' She was wiping up the spilled coffee with a Wettex. 'I'm coming to the conclusion that I didn't know Terry at all. Conclusion. He used to say, a joke, that a woman never came to a firm conclusion till she died. I used to throw this at him.' She held up the Wettex.

Malone wondered how Lisa would have reacted to Kornsey's piece of male chauvinism; but Leanne Kornsey had uttered it without any apparent resentment.

He tried for one last time to pierce this woman's total acceptance of her husband: 'Mrs Kornsey, didn't you ever query *anything* about your husband's past life?'

She took her time, not wanting to open up too much of herself: Malone had seen the same self-protection countless times, not always with women. 'I sometimes wondered if there'd been another wife before me. But I – I didn't wanna know, you know what I mean? Well, no, mebbe you don't. I – I've never had much luck with men, not before Terry. I was married once – it was a disaster, I try not to think about it. Then there were a coupla others . . . Then Terry came along. A woman gets to my age, she doesn't query her luck, right? D'you gamble? I do. Not big, I just play the poker machines down at the club. When you hit the jackpot on the pokies, you don't question your luck. It was the same with Terry, he was my jackpot. He was kind and loving and – *permanent*. Or so I thought.'

'When your husband left the house, the day he disappeared, how did he go?'

She paused on her way to the sink to wash out the Wettex. 'How d'you mean?'

'The day I came here to tell you we'd found his – his body, his Mercedes was in the garage. So was your Honda. So how did he leave? Did you see him go?'

'He took the dog out for a walk. It's something, isn't it, when the last words your husband says to you is, I'm taking the dog for a walk.'

'Did the dog come back?'

She shook her head. 'They probably killed it, too. He was a gentle dog, a real sook, he wouldn't have attacked anyone. We had all the windows barred and the security doors and a dog that would've slobbered all over anyone who tried to break in.' She was melting the irony; which was preferable to seeing her weep. 'You sure you don't want more coffee?'

'It's time we went. Get your niece over here as soon as you can. If anyone calls you, or comes to the door, someone you don't know . . . '

'You've already warned me. I still can't believe this has happened –' She had put her glasses back on, but now she took them off again; Malone saw the beginning of tears. 'I'll be careful.'

'And, Mrs Kornsey –' He didn't want to mention the twenty-five million; but: 'Tell your solicitor to go easy for a while. If there's anything coming to you out of your husband's estate, you'll get it eventually.'

'I'm not hungry for it,' she said defensively.

He wondered how hungry she would be if she knew of the twenty-five million; but that was judging her by the standards of too many others in this case. 'Take care,' he said, and he and Clements were ready to leave.

'Do you like marmalade?' She gave them each a jar. 'It was

236

Terry's favourite, said he'd never tasted a decent jam all the time he'd lived in America.'

Driving away, Clements said, 'You think they'll try to get to her?'

'I don't know. Let's go and see Douglas Fairbanks. I should've brought my autograph book.'

'You think your kids would know who Douglas Fairbanks was? Even Junior? They wouldn't know who Clark Gable was.'

'You've got him on your mind since that estate agent said you looked like him. You going to grow a moustache?'

It was the sort of prattle that helped them unwind; they had both been tense while they were with Leanne Kornsey, not wanting her to break up on them. Prattle does more than fill empty air.

The main street of Hurstville was chock-a-block with parked cars. Clements pulled into a No Parking zone and a parking warden appeared out of nowhere like a grey genie. 'Not there, mate. Move it.'

'Police.'

'Okay,' said the warden, a huge Fijian who looked as if he could have picked up the Commodore and carted it away under his arm. 'But it sets a bad example.'

'You sound just like my mother.'

The two detectives went into the building next to the Treasury bank, where Malone had visited last week, went up a flight of stairs and into the offices of Douglas Fairbanks, Solicitor. A grey-haired woman, old enough to have been a fan of Fairbanks Junior, took them into an inner office.

Fairbanks, as Leanne Kornsey had said, was as dull as dishwater. There was nothing about him that suggested he might leap over his desk to greet them, that he might even leap over a flooded gutter. In the latter case he would take off his shoes and socks, roll up his trousers and wade through the water, mentally composing a stern letter to the local council. He was in his fifties, with wispy grey hair, of stout build and a bland face that looked as if it had never known excitement, not even in love-making. His voice was thin and reedy, a silent film star's voice.

Malone explained the reason for their visit. 'How did you know where to look for Mr Kornsey's estate?'

'He left a will.' Fairbanks' elbows rested on the arms of his chair, his long but plump fingers locked together.

'May we see it?'

'You know better than that, Inspector. It's in probate.'

'Is everything left to the widow?'

The solicitor hesitated, then nodded. 'Yes.'

'Are Sue City Investments and Hannibal Development mentioned in the will?' said Clements, who had a better memory for such details than Malone.

'Yes.'

'Mr Fairbanks,' said Malone, 'we respect client confidentiality, but your client is dead and we're trying to find out who killed him.'

'My client is now Mrs Kornsey.'

'You're getting to be a pain in the arse –' said Clements.

'It's a lawyer's talent.' There was no smile, not even a twist of the lips, so there was no way of knowing if Fairbanks had any sense of humour.

'We're also trying to prevent Mrs Kornsey from being killed,' said Malone.

That stiffened the locked fingers. 'H'm. That makes a difference, doesn't it?'

'Especially if they come bounding up those stairs outside, like the villains in your grandfather's movies,' said Clements.

Even then Fairbanks didn't smile. 'Those sort of jokes are a *real* pain in the arse.'

'Righto, let's say we're even-Stephen on who's a pain.' Malone was losing patience, as he often did with lawyers. 'Let's agree it'll be no joke if Mrs Kornsey goes the same way as her husband. And it's likely to happen if you start scratching around too deeply into where Mr Kornsey's money is stashed away. How well did you know him?'

The lawyer unlocked his fingers. 'Hardly at all. I saw him

only twice, to my recollection. He played everything close to his chest, he reminded me of those gangsters you see in American films.'

'He was one,' said Malone.

'Oh. Are you going to tell me more? No? All right, then. He came in and asked me to make out a will, just a few lines leaving everything to his wife. Then he came back a week later and signed it. He left a sealed envelope with me, said it was a list of everything he owned, but I wasn't to open it till his death.'

'When was this?'

'A month ago. The next I heard of him was the report the other day in the newspapers of his death. I gave his widow time to get over the shock, then I got in touch with her.'

'Is she on your back to get everything cleared up in a hurry?'

'No. But I have the feeling she will ask me to account for every penny. She's a lady who likes everything neat and tidy. Well ordered.'

Except for the huge hole in her life. 'Let's keep it neat and tidy. Ease off till we clear up the murder. Otherwise you might be risking her life.'

One of the plump fingers scratched the plum nose. 'Am I likely to be receiving a visit from whoever killed Mr Kornsey?'

'Probably not. But like I said, don't scratch too deep.'

On their way down to the street Clements said, 'He doesn't know about the twenty-five million.'

When they got out to their car the traffic warden was writing out a ticket for a car parked in front of the Commodore. 'You see? I told you you were setting a bad example.' He gave them a huge smile, a metre of teeth. 'You make good bait. This woman fell for it.'

'How do you know this is a woman's car?'

'It's parked a short walk from the kerb.'

Another huge smile. Male chauvinism knew no national boundaries.

Malone was having dinner, steak-and-kidney pie with two veg, a glass of Hunter red and with poached pears to follow, when the phone rang. He looked at his three children. 'If that's for any of you, hang up. We're going to finish dinner together and in peace.'

'I'll get it.' Maureen went out to the kitchen. She had a few moments' conversation with someone on the other end of the line, then she came back into the dining room. 'It's Uncle Russ. I asked him when he and Romy are getting married.'

'Why don't you mind your business?' Malone pushed back his chair.

'It *is* our business.'

Malone went out to the kitchen, picked up the phone. 'I'm in the middle of dinner. This had better be important.'

'They've found the Viet girl, Kim Weetbix. Killed the same way as Rob Sweden, the puncture in the back of the neck.'

'Where did they find her?'

'She was dumped on Mrs Kornsey's front doormat.'

Jack Aldwych had brought Emily Karp to dinner in the Gold Room at the Hotel Congress. The waiters were too young to know who he was or had been. The maitre d', if he knew, didn't care: business had been so bad all this year that even Pol Pot would have been welcome, with or without his American Express card. Emily, beautiful and elegant in black silk, did the unexpected: she didn't order the most expensive items on the expensive menu nor did she ask for French champagne. 'Just a glass of the house white.'

Aldwych smiled, pleased with her. 'Give the lady the best white you have. Australian.'

'Sir, we have splendid French whites. Perhaps a Montrachet?'

'Australian,' said Aldwych and gave him his killer's look. The maitre d' went away, his blood turned to mineral water, and Aldwych smiled again at Emily. 'There are two kinds of conmen who never get locked up, head waiters and fashion designers.'

'I was a fashion designer, once. Till I married.'

'I know. I got Juliet to tell me all about you.'

'You think I'm a conwoman? Or was one?'

'Not now. You would've been when you were a designer. I read it somewhere, fashion is for sheep who like a conman as their shepherd.'

'*Vogue* would put out a contract on you if they heard you say that. Were you ever a conman?'

The young waiter, bringing fish-knives, managed not to drop his eyeballs on the table. Aldwych waited till he had gone: 'You don't mind being with an old crim?'

'I might, if you hadn't told me you'd retired.'

'No, I was never a conman. I didn't have that sorta brain. Early in the piece I was a bash artist, what you'd call a thug. I was pretty nasty.' He had a certain honesty about his youth that some of the elderly manage to carry without embarrassment. 'Then I graduated, I learned to leave the rough stuff to others. I became a general, I planned things. I could of run the Gulf war if they'd asked me,' he said with self-mocking conceit. 'Being a successful crim is all strategy and tactics, that's all, just like running a war.'

'Maybe you'd be better than the police at solving the murder of Ophelia's stepson.'

'Maybe. But I dunno if it's any of my business, not any more. Once I made sure my son Jack wasn't gunna be dragged into it . . . ' The maitre d' had not come back, but had sent the wine waiter, who held out a bottle for Aldwych's inspection. 'I wouldn't know one label from another, son. But if it's no good . . . '

The wine waiter got the message, but, given to waiter's hyperbole, made the wrong recommendation. 'I'd stake my life on this one, sir –'

241

Aldwych smiled, winked at Emily. 'I'd already done that for you, son.'

After the waiter, with shaking hand, had poured their wine and gone away, Aldwych said, 'Do you mind me playing the old terror like that?'

'Just so long as you don't overdo it.'

She was enjoying his company; but then almost any company was enjoyable. She had lost her husband five years ago, her only son ten years ago; she had loved them both with perhaps too much love; their deaths had left a hollowness in her. She had been left with very little money and it had been too late for her to go back into fashion; tastes had changed, which they do every year in fashion, and she would have had to gallop to have caught up. Women in their fifties never look attractive galloping; she had settled for a slow walk, which attracts more invitations from men than a quick trot. She never took expensive gifts from men; she was promiscuous but honest and selective. She lived frugally at home, but no one ever got rich by economizing. So she was an always available dinner companion, even if people talked about her. She reasoned they would have talked about her if she had remained at home in the lonely flat and she preferred gossip to pity. She was, as she said, a lady but only just.

'Do you think the police will solve the murder?'

Aldwych toyed with his smoked salmon. The Gold Room was a hangover from the boom years of the Eighties, when extravagance had been mistaken for a virtue, when designers thought they had been let loose in Byzantium. The crystal was gold-rimmed, the plate gold-patterned: the smoked salmon was spread on a gold grid. 'Eventually they will. The man in charge is one of the best, Inspector Malone. He won't give up. Did you know young Rob?'

'Yes, I knew him. I couldn't stand him, though he was always charming to me. But he wanted to go to bed with every woman he met.'

'Including you?'

'No, I was just out of his age group. But he didn't mind a

242

middle-aged woman, so long as she wasn't sagging in the wrong places.'

'Like the Bruna sisters?'

She looked at him above her gold-rimmed soup spoon. 'You don't miss much, do you?'

'Are you saying he went to bed with them? All of them?'

'Not with your daughter-in-law.' She had suddenly recognized that in certain things he was strait-laced; under the criminal was a Methodist struggling to get out. She was not a good liar, but she managed to convince him: 'No, not Juliet. Nor Rosalind, I'd say, though I'm not sure. But Ophelia . . . '

'Why her?'

'Jack, what do you know about women?'

He grinned, not afraid to be honest with this woman. 'Not much. You never learn much from hookers, not unless you're their pimp. I ran a string of brothels, but I never thought of myself as their pimp. I was the managing director.'

Roland, her husband, would never believe this conversation if he were alive and she could tell him; Roland had been a senior executive with a trustee company, handling trusts for old ladies who, if they knew anything at all about brothels, believed they were women's co-operatives. Pimps were girls who had told tales on them in school. Roland had not been as innocent as the old ladies, but he had been a sweet gentle man who looked for the best in everyone. Since his death she had been out with and into bed with crooked politicians, crooked lawyers, crooked bankers; but none of them had been killers or run brothels. She had to treat Jack Aldwych differently from all the others.

'Ophelia thinks the world is her oyster. She would never miss an opportunity, no matter what the opportunity was. Cormac is an old man . . . Are you offended at me saying that?'

'Emily, I *am* old. Why should I be offended?'

'Male vanity.'

'I'm not gunna put the hard word on you, love. I'm too old for that, so if you had your hopes up – Did you?' He smiled,

243

enjoying her almost as much as if making love to her. 'I wouldn't wanna die on top of a woman. We had that politician of ours who did –'

She nodded. 'I know the lady in question. It was a nightmare for her.'

'I won't ask who she was. There was an ex-governor in the States, too, you would of read about him. That must of been funny. The woman in that case, she called his minders and they went rushing to his place. He was naked and they tried to put his clothes back on before they called the ambulance. But they couldn't get his shoes on – Did you know it's almost impossible to put shoes on a dead man? It's got something to do with the way the bones of the foot set. There's a moral there. Over a certain age a man should always make love with his shoes on, just in case . . . I wanna die with dignity. Some men think it'd be a wonderful way to go, while making love.' He shook his big head. 'Not me. I think it'd be the most undignified way to go.'

'It wouldn't be very dignified for the woman, either,' she said and they both laughed. 'How'd we get into this conversation?'

'You were telling me about Ophelia. And Cormac.'

'He's too old for her, he couldn't keep up with her. Not in bed.'

He waited till the waiter had put their main courses in front of them, rack of lamb for her and fish for him. 'You're full up tonight?' He had looked around the suddenly crowded dining room.

'Yes, sir,' said the waiter. 'It's a change. There's an international bankers' convention. Mint sauce, *madame*?'

When the waiter had gone, Aldwych said, 'How do you know what goes on in their bedroom?'

'Ophelia can't help boasting. Not directly, she doesn't exactly come out and tell you what she's done. But another woman can tell. She's had half a dozen lovers since she married Cormac. I'll bet Rob was one of them.'

'Are you saying she might have had a hand in killing the

young bastard?' He asked the question as casually as he might have asked her if she was liking her lamb.

She was shocked at how she had let the conversation run away with her. Because he was an old criminal, must they talk of things criminal? But then the businessmen she had gone to dinner with had talked business, the horse trainer had talked horses. 'No. I wouldn't accuse anyone of murder unless I actually saw them do it.'

'That's always a dangerous thing, seeing someone commit murder.' The ocean trout was over-cooked, but he wouldn't embarrass her by sending it back. Shirl wouldn't have let him. 'If ever you see a murder, turn your back and walk away.'

You couldn't ask for anyone better than he to give that sort of advice; but she didn't say that. He went on: 'She didn't kill him, it was a professional job. Unless she paid to have it done.'

She felt a mixture of queasiness and excitement; the rack of lamb was under-cooked, she could see blood. 'We shouldn't be talking about a friend like this –'

'She's no friend of mine. But I like Cormac – I'd hate to see him mixed up in anything as dirty as murder.'

'He was almost killed himself.'

'A rich man's risk.'

'Did you only rob the rich?'

'What's the point in robbing the poor? Like the Bible says, the poor are always with us. But they're bloody useless if you're trying to make a living.' He was a reactionary, the only sensible stance for a professional criminal. He had no time for the welfare state; it only encouraged bludgers. Socialism bred its own crims, members of the ruling clique; there was no place for outsiders; he was amused when he read that the only successes in the old Soviet Union, now that socialism was dead, were the Russian Mafia. 'Cormac copped it because he advertised he was rich.'

'No, Jack, he's always been discreet about how much he is worth.'

'That was before he married Ophelia. Jack Junior told me about him. He never had a private jet, he didn't own a string

245

of polo ponies, he didn't let the world know when he bought a valuable painting. He had a yacht, I think, but Jack tells me he was only part-owner of that. Then Ophelia comes along and next thing they've got that penthouse in The Wharf and a new place in the country and the Bentley . . . I dunno what he thought of it all, he'd be too conservative to tell you anyway, but Ophelia made sure of the advertising. Muggers like those kids who tried to burn him, they go by appearances. He *looked* rich, so they did him.'

She looked around the dining room, now full. 'You look like a rich man. Aren't you afraid the muggers might – *do* you? Or do they all know who you are and they wouldn't dare?'

'Today's muggers and street kids wouldn't know me from Ned Kelly. I was before their time. I take my chances, like everyone else. There's gunna be more and more muggers, the world's going to the dogs. History repeats itself – I read that. The only difference now is you got muggers and hookers out in the suburbs. It wasn't like that in my day.'

Then they got off mugging and murders and crime in general; the subject bored him after a while. But Ophelia Casement stayed in a corner of his mind, suddenly a suspect. It shocked him that he was thinking in terms of justice, like a policeman.

He paid the bill with cash, as he always did; credit cards were like fingerprints. He left no tip, which would have upset Shirl; he hadn't liked the condescension of the waiters, which Shirl would have counteracted by over-tipping. As he and Emily walked out of the dining room several diners turned to look after them. Like a true male chauvinist he was all at once immensely proud of the beautiful woman he was escorting; he saw her through the eyes of the men staring at them, not through those of the women. Some of the latter, recognizing Emily from the Sunday social pages, marvelled at how she carried her age. None of them, men or women, recognized Aldwych. His minders had always smashed the cameras of anyone who tried to take photos of him. Photos of him *had* appeared in the newspapers, but he had always been walking away from the camera.

246

As they waited outside the lobby of the hotel for their hire car, another hire car, a stretch limousine, drew into the kerb. Aldwych glanced at it, wondering why anyone would want to ride in anything so conspicuous. He grinned at Emily. 'Would you have come out with me if I'd called for you in that battleship?'

Then three men, all Japanese, came out of the hotel lobby, down the steps and into the car. Two of them were middle-aged; the third was the young Japanese who had abducted him. They got into the limousine, disappearing behind its dark windows and the long car drew out of the driveway and into the street. But not before Aldwych had noted its number; he took out a small notebook and biro and wrote it down. Then he was aware of Emily looking hard at him.

'Do you often do that? Take down a car's registration?'

He smiled. 'It's a hobby, like train-watching. Here's our car.'

'Have you got *its* number?'

His smile broadened. He knew now that if he had met Emily twenty years ago he would have been unfaithful to Shirl. The thought hurt him, so that the smile was more a grimace.

4

This late in the evening the morgue was deserted, at least of the living. Malone walked down the long main room towards the murder room, past the stainless steel tables now washed clean of the blood and tissue of the day. Insect-killers hung from the ceiling like blue honeycomb and on one wall a row of white rubber aprons were draped like corpses that had been gutted. The air reeked of death, disguised as disinfectant.

Romy Keller and Clements were in the murder room with the body of Kim Weetbix. It lay on a stainless steel table under the bright light of a green-domed lamp. Face down, arms by her side, Kim looked much thinner than she had in life.

'I haven't touched her yet.' Romy, in a white coat but with no rubber apron, blew a kiss to Malone across the corpse. 'I'm waiting on the HIV or hepatitis test. I don't think it matters – the autopsy, I mean. She was killed the same way as Mr Sweden and Mr Kornsey.'

She lifted the short hair on the girl's neck and Malone saw the small wound. 'Who found her, Russ? Mrs Kornsey?'

'She came back to the house, she'd been to pick up her niece, and there was this girl on her doorstep. Just dumped there on the mat. She's hysterical, Mrs Kornsey, so the local D's said. I didn't go out to see her –'

'Leave her, her family will look after her. Why'd the buggers do this to her? Is it some sort of warning?'

'I'd say so. Telling her to lay off, not try for the twenty-five million.'

Romy had been listening to this without comment, but now she whistled softly. 'Twenty-five *million*? This girl was mixed up in something as big as that? I thought she was supposed to be a street-kid?'

'She was. If she knew anything about the money we're talking about, it was by accident. Maybe whoever killed her thought she knew more than she did.'

'She'd been tortured. There are burns, they look like cigarette marks, on her breasts. And there are bruises on her arms – she'd been pretty heavily handled.'

Malone leaned with his back against the wall looking at the thin pitiful body; it looked more yellow than white, as if her mother was asserting herself. He knew nothing of the girl's background, but he guessed it had been neither happy nor promising. But she had not deserved to finish up, tortured and dead, on this table in this pitiless room. 'I don't suppose there'll be anyone to claim the body for the burial?'

Clements shrugged. 'Who? Some street-kid?'

'Do you expect to find anything, Romy, when you do the autopsy?'

'Not really. All that'll help you is what you see there.'

'Anything in her clothes?'

'I've got the PE guys on that,' said Clements. 'Fibres, dirt, anything. But I don't think we're gunna come up with anything

248

that'll help. There was nothing in her pockets, not even a handkerchief.'

Malone heaved himself off the wall. He could feel the weight of these cases building up; he was an unwilling weightlifter as the kilos were added to the bar. 'We'd better mount security on Mrs Kornsey, we don't want her finishing up in here.'

Romy was attaching a label to one of Kim's big toes. 'I'll park her in the body room till morning.'

'And let's hope nobody comes trying to steal her,' said Clements.

Romy pushed the wheeled table out of the murder room and down the long main room. She looked back as the men followed her. 'Has Russ told you we're being married in July?'

Malone waited for the corpse to roll over and sit up. 'No. When did you decide that?'

'While we were waiting for you back there.' She jerked her head back towards the murder room. 'We want you to be the best man and Lisa matron of honour and the girls to be our bridesmaids.'

They had reached the door to the body room. She unlocked it, pushed the table ahead of her and the three of them went into the chilled room. 'Will you?' She gestured for the men to help her move the body on to one of the shelves. 'I'll talk to Lisa later.'

'Why couldn't you have talked to me later?' Kim was a cold dead weight on Malone's hands. 'Where are you holding the reception? In here?'

'Droll.' Then she looked at the two men. 'Sorry. Have I upset you too, *liebchen*?'

Clements grinned. 'Wait'll I tell my mum. She proposed to my dad while he was castrating a sheep.'

In the Police Minister's office the possibility of political murder, which is merely a misdemeanour and not a felony, was being canvassed.

'Derek, listen to me,' said Hans Vanderberg. 'I'm doing the decent thing, I'm offering you an honourable way out. That doesn't happen often in politics, does it?'

'Hans, you're holding a gun at my head and you're doing the decent thing? Come off it, cut out the crap.'

The Dutchman was unoffended; insults, blunt talk, were his conversational forte. He could be annoyed if an opponent impugned his dishonesty, but that was only because it spoiled the political game. Idealists, sticklers for the truth, were the bane of his life.

'You can resign, like I said, you can say your son's death has been too much for you. Who's gunna be wise? You've been in parliament long enough, you've gotta be getting how much superannuation? Not to mention what we've been talking about.'

'You've already mentioned that. Twice. Where did you get your information?'

The old man smoothed down his quiff. 'Derek, where does anyone in our game get their information? The walls don't only have ears, they've got lips, too. Don't you hear the whispers? I've got friends, you got enemies. And vice versa. A friend of mine and an enemy of yours told me about your insider trading. Four million dollars, that's better than the going rate to buy one of us.'

'You mean a Labor man?'

The Dutchman smiled, a horrible sight. 'I mean any politician, meaning you government fellers. Us on the Labor side can't be bought, you know that. I've never taken a penny.'

Which, unfortunately, was true. Sweden knew that many things could be charged against the Opposition Leader, but a charge of taking a bribe would never stick. 'You could never prove anything, Hans.'

'Who needs proof? You throw a little mud, someone picks it up and adds to it, pretty soon you've got a mud-bath and you're in it up to your neck.'

He sat back, sipped the mineral water that he had asked for, looked around the Minister's office. When his party had been in government and he had been Police Minister as well as Premier, he had operated out of the Premier's office downtown. Once back in power he would give this room back to the police administration; it would be a good public relations ploy. He must be getting old: there had been a time when he had scoffed at the idea of public relations. But that had been in the good old days before the rise of pressure groups and that double-headed, brainless monster, the swinging voter.

Sweden, for his part, saw nothing of the room but only this vindictive, unscrupulous old man opposite him. Well, maybe not unscrupulous: what he was suggesting was legitimate politics. It was, of course, murder: resign or I'll cut your throat. But Sweden had read enough history to know that when it came to a question of power, the voting booth was only a prop in the drama. In his own party throats had been cut and backs stabbed; he himself bore previous scars. But he did not want to be murdered now, not now.

'Hans, if I resigned, you fellers couldn't win my seat. It's been ours for years.'

'Oh, we can win it all right. We'll get an Independent to run, they come in useful sometimes –' He had the party politician's contempt for any Independent running for office, all they did was clutter up the place and most of them, as he had been heard to say, didn't know their arse from their green thumb. 'He'll take enough votes away from you fellers and we'll sneak in. We've done our sums, mate. We win your seat, then we're all square in the Assembly and we'll demand an election. Then we'll gallop in.'

Sweden took his time; after all, one doesn't go bungy-jumping without making sure the rubber rope will stand the strain. 'Hans, I'm not going to resign. Try your luck, throw your mud. But if I resigned now, it wouldn't say much for me

251

as Police Minister nor for my faith in the police. I want my son's murder solved and I'd cut my throat before I'd let you announce it as Police Minister.'

Vanderberg shrugged, put his glass down on the desk. 'Have it your way. I see your point, I'm a father m'self. But you blokes are buggering up this State and it's my duty to see you don't bugger it up even more.'

'Bullshit, Hans. Your only idea of duty is what you pay on a bottle of Bols gin when you bring it into the country.'

'Maybe.' The old man grinned again. 'But it sounds good, doesn't it? Have a second think, Derek, I'll give you another day or two. There's nothing personal in this, y'know. You were just the easiest target. You haven't done a bad job as Minister, the little time you've been in it.' Then he stopped, his grin widening till it looked as if his jaw might fall off. 'There's an alternative. You could resign from your crowd, cross the floor and become one of ours. We're all birds of a birdcage these days, the voters dunno the difference between us, not since we got rid of our Loony Left. Have a think about it. Give my regards to your wife.' He was at the door when he turned back. 'Incidentally, if the police solve the murder and it's close to home, what're you gunna do? Maybe you'll have to resign after all.'

Then he was gone, the door shut behind him. Sweden went limp in his chair, his hand reaching automatically for the button on his desk. But then he remembered that all his staff, including Tucker, had gone. Vanderberg had waited till he was sure there would be no interruptions. Sweden was alone with his pictures of himself and Rosalind in the Dunhill frames on his desk and on the bookcases behind him. He closed his eyes and, to his surprise, saw his first wife, Rob's mother, on the darkness of his lids. He suddenly wished she were alive, to help him as she so often had in the past.

Chapter Fourteen

◆◆◆◆◆◆◆◆

1

'Scobie, are these calls taped?'

Aldwych hadn't named himself, but Malone had recognized the voice. 'No, Jack. We only do that with politicians and smartarse lawyers. What's on your mind?'

'If ever you call me up before ICAC, I'll deny I ever spoke to you. I couldn't go to my grave, people thinking I was a dog.'

'You going to dob someone in?'

'I dunno. Yeah, I guess I am. Last night I was at the Congress, the hotel. On my way out I saw the young Jap who took me for that ride the other day. He was coming out with two other Japs, older blokes. They got into a stretch limo, a hire job, and drove off. You want the number?'

Malone never let excitement boil his blood; too often, tip-offs and stumbled-upon clues had led nowhere. 'Go ahead.'

'It's HC –' Aldwych gave him the number. 'The hire company'd have a record of who hired it.'

'Thanks, Jack.' A cop always loved having a crim tell him how to do his job. 'If we pick up the young bloke, I'll want you to identify him.'

'What for? He just took me for a drive. I'm not laying any charges, Scobie. I'm only telling you about him because it might help you clear up them murders you're working on.'

'There was another one last night. The young girl who tried to burn Cormac Casement.'

'I read about it this morning. They're keeping you busy.' Aldwych hung up abruptly, as if still suspicious his call was being taped.

Malone put down the phone and stared out through the glass wall of his office at the outer office. The linked cases were now all co-ordinated into the one investigation and Peta Smith had set up a room across the hall where charts, diagrams and photos gave facts but no solution, where the police work was on display. And now it might all fall into place on a single clue given by an old crim. Malone had to smile, though it hurt.

Last night, when he had got home, he had phoned the Riverwood police station near Lugarno and suggested a twenty-four-hour watch be kept on the Kornsey home. 'Is that an order, Inspector?' said the senior constable who had taken the call.

'It's your beat. You want a second murder to keep you going?'

'Well, I'm not *au fait* with the ramifications, sir –'

Malone could just hear the old-timers, Jack Greenup and Thumper Murphy, being *au fait* with the ramifications. Education was replacing the sledgehammer. 'Talk to your patrol commander. All I'm doing is recommending you take care of Mrs Kornsey's safety.'

When he had got off the phone in the kitchen, Lisa, sipping a cup of hot chocolate, had looked at him with concern. 'You sound as if you have whatever-you-call-it on your liver.'

'Shit.'

'Yes, that's it. I always have trouble remembering four-letter words.' But she leaned back as he passed behind her chair, put up her face to be kissed. 'Darling, this one is getting you down.'

'Don't they all?' He made himself some chocolate and sat down opposite her. 'The trouble is, with this one I'm not sure the killing has stopped.'

'Can you do anything to prevent more killing?'

He shook his head. 'We can try to stop Mrs Kornsey being killed, but that's about all.'

There was the sound of a key in the front door and in moment Claire came down the hallway and into the kitchen. 'Oh, you're still up.'

'Dad's only just got in,' said Lisa. 'Someone hit you in the mouth?'

Claire grinned with embarrassment, wiped the smeared lipstick from her mouth. 'There, that better?'

'How's Jay?' said Malone.

Eighteen months ago Jason Rockne's mother and her lesbian lover had murdered his father. The two women were now doing life and the boy and his younger sister were living with their grandfather and their stepgrandmother. Jason had gone through a terrible trauma, an horrific jungle of emotions, but somehow he had kept his balance. It pleased Malone, who had arrested the mother, that Claire, his daughter, had helped the boy through his crisis. The pleasure came from pride in Claire, not from the prospect of any future in their relationship. She was only sixteen and he was sure the next four or five years were lined with young men, each of whom would be the love of her life till she would settle for some bastard whom, Malone knew with certainty, he would hate on sight.

'He's okay.' Claire sat down with a glass of milk. 'He's finding uni. hard, he says. He's not sure now that he wants to do chemical engineering when he graduates.'

'What does he think he'd like to do?' said Lisa.

Claire looked sideways at her father. 'He thinks he'd like to be a cop, a detective.'

'Jesus!' Malone put down his mug, somehow managing not to spill any of the chocolate. 'Why? You'd think he'd seen enough of cops to do him for the rest of his life.'

'I told him that. He just says he's more interested in human nature than he is in science and chemicals.'

Lisa said quietly, 'He sounds as if he's still trying to work out what made his mother do what she did.'

'That's what I thought,' said Claire. 'But I didn't tell him.'

'If he's interested in what makes human nature tick,' said Malone, 'tell him to be a school teacher. Kids simplify everything that adults eventually do.'

'Kids don't murder. Except the psychopaths.'

'There are more of them around now than you realize.

Maybe not at Holy Spirit, but they're around. And not all of them are psychos. You don't have to be one to belong to a colour gang.'

He was concerned at the increasing violence in schools; so far he had not been called in on a school homicide, though he expected a call any day. Then his theory would be tested that kids simplified everything that adults did. In the meantime a collection of adults were pulling him through a maze that no schoolyard would ever resemble.

'I'm going to bed.'

As he went through towards the front bedroom he heard Claire say, 'He looks tired. *Old.*'

'Perhaps you should invite Jay around to see him when he looks like this,' said Lisa. 'It might change Jay's mind about being a detective.'

Malone had not slept well last night and now here he was in his office with Jack Aldwych having just added another twist to the maze. He was staring into space, as if asleep with his eyes open, when Clements, lounging against the door jamb, said, 'You want me to come back later?'

Malone shook his head, like a dog coming out of water. 'Sorry. I was in a maze then –'

'A daze?'

'No, a – forget it. You got anything?'

Clements remained lounging in the doorway; he, too, looked tired. Since his engagement Romy had somehow succeeded in smoothing out his rumpled look; but this morning he appeared in need of a good steam-pressing, especially his face. It was lined and baggy, as if it, and not the rest of him, had lost weight overnight.

'Romy's just called. Kim was HIV-negative, so she's done the autopsy. Kim must of insisted on safe sex with that creep Kelsey. It's official – the same MO as they used on Rob Sweden and Kornsey. It's a message, all right. Do we pass it on to the others in this mess?'

'Maze.'

'Eh?'

256

'Maze. That's what this is. If we pass on the message – who to? Casement, his wife, Sweden, *his* wife, the Aldwyches? – are we going to have one of them suddenly head for the bush? If the Japs, the *yakuza*, have organized these killings, I don't think I want to know. Tibooburra may not be a bad option, after all.'

'You're putting your money on Mr Tajiri? We dunno if he even exists, nobody's ever met him.'

'He exists. Jack Aldwych has just been on to me. Last night he was at the Congress Hotel, he saw the young bloke who took him for the ride. He was with two other Japs. They went somewhere in a stretch limousine, number –' He handed over the scrap of paper on which he had noted the number. 'Get Andy on to it. I want to know where the limo driver took the three Japs.'

Clements took the piece of paper. 'While Andy's working on this, I'll get on to the Congress. There's a girl on the reception desk I took out a coupla times. She'll let me know what Japs are staying there.'

'I wish I had your contacts. What're you going to do when you're married? Girls don't give information to married men, not nice girls.'

Clements was back in five minutes, no light of hope in his big face. 'There are seventy-eight Japanese staying at the Congress. I'd forgotten – they own forty-nine per cent of it. But –' He seemed to be trying to lift the bags in his face. 'Fourteen Japanese booked in yesterday. Four married couples, four businessmen in a party, and two businessmen who came in as a pair. Mr –' He glanced at his notebook. 'Mr Kushida and Mr Isogai. They were booked in from Tokyo by their firm, the Kunishima Bank.'

'Bankers? Who do bankers usually come to see?'

'Other bankers? I think we're gunna find out that that limo took those three Japs to see someone at Shahriver International. Maybe Kunishima owns part of Shahriver.' He was suddenly revived; he put his head out of the door and yelled, 'Andy! How's it coming?'

Andy Graham appeared in a moment. 'No problems, mate.

The limo belongs to Sundance Hire Cars, out in Rosebery. The driver was a guy named Barker, it was booked to the Hotel Congress, to the account of a Mr Kushida and he took Mr Kushida and two other Japs to The Wharf apartments.'

2

Malone and Clements looked at each other. 'Sweden or Casement?' said Clements.

'Casement. Another bank. Thanks, Andy.'

'No worries.' Graham galloped away.

Malone rose to his feet. 'I don't think we'll report this one to Zanuch or the Minister till we've checked it out.'

All the way down to Circular Quay he wondered if he really wanted to find a connection between Cormac Casement and the Japanese, especially if the latter were *yakuza*. He liked the older man, respected him. Though Malone was a gentle radical, he had some conservative traits; he admired some of the older ways and standards. If Casement had gone against the grain of generations, Malone knew he would not feel any satisfaction from confronting the older man with it.

The doorman at The Wharf told them that Mr Casement was across the road at his office. 'He's back at work, he says he's much better. I spoke to him this morning. You got the two young bastards who tried to burn him, that right?'

'No,' said Clements. 'Someone got to them first.'

'Same difference, so long's you got 'em.' He went back behind his desk, secure in his judgements.

Across in the Casement building Mrs Pallister, on the phone to Malone downstairs at the security desk, was quite adamant that Mr Casement couldn't see them. 'He has someone with him right now and he has a board meeting in half an hour. It's out of the question, Inspector. Call me this afternoon and I'll see if I can fit you in around five.'

She hung up and Malone grinned at the security man. 'The Wicked Witch says for us to go right on up.'

258

'You must have a way with you,' said the security man. 'She gave me specific instructions the Old Man was seeing no one today.'

'It's the police charm school. We're both graduates.'

He and Clements rode to the fiftieth floor, stepped out of the lift and tried their charm on the girl on the outer desk. She looked at them dubiously. 'He has someone with him.'

'Japanese?'

The question seemed to puzzle her. 'Japanese. No. No – it's *Mrs* Casement.'

Malone wondered if that was a bonus; but it was too late to back out now. 'Tell Mrs Pallister we're here. It'll make her day.'

The receptionist smiled at that, but said nothing. She went through into the inner office and was back a moment later with Mrs Pallister, the latter ready for battle: 'I told you Inspector –'

'I know what you told us, Mrs Pallister, but that's not the way we work, being told when we can and cannot see customers. Now let Mr Casement know we're here and we'll stay here till he sees us.'

She glared at him for a moment; but she was too well-bred to give way to anger in front of her junior. She spun round and disappeared. The receptionist blew out a soft gasp. 'You haven't made *my* day. She'll be in a terrible mood now.'

'Sorry. Join the police force. We're always in a good mood.'

Mrs Pallister came back. 'Mr Casement will see you. But remember – he has a board meeting in half an hour.'

'He may have to miss it. Thanks, Mrs Pallister. We're just like you, y'know, only doing our job.'

She was not appeased; her loyalty had only one direction. She opened the door to Casement's office and ushered them in. 'The police,' she said and made it sound as if she were introducing the Gestapo.

Casement sat at his desk. Ophelia sat beside him, her chair close to his. Here we go, thought Malone, the battle lines drawn.

259

Ophelia said, 'You seem to have a habit of barging –'

But Casement put a hand on her arm; the fingers, still brownish-yellow from the dressing, seemed to claw at her. 'Let's hear what the Inspector has to say.'

'May we sit down? Sergeant Clements and I may be here for some time.'

'Of course.' Casement's glasses had been on his desk; he picked them up and put them on. He had looked aged without them; now he looked vulnerable, a man hiding behind clear glass. 'Has something come up, something to clear up this whole damn mess?'

'We're not sure. You read about Kim Weetbix's murder? The girl you refused to lay charges against? Or anyway to identify.'

Casement nodded. There was silence for a moment, then with some asperity but quietly he said, 'You're not blaming me for her death, are you?'

Malone, one eye on Ophelia, said, 'If she were still in custody, she'd still be alive.'

'That's preposterous –' But again Ophelia had her arm pressed by her husband's yellow claw.

'You haven't come here just to accuse me of that, Inspector.'

'No. I just thought you might like to live with it.' All the sympathy Malone had felt on the way here for Casement had abruptly evaporated. 'No, we're here to ask you about some Japanese visitors you had last night.'

'What Japanese?'

Malone left the details to Clements, who had them at his tongue's tip: 'A Mr Kushida and a Mr Isogai, both from Kunishima Bank in Tokyo. The other Japanese, we think, was Mr Tajiri.'

One hand was still clutching Ophelia's arm, a silencer; the other was toying with a silver paperweight. It was a yacht on a heavy base, and Malone wondered if it was a model of the boat Casement had once raced. A reminder of carefree days . . . 'Have you had me under surveillance?'

'Why should we do that, Mr Casement?' said Malone. 'No,

we just did our job. Detective work. Was the third man Mr Tajiri?'

He was watching Ophelia, waiting for the enquiring look at her husband; but there was none. The indignation had gone, too; her face had closed in, the beautiful eyes wary and dark. He had a sudden moment of indecision: what if the Japanese had come to see *her*?

'We think,' said Clements, the change bowler, 'Mr Tajiri had something to do with the murder of the two kids who tried to burn you. And that makes us think he might also have had something to do with the murders of Rob Sweden and Mr Kornsey.'

Malone remarked that Ophelia didn't ask who Mr Kornsey was; her husband must have filled her in on all the *personae* in this mess. Maze. 'If you can put us in touch with Mr Tajiri, Mr Casement, maybe we can clear up all the murders. Your brother-in-law is on our backs to do that.'

'You have a sharp tongue, Inspector.' But Casement made the comment almost as an aside, something to fill the void while he thought what he really wanted to say. Then he took his hand off his wife's arm, folded one hand gingerly within the other and said, 'The other gentleman's name is Itani, not Tajiri. At least that's how he was introduced to me.'

'And Kushida and Isogai, you've met them before?'

A slight hesitation: 'Yes.'

'Would they have anything to do with the missing twenty-five million?' The sum rolled off his tongue without effort; it was remarkable how other people's money was not as valuable as your own.

'Why should it concern them?'

He's fencing, thought Malone; who had fenced with the best of them. He turned to Ophelia. 'Were you at the meeting, Mrs Casement?'

'Only as a hostess,' she said coolly. 'I wasn't privy to what was being discussed.'

Privy: she might have been coached by a lawyer. 'So the murders weren't mentioned.'

'You have a blinkered view of business discussion,' said Casement.

'The Japs didn't even comment on the attack on you?' said Clements.

'Well, yes. But only in passing. The *Japanese* are very polite about other people's affairs.'

'So are we,' said Malone. 'Except in a case of murder. Or five murders – no, six. There's one you probably don't know about, a girl who worked for one of the companies Mr Tajiri was connected with.' Casement showed no reaction and Malone went on, 'You're stonewalling. Do you want to send for your lawyer and we'll really get down to cases?'

'We might send for my brother-in-law,' said Ophelia, 'and have you taken off this case.'

'That would suit me.' But it wouldn't; all at once he wanted to stay with this. Tibooburra receded into the dust-haze of the far north-west. 'But it wouldn't look good if ever it got into the papers. Let's stop threatening each other. Sergeant Clements and I might walk out of here with no satisfaction, but we'll come back. Again and again. That's the way we work.'

There was a knock on the door and Mrs Pallister looked in. 'Mr Casement, there is the board meeting –'

Casement stared at her as if not recognizing her; then he collected his thoughts and his options. 'Call them and tell them to start without me, Alice. I'm going to be delayed.'

Mrs Pallister gave the two detectives a look that should have sent them to Tibooburra, had she known about it; then she closed the door. Ophelia said, 'I think we should send for Henry Gower, darling.'

Gower was the senior partner in the city's most prestigious law firm; he would be a tank-trap. Malone was relieved when Casement, almost wearily, said, 'No. We don't want any outsiders . . . Inspector, the Kunishima Bank owns twenty-five per cent of Casement Trust. Mr Kushida and Mr Isogai were here regarding the missing twenty-five million. They are understandably concerned.'

'And Mr – what was his name? Mr Itani? What's his role?'

'He is their local representative.'

'Does he have an office here in this building?'

'No-o. Kunishima has no office here in Sydney.'

'Mr Casement, you are bull – you are stringing us along. Mr Itani abducted Jack Aldwych two days ago, at gunpoint. He took him for a ride, as they used to say in gangster films, but didn't bump him off – as they also used to say.'

'Jack Aldwych? They kidnapped *him*?'

'Laughable, isn't it? We don't think Itani – or Tajiri, whatever his real name is – we don't think he quite knew what he might be starting. He knew who Jack was – I don't think he knew how much clout Jack still has. If Itani is Kunishima's rep in your bank, he's not doing much for the reputation of Casement Trust.'

There was silence for a long moment; now Ophelia reached for her husband's arm. 'You'd better tell them, darling.'

Casement shook his head without looking at her. He took off his glasses again, was abruptly almost old enough to be her grandfather. Age had engulfed him. Beyond the window autumn, it seemed, had already succumbed to winter; the Harbour came and went behind gusts of cold rain, the arch of the Bridge was a mocking grey rainbow. He shook his head again, but this time in despair.

'Inspector –' He was having difficulty getting his words together. 'How much of what I tell you goes into your report?'

'That depends.' Malone was as cautious as any banker approached for a loan; or as cautious as a banker should be. The city's banks were riddled with executives who had shown no judgement. But Casement Trust had never figured in the bad news of the boom time. 'Tell us what you have to say. No notes, Russ,' he said to Clements, who had his biro at the ready. 'Not yet.'

'The police make deals with criminals, I understand,' said Casement. 'It's happening right now in ICAC.'

'Are you a criminal?'

'God, what a question!' Ophelia reached across the desk towards the silver paperweight; then thought better of whatever she had in mind. 'My husband is trying to *help* you, for Christ's sake!'

'Go ahead, Mr Casement. We could do with some help.'

Casement heaved a sigh; it seemed to come from his toes, it took so long. As chairman he had never had to deliver a report like this: 'Kunishima bought into Casement Trust just over two years ago, when money was still flowing out of Japan. They had the necessary government approval, but we didn't make any public announcement – we're a privately owned bank. And two years ago there was so much going on in the headlines, the newspapers took no notice of us. We've always worked on the principle that what is our business is nobody else's business.'

'Get to the point, darling.' Ophelia was leaning forward, pressed against the desk. She was more on edge than her husband, who now appeared listlessly resigned.

Casement glanced at her with irritation, but made no comment. Instead he looked back at Malone and said, 'We had checked on Kunishima, naturally, the usual due diligence. They were a new bank, they'd been going on only eight years, but their capital was solid and so was their reputation. We were not diligent enough, it turned out. We never traced their capital back to its source. Kunishima Bank is owned by one of Tokyo's *yakuza* gangs. In other words, the *yakuza* own twenty-five per cent of Casement Trust.'

The confession exhausted him. He put out a hand for the glass and jug of water on the silver tray behind him, but seemed unable to raise himself to reach it. Ophelia poured him a glass of water, handed it to him and stroked his arm. Her concern for him was genuine, not an act put on for the two detectives.

'Are Kushida and Isogai *yakuza* men?'

'You mean are they gangsters? I don't know.' Casement sat up, tried to re-gather some strength. 'Obviously they are employed by the *yakuza*. But they are bankers, they understand the business.'

'Why are they here?'

'Ostensibly for the bankers' convention that starts tomorrow.

264

Tonight, actually – there's a cocktail reception. The real reason is the twenty-five million. The *yakuza*, it seems, don't like that much money being stolen from it.'

'Did the *yakuza* kill Rob Sweden and Terry Kornsey?'

Casement again put on his glasses, took his time about setting them straight, as if they were a new pair. 'I wouldn't know. We only talked about banking matters. Including the stolen money, of course.'

'They know where the money is?'

Casement nodded. 'In Hong Kong, they say it's still there. They're applying pressure on Shahriver International.'

Malone looked at Clements. 'I'd enjoy watching that . . . Do you think the money will be returned?'

'I think so. The *yakuza* seems to have more influence than any bank or even the banking system.' Casement's cynicism sounded more despairing than weary.

'We didn't ask you the other night –' The omission had not been deliberate. This case had more questions than he could remember in any other investigation; his mind was like a too-full sack, questions were lost in the corners of it. 'Did you know before Rob Sweden was murdered that he was the thief? I mean, did you personally know?'

'No.' The answer was direct, but Malone did not miss the stiffening of Casement's arm under his wife's hand.

'Did you know about Terry Kornsey?'

'I'd never heard of him.'

'Have your *yakuza* friends told you anything about him?'

'That's going too far!' Casement jerked his arm from under Ophelia's grasp, sat up straight, leaned forward aggressively.

'What else would you call them, Mr Casement? Business associates? Acquaintances? Your *yakuza* acquaintances, have they told you anything about Mr Kornsey?'

The battle lines faced each other across the desk. Then Ophelia said, 'You'll be off this case by this evening, Inspector, I promise you. We've had more than enough!'

Rain suddenly beat against the window, like soft bullets.

'No,' said Derek Sweden.

They were at lunch, the three Bruna sisters and their husbands. It was a monthly ritual, something that Sweden only attended because of his devotion to Rosalind. Each of the sisters took it in turn to be hostess; this month it was Rosalind's turn. He had waited for her to suggest that it be cancelled; it was too soon after Rob's burial. But she hadn't and when he had broached the idea, she had said no.

'No, my darling. I believe in routine, that it keeps one's life together. I'm no gypsy, like 'Phelia and Julie –' He had once, only half in jest, called all Roumanians gypsies; she had taken him seriously, which in a voter is sufferable but not in a wife. 'We go on with our life as before. I know how much you miss Rob –'

'I don't,' he said truthfully, surprised that it *was* the truth. 'I will, in time, I suppose. We never loved each other, not the way a father and son are supposed to. Not the way you love Adam,' he said flatteringly, though Adam Bruna gave him a pain in the arse. 'Or he loves you. No, what I hate, what *kills* me, is the way he died. Jesus, no parent expects his kid to be *murdered*! Murdered and then thrown – like the cops said, *tossed* – off our balcony! Christ, every morning I get up, since that night, I pull back the curtains in our bedroom and there's the balcony . . . '

'We'll move into one of the other bedrooms –'

'Which one? The police say he was actually killed in the second bedroom. Maybe it all started in one of the other bedrooms, in the living room – who fucking knows?'

She had walked round behind him, put her arms round his neck as he sat in his chair in the study. 'My darling, do you want to move out of here?'

He stroked her arm absently. 'You'd hate that, wouldn't you?'

'Yes.'

'We'll stay.' He lifted his face, kissed her as she bent her head. 'Okay, we'll have the lunch. We'll stick to routine.'

And now halfway through the luncheon, served by the temporary cook Rosalind had found to replace the missing Luisa, Ophelia had asked him to have Inspector Malone and Sergeant Clements taken off the investigation. 'No,' he said emphatically. 'I can't do that. I've been a Minister of three other departments and I've been able to interfere – Ministers do that, if they're doing their job properly. But not with the Police – you interfere there and you're up against a culture you can't beat, you can't win. You pull your head in and you work with your Commissioner and the Deputy Commissioner and the seven Assistant Commissioners and you get along, you get things done. Bill Zanuch tells me Malone is the best man in Homicide and if anyone is going to find out who murdered Rob it'll be him. And I'm sure you, and all of you here, are like me – you want to find out who killed him. So, no. Malone stays, I won't interfere.' He looked down the table at Cormac Casement. 'You agree, Cormac?'

'Of course,' said the older man, intent on his food.

'You haven't asked me,' said Jack Aldwych Junior, 'but I agree with you. Dad thinks Malone is tops.'

'He'd know,' said Juliet, but said it sweetly.

'But he's hounding Cormac!' Ophelia had pushed her plate away untouched.

'Is he, old chap?' said Sweden. 'Hounding you? I can have that stopped.'

'No, let it lie. I think things are coming to a head.'

'Tell us!' Juliet leaned forward. 'What are luncheons for, except gossip?'

'Easy, love,' said Jack Junior. 'This is too serious for gossip.'

Sweden looked at the younger man. He had not made up his mind about Jack Junior; perhaps there was more shrewdness there than he suspected. Or perhaps it came of comparing him to his old man, which was unfair. He had the sudden crazy thought that, when it came to Hans Vanderberg and his threat, he should turn to Jack Senior for advice.

'Nothing will come to a head,' he said, 'till we find out who murdered Rob.'

'And the others?' said Rosalind, who kept count.

Sweden nodded almost absently. 'Yes, and the others.'

'Let's hope there are not still more,' said Casement, thinking of the phone call he had received just before coming to the luncheon.

4

'We shall have to eliminate him,' said Tajiri. 'He is weakening. If the police keep coming back to him, he is going to tell them too much.'

'If he hasn't already told them too much,' said Belgarda. 'How did he sound when you called?'

'Upset. He said something about conscience, but I didn't catch it and he wouldn't repeat it.'

They were speaking English because neither knew anything of the other's language. They were in the living room of the house Tajiri had rented on a short-term lease in a quiet street in Roseville. The Japanese community in Sydney lived mostly on the North Shore because of the proximity of the school for Japanese children in Terrey Hills; another Japanese man, even one without a family, moving into the neighbourhood would not cause comment amongst the native residents. Of course, were it known that he was a member of the *yakuza*, he would have been asked, as with any of the native crims, to move south of the harbour, where tolerance was looser.

'I want to go home,' said Teresita Romero in Spanish.

Tajiri did not like women, though he was not homosexual. He was a man of strong prejudices, of contradictions, too; but most of the time he managed to keep both under control. He had not been born into a life of crime; his father, a hardware merchant in Osaka, had been primly honest. Wanting a son who would sell more than nuts and bolts, he had sent him to Tokyo University to study economics and perhaps get a job for life with Mitsubishi or Nomura Securities. But at university Kenji Tajiri had discovered that honesty might be the best policy but was not always the best-paying proposition. He knew that in the Japanese social system one had to climb the ladder a rung at a time, a lengthy ascent that did not appeal to him. He was young and ambitious and he had looked around for a milieu that would appreciate his talents. Crime is a profession in which, like all systems, there are ladders; but on its ladders not all rungs have to be climbed. Tajiri joined the *yakuza*, after arranging a proper invitation.

He liked the companionship of men, but his intelligence and education had taken him out of the gang environment, out of the bath-house camaraderie, and left him high and dry and lonely, a treasured tool of the bosses. Unlike some of his *yakuza* brethren, he had never developed a samurai mentality. He had read the *Hagakure*, but had never thought much of that bible's precepts. He had never seen any dignity in 'clenched teeth and flashing eyes'. He did not believe that it was wrong to have strong personal convictions. He did not have a strong belief that death was preferable to dishonour. He did, however, believe that murder was often necessary; so long as someone else committed the murder. But he had not been happy when his bosses in Tokyo, sensing a growing mess in their investment here in Australia, had sent him out to clear it up. Too often left to work alone, his grasp was slipping on that staff of the Japanese male, loyalty. He had only one tattoo on his body, a pair of clasped hands on his chest, and even that, it seemed to him, was beginning to fade.

He had arrived in Sydney after Lava Investments had already been established in its offices. By then it was known that there was a leak between Casement Trust and Kunishima Bank; driblets had been transferred to Hong Kong, testing the water, as it were. It had taken Tajiri some weeks to discover the mastermind behind the scheme; it had not taken much effort to mark Rob Sweden and then trace back to his control, Terry Kornsey. After that, the task had been turned over to Belgarda. The man was a natural-born killer.

'I want to go home,' Teresita repeated.

'What did she say?'

'She said she wants to go home,' said Belgarda. 'To Manila, she means.'

Tajiri, too, wanted to go home, to the small apartment in Akasaka, where he wore a mask of respectability that the other tenants in the building accepted. But it would be a weakness to confess that he was homesick, even though every day here in Sydney amongst the barbarians was a small purgatory, a Christian concept he had read about and which he now understood, here amongst the so-called Christians.

He had rented this house for a month from a Japanese family which had gone home on leave. It was furnished Australian style, with wall-to-wall carpet, heavy chairs and a couch that smelled of dog, and dark-flowered wallpaper; his countryman had explained, apologetically, that the owners were an elderly couple who had built and furnished the house right after World War Two – 'when, as they explained to me, we were still enemies,' his countryman had further explained. 'You will find that Australians think they are diplomatic.'

Whatever pictures had been on the walls had been removed and been replaced by classical prints by Sanraku and others. Around the prints were the oblong patches on the wallpaper where the owners' pictures had hung, like a ghostly reprimand for having interfered with the local atmosphere. Tajiri, a meticulous man, wondered why his countryman had not bought frames large enough to cover the patches.

'Is she afraid?'

Belgarda looked at Teresita. He had shaved off his moustache and, thought Teresita, looked weak and not as handsome. She had come to Sydney as the bride of a local ocker, a term she had not understood until she had had to live with it. When she had met Jaime Belgarda at a Spanish club she had immediately left her gross, vulgar, beer-swilling husband and moved in with him, soon becoming the secretary at Lava Investments, a job that required no qualifications other than to look pretty and ask no questions. Her husband had come looking for her, but Belgarda, without arguing with him, had killed him with a knife. It had shocked her to see that Jaime could kill without compunction, but by then she had been in love with him.

'Are you afraid?' Belgarda said now, and in Spanish.

'Speak English!' snapped Tajiri.

'I asked her if she is afraid. Are you?'

Teresita shook her head, too afraid now to say yes. Home, the bar in Ermita where the Aussie ocker had found her, all at once looked appealing. 'No, just homesick.'

Belgarda nodded and smiled at her. He did not love her, but he always treated her gently; when he eventually tired of her, as he would, he would not get rid of her by killing her. His own mother, Lily, had been a bar-girl, not in Ermita but out by Subic Bay. He had inherited his politeness from her. She had invariably been polite, even when on her back or in a dozen other positions; she had re-written the Kama Sutra according to Emily Post. The sailors from Subic Bay, being American and naturally polite, had flocked to her for instruction. With the money she earned she had sent her son to university to study medicine. He had lasted one semester, being expelled when he had threatened a professor with a scalpel when he had been disturbed in bed with the professor's wife.

Armed with a little medical knowledge and faked papers, he had then been taken on as an assistant at the morgue in Makati in Manila. He had left there after a year, seeing no future amongst the dead. He had then started as a salesman for Pinatubo Engineering. He had soon established himself as a successful salesman: in a land where bribery, under President Marcos, was endemic, he had become a specialist in the greased palm. Two years ago he had been transferred to Sydney to take charge of Pinatubo's Australian operations. Six months ago his Manila boss, on a visit to Sydney, his tongue loosened by the local shiraz, had told him that Pinatubo was owned and controlled by the *yakuza*. The information had not frightened him: he was supremely confident that, no matter who his bosses were, he was his own man. When Tajiri had arrived and told him some murder might be necessary, he had laid down only one condition: that he be paid more. Tajiri had agreed without reference to Tokyo. Against the missing twenty-five million dollars, a few thousand dollars in blood money was only petty cash.

'Just homesick,' said Teresita.

Tajiri gave her a smile, a concession. 'So am I. I think we can all go home soon. But first, we have to get rid of Mr Casement.'

'How do we do it?' asked Belgarda, the journeyman killer. 'When?'

'As soon as possible. Could you kill him in a crowd?'

Teresita sat staring at the wallpaper, shutting her ears against the men's voices. She had been here at the house for four days and only now did she remark that the flowers on the wallpaper were lilies, the flowers of death.

Chapter Fifteen

✦✦✦✦✦✦✦✦✦

1

'Jack, do it as a favour,' said Malone.

'Scobie, I've never pointed the finger at anyone in my life. I wanted something done, I did it m'self or had someone do it for me.'

'Jack, you're *retired*. You keep telling me. All I want you to do is come to this cocktail reception this evening at the Congress and, if he's there, pick out Tajiri for me. We'll do the rest.'

'I'm no banker, they'll never let me in –'

'Jack, you look like the governor of the Reserve Bank. You've got it all – the three-piece suit, the silver hair, the look of knowing all the answers that the rest of us don't. Come on, Jack. You owe me.'

'Owe you? What for?'

'I've never pinched you, have I?'

Aldwych laughed. 'Okay, you win. I'll be there, I'll come with Jack Junior and the daughter-in-law. They've been invited, all the clan. I gather Ophelia arranged it, never misses a social occasion. Will you be there? How're you gunna pass as a banker?'

'I'll try posing as a conman. Not long ago banks welcomed them with open arms.'

Malone and Clements, dressed in their Sunday best, had shown their police badges at the door to the main ballroom of the Hotel Congress and the usher had shown no surprise. 'Just a security measure,' Malone had said, making no mention of Homicide, and the usher had been satisfied with that. Bankers, from what he had read, had recently become paranoid about security.

'Are John and Andy here?'

'They were coming in through the kitchen,' said Clements. 'There they are. John looks more like a banker than you or me, but Andy looks like a bank *clerk*.'

The two junior detectives, at the rear of the big room, saw their seniors and just nodded across the heads of the rippling crowd. The air was a babel of voices, though English, the *lingua franca* of finance, predominated. The French, *naturelle-ment*, were speaking only French; *ils ne pouvaient pas compren-dre pourquoi les autres ne faisaient pas la même chose*. The Americans, articulate only in four-letter words during their work-day, were having difficulty with their vocabulary in the company of women other than their secretaries and wives. The British, stiff-upper-lipped, were resisting advice from the Russians on the Royal family: 'No revolution! It does not work!' The Italians and other assorted Latins were pinching bottoms, not all female. The Germans and the Japanese were politely congratulating each other on the possibility of a new Axis. And the Australians were becoming increasingly garru-lous as they discovered bankers from other nations who were even more heavily loaded with bad debts than themselves.

Malone turned round in the crush and found himself face-to-red-face with Harold Junor, who looked as if he had fortified himself with several whiskies before arriving. 'Inspector! On duty?'

'Sort of. You hear from Mr Palady?'

'Matter of fax, yes. Sorry. Fact. I got a fax in just before I left the office. In code, of course. Old Ishmael has a thing about codes. He once worked for the CIA, did you know that?' His tongue was whisky-oiled, Scotch but with no burr. 'Takes all types to make the CIA . . . Anyhow, the gist of the fax was that everything's been sorted out in Hong Kong. The money's on its way back. I gather the Honkers boys got an offer they couldn't refuse. From the Japs, savvy?'

Malone nodded. Junor melted away, some feat considering

his bulk, and Malone was left alone. He scanned the crowd till he found Cormac Casement in the midst of a small group of men in a far corner. At the instant he saw the banker, Casement saw him. The older man's glasses flashed as he raised his head, then he said something to those around him, left them and came towards Malone.

He was blunt: 'What are you doing here?'

'Just looking.'

'Looking for what?' Casement seemed nervous, ill at ease.

'Mr Tajiri, maybe. Are Mr Kushida and Mr Isogai here?'

'I haven't seen them. There are private parties, I understand, in some of the suites.'

Then Ophelia's party surrounded them. The three Bruna sisters attracted their usual attention, even from those who didn't know them. Their beauty, their dressing, always drew the eye, but there was something more: someone else's malice always adds extra burnish to the object. Under the froth of gossip there could be heard, faintly, the whisper of envy. The men, Sweden, the two Aldwyches and Adam Bruna were just background to their women, plush to the diamonds.

'I'm surprised to see you here, Inspector,' said Ophelia.

'Just keeping an eye on our deposits,' said Malone, smiling to show he wasn't spoiling for another fight. 'All these bankers . . . Do customers ever get invited to these conventions?'

'Do bookies ever buy the punters a drink?' said Sweden.

'They all look so sleek and successful!' said Bruna, who looked sleek and successful. 'One imagined they would all be down-in-the-mouth, out-at-the-elbows. The world must be picking up. Perhaps people will start buying paintings again!' He brightened, like a suddenly restored fresco.

'Whoever thought I'd be hobnobbing with them?' said Jack Aldwych. 'I wonder what some of the local ones'd say if I walked up to 'em and said I'd held 'em up back in the old days?'

'Let's try it,' said Juliet, eager for fun and mischief. 'Point one out.'

'For God's sake, Julie!' But Rosalind included Aldwych in her disapproval.

'Relax, dear, I know my place.' He took Malone's arm and eased him away from the group. 'I'm here with your gun at my head, you know that?'

'All you have to do is point him out, Jack. The Jap. Casement's no help, he won't play ball at all.'

'I wonder why?'

The two tall men looked at each other; then Malone said, 'Jack, I think your relative-by-marriage is up Eastern Creek without a bike.'

'Is that the polite version of up shit creek without a paddle?' Eastern Creek had been a government-financed speedway venture that had been a disaster. 'I think you're right about him, but I dunno the details. Do you?'

'Some of them. Did you know the *yakuza* own twenty-five per cent of Casement Trust?'

'Yes. I've known it for a year or more, I got it from Les Chung. He got it from his mates in the Triads. They ever get together, the *yakuza* and the Triads, the Mafia can call it a day. Don't buy shares in Cosa Nostra. When did you find out about the *yakuza*?'

'This morning. I should've come to you first, the day all this mess started.'

'You think I'd have told you anything?' Aldwych shook his head. Then he paused, his head held stiffly, his eyes squinting.

'You see him?' Malone looked in the direction of the old man's gaze.

Aldwych continued to stare for a moment, then he shook his head. 'No, not the Jap. I thought I saw the other bloke, the one who drove the car, but no, I guess I was mistaken. You know how it is, you see someone, there's something about them . . . '

'Jack, I'll bet you've never missed identifying a man, ever. You want to point the finger at someone, you could identify an Abo at a hundred yards in a coal mine. Who were you looking at?'

'He's disappeared. Slim bloke with glasses, he might be the one who drove the car. He had a mo the other day, but I don't think he's got one now. He's in a light-coloured suit, doesn't look like a banker.'

Malone nodded admiringly. 'You're on your own, Jack. You notice the colour of his eyes from here? Excuse me, I'll be back.'

On the other side of the room, behind one of the huge flower urns that flanked the room, Jaime Belgarda saw the tall younger man leave Jack Aldwych and come pushing through the crowd. He had been shocked to see Aldwych at this bankers' function; he knew the old criminal's past record and he hadn't expected him to be a guest amongst these pillars of world banking. Of course back home in Manila the law-abiding and the lawless mixed with familiarity because corruption laid on a common veneer. But here in this Sydney ballroom Aldwych, though he looked like a banker, should have been as out of place as an Ermita pimp.

He had felt safe up till now. The horn-rimmed glasses and the hairless upper lip had changed his appearance; a dude all his life, his only mistake had been to wear the sharp light-grey suit amongst all the dark greys and blues. He carried a folded short-handled umbrella, but that didn't make him conspicuous; it was raining heavily outside and he had heard arriving guests complaining about having got wet. The umbrella was his weapon, an air-gun that could shoot a dart with sufficient force to penetrate a layer of clothing and lodge in the intended target's flesh. The dart was tipped with Ricin, a fast-acting poison that had first been used to dispose of a Bulgarian dissident in London back in 1978 and had been used selectively since by the more cultured assassins of the world's espionage clubs. Belgarda, who had had medical training, was about to use it for the first time and looked forward to the opportunity. Tradesmen, even killers, know the pleasure of a new tool.

As he saw the tall man (a policeman he wondered?) approaching, he slipped away from behind the big urn and lost himself in the crowd. He worked his way round the perimeter of the room towards Casement and the group around him. The glasses worried him: they were just clear glass and not prescription lenses, but the thick frames distracted him. Tajiri had insisted that Casement had to be eliminated this evening, before he cracked and started talking to the police or the Securities Commission. Tajiri, of course, had stayed safely at home, but Belgarda didn't resent the fact. Tajiri was squeamish about actually witnessing a killing and had seen none of the other murders. It was a pity because Belgarda liked those who employed him to see and admire his work.

The deed would have to be done quickly. He had lost sight of the tall man, but he knew he was somewhere in the crowd. Whoever had organized this reception must have anticipated only a percentage of acceptances to the invitations; instead of which it seemed that one hundred per cent had come along and brought their relatives into the bargain. He remembered Tajiri's comment that Australians were the greatest freeloaders in the civilized world; this evening he was grateful for the natives' fetish for a free drink. He moved amongst them, continually glancing back to see if the tall man was following him.

Malone, losing sight of his quarry, had paused by John Kagal, who could have passed for the youngest bank president in the room. 'Jack Aldwych has picked out a feller he thinks may be one of those who took him for a ride the other day. Horn-rimmed glasses and a light-coloured suit.'

'I saw him, he looked like an SP bookie.' Kagal was a sartorial snob. 'Who is he?'

'Haven't a clue. But he could be the feller who ran Pinatubo Engineering, Belgarda – I'm only guessing. Get Andy, then you and he work that side of the room, I'll go this way. If you get to him, take him quietly.'

'What if he's armed?'

'Let him go, at least till he gets outside. Bankers have had enough potshots taken at them. Metaphorically speaking.'

Kagal grinned. 'Wouldn't life be grand if all shots were just metaphorical?'

On the far side of the room the Casement party had attracted a clotting of the crowd. Cormac himself had revived under the attention and respect given to him, an Establishment icon; flattery, though temporary, is a splendid cement for covering up cracks. Ophelia, basking in the glory of being *Mrs* Casement, felt cheated that the reception was due to end at nine; she was a marathon runner when it came to the limelight. Juliet fluttered from male to male, a butterfly who knew just how long to hover at each stamen. Rosalind, more subdued, as befitted a politician's wife, was polite to those who spoke to her but looked worried.

'What's the matter with 'Lind?' Aldwych and Sweden stood a little apart from the crush.

The Police Minister sipped the orange juice he had asked for in preference to the champagne. 'Things are piling up on us, Jack. I imagine it's what gang warfare was like in your day.'

'Derek, you could never imagine what it was like in my day. We never stabbed each other in the back, it was always up front. You look up the newspapers on it. A bloke was killed, he was always shot from the front. Who's after you? The Dutchman?'

Sweden nodded, smiled wryly. 'You wouldn't like to come out of retirement, handle him for me?'

'He got something on you?'

Sweden nodded again, but offered no explanation. 'He expected me to buckle under. I'm not going to.'

'I'd like to help, if I could. The last thing I want is a Labor government back in. The buggers are always talking reform. You blokes almost ruined things, looking for the underprivileged vote. Let the Salvos look after them. But I can't do much about Vanderberg, Derek, not now I'm reformed. Well, *retired* . . . How're things going, Adam? Sold any paintings?'

Bruna had materialized, his usual mode of entry. 'Some Japanese have promised to come to the gallery tomorrow evening. I tried the Chinese and the Arabs, but the Arabs are crying poor mouth and the Chinese look surprised we have any artists. The Americans are only buying Aboriginal art. They think it's kerygma-stirring, whatever that means.' He looked around, raised his glass of champagne to the room at large. 'Let us hope that all these wonderful bankers can discover loose change again.'

Jack Junior joined the three men. 'You listen to these guys, everything that's gone wrong, they blame on everyone else. Mostly you politicians,' he told Sweden. 'All around the world, you're the ones who brought us to our knees. Rosalind is putting them straight.'

'She'll do a better job than I would,' said Sweden, sounding as if bankers' opinions were the least of his worries.

Jack Aldwych was surveying the room. He was wishing he had brought Emily Karp with him, to take her to dinner afterwards and enjoy her company; but if he was here to play scout for Malone he did not want her involved in any risk. It was some years since he had been involved in a situation like this and it irked him that he was not in control. He was not surprised that he had not seen the Japanese here this evening, but he wondered why the other man (the Filipino?) had put in an appearance.

He turned, caught Cormac Casement's eye and smiled at him. Then behind Casement he saw the man in the light grey suit push through the crowd and bend his arm. Laid along the man's forearm was what Aldwych at first thought was a sawn-off shotgun. Then he saw that it was a short-handled umbrella, the base of it with a barrel-like opening in it.

2

A few steps short of his intended death, Casement had a sudden recurrence of the unease that had plagued him since the late-morning phone call. All day memories, like iron filings, of a certain night had jabbed at him:

After Ophelia had gone to the opera he had gone downstairs and pressed the bell on the Swedens' door. It had been opened by Rob Sweden, who had blinked as if he didn't quite believe who his visitor was. 'Cormac?'

'Expecting someone else? Ophelia, perhaps?' He pushed the door wider and walked in. 'Close the door, Rob. You and I have something to talk about.'

'I'm expecting someone –'

'Another girlfriend? Close the door, Rob.'

He walked on into the big living room, went straight to the marble-manteled fake fireplace, turned round and stood with his hands behind his back. Even in his own mind's eye he looked like a stern Victorian father, but he was establishing the stage. None of Rob Sweden's guile was going to be allowed sway.

'Look, Cormac, I don't want to be rude –'

Jesus, thought Cormac, how do mature women fall for this callow young bastard? The young man had looks, no doubt: strong jaw, aquiline nose, blond hair cut rather long: Casement, a poetry reader, was reminded of photos of Rupert Brooke. He was tall and well-built and always just the right side of being too well-dressed. Only his eyes let him down: so busy looking for the main chance, they suggested furtiveness. He had the gift of the gab, had supreme confidence in his own charm and, though he hid it well, equally supreme contempt for anyone over forty. Except women.

'Is the maid home?'

'No, I gave her some money to go out –'

'You have all the gall in the world, haven't you? Setting up assignations in someone else's place. Did Ophelia meet you here?'

'Assignation? Cormac, I don't know what's got into you – you keep mentioning Ophelia –'

'No crap, please. I *know*.' He straightened his glasses with one hand. He had beautiful hands for an elderly man and Ophelia insisted that he had them cared for regularly. 'Rob, I don't think you appreciate my position. I have some standing in this community, I'm not one of the Johnny-come-latelies who clutter up this country. You cuckold me –'

'For Crissakes, cut out all this old-fashioned crap!' Rob lost his temper; or made a pretence of it. 'Assignations, cuckold – Jesus, that went out with – with –'

'With modern education? Perhaps you're right.' He did belong to the old school; when school, in his eyes, taught you standards. He had resigned from the Senate of Sydney University a couple of years ago because he could not stand the new young professors. 'All right, I know you've slept with Ophelia. And maybe your stepmother and Juliet, for all I know. And a dozen other men's wives. I came down here to tell you it's finished, all over. I would kill you before you got near my wife again. But that's only part of why I'm here –'

Then he was aware of the three hooded men who had come in from the rear of the apartment and stood in the archway that led into the living room. At first he thought they were some sort of back-up to Rob, but then the young man turned round and he took a step backwards in shock. Rob looked over his shoulder at Casement.

'Jesus, what's going on? What the fuck're you gunna do to me?'

'It has nothing to with Mr Casement,' said the shortest of the three hooded men. 'We're going to kill you, but we're not working for him.'

Casement was the first to recover. 'Who are you working for?'

'That may explain itself when we tell Mr Sweden why we're going to kill him.' The spokesman had a soft, thin voice with a slight accent. He was well-dressed; no, *nattily*-dressed, thought Casement. He even wore gloves; then Casement saw that they were white surgical gloves. 'Mr Sweden has stolen a lot of money. Or perhaps you know that?'

'Yes, I know.' He also knew now who had sent these killers; and was horrified. 'That was the other reason I came down here, Rob. The twenty-five million you stole.'

Rob had taken a step towards the front door, but the two larger men had moved round in front of him. One of them had produced a gun and with gloved hands was screwing a silencer to it.

'Aw, come on, for Crissakes! It's only money, I'll give it back – none of it's been touched –' He whirled back to face

Casement. 'Cormac, don't let them kill me! Jesus, man, why? I don't deserve to be killed – shit, guys are stealing money every fucking day –'

Casement was disgusted at the collapse of the younger man. But he looked at the hooded leader. 'Let him go. If he brings the money back –'

'It's too late, Mr Casement. We've already killed his accomplice – we have to play fair. It wouldn't be cricket, isn't that what you say?'

'His accomplice?'

'Sure, didn't you know? A Mr Kornsey. Well, actually, his real name was Bassano. An American, ex-Mafia – a canary, as they call them, he sang to the FBI –'

Casement felt he had been cut adrift in a sea of which he had no maps; but he turned to Rob again. 'Someone put you up to it? I just couldn't believe you'd have the imagination to steal as much as twenty-five million.'

He was not surprised when Rob did not accept the chance to blame someone else; the young man's ego was as big as his fear. 'No, he didn't put me up to it! But Mafia? Christ, I didn't know he had those connections! I was handling futures for him – he was perfectly legit, I thought . . . Then –'

'Then?'

The three hooded men were still and silent. One of the big men had moved impatiently, but the leader had waved a restraining hand. A wind had sprung up outside and moaned through an unseen open window.

'Then he came to me with this idea. Okay, it *was* his idea. A third to him, two-thirds to me. I transferred to the bank . . . It was all so much easier than I'd thought it'd be, moving the money . . . He was coming here tonight, he was the one I was expecting, not some girl –'

'On the futures exchange, he paid you off for laundering money for him?'

Rob reluctantly nodded.

'And you thought he was legitimate?' Casement shook his head; he and Rob could have been alone. 'If he's Mafia – or even ex-Mafia . . . You wouldn't get the two-thirds. You're naive, Rob. And ignorant. What you don't know is that twenty-five per cent of my bank is owned by the Japanese *yakuza*. They're the ones who have sent these men. You're out of your depth, Rob. So am I,' he said, suddenly weary, and sat down on the arm of the couch behind him. He looked at the hooded men. 'Do you have to go through with this? If we get the money back?'

'I'm afraid so, Mr Casement. It's a matter of honour. Our friends are very strong on honour.' Behind the hood Casement imagined a smile; the black silk fluttered as if there might have been a soft laugh. 'Before we came in here we heard what you said about Mr Sweden and your wife. You said you would kill him if he went near her again. That's a matter of honour, isn't it, Mr Casement?'

'I never meant I'd actually –' But he would: he could never face losing Ophelia, to Rob Sweden or any other man. He nodded absently at the gun in the hand of one of the larger men. 'You're going to kill him with that?'

'Ah no, something subtler,' said the leader and removed what looked like a scalpel from a thin case he took from his pocket. He had moved closer and Casement could smell perfume on him, something he abhorred in a man.

'Get fucked!' From somewhere Rob dragged up some defiance.

The leader nodded and the man with the gun moved in on Rob and put the silencer to his head.

'Not in here!' Casement stood up on weakened legs. 'I'll go –'

'No, sir, you stay here till it's done!'

The leader jerked his head and led the way out of the living room, the man with the gun pushing Rob ahead of him. The third man stayed with Casement, who sank back on the arm of the couch.

He said, 'Are you going to kill me, too? I'm a witness.'

'I dunno what the orders are on you, mate.' His voice was muffled, but distinctly Australian. 'Just sit and we'll find out, okay? Nice place this, eh?'

'It's comfortable. Or it was, till tonight.'

'You got a sense of humour.'

'Have I? I wasn't trying to be funny.' There was a cry of pain from an inner room; he started, remained stiff a moment, then his spine crumpled again. 'Is it going to be bloody? I mean, blood everywhere? His father shouldn't come home to find him like that –'

'No worries, mate. It'll be neat. I seen him do the Yank, you wouldn't believe how neat.'

'I'm not used to this sort of thing.' He had not seen the victim of a violent death since, as a junior officer, he had served in New Guinea in the last year of that war.

The hood nodded: sympathetically?

Then the other two hooded men came back into the living room. 'It's done,' said the leader. 'Now we have to toss him off the balcony. An accident,' he explained as Casement looked enquiringly at him. 'My employers prefer it that way. It'll read better than the son of the Police Minister being murdered.'

'Won't the police find out how you really killed him?'

'I don't think so. The police are always satisfied with the obvious.'

Casement felt momentarily light-headed: he was dreaming this conversation. Then his banker's mentality took over: accounting had to be done: 'What about – what was his name? The Mafia man. Was his death an accident, too?'

'No. I used the same method.' He was wiping the scalpel on a tissue. The smell of his perfume was stronger, as if, though he still sounded cool, excitement had heated him. 'You two, toss Mr Sweden off the balcony. There's one off the main bedroom. Make sure you don't drop him on someone.' The two men went out of the room and the leader, putting the scalpel back in its case, gave his attention again to Casement. 'Mr Bassano is on a park seat out at Canterbury. I think it would be a good idea if you forgot he was ever mentioned.'

'You killed him the same way?' Casement nodded at the slim case.

The leader put his forefinger to the back of his neck. 'In here. I once worked in a morgue. It is a very good training ground for studying how to eliminate people.'

Casement said, careful with his words, 'I think you have made a mistake. If we can't keep secret what's been stolen from our bank, our friends won't like it if the Mafia, even ex-Mafia, is linked to the theft. I think you're wrong about the police, our police. They're not always satisfied with the obvious. And Rob is – was the Police Minister's son.'

One can't see doubt through a hood; but a man's hands often give him away. He bounced the scalpel case on his gloved palm. 'Perhaps you're right.' The two big men came back into the living room. 'Done?'

'Done,' said the man who had talked with Casement. 'He's down on the footpath, we missed the cars parked down there. We better get going. Someone finds him, the place'll be humming with coppers.'

'We have something else to do,' said the leader. 'We have to go back to Canterbury to see if the cops are humming about Mr Bassano. Or we may have to pay a visit to the morgue, if they've already collected him. We have to find him and re-kill him.'

'Jesus! I done some jobs, but this is fucking bizarre!'

'Goodnight, Mr Casement,' said the leader. 'Have you touched anything in here? Had a drink or anything? Fingerprints,' he explained. 'We don't want you connected with any of this.'

'No. No, nothing. I – I may have touched the door as I came in –' *Good God, they're teaching me how to think criminally!*

'Better wipe the door,' the leader told one of the men. 'Mr Casement, I think you should now go up to your own apartment and leave this to us. It's in your own interests to forget what you saw tonight. I'm sure our friends would remind you of that if you should be careless.'

Casement had done as he was told. He went back upstairs to the penthouse, poured himself a stiff drink, sat down and stared out at the harbour, feeling the foundations of himself slowly crumbling away as the terrible realization hit him that he had become an associate to murder.

And now, here in the ballroom of the Congress, he smelled the perfume again. He turned round, saw the slim man in the horn-rimmed glasses and the light grey suit, saw the thing that looked like a cloth-covered gun and knew it was all over. And in that instant Malone came in from the side, hit the man's arm and knocked it upwards. There was a faint explosion of air and something silver flashed in the overhead lights, then buried itself in the plaster cheek of a cherub on the decorated ceiling. The man struggled, but Malone, standing close to him, had produced his gun and was jabbing it into the man's side.

'No fuss, understand? Let's go quietly. Sorry about this, but you're done for, sport.'

Chapter Sixteen

◆◆◆◆◆◆◆

1

Two days later Malone sat in the Police Minister's office with Sweden and Assistant Commissioner Zanuch.

'We went to the house where Belgarda's been staying, in Roseville. It had been rented by a Japanese, who we guess was Tajiri. The place was empty. But we found a gun, a Russian make, a Makarov. Ballistics have identified it as the gun that killed three of the victims. We also found a scalpel, we can't prove it's the one that killed your son, but we can present it as circumstantial evidence.'

'What's Belgarda got to say?' asked Zanuch.

'He's not saying anything, sir, but we have enough on him for any magistrate to commit him for trial. He'll go down, for sure.'

'You got nothing at all out of him?'

'Well, not much. We did find out, Mr Sweden, that your maid was the one who'd left the back door to your apartment open for him. She'd been planted on you when they first found out Rob was your son.'

Sweden, from the moment Malone had entered his office, had said virtually nothing. When Belgarda's arrest had been headlined in yesterday morning's newspapers, sharing almost equal space with the US bombing of Iraq, one of the first on the phone to him had been Hans Vanderberg:

'All right, Derek, don't you worry about what we talked about the other night. I know when to score points and when to kick the ball out of play. You're a hero, the coppers have done you proud. Now's not the time for me to be screwing

288

your balls off in the scrum. But watch out, Derek, I'm not dead yet. You could be, though, there's always tomorrow.'

Now Sweden said to Malone, 'Will he talk once he's in court?'

Malone glanced at Zanuch, then looked back at the Minister. *Watch your tongue here, son.* 'I don't know, sir. If he doesn't, I think the Crown Prosecutor will. The Crown's case is going to look better if it gives a reason for Rob's murder. Your son was a thief, sir, there's no getting away from that.'

For a moment Sweden's face hardened; but it was Zanuch who said, 'There's no need to rub it in, Scobie.'

'That's not what I intended, sir. But this whole thing's been pretty dirty. We've had five – no, *six* murders. We keep forgetting about the girl who worked for Belgarda in his office – she obviously found out more than she was supposed to. And the morgue attendant, Frank Minto. He's the one I'm sorry for, he had absolutely nothing to do with this, he just happened to be in the way. He was killed because Belgarda liked killing. We've picked up the two heavies who helped Belgarda. They're locals, Kenny Sturgess and George Paderewsky – one of 'em, maybe both, will talk if they can make a deal. It's all going to come out, one way or another.'

'What about Casement Trust and their being partners with the *yakuza*?'

Malone shrugged. 'That's Mr Casement's problem. My job's homicide.' It was another of their small challenges; but he was tired and wanted to be out of this room. 'He could have been more helpful at the start.'

Casement had been no help at all even at the end. After Belgarda had been taken away by Kagal and Graham, Malone and Clements had suggested they go back to The Wharf with the Casements. There the two detectives had tried to get Casement to open up, but the old man, shaken by how close he had come to death for the second time, had given them nothing.

'Please –' Ophelia was grateful to Malone for having saved her husband's life; but now he needed further saving. 'Leave us alone for this evening. It's been too much –'

'We just want to know why Belgarda was trying to kill you, Mr Casement.'

Casement shook his head, still seemingly dumb with shock. Ophelia said, 'Please go. Perhaps my husband can talk tomorrow . . .'

The two detectives had left the Casements, he clutching her arm as if she might steal away from him, she stroking his hand as she might have a child's. Going down in the lift Clements said, 'How much do you reckon he hasn't told us? Won't tell us?'

'I think he knows what happened the night Rob was murdered. Belgarda said something when I was hustling him out of the ballroom – he said, "I should've killed him the first night." I dunno, maybe Casement was in on the killing.'

'He's afraid of losing his wife.'

Malone looked at him a moment; then he nodded. 'You're probably right. Would you kill to keep Romy?'

'That's a bastard of a question . . . But *he* would. The thing is, I don't think he would ever lose her. She might play around, but she'll never leave him. She's reached the top of the tree, why slide down?'

'You're pretty cynical about women.'

'Only some of 'em. I'm the same way about some men.'

They went out of the apartment building, round the corner to their car. Clements, without realizing it, had parked the car right at the spot where Rob Sweden had crashed into the pavement. The white outline of the body and the blood had been scrubbed away, feet had trodden the ghost into the ground.

Now, on the second day, Malone stood up, dismissing himself. 'If I say it myself, sir, I think we've done a good job. The newspapers are satisfied with it, for once they're not criticizing us. I think we should leave it as it is. The full report will be on your desk in the morning, Minister.'

'Thank you,' said Sweden; he sounded anything but ministerial. 'And thank you, on a personal level.'

Outside in the corridor Zanuch said, 'He's spoken to me about recommending you for a commendation.'

'Tell him to forget it. That'll take time, commendations always do. By then the case'll be forgotten, there'll be something else. Let it lie.'

'You're more of a diplomat than I suspected.'

Malone relaxed, smiled. 'Not really. When I was playing cricket, there were times when you knew you couldn't win. You played for a draw.'

2

'We're going to be married on the thirty-first of July,' said Romy. 'A Saturday.'

'Why don't you make it the last Saturday in June? That gets you into this financial year and Russ can claim a full tax allowance for a spouse.'

'Oh God, Dad, that's really *gross*!' Both Claire and Maureen thumped him. 'Mum, how can you *stand* him?'

It was a week later and Malone had brought Lisa and the children and Clements and Romy here to the Golden Gate for dinner. It was Lisa who had insisted on the venue – 'We all like Chinese and it's the best Chinese restaurant I've been to. French cooking is wasted on Maureen and Tom and we're not going to Pizza Hut.'

Belgarda was still in custody, bail refused. His heavies, Sturgess and Paderewsky, having made a deal with the Director of Public Prosecutions, had been granted bail. Teresita Romero had been picked up, but, because nothing could be proved against her, she had been released and, as far as Malone knew or cared, she was now somewhere between Sydney and Manila. Tajiri had disappeared and it was assumed that he had somehow got out of Australia and was back in Tokyo. It irked Malone that he had never seen the man who had masterminded all the murders; he was known only by appearance to Cormac Casement and Jack Aldwych. Neither of whom, for his own reasons, would ever sit down and try to match him with an Identikit picture. Belgarda's trial still had to come, but the maze had been solved and all the work now lay with the DPP.

Autumn's cool had turned to winter's chill; it was a good night for hot food. The meal was almost finished when Aldwych and a white-haired woman rose from a back booth and came down towards the front door. They paused by the Malone table and Clements introduced Romy. 'My fiancée.'

'This is Emily Karp, a friend.'

Malone had not seen Aldwych since the day after Belgarda's arrest. He had driven out to Harbord to see the old crim, but Aldwych had been adamant he would not give evidence at any trial. 'No, Scobie. You got the bugger in the act – he was trying to kill Casement. You don't need anything from me. No, mate, definitely no. I'm trying to cultivate respectable friends now. They don't wanna read about me being mixed up with a multiple killer.' He had had the grace to smile.

Malone wondered now if Emily Karp was the respectable friend. He smiled at her, appreciating her. 'A pleasure meeting you, Mrs Karp.'

She said a few words to Lisa and the children. Aldwych stepped round her and leaned down to speak quietly. 'It's all been taken care of, Scobie. The bill. I owe you, remember?' He winked and straightened up.

Malone didn't demur. All had indeed been taken care of. Well, almost. Loose threads are in the weave of any cop's life.

Kirribilli
August, 1992–July 1993

292